D0260781

A2

50p

The Accident Man

The Accident Man

TOM CAIN

BANTAM PRESS

LONDON • TORONTO • SYDNEY • AUCKLAND • JOHANNESBURG

TRANSWORLD PUBLISHERS
61–63 Uxbridge Road, London W5 5SA
A Random House Group Company
www.booksattransworld.co.uk

First published in Great Britain
in 2007 by Bantam Press
an imprint of Transworld Publishers

A CIP catalogue record for this book
is available from the British Library.

ISBNs 9780593058053 (cased)
9780593058060 (tpb)

Addresses for Random House Group Ltd companies outside the UK
can be found at: www.randomhouse.co.uk
The Random House Group Ltd Reg. No. 954009

The Random House Group Ltd makes every effort to ensure that the papers used in its
books are made from trees that have been legally sourced from well-managed and credibly
certified forests. Our paper procurement policy can be found at:
www.randomhouse.co.uk/paper.htm

Typeset in 11/14 pt Caslon 540
by Falcon Oast Graphic Art Ltd.

Printed in the UK by CPI Mackays, Chatham, ME5 8TD

2 4 6 8 10 9 7 5 3 1

Mixed Sources
Product group from well-managed
forests and other controlled sources
www.fsc.org Cert no. TT-COC-2139
© 1996 Forest Stewardship Council

Author's Note

The Accident Man was inspired by real events, the worldwide reaction to them and the ongoing speculation that surrounds them. Wherever relevant, I have endeavoured to respect the facts as they are known. Nevertheless, this is explicitly and unambiguously a work of fiction. I am categorically *not* claiming to reveal some supposedly genuine conspiracy that has somehow remained undisclosed or suppressed up to this point. An investigative journalist or police detective tries to uncover the answer to the factual question 'What happened?' Writing as a novelist, I have tried to use my imagination to devise an answer to a very different, hypothetical enquiry: 'What if . . .?'

Prelude

The night air was weighed down with heat, and the sea rippled lazily against the pebbled beach.

There was a guard on the wooden jetty, but it was past ten o'clock with no moon in the sky, so the man with the AK-47 did not see Samuel Carver as he swam beneath the Adriatic waters, didn't hear him as he surfaced beneath the jetty, didn't detect Carver's presence just beneath his feet.

Slowly, silently, Carver made his way up towards the shore, where the water was shallowest. He took off his mask, flippers and the buoyancy vest to which his air-tank was secured. He clipped the mask and flippers to d-rings on the side of the vest, then gently slipped the diving gear back into the water, letting it settle on the seabed.

Carver waited till he heard the sound of the helicopter in the distance before he moved to his starting position by the foot of the ladder that led down to the sea at the deep end of the jetty. He was counting on human nature. When the chopper passed overhead, the man would look up. Anyone would, particularly if his boss was onboard.

There were two waterproof pouches strapped to Carver's thighs. As the noise of the rotors reached the high point of its clattering crescendo, he opened one of them and extracted a standard veterinarian's air-pistol. He let the glow from the helicopter's landing lights pass overhead. Then he took a deep breath, gripped the side of the ladder and pulled himself upwards.

He landed flat on the planking and looked up to see the guard still watching the Bell 206 Jetranger as it hovered about four hundred metres away before dropping down to land at the villa's private helipad. The man's back made a perfect target for the tranquillizer dart Carver fired from his gun. He dashed forward and caught the guard before he fell, making sure that there was no sound as the body hit the deck. He removed the dart and threw it into the water. Then he moved forward into the estate, preparing himself for the job he had to do.

Samuel Carver made very bad accidents happen to even worse people. His current target was a forty-three-year-old ethnic Albanian called Skender Visar. The official term for Visar's business was people-trafficking, but Carver preferred a more traditional job description. As far as he was concerned, the Albanian was a slave trader.

Visar shipped human beings in containers from China, Africa and the former communist states of Eastern Europe. He sent men to work as indentured labour in fields and sweatshops, doing jobs that westerners now felt were beneath their dignity. He bought women from families so impoverished they would sell their own kith and kin; he then beat them into submission, strung them out on drugs and worked them mercilessly in the brothels, bars and massage-parlours he owned across Europe and the United States. Few slaves lasted more than two or three years, but Visar didn't care. By then they had repaid the cost of their purchase, transport and pitifully meagre upkeep hundreds of times over. And there were always more, countless thousands more, where they came from.

Slavery was crime's growth industry, its profits rapidly catching up with those to be made from illicit weapons and drugs. In some ways, the business model was far smarter: you could sell a gun or a gram of cocaine only once; you could sell a sex-slave ten times a night. But easy money bred tough competition. Visar lived in a permanent state of professional paranoia, constantly on the lookout for enemies, alert to every possible threat to his position, whether real or imagined.

He'd been taking a break on his 180-foot yacht, cruising the Dalmatian coast of Croatia with his family, when he heard that one of his senior lieutenants, Ergon Ali, had been trying to cut a deal with a rival boss. The information was false, planted to deceive, but it had the desired effect.

Visar sent a four-man team to the Berlin strip-club that served as Ali's base. They knocked Ali unconscious with the butt of a Mossberg pump-action shotgun, bundled him into the trunk of an S-class Mercedes, shot him full of heroin and hit the autobahn south. Fourteen hours later they arrived in Split, the Croatian seaside town that had once been the favoured summer resort of the emperors of Rome. Visar's men topped up Ali's dose to keep him quiet, then drove their Merc on to the ferry to the island of Hvar, sticking it next to a camper-van filled with Australian students on a round-Europe tour. They spent the three-hour voyage in the ferry bar, matching the Aussies beer for beer. The only other occupant of the bar was sitting in the corner, a bearded man in a battered Panama hat, with a pair of binoculars round his neck, eking out a pot of tea and studiously consulting a book about bird-watching.

When Visar's men reached the villa, they dumped Ergon Ali, bound and gagged, in the cellar. They did not want to waste their boss's time, so they spent the rest of the night and all the next day beating, electrocuting and half drowning the man who had once been their friend. Only when they felt that Ali was about to crack did they call Skender Visar to inform him that everything had been prepared for his arrival. By the time Visar hung up, the blades on his helicopter had already started to turn. He was on his way to apply the finishing touches to Ergon Ali's interrogation. And Samuel Carver, bird-watching now far from his mind, was waiting for him.

*

Carver crouched in the shadows to the side of the helipad. Visar and his bodyguard had already walked up towards the main house where Ergon Ali was awaiting his fate. The pilot stayed behind for a few minutes to shut down and check his aircraft, then he too made his way up the path. Carver waited until he was sure that the area was deserted, then slipped across the pad to the silent machine.

The Bell 206 was the workhorse of the skies, first put into service in 1967 and barely changed since. The rear of the aircraft consisted of a long tail-boom, at the end of which sat the tail rotor and the vertical stabilizer, which stuck out above and below the boom like the angled fins of a shark. This stabilizer was attached to the rest of the helicopter by four bolts, arranged in a rectangle.

Carver put on his gloves, reached into the second thigh-pouch, took out an adjustable wrench and removed the bottom two bolts. Then he used a mini-saw to cut halfway through each one, making them significantly weaker. He screwed them back into the housing, taking extreme care not to snap them in two. Next he unscrewed the top pair of bolts, exactly as before. But this time he cut right through them, up by the head. He put the shafts back into his pouch, then used tiny blobs of Blu-Tac to stick the heads of the bolts back on the vertical stabilizer, exactly where they had been before. An inch-by-inch inspection of the helicopter would reveal what Carver had done. But his work would certainly pass a tired pilot's cursory pre-take-off check.

He ran through the whole procedure one more time in his mind, making sure he had done everything that was required, and then made his way back to the jetty. By the time the guard woke from his slumber, Samuel Carver was long gone.

Ergon Ali took a long time to die, protesting his innocence and loyalty to the end. It was dawn by the time Skender Visar got back onboard his helicopter. He was tired and preoccupied, fearing a dangerous, costly gang-war and wondering who would be next to betray him. He wanted to get back to his boat. His pilot had no desire to anger him further, so he rushed through his take-off procedures and got the Bell off the ground as fast as possible.

They were five miles out to sea when the vibrations started. The pilot's instincts told him to turn back, but he knew Visar would not allow it, so he picked up speed, hoping to get the trip over and done with as soon as possible.

As the helicopter accelerated, air started rushing ever faster around the vertical stabilizer, pushing it from side to side. If all four assembly bolts had been solidly in place, they would have kept the stabilizer upright and motionless. But with the top assembly bolts gone, the weakened bottom bolts became a hinge around which the stabilizer started to flap. And the more the pilot piled on the speed, the more extreme that flapping became.

When the helicopter took off there was a clearance of about a foot between the stabilizer and the tail rotor. But with each vibration that distance decreased: ten inches . . . six . . . three . . . closer and closer until it collided with the spinning blades in a screaming impact of metal on metal, instantly jamming the rotor like a broom-handle shoved between the spokes of a bicycle wheel. The sudden, total deceleration ripped the rotor-blades away from the helicopter, the two remaining stabilizer bolts snapped like breadsticks, and the entire tail assembly was sent plummeting down towards the waters of the Adriatic Sea, burnished to a gleaming copper by the rays of the rising sun.

The helicopter now began to spin round and round at ever-increasing speed. Skender Visar, who had calmly supervised the death and degradation of so many human souls, reacted to his own impending doom with an animal howl of terror. The pilot simply switched off the engine, leaving the main rotors to auto-rotate like the blades of a windmill. For a brief moment, calm was restored. The cabin stopped spinning. Visar grinned feebly in a desperate attempt to disguise his cowardice. The pilot began to send out a mayday message, calling for rescue.

A Bell 206 Jetranger under auto-rotation descends at a speed of 17 miles per hour. With an experienced pilot at the controls, the chances of survival are good, even when landing on water. But Carver had banked on something else. A helicopter's tail rotor is powered by a driveshaft that runs from the engine along the tail-boom, but the power can't be transferred from the shaft to the rotor without a gearbox. This box is a heavy hunk of metal that sits at one end of the boom, acting as a counterweight to the cabin and engine at the other end. So when the rotor was ripped away from the helicopter, it yanked the gearbox out of its moorings and left it dangling off the driveshaft at the open end of the shredded tail-boom. It stayed there for ten, maybe fifteen seconds, pulled by gravity and pummelled by the wind. Then the connection to the driveshaft gave way and the gearbox joined the debris tumbling to the sea.

Without its weight, the Jetranger lost any semblance of balance. One second the pilot was looking at the sky; the next he was pointing straight down at the sea and the chopper had ceased to be a functioning aircraft, becoming instead a glass and metal coffin plummeting towards the churning waters. All the pilot could hear was the manic rush of the air and the death-scream of Skender Visar.

Samuel Carver was fast asleep when the people-trafficker died. Hours earlier, he'd swum back to the rented motor-boat he'd moored just around the headland from the bay where Visar's villa lay. He'd peeled away the wetsuit, dried himself off and changed into a pair of jeans and a loose cotton shirt. He'd then returned to the tourist resort of Hvar, where he was staying, moored the boat and had a late dinner in a restaurant down by the seafront. Carver ordered grilled seafood and a chilled bottle of Posip Cara, a fresh white wine from the neighbouring island of Korcula. He ate at an outside table and watched the girls go by. Then he walked back to his hotel, just like any other tourist, bidding goodnight to the night-porter before making his way to bed.

The next day Carver breakfasted on fresh bread rolls and sweet black coffee before he checked out, paying in cash. He boarded a ferry bound for the Italian port of Pescara across the Adriatic, just another anonymous foot-passenger at the height of the summer season. Once he got to Italy, he bought a train-ticket home – no documentation or ID required, no record kept of his journey, cash accepted without question.

Carver travelled first-class. He read a book that wasn't about bird-watching. He joined in the conversation when fellow passengers felt like talking, stopped along the way for a couple of decent meals. He did everything he could not to think about what he'd just done.

Ten Days Later

1

The man smiled to himself as he walked into the walnut-panelled room, relishing the cool of the air-conditioning after the blazing August heat. He pushed his sunglasses off his face, up over the thinning black hair that he kept cropped close to the scalp. The semi-darkness, too, came as a relief. The peoples of the cold, gloomy north might be happy to spend their summer holidays roasting their milky skins to a crimson crisp, but he was a child of the sun, so he respected its power and sought the shade at midday.

He had only a few minutes to himself. Soon he would be expected back outside, where the servants were laying a table for lunch under a white canvas awning that flapped in the Mediterranean breeze. He walked across the room, feeling the soft thickness of the custom-woven carpet under his bare, olive-brown feet. His jeans and T-shirt were simple but very expensive, Armani rather than Levi. His watch was a Cartier Pasha. He took such things for granted. His entire life had been spent inside the cocoon that money provides for the children of the rich.

Yet for all its privilege, inherited wealth carries with it the stigma of being unearned. To outsiders, he was a mere playboy, a parasite feeding off his father's achievements. He planned to change that. Very soon, the whole world would be talking of what he had done. A smile crossed his lips as he anticipated what was to come, pressed a button and speed-dialled a London number.

'We must talk,' he said to the person on the other end of the line. 'Be ready on Monday. I have important news, good news about . . .' He hesitated, trying to find the right words, knowing that others might be listening. 'Let's just say, our mutual friend.'

The man's attempt at discretion was futile. His conversation was picked up by the giant radomes scattered across the bleak Yorkshire landscape at Menwith Hill, where Echelon, the global surveillance system run by America's National Security Agency, intercepted countless telephone and email messages every day. From there, a signal was sent via a satellite, in orbit 19,000 miles above the earth, to the NSA headquarters at Fort Meade, Maryland. Cray YMP super-computers, capable of almost three billion operations per second, sifted through the never-ending multilingual babble. Like a prospector panning for gold, the Crays picked out nuggets from the onrushing stream. They sought key individuals, trigger-words and -phrases to be flagged up for further investigation.

Data gathered by Echelon was also sent to British Government Communications Headquarters, commonly known as GCHQ, on the outskirts of Cheltenham, Gloucestershire. More computers plucked yet more information from the human torrent. That information was passed on to the Ministry of Defence, the Foreign Office and the law enforcement and intelligence agencies.

Fiona Towthorp, an attractive, freckle-faced woman of forty, worked as a senior intelligence analyst at GCHQ. She had just spotted an item she knew her masters would covet. But when she picked up the phone, the number she dialled had nothing to do with Her Majesty's Government. The line was encrypted at a level even Echelon could not decode. This call would never be overheard.

'Consortium,' a man's voice answered.

'I have a message from the corporate communications department,' said Towthorp. 'There's something the chairman needs to know.'

Towthorp was put straight through.

2

They came for Carver in the morning. He'd got the call the night before, just as he was turning out the gas lantern that provided the only illumination in his sparsely furnished mountain hut.

'Carver,' he'd said, not bothering to disguise his irritation as the GSM phone shrieked for his attention.

There were no formalities or introductions from the voice on the other end of the line, with its flat Thames Estuary accent. 'Where are ya?'

'On holiday, Max. Not working. I think you know that.'

'I know what you're doing, Carver. I just dunno where you're doing it.'

'Guess what, there was a reason I didn't tell you.'

'Well, I may have a job for you.'

'No.'

Max ignored him. 'Listen, I'll know for sure within the next twelve hours. If it happens, trust me, we'll make it worth your while interrupting your hols. Three million dollars, US, paid into the usual account. You can have a nice long break after that.'

'I see,' said Carver, flatly. 'And if I refuse?'

'Then my advice would be, stay on your holiday. And don't come back. It's your choice.'

Carver wasn't bothered by the implied physical threat. But he didn't want to lose his major client. This was his job. It was what he did best. And no matter how often he thought about packing it in, he still didn't want a competitor taking his work. One day, maybe soon, he would be ready to quit, but it would be on his terms, at a time of his own choosing.

'New Zealand,' he said.

He cursed to himself as he turned off the phone and put it back on the bare wooden table that stood next to the steel and canvas bedframe where he'd laid his sleeping bag.

Samuel Carver had the lean, spare look of a professional fighting man. His dark-brown hair was cut short. A dozen years in the Royal Marines and the Special Boat Service had left his face etched and weatherbeaten. A fierce determination was evident in his strong, dark brow, bisected by a single, deep concentration-line. Yet his clear green eyes suggested that Carver's physical intensity was always guided by a calm, almost chilly intelligence.

He tried to rationalize what he did as a form of pest control, unpleasant, but necessary. After the Visar job he'd looked, as he always did, for a place where he could wind down and try to clear his mind of what he knew, but did not want to admit: that every additional killing, no matter how many lives it saved, no matter how logically it could be justified, added a little more corrosion to his soul.

He'd ended up on the far side of the world, in the Two Thumb Mountains of New Zealand's South Island. Aeons ago, when all the continents of the earth were one, the Two Thumbs had been part of the same chain as the Peruvian Andes and the California Sierras. The mountains had moved several thousand miles since then, but not much else had changed. There were no nightclubs, restaurants or chalet-girls, no newspapers or TV, no lifts, instructors or nursery slopes. For Carver, that was the whole point.

He had come in search of absolute solitude and an existence

pared down to its simplest elements. He wanted to purge the shadow of death from his mind with raw speed, physical sweat, empty sky, blinding sun, air and snow as cold and pure as vodka straight from the freezer. He hadn't shaved in a week. He hadn't washed much, either. He probably stank like a rhino. Why worry? It had been a long time since there'd been anyone to smell good for.

The chopper came from the east, in the first faint rays of the rising sun before the last star had gone. Carver saw it away in the distance, caught between the blue-black sky and the icing-sugar snow. He didn't need to pack. Inside his ski-jacket he wore a black nylon money-belt. Its pouches contained four different passports, each with two matching credit cards. There was also a spare phone and $20,000 cash. Gold cards were all very well, but Carver had yet to go anywhere that didn't accept US green.

A little blizzard of snow flurried in the air as the helicopter landed, fifty metres away. Carver watched it touch down. Christ, it was another Bell. An image flashed into his mind of a Jetranger crashing, sounds of screaming, an almost physical impression of terror. He closed his eyes for a second and muttered to himself, 'Get a grip.' Then he eased the zipper on his jacket and walked over, loose-limbed but watchful for any sign that he'd been set up.

'G'day,' the New Zealander co-pilot shouted over the clattering pulse of the rotor-blades. He held out a hand and pulled Carver onboard. 'They said we either had to pick you up or kill you. Glad you ticked Box A.'

The smile on the co-pilot's face was broad. But his eyes were flat and expressionless.

Carver grinned back, playing the game. 'I'm glad too,' he shouted back. 'You might have got hurt.'

He slumped into his seat, fastened the safety-belt, put on his headset and sighed. So much for his holiday. He hadn't even had time for a decent cup of coffee and already he was knee-deep in bullshit. He rubbed his thumb and forefinger back and forth along his forehead. He'd had nothing to do for a week but ski and sleep. He should have been rested and refreshed. Instead he felt tired to the bone.

Less than two hours later, Carver was on a brand-new Gulfstream V, climbing to 40,000 feet, flying north-east out of Christchurch, en route to Los Angeles, some 5,800 nautical miles away. The GV was the longest-range private jet in the world, but by the time it got to California, the plane would be gliding. It would sit on the tarmac just long enough to refuel and pick up a new air-crew, then take off again for Europe.

There was a shower onboard. Carver cleaned up, shaved and changed into a soft, shapeless grey tracksuit handed to him by the flight attendant. 'I hope it's the right size. They gave me your measurements . . .' She paused. 'But you never really know whether something fits until you try it on.' She was a pretty brunette with big brown eyes, soft full lips and a glossy ponytail. She spoke in that way girls do Down Under, rising slightly at the end of every sentence, turning each statement into an ingratiating question. Now she stood in front of Carver with her weight shifted to one side, her hips cocked and the dark-blue fabric of her snug, knee-length skirt stretched tight across her thighs. She was looking at him appraisingly, with a smile that suggested she was happy with what she saw. Either she really liked him, or her job description included a fuller range of executive services than your average trolley-dolly. Carver considered the latter option. Both he and the girl worked for people who believed that anything could be paid for. He'd been bought. Presumably she could be too.

'What's your name?' he asked.

'Candy,' she said.

Carver couldn't stop himself laughing. The girl even had a stripper name to go with her professional seduction routine. But then she surprised him, by blushing.

'No, really. It's short for Candace.'

He realized he'd missed a third possibility, that Candy was a nice kid trying to brighten up her working day with a bit of mild flirtation. The way normal people did. Christ, he was a cynical bastard these days. When had that happened? Stupid question: he knew exactly when. He could time it down to the last minute. It suddenly struck him that his jaw was clenched and his teeth were grinding together with a tension he could not begin to explain. It was far too soon for the nerves that usually preceded any deadly action. This was something else – a message from his subconscious he wasn't able to decode. Perhaps he just didn't want to.

Carver had spent the past few years trying not to look too far inside his head. He told himself it was basic military pragmatism. Concentrate on what's in front of you, worry about the stuff you can control, forget about everything else. Well, there was a girl in front of him, and he could control his bad attitude. He and Candy were going to be stuck together in a pressurized metal tube for the next twenty-four hours. The least they could do was be polite to each other.

He gave a quick shake of his head, ridding it of unwanted thoughts.

'Sorry,' he said. 'I was out of line.'

'No worries. Can I get you anything, a bit of breakfast, coffee?'

'Sure, that would be great. Thanks a lot.'

Ten minutes later, the target details were faxed to the plane.

Subject: Ramzi Hakim Narwaz
Nationality: Pakistani (French mother)
Age: 41
Height: 5 foot 11 inches (182 cm)
Weight: 190 lb (86.4 kg)

Subject belongs to one of Pakistan's wealthiest families, was educated at Le Rosey school, Switzerland, is based in Paris and is completely at home in upper echelons of European society. He is married (wife Yasmina comes from a rich Lebanese family) with one son, Yusuf. Drinks alcohol, but seldom to excess. Some social drug use. Discreet, but regular extra-marital sexual activity, typical of a rich, westernized male.

This lifestyle is just a cover. Subject, who is highly intelligent and has poor relations with his father, was radicalized by mullahs at various mosques in north and east London, while a student at the London School of Economics. Subject has become an active and increasingly influential player in a growing network of extreme Islamic terrorist cells.

Monitoring of telephone communications by US intelligence, coordinated through the joint CIA/FBI anti-terrorist unit, codename 'Alex', shows regular contact between Subject and suspected associates of terrorist movements. These include Konsojaya founders Wali Khan Amin Shah and Riduan Isamuddin (alias 'Hambali'); Nairobi, Kenya-based suspect Wadih el-Hage; and several suspects in the Manila, Philippines-based 'Bojinka' (Big Bang) plot, which intended to bomb twelve US-bound planes.

Recent bank transfers to and from Subject's accounts show much greater than usual activity. Subject is strongly believed to be planning a major terrorist assault in Europe, almost certainly in the UK. This assault is believed to be imminent – days, rather than weeks. Telephone intercepts indicate that he will be leaving his family on holiday in the South of France and returning to Paris within the next twenty-four hours.

There is a clear danger to both military personnel and civilian lives if Subject is allowed to proceed with activities. *He has therefore been selected for immediate action.*

A second fax arrived soon afterwards. It notified Carver that $1.5 million had been wired to his numbered account at Banque Wertmuller-Maier de Genève. Whoever his employers were – and Carver had no great desire to find out, any more than he wanted them to know too much about him – they always paid on time, and in full.

Max called again when the plane was over the western USA.

'So where are you now?'

'Half an hour out of LA,' Carver replied. 'The pilot's putting his foot down. Should be on the ground in a little over ten hours.'

'Right, so that'll make it seven thirty p.m. Central European Time. We don't expect much action before midnight, so that's fine. But there's something else we need you to sort out first.'

Carver was several thousand miles away, speaking through a satellite phone. But his anger got through just fine. 'You're joking. Two jobs? Both improvised? You must think I've lost the will to live.'

'Don't worry, the second one's just routine,' Max said. 'Back-up in case the first strike doesn't work out. Our friend has another property he uses for private meetings – personal and professional, if you follow my drift. If he feels under threat, he'll use it as his safe-house. Except you'll have made it unsafe, won't you? Don't worry, we've got the code to the alarm system. It's a piece of piss.'

Carver sighed. It didn't matter what you did for a living. In the end, you took the same crap from the people who paid your wages. He listened as Max described the little love-nest where Ramzi Hakim Narwaz liked to conduct his private business. This was one Islamic terrorist who took his cover as a decadent apostate really seriously. It was an Oscar-winning performance.

A few minutes later, the floor-plans and wiring schematics of the Narwaz apartment came through on the Gulfstream's fax. It took Carver half an hour to work out what he was going to do. The next time Max made contact, he had his equipment list ready. He listed the transport, weaponry, explosives, timers, fuses and tactical equipment he'd need, then got down to the finer details.

'I'll need a small tin of lubricating oil – 3-in-1, something like that. Then get me half a dozen small-size plastic freezer bags, self-sealing; a plain black bin bag; a mechanic's torch with a head-strap;

a pair of scissors, industrial ones with three-inch ceramic blades; a screwdriver, wire-cutters, a roll of gaffer tape, a can of air-freshener spray, a bottle of Jif cleanser, a few pairs of thin latex gloves and a Mars bar.'

'Why the hell do you need a Mars bar?'

'To eat. I've got a sweet tooth. And come to mention it, why not get me a takeaway pizza?'

Max did not bother to keep the sarcasm out of his voice. 'Whatever you say, mate. Any favourite toppings?'

'I couldn't care less,' said Carver. 'It's the box I'm interested in. Second thoughts, don't worry. I'll get it myself. I'll be needing a decent meal.'

3

Carver's plane landed at Le Bourget airport, a few miles north-east of Paris, France, and taxied into a private aviation hangar. When Carver reached the bottom of the steps, a maintenance engineer handed him an envelope and a large carrier bag. Inside the envelope were a parking ticket, with the space-number written on it, a Honda motorbike key and the key to a locker in the terminal building. The carrier bag was filled with clothes. Carver carried it back up into the plane and got changed.

Max had given him black cargo pants, black T-shirt, black nylon bomber jacket, black trainers, black helmet. The rest of the gear he'd asked for was in a backpack, stowed in the terminal locker. It was just as black as everything else.

The bike that awaited him in the car park was a debadged Honda XR400. It was a trail-bike, designed for rutted country paths rather than city streets, as skinny and high-stepping as a whippet. But it was ideal for Carver's purposes. If the operation went wrong and he needed to get away fast, he wanted a machine that could go where police cars and their heavy, powerful bikes would have a hard time following him.

Five minutes after leaving the airport, Carver stopped at a roadside pizza-parlour and ordered a takeaway. While it was being cooked, he went looking for the bathroom, carrying his pack with him. There were two individual cubicles, each with a toilet and basin, and he made his way into the nearest one. He got out the gun he'd specified, a SIG-Sauer P226 pistol, with a Colt/Browning short-recoil mechanism and no safety-catch. There were twelve Cor-Bon 9mm 115 grain +P Jacketed Hollowpoints in the magazine. The SIG was the British special forces' pistol of choice for anti-terrorist and undercover work. Carver had used it on countless military operations and had stayed with it ever since. Now, as always, he stripped his gun, checked it and reassembled it. The whole process took him less than a minute. On one level, it was a basic precaution to make sure the weapon functioned; but it was also a ritual that helped him focus on what was to come – like a warm-up for an athlete, moving into the zone, getting his game-face on.

Next, Carver plugged the washbasin. He reached into his knapsack, took out the can of 3-in-1 and poured its contents into the basin. Then he reached in again, removing a small brick of what looked like grey modelling clay. It was C4 explosive – plastique. He put the C4 into the basin and started kneading it, mixing the oil and plastique together, like a baker working his dough. He ended up with a sticky, pliable putty that by itself was completely safe. It could be moulded into any shape and stuck to any surface. You could shove it in small plastic bags – just as Carver now started to do, having divided it into four equal quantities – hit it, burn it, even shoot it full of bullets and nothing would happen. But put a fuse, a blasting-cap or a timer into it and suddenly you had a bomb.

Once the bags of explosive putty had been stashed in Carver's knapsack, he got out the cleanser and poured it all over the basin, removing any traces of oil or C4. He set the taps on full blast to rinse it all away, and binned the bottle. There was still a slight smell of oil and plastique in the air, so Carver sprayed air-freshener around the tiny room then junked that can too. A man was waiting outside as he left. Carver shrugged his shoulders apologetically, held his nose and murmured, 'Excuse me.'

He collected his pizza and ate half of it in the car park outside. The rest he threw away in a dumpster. He kept the box, mounted the Honda and headed south into Paris.

The apartment was on the Ile St Louis, one of the two islands in the middle of the River Seine that sit virtually at the dead centre of the city. The street outside was filled with tourists enjoying the island's relaxed village atmosphere and the warm, late-summer evening. They wandered along, taking their time, stopping to look in shop windows or to check out the menus of the restaurants and cafés dotted along the pavements.

Carver parked his bike and got off, still wearing his helmet, carrying the pizza box. Anyone who spared him a passing glance would just see a deliveryman. Only a very sharp eye indeed would spot that he had on a pair of latex gloves as he walked up to the front door of the eighteenth-century building where Ramzi Narwaz entertained his lovers. A few seconds' work with a set of skeleton keys got him in.

He looked around the ground-floor lobby, familiarizing himself with its layout, then walked down it to a back door that led into a bare courtyard with a row of rubbish bins down one wall. Directly opposite him an archway opened out on to the street at the back of the building. Relieved to see that there was more than one way out, Carver got rid of the pizza box and went back into the building.

The apartment was on the top floor, up several flights of stairs. Once again the locks were no barrier. Carver stepped into a central hallway, with a floor-to-ceiling window at its far end. It was almost dark outside, but the streetlights gave off enough illumination to enable Carver to see his way around.

The moment the door was opened the burglar alarm warning had started beeping, set off by a standard magnetic door contact. Carver had thirty seconds before the alarm went off. A small control-pad was fixed to the wall immediately to the left of the door, just as the plans he'd been sent had promised. The code, too, was exactly as Max had said. The beeping stopped.

Ahead of him, leading off the hall, was a short passage, lined with cupboards. The left-hand side was broken by a door, which opened on to a tiny kitchenette. Carver turned the other way and opened the cupboard on the right-hand side of the passage. There were a couple of winter coats hanging up. Behind them was the white metal box that contained the heart and brain of the apartment's alarm system. He gave a satisfied nod, then closed the cupboard door.

At the far end of the passage was a large, open-plan living-room. The place was classier than Carver had been expecting, given the kind of man who owned it and what he used it for. There were no flashy glass-and-chrome tables, no mirrored ceilings or semi-pornographic nudes. Instead, the room had pale walls, with an antique wooden dining table at one end, decorated with a vase of fresh flowers. Beyond it, three large, creamy sofas were ranged around a Persian rug. Other than that, the floors were bare wood, echoed in the massive, black wooden beams that supported the ceiling. A fireplace was set into the far wall, next to bookshelves that housed a mini hi-fi system, a couple of rows of books and a small collection of crystal vases, small pots and miniature sculptures. Two infra-red motion detectors blinked at him from opposite corners of the room, there to catch intruders coming in through the windows.

Carver put his pack down in the middle of the floor, extracted the torch, strapped it around his head so that both his hands were free and took a long, detailed look at the hi-fi. He banged his hand against the wall behind it, checking to see that it was a solid, load-bearing structure. Satisfied that it was, he returned to the pack and removed the screwdriver, the wire-cutters and three small, oblong plastic cases, each roughly the size and depth of a paperback book but very slightly curved along their longer sides. These were M-18 Claymore anti-personnel mines, configured for remote detonation. Each consisted of a kilogram slab of C4 explosive, around which were wrapped seven hundred tiny steel ball-bearings, encased in a polystyrene and fibreglass outer shell.

He lifted down the mini hi-fi, unscrewed the back of the speaker cabinets, opened them up and cut away the speaker units themselves. Then he placed a Claymore inside each of the empty cabinets, closed them up again and replaced them exactly as they had been, complete with leads from the amplifier. When they went off, the deadly pellets would be fired in an arc across the room and through the flimsy partition walls that separated it from the kitchenette and the hall. Anyone in their way would be shredded into bite-size chunks. Carver tucked his screwdriver and wire-cutters away in his outside thigh-pocket and took another look at the finished job. The switch was undetectable. If Narwaz turned on his hi-fi within a minute of walking into the apartment, he might be suspicious when no sound came from the speakers. But then, if Narwaz came back to the apartment that night, he'd just have survived an assassination attempt. He wouldn't be in the mood for music.

Carver was working without undue haste, settling into a steady rhythm that would get him out of the apartment as quickly as possible without rushing into careless mistakes. He picked up the pack and walked from the room, down the passage and across the hall to the bedroom. Again, the walls were pale, the floors wooden, the window and curtains full length. This time there was just one motion sensor. The bed was the one extravagance in the place, a magnificent piece of Victorian brass, its gleaming rails topped by extravagant swirls of twisted metal.

Carver was about to move on when something caught his eye at the end of the bed. When he shone his torch on it he realized it was an overnight bag. The pattern on the fabric was Louis Vuitton. It was open, and half filled with women's clothes. Nearby was a small, shiny Chanel carrier bag. A pair of white jeans had been thrown on the bedcover next to a short denim jacket. Two slip-on Keds sneakers, in matching white, were lying on the floor next to the bed. Carver walked around the bed and over to another door that led into the en-suite bathroom. On the shelf above the basin there were a couple of bags, one filled with make-up, the other, bigger one stuffed with shampoo, body lotions and other bathtime paraphernalia.

The discovery jolted Carver out of his smooth, complacent

routine. Max hadn't told him that Narwaz had a girlfriend in town. She'd obviously arrived, changed and then gone out again. If she was with Narwaz now, she was going to die with him tonight. Carver pulled out his phone and dialled a UK-based mobile line.

'You didn't tell me about the woman.'

'Why would I? Makes no difference to the mission.'

'It makes a difference to me. I came here to eliminate a serious terrorist. The girlfriend's a civilian. You know I don't hit civilians, Max.'

Carver heard a laugh come down the line.

'Course you do. You just don't like to admit it. That Albanian – you think his helicopter flew itself? He had a pilot, Carver.'

'The pilot knew what he was doing. He was getting paid.'

'Oh, what, and the bird isn't? Look, it doesn't matter if the target has a girlfriend, a driver, a bodyguard or his entire family with him. I don't care if he invites the Dagenham Diamonds drum majorettes round to his gaff for a party and we blow them all to smithereens. This mad bastard wants to start a holy war. There could be millions of lives at risk. So he has to go. The collateral damage is not our problem.'

Carver said nothing. He'd spent his military service fighting blood-soaked dictators who lost wars but stayed in power. He'd gone after psychopathic terrorists who somehow morphed into peace-loving politicians, greeted with handshakes at Number 10 and smiles on the White House lawn. He and his men had seized countless old freighters and fishing-boats filled with drugs or guns. But it never made a damn bit of difference. No one ever paid for what they'd done. No government ever stopped them doing it in the first place. Now he was able to trade with the bad guys in their own currency. He believed he made the world a better, safer place. Sometimes people got caught in the crossfire. That was the price of doing business. He forced his doubts out of his conscious mind, locking them up in the same mental dungeon where so many of his scruples, fears and emotions had been shut away.

Max broke the silence. 'You still with me there, mate? Cause if you're not up for this job, just tell me now. I can't have anyone screwing this up.'

'Tell you what, Max. Why don't you come down here? Walk through the front door and wait sixty seconds. Find out if I'm up for it yourself.'

'That's more like it. For a moment there, I thought you might have lost it. You're not losing it, are you, Carver? I'm starting to worry about you.'

'Piss off, Max.'

Carver's tone was aggressively self-confident. Inside, though, he asked himself whether Max might be right. Was he losing it? In terms of straightforward competence, he was certain the answer was no. He kept himself in good shape; he didn't throw away his money on drugs or divorces; he wasn't one of those military relics who hung around the pubs of Hereford and Poole telling pathetically exaggerated war-stories to other old soldiers as lost and purposeless as themselves. So no, he hadn't lost his ability to do the job. But maybe he was losing the taste for it. He'd long ago concluded that his strength had nothing to do with muscles, guns or explosives. It lay in his mind and his eyes, in the force of his will and the certainty of his purpose. Somewhere inside him, there was a well of barely acknowledged anger and loss that had always driven him on. But if that well ran dry, if that strength of will should ever be diminished, well, what then?

This really might be his last contract, after all. So he'd better make it a good one. And come out of it alive.

The third mine went in the bedroom, taped to the wall at the head of the bed and covered up with pillows. The woman's bag was right next to Carver as he worked. He caught a faint trace of her scent, rising from her clothes. He wondered whether she knew the truth about her lover. Did she follow the same cause? Or was she just a pretty girl about to die because she let a wealthy man seduce her?

'For Chrissakes,' he muttered to himself. 'Focus.'

He still had another three devices to put in place – the freezer bags filled with explosive putty. He taped one inside the cistern of the toilet, then stuck a tiny radio-detonator into it. A second bag and another detonator went inside one of the eye-level kitchen units. The claymores should penetrate the room, but he wasn't going to count on it. Too many targets had survived assassination attempts because bombs turned out to be less deadly than their users had planned. You needed to kill them twice, just to make sure. A final bag with detonator was secured beneath a console table in the hall. Every room in the apartment had been turned into a killing field. Now he just had to make all his bombs go off.

He returned to the sack and removed a small plastic box the size of a mini radio. Two wires protruded from the bottom of the box, and on the top were an extendable aerial, an on–off switch and a tiny red power-light. He went back to the coat cupboard, opened up the main alarm-system box and wired his little box into the same terminals as the door sensor. Then he switched it on. The red light at the top of the box began to pulse. The unit was on standby.

When the apartment's alarm system was activated, the unit would be fully switched on. Any break in the alarm circuit, such as the opening of a door, would trigger a switch inside it, setting off a sixty-second timer. But unlike the alarm, it couldn't be turned off. Tapping the code into the control panel made no difference. The timer just kept counting down the seconds till it reached zero and sent its deadly signal to the explosives hidden around the apartment.

The trap was set. Carver took off the torch and put it back in the pack, along with the rest of his equipment. He retraced his steps around the apartment, making sure that everything was exactly as he had found it and nothing had been left behind, then he moved back out the way he had come in, resetting the alarm as he went. The next time anyone came in through the front door, the whole place would blow.

At the bottom of the stairs, Carver turned towards the back door and went out into the courtyard. He took off his pack and extracted everything he'd need for the rest of the operation, along with the black bin bag. He opened it up and put the pack and its remaining contents inside, then walked down the street to an alley beside a local bistro and slung it into a huge metal bin, burying it beneath a layer of restaurant rubbish.

As Carver made his way back to his bike, he called Max.

'The apartment's fixed. Where do you want me now?'

He received his instructions, making sure that he was absolutely clear about every stage of the operation. For now, at any rate, those moments of weakness in the apartment had passed.

4

Less than a mile from the apartment Carver had booby-trapped, two men with false names were going about their work in a building with bogus ownership papers. One of them was known to Carver as Max. His face had the deep-lined, half-starved look of a jockey or a Rolling Stone. His steely hair was cropped tight to his skull. He wore rimless glasses, a charcoal suit, a white linen shirt and a pale-mushroom knitted tie.

His stark modernity looked out of place in his immediate surroundings. He had just walked into the drawing-room of an eighteenth-century townhouse, decorated with lavish extravagance. It had 12-foot ceilings, a marble fireplace, antique furniture, ancestral portraits with heavy gilt frames, and oversize picture books and glossy magazines artfully piled on inlaid coffee tables. Whoever chose the decorations had been trying to evoke the grandeur of a bygone age. There wasn't a curtain, a lampshade or a seat-cover in the entire place that didn't have a fringe or tassel dangling from it somewhere.

Max looked around in distaste. The place looked like a bloody museum. He turned his attention to the middle-aged man in beige cords, green sweater and pale-blue button-down shirt standing by the unlit fire, holding a glass of whisky. The man was stocky, powerfully built, just starting to run to fat as time, gravity and lack of exercise took their toll.

'I got news from Carver, sir.'

The other man's job title was operations director. Some of his staff referred to him as 'OD'. When he wanted to give an impression of friendship, he told people, 'Call me Charlie.' But Max preferred 'sir'. He never liked getting chummy with his bosses. They started taking liberties if you did. Keep it nice and formal, then everyone knew where they stood.

'How's he getting on?' asked the operations director.

His voice sounded tired. He ran a hand through his hair and down the back of his neck. He'd had less than three hours' sleep in the past forty-eight. They'd been working fast, under pressure, cutting too many corners. Max wondered whether the old man was any longer up to it.

'Fine,' he said. 'Just one thing, though. Looks like he's had a sudden attack of conscience.'

'Really? How so?'

'He's worried innocent people might get killed.'

The operations director laughed, composing himself when he saw the disapproval on Max's face. 'Sorry,' he said. 'Tension must be getting to me. But you see the irony, surely.'

'Oh yes, I see that.'

'Right then, are the Russians in place?' He gave a sharp, frustrated sigh. 'I don't like using new people on a job like this. Still, the chairman assures me they're top-notch. He must know what he's talking about.'

'They're in position,' said Max. 'And the observation teams are ready. Once there's a sighting, we'll be ready to move at once.'

'Excellent,' said the operations director. 'Let's wait for the show to begin.'

Sunday, 31 August

5

The time was a quarter past midnight. Samuel Carver stood astride the Honda, waiting to go into action. He glanced down at the black metal tube clipped to the bike behind his right leg. It looked like a regular long-barrelled torch, the kind police or security guards use. It was, in fact, a portable diode pump laser, otherwise known as a dazzler. Developed as a non-fatal weapon for US police forces, but taken up with deadly enthusiasm by special forces around the world, it emitted a green-light beam at a frequency of 532 nanometres. Its nickname, though, was misleading. When this light shone in somebody's eyes, they weren't just dazzled. A green-laser beam left anyone who looked at it disoriented, confused and temporarily immobile. The human brain couldn't process the sheer amount of light data flooding through the optic nerves, so it acted like any other overloaded computer, and crashed.

Night or day, rain or shine, a dazzler was an accident's best friend.

It would only be a matter of seconds now. Carver was positioned by the exit of an underpass that ran beneath an embankment on the northern side of the Seine. If he turned his head fractionally to the right, he could look across the river at the glittering spire of the Eiffel Tower darting up into the night sky. It was past midnight, but there were still a few pleasure-boats out on the water. If Carver had been the slightest bit interested, he'd have seen the lovers standing arm in arm by the rails, looking out at the City of Light. But Carver had other things to think about. He was looking towards the far side of the underpass. All he cared about was the traffic.

The time had come. He took a deep breath, then let the air out slowly, dropping his shoulders, easing the muscles, twisting his neck and rotating his head to loosen the top of his spinal cord. Then he looked back at the road.

Several hundred metres away, beyond the entrance of the underpass, he saw a black Mercedes. It was travelling fast. Way too fast.

Behind the Merc was the reason for its desperate speed. A motorbike was chasing it, buzzing around the big black car like a wasp around a buffalo. There was a passenger riding pillion, carrying a camera, leaning away from his seat and firing his flashgun, apparently oblivious to his own safety. He looked for all the world like a paparazzo, risking his neck for an exclusive shot.

'Nice job,' thought Carver, watching the speed team. He started his bike and got ready to move.

For a second, he imagined the passengers in the car, urging their driver to pull away from the relentless pursuit of the bike.

Everything was going to plan. Carver rolled downhill, towards the road leading from the underpass. As he reached the junction with the main road, a grey Citroën BX hatchback emerged from the underpass. Carver let it go, noting the two Arab men in the driver's and passenger's seats. Another car went by, a Ford Ka. Then Carver rode his bike out into the middle of the road.

He crossed to the far side of the carriageway, then turned the Honda into the flow of the oncoming traffic and dashed forward about a hundred metres to the mouth of the underpass. There was a line of pillars down the middle of the road. They supported the tunnel roof and separated the two flows of traffic. He stopped by the last pillar and reached down to unclip his dazzler.

Something caught Carver's eye. At the mouth of the underpass, coming towards him, was a battered white Fiat Uno. It was doing the legal speed, 50 kilometres per hour, and therefore going less than half as fast as the car and bike racing towards its tail.

Carver's eyes narrowed as he pulled out the laser. His mouth gave a quick twitch of silent irritation. This wasn't part of the plan.

The Mercedes and the motorbike were closing on the little white car at breakneck speed. There were a hundred metres between them. Fifty. Twenty.

The Merc came roaring up behind the Fiat in the right-hand lane, then swung left, trying to overtake it. The bike-rider had no option. He had to go round the other way, squeezing between the right-hand side of the Fiat and the tunnel wall. Somehow, he shot through without a scratch, rocketing out the far side of the Fiat. The Merc wasn't so lucky. The front of the car, on the passenger's side, caught the Fiat from behind. The Merc smashed through the Fiat's rear lights and crumpled the thin metal of the Fiat's rear panels.

The tunnel walls echoed to the cacophony of screaming engines, smashing plastic and tortured metal. But inside his helmet, Carver felt isolated, unaffected by the chaos that was rushing towards him. He could see the driver of the Mercedes struggling to regain control as his vehicle careered across the road. The guy was good. Somehow the car straightened out. Now it was coming straight towards Carver.

Carver stood as immobile as a matador facing a charging black bull. He raised the laser, aimed at the windscreen of the car and pressed the switch.

The blast of light was instantaneous. A beam of pure energy exploded across the ever-narrowing gap between Carver and the onrushing Merc. It took only a fraction of a second, then the beam was gone.

The Mercedes lurched to the left. Somewhere, deep in the unconscious, animal part of the driver's brain, some sort of alarm signal must have registered. He slammed his foot on the brakes, desperately trying to stop the car.

He had no chance. The two-ton Mercedes smashed into one of the central pillars, instantly decelerating from crazy speed to total immobility. Its bonnet crumpled, exactly as it was supposed to, absorbing some of the force of the impact. But there was just too much speed, too much weight, too much momentum. The shattered car bounced off the pillar and slewed across the road, spinning round as it went. It finally came to a halt in the middle of the road, facing back the way it had just come.

The front of the Merc looked like a Dinky toy hit by a baseball bat, with a gigantic U-shaped depression where the bonnet and engine-bay had been. The windscreen was shattered, as was every other window. The driver's-side front wheel was splayed outwards, and on the other side the wheel had been jammed into the body-work. The roof had been ripped from the passenger side, thrust down into the passenger compartment and shifted two feet to the left. The pressure from front and top had forced all four doors open.

There was no sign of movement from the passenger compartment. Carver knew that the chances of anyone surviving that kind of an impact were minimal. In the corner of his eye he saw a car drive past him, on the other side of the road, going into the tunnel, past the Mercedes.

Meanwhile, the Fiat was completing its journey out of the tunnel. Carver caught a glimpse of shock and terror on the driver's face. Then he noticed something else. There was a dog in the front seat. It had its tongue out, panting happily, oblivious to the destruction disappearing behind it.

Carver strapped the laser back on the petrol-tank of his bike. He was tempted to go down and check the wreckage to make sure the target was dead, but there was little point. In the unlikely event that anyone had survived such a devastating impact, there was nothing Carver could do about it without leaving some sort of forensic trace. And even if Ramzi Hakim Narwaz was still alive, he wasn't going to be plotting terrorist activities any time soon.

It was time to go. At the far end of the tunnel, Carver could see a couple of pedestrians, standing and watching, unable to decide whether to walk any further towards the scene of the accident. In the distance he could hear the mosquito whine of motorbike engines. People were coming. They would have cameras. They would be followed by cops, ambulances, fire engines.

Carver didn't want to be around when they got there. He needed to get away before anyone figured out that this wasn't just an unfortunate accident. He swung the tail of his bike round 180 degrees and headed back up the exit ramp of the Alma Tunnel.

6

The other motorbike pulled up two hundred metres further up the road, on the Avenue de New York, just beyond the vast neo-classical expanse of the Palais de Tokyo, home of the Paris Museum of Modern Art.

Grigori Kursk placed his feet on the ground astride his Ducati M900 Monster, sat upright and raised his visor. There was a predatory smirk on his face and his eyes burned with the rapacious hunger of a man for whom killing was not just a job, but a compulsion – one that he would gratify whether he was paid to do so or not. He turned to look at his passenger, who was just stowing the camera in a pannier on the side of the bike.

'Did you see that?' he crowed, speaking in Russian. 'Did you see the look on that driver's face? The poor bastard didn't know what to do. Well, he's just French pâté now!' He paused for a second, then continued more calmly, getting back to business. 'OK, that was just as easy as I promised. Now, let's pick up the other half of the money.'

'Just pick it up fast, I'm in agony back here,' his passenger replied. 'My knees are up around my ears.'

Kursk laughed. 'Ha! I thought you liked it like that!'

He drove on another few metres till he found a gap in the parked cars just big enough for the bike. He positioned himself facing outwards from the curve, giving himself just enough clearance to see the exit of the tunnel. He then took a night-scope from the chest pocket of his biker-jacket and held it up to his right eye, through the gap in his helmet. He was looking for the man who'd been astride the bike at the far end of the tunnel.

Kursk knew two things about this man. He was ex-British special forces. And he was their next target.

7

Carver's route out of town was simple. He planned to follow the river till he reached the *périphérique*, the autoroute that ringed Paris, then to circle the city anti-clockwise before hitting the A5 autoroute, away from the city to the south-east. He'd be over the Swiss border before dawn.

He was just about to open the throttle when a flash of light caught his eye, no more than a hundred metres ahead, a reflection off a glass lens. It was only there for a fraction of a second, but that was long enough to draw Carver's attention and alert him to the curve of a bike-wheel protruding from behind a parked car.

Someone was watching him. And he was riding straight towards them.

Carver needed to get off the road. He looked to his right. There was a turning. No good – a dead end. There was only one option now. He swung the Honda on to the broad expanse of pavement and raced past a line of trees and a low, black-painted iron railing that provided some sort of barrier between himself and whoever was waiting for him.

To his right loomed the grey-white bulk of the Palais de Tokyo, its wings wrapped around a vast expanse of open plaza that rose uphill on four levels, separated by flights of shallow steps that stretched the full width of the building. At the very back ran two rows of tall classical columns, raised on a high pediment between the two wings. Behind them was the Avenue du Président Wilson, which would give him another route out of town.

Carver swerved towards the giant building, aiming the bike at the pediment. He hugged the curved wings of the plaza, racing past a knot of skateboarders huddled round a glowing joint, who looked at him in stoned bafflement. As he hit the first line of five steps, he rose in his saddle, letting his legs and arms act as shock-absorbers as the Honda juddered up and over the obstruction.

With his helmet on and the engine screaming, Carver didn't hear the gunfire. He just saw a spark of light in the corner of his eye, followed instantaneously by the impact of bullets smashing into the back of the bike, punching holes in the rear mud-flap and blasting through the exhaust pipe. Behind him, the skateboarders were woken from their trance. A couple threw themselves to the ground. The rest just ran, screaming in panic across the expanse of open stone.

Carver crouched over the handlebars, pressing his head down as low as possible as the wall next to him erupted in a spattering of miniature explosions, little puffs of stone fragments and dust. He had nowhere to go but straight ahead. Jinking his bike from side to side, he raced across the paving, then hit the next set of steps.

He was in a muck sweat now, almost pulling the machine beneath him over the steps through sheer physical effort and bloody-minded determination. But as his body rocked back and forth in the saddle, his mind was working on another problem. Who was shooting at him? The obvious answer was someone working with or for Ramzi Narwaz. But if he had protection, why hadn't they defended his car? It had to be someone else. And unless the assassination party had an uninvited guest, that left only one alternative.

*

'Shit!'

Kursk shook his head in disgust and shoved his Mini Uzi submachine gun back in his jacket. He had been forced to shoot twisted round in the saddle of his bike, which was pointing in the wrong direction, away from the plaza where the Englishman was making his desperate attempt at escape. There were trees in the way, and he was aiming at a moving target. He was just wasting ammunition.

Then he looked again. The Englishman seemed to be riding into a dead end, trapping himself at the far end of the inverted U-shaped plaza, beneath a wall at least four metres high. Kursk saw that there were more steps rising, much more steeply this time, diagonally up the side of the wall. Mother of God, was the man planning to ride up those as well?

If he did, Kursk would not be able to follow him. His bike wasn't built for that kind of stunt. Not with a passenger onboard. Of course, he'd have time to get off the bike, set the gun to fire single-shot and aim at leisure as his target struggled upwards. But the range would be well over a hundred metres. At that distance his gun, designed for close-quarter work, had greatly reduced stopping-power.

There was another issue. Suppose he put enough shots into the Englishman to kill him. Kursk would still be left with a body on the steps of a public building, with witnesses to the shooting, less than four hundred metres from the initial crash. Even for the guys who'd hired him, that would be hard to cover up.

He swore under his breath. Things were getting ragged. Kursk had to get one move ahead of his opponent.

'Hang on,' he said to his passenger.

The Ducati roared back to life as Kursk pulled out on to the Avenue de New York. He drove another few metres down the road, then made a right into a side street and roared uphill, beside the Palais de Tokyo. Now he was running parallel to Carver, separated by the bulk of the building, heading away from the river. But he'd be closing on his quarry soon enough.

*

At the far side of the plaza, Carver had got to the foot of the pediment steps. He revved the bike, prayed that its low-gear grunt was as good as advertised, then hurled himself at the steps, heaving the handlebars and pushing with his thighs, as if forcing an exhausted horse over a series of fences. The engine screamed in complaint at its mistreatment. But it kept going up. Finally, with one last howl of protest, it made it to the top, spun its rear wheel for a second on the slick marble surface, then raced forward, between the columns, out on to the tiny semi-circle of the Place de Tokyo, which led directly to the Avenue du Président Wilson and—

'Damn!'

Carver needed to turn left, across the oncoming traffic, into the far, right-hand lane of the road. That was the way to the *périphérique.* But there were two solid lines of parked cars, backed by trees, running down the middle of the road, blocking his way.

Then, emerging from a side street about fifty metres to his left he saw the same bike that had been chasing the Mercedes. It was a big, powerful machine but it looked like a scooter beneath the massive bulk of its rider, who dwarfed the passenger riding pillion. Their two heads scanned from side to side, then the smaller man tapped the rider on the shoulder and nodded down the road in Carver's direction. The rider responded immediately, turning right and gunning it downhill.

By then Carver was already blazing down the road. He'd answered his own question. Max had set his people after him. But why would he want him dead? Carver ran through the alternatives in his mind as he sent the Honda's engine back into the red zone, ignoring traffic lights, and swerving in and out of traffic coming out of the cross-streets.

Was it the money? Three million bucks was a lot to splash out on one job. If Max got him out of the way, he could keep the unpaid half of the cash for himself.

Parisian drivers don't give a damn, but even they hit their brakes at the sight of a motorbike racing across their front fenders. Carver weaved between cars as they skidded to a halt, rear-ending one another in a cacophony of shrieking brakes, squealing tyres and furious French insults. That suited him fine. Every stopped car was just one more obstruction slowing down the men on his tail.

Had Carver outlived his usefulness? It had been pretty clear from their conversation that this was the last job he'd be doing for a while. Max might want to tie up all the loose ends.

At the bottom of the road, the avenue opened on to the Place de l'Alma. That, in turn, led past the Alma-Marceau metro station to the Pont de l'Alma, or Alma Bridge. The Alma Tunnel ran crossways underneath. In Paris, when they found a name they liked, they stuck with it.

Or was there some other reason Max needed him out of the way, something to do with this operation? But what made this operation so different from the rest?

He bore right across the Place de l'Alma, passing right over the car-smash he'd caused just a few minutes earlier. As yet there were no ambulances, no police cars' flashing lights. At ground level, there seemed no sign at all of any accident.

Carver hit the bridge a hundred metres, maybe a little more, ahead of the Ducati, heading across the River Seine. He was going to make a right and get on to the autoroute that ran along the south bank of the river, making for the *périphérique*, just like before. But he realized that would be crazy. The Ducati was a much bigger, more powerful bike. Even with two onboard it would soon run him down on the open road. He needed a battleground where he could fight his attackers and win.

And then he saw it.

On the far side of the bridge, across the other side of the road, stood a small white kiosk surrounded by low hedges. It looked like a giant geometric mushroom: a short, squat tower topped by a wide, gently sloping octagonal roof. Just in front of it stood a blue sign that read VISITE DES ÉGOUTS DE PARIS.

Carver grinned. He knew what that was. And it would do just fine.

Ahead of him he could see a long articulated bus, its two halves held together by a rubber concertina. It was about to turn left, off the main road that ran along the Left Bank, on to the Alma Bridge, going back the way Carver had just come. He needed to get across the road. The bus would cut right across his path. He played one last game of chicken, turning his bike hard left, skidding across the path of the oncoming bus, sensing its bulk loom above him, seeing the look of horror on the driver's face.

The bus screeched to a halt in mid-turn. Or at least its front half did. The rear end kept going, fish-tailing as the link between its two halves acted as a hinge, slewing the bus around to the right. Somehow, the driver brought the bus under control before the momentum of the spin flung it on to its side. But now it was sprawled across the bridge, with traffic piling up around it. A perfect roadblock.

Carver brought his bike to a halt beside the kiosk. He jumped off, pulled off his helmet and grabbed the laser-torch.

Next to the kiosk, a low, white metal gate guarded a stone stairway that spiralled underground. A sign on the gate said ACCÈS INTERDIT – entry forbidden. He kicked open the gate then headed down the stairs.

8

The first underground sewer was dug beneath the streets of Paris in 1370; now there were 1,300 miles of tunnels beneath the city. Known as *les égouts*, they carried away 1.2 million cubic metres of water and waste a day, and they directly followed the lines of the roads above. Every tunnel was signposted with the name of the avenue, boulevard, street or square whose filth it removed.

If you wanted to have a gun battle right in the middle of a major city without anyone noticing, the sewers were the place to have it. But Paris went one better. It didn't just have sewers, it had a sewer museum, a concrete-and-steel warren of tunnels and chambers, right underneath the south end of the Alma Bridge.

Carver scuttled down the narrow stairs, bare concrete walls on either side. At the bottom, the passage turned sharp left. In front of him was a solid steel door. On it was a white sign with a red banner across it announcing DANGER. Below the sign a padlock held a massive bolt in place.

He put a bullet through the padlock, blowing it open, then pushed against the door, which swung away from him into a pitch-black void filled with chill, damp air that smelled of drains. He turned on his dazzler, twisting the end to widen the beam, filling the black void with a ghostly, radioactive green glow. Ahead, the passage seemed to open up into a low, broad chamber.

There was another lock on the inside of the door, operated by a metal wheel. Carver closed the door and turned the wheel. There wasn't much chance the guys who were after him would come in that way. Only an idiot would charge down a narrow, dark corridor towards a man known to have a dazzler, and almost certainly a gun as well. They'd find another way in. Even so, it never hurt to cover your back.

Carver walked on into the sewers, his torch in his left hand, the SIG-Sauer in his right, trying to work out the direction from which his enemy's attack would come.

The first chamber consisted of two old sewer-tunnels that ran side by side. The sewer was filled in with concrete to make a flat floor. The wall between the tunnels had been punctured by a series of low egg-shaped arches to make a single space. Carver walked through one of the arches, then hurled himself to the ground, bringing his gun to bear as he rolled across the concrete. To his left, in the shadows on the edge of the green torch-light, he'd seen a group of figures in boiler suits and miners' helmets. It took him half a second to realize they were waxworks, part of the museum's exhibition.

He got up sheepishly and dusted himself down. To his right there was another, smaller tunnel. A notice said THIS WAY FOR THE TOUR. Carver followed it and went deeper into the tunnel.

Grigori Kursk had reached the far end of the Alma Bridge a few seconds after Carver. He'd tracked the Englishman right up to the point where he'd pulled that crazy stunt in front of the oncoming bus. By the time the bus had got out of the way, he'd lost him.

For a second he thought the man had got away. Then, across the far side of the road, he saw Carver's bike abandoned next to the kiosk. He drove the Ducati on to the pavement at the end of the bridge, parking it next to a waist-high metal cage that stood over an open manhole. Beneath the cage a metal spiral staircase descended into the ground.

Kursk gestured to his partner to approach the Englishman's abandoned bike from the right. He moved left. The two of them dashed across the bridge. Kursk ran round the front of the stranded bus, while his partner darted between the bus and the cars piling up behind. As they approached the bike they saw no sign of its rider. Then Kursk noticed the open gate and the concrete stairway behind it.

He stared at the signs on the kiosk, trying to work out what they meant from the mass of different languages and symbols. OK, so this was some sort of visitors' entrance to something. Which presumably meant somewhere there had to be an exit, or maybe a fire escape. Which would need a manhole. Beneath his helmet, Kursk grinned. Now he knew how to beat the Englishman.

He gave his instructions to the other black-leather-clad figure, then jogged back across the bridge to where his bike was parked against the metal cage. The top of the cage was hinged in the middle. One half opened up to allow access to the manhole underneath, and it was held in place with a padlock and chain. Kursk took off his helmet, reached into the bike's top-box and pulled out a tool-kit in a black, roll-up nylon pouch. From this he removed a small pair of bolt-cutters, casually leaned over the cage and cut the links of the chain. He lifted the hinged lid of the cage, stepped over the side-railings and started to walk down the metal stairs. Once he was below ground, he reached into his jacket and took out his gun before clipping a small black torch on to a mount on top of the barrel.

At the bottom of the shaft there was a double door that shone scarlet in the beam of the torch. It was an emergency exit, opening out, towards him. Kursk fired a three-bullet burst into the locking mechanism. The sound of the gunfire reverberated away into the darkness. The Englishman was bound to hear, but that was good. Kursk did not want to waste time wandering around the sewers of Paris, playing blind-man's bluff. He'd far rather draw his opponent on, tempting him into an ambush. But he still had to find a way of setting up that ambush.

He pulled open the splintered door, walked a few paces forward and entered a sort of man-made cave, maybe fifty feet square and twelve to fifteen feet high. He could hear the sound of rushing water somewhere beneath him. The torch tracked across the concrete floor until it came to an inset metal grille running the full width of the cave, maybe six feet across. A thick brown soup of sewage and drainwater was running beneath it, filling the air with a heavy fecal smell. And people actually paid to come down here?

Kursk looked around for cover. The huge space was almost entirely bare. The only means of access to the cave were two tunnels, one narrow and floored with concrete, the other broader, with another grille-floor, directly over the open sewer. They ran away, a few feet apart, to the left.

On the right was an alcove. Its far wall had a great circle cut into it, maybe ten feet in diameter. In the middle of the circle, held on a low wooden frame, was a gigantic black sphere, like a huge cannon ball, so high that Kursk could not reach its top. There was a scale model of the ball down on the floor, demonstrating that it was made of wooden planks, with a hollow core. An illustrated notice showed how the ball had once been used as a cleaning device, dragged through the main sewers, bashing against the sides and knocking the crud from the walls. Kursk scanned the notice. He examined the ball and the way it was held on its frame. OK, now he had a new plan.

Carver had heard the muffled echo of gunfire in front of him, somewhere in the distance, just as he emerged from a low, narrow tunnel into an underground plaza. He swept his torch round and tried to get his bearings. It looked like some kind of a junction, where a warren of underground routes converged at a single point. On all sides there were arches beyond which he could see nothing but the blackness of passageways disappearing into the depths. But the only tunnel that interested Carver opened directly ahead of where he was standing. He was sure the gunfire had come from its far end.

He moved forward, accepting the implied invitation. Whoever had fired those shots had wanted them to be heard. Carver understood completely: he wanted to get this over and done with too. There was something almost reassuring about the absolute nature of the game they were playing. All the whys and wherefores could be forgotten. He just had to kill the other guy before the other guy killed him. It was a simple, straightforward task. He liked that.

A dozen paces down the tunnel, there was an opening on the left. From it, Carver could hear the sound of rushing water, moving much faster than anything he'd heard so far. He stopped by the opening, flattening himself against the wall. He took a deep breath to calm his pulse, and placed his left hand holding the torch directly under his right hand holding the gun, so that each steadied the other. Then he stepped out into the open, feet apart, legs bent, arms straight out in front of him.

There was no one there. In front of Carver stretched another, much bigger tunnel. From the ceiling, placards and display cases were suspended in mid-air on steel wire, the whole history of the Paris sewers stretching away into the distance. Directly underneath all the displays, thick steel mesh covered a working, gushing sewer. That was where the noise of water was coming from. To the sides, along the walls of the tunnel, concrete walkways kept visitors firmly on dry land.

Carver stepped back into the cross-tunnel and walked on. There was still water flowing all around him, but much more sluggishly now. And the smell was suddenly more intense, a nauseating stench of human waste.

Ahead, a massive pipe hung from the ceiling, banded with striped warning-tape to prevent people banging their heads. Beyond it was another junction, where the tunnel split in two. The left-hand fork was a narrow tube of concrete; the right-hand one was wider, with a walkway running beside a sewer covered with a raised metal cage. Carver went left. There was no big strategic logic, he just figured the concrete tunnel would smell less rank.

Carver shifted the torch-beam left and right as he went, listening intently for any sound of human movement. He almost fell into the huge open space at the end of the tunnel, stopping himself just in time before he crashed on to the floor. He pulled back a couple of feet, wondering why there hadn't yet been a shot. The hostiles must be close now. Why didn't they fire? Had they gone down the other way without him noticing? Was he outflanked?

He shone the torch back the way he had come. No one there. He turned again, hands together, stepped out into the space and . . . nothing, just a cavernous emptiness. He stepped forward a few more paces. The beam of the dazzler caught a vast black ball in an alcove and the splintered body of a half-open red wooden door, through which Carver could see stairs curving up to ground level. That was how his enemy had got in, but where the hell were they?

Carver stepped forward, stopped, then began a slow, deliberate rotation, sweeping the whole space with light, his gun following the dazzler all the way. He was halfway round when he heard a grunt behind him, a human sound, like a weightlifter struggling to shift a massive load. It was immediately followed by the creaking of wood under pressure. Carver spun round just as the massive spherical mass came free from its housing and started rolling towards him. He fired four shots straight at the giant black ball, but the bullets ricocheted off the wood, leaving barely a mark on the rock-hard surface, the reverberating gunfire mixing with the deep, hard rumble of the ball against the concrete.

He turned to run back towards the mouth of the narrow tunnel, just a few feet away, but slipped on a patch of water on the bare concrete floor and stumbled. The ball was almost on top of him. Desperately, Carver scrabbled to his feet, dropping the dazzler, which was crushed beneath the ball like a tin can beneath a jack-boot. The man-made cave was plunged into darkness, and Carver threw himself back into the tunnel. He heard the giant ball smash against the entrance, too big to penetrate any further.

Frantically, he dashed into the pitch-black void in front of him. He shifted his gun into his left hand and placed the fingers of his right hand against the wall to act as his guide. He was totally blind, but he forced himself to sprint flat out into nothingness, though every instinct screamed at him to go slowly.

He reckoned the tunnel was about twenty paces long. Then came the junction. The other guy would be coming that way. Carver listened. He could just hear one set of slow, steady, watchful footsteps – the steps of a man who wants to hunt down his enemy without becoming the prey himself.

Carver looked left and saw a faint torch-beam emerging from the darkness. It was sweeping from side to side as the man behind it searched for him. He turned towards the opening of the other tunnel and fired three quick shots. He wasn't expecting to score any hits, he just needed to force the other guy to take cover, even for a few seconds.

He could still make this work. He turned again, reached for the wall, and ran on into the blackness.

Kursk was on the offensive. He had forced his enemy to retreat and smashed his most important weapon. Without the dazzler to light up his target, the Englishman's gun was far less of a threat. Now Kursk had to press home his advantage.

He had gone no more than five paces down the other tunnel, walking parallel to the one down which the Englishman had fled, when he saw the glint from the pistol barrel in the torch-beam. Kursk flung himself to the ground as three bullets ricocheted off the walls around him. The moment he hit the ground, he switched off the torch, making himself invisible again.

He heard the Englishman's footsteps moving away from him, fast. Kursk turned the torch back on and kept going to the end of the tunnel. He saw the pipe with its striped tape, but beyond that, nothing. The Englishman must have turned off the passage somewhere, gone down another way.

Ahead on the right, Kursk could see the arch of another tunnel, from which came the sound of fast-moving water. He ran towards it, then, without stopping, flung himself to the floor, rolling across the open arch, firing into it as he went. As he reached the far side, two bullets smashed against the wall, showering him in dust and concrete chips. Well, that answered one question. The Englishman had found a new bolt-hole.

As the echoes of gunfire faded away, Kursk thought he could hear something over the sound of water: a scuffling movement in the darkness, then a louder bang and a muffled curse. It was all he could do not to laugh. The poor bastard had bumped into something, trying to run away in the darkness.

OK, time to see where the Englishman was hiding. Kursk got to his feet, then sprinted back across the open archway, holding his blazing gun away from him so that anyone aiming at the torch would not hit him. This time he looked down the tunnel and saw the boards and display cases suspended between the ceiling and the metal-grate floor. Maybe the Englishman thought he could hide behind them. Well, he'd see about that.

He switched off the torch. All trace of light disappeared. Now they were both blind. He slipped to the floor and slid on his belly to the centre of the archway. Then he moved forward until he could feel the surface beneath him change from concrete to metal. A blast of chill, damp, fetid air hit him from the sewage-water racing beneath him. He reached forward and felt the first wire, as taut as the guy-rope of a tent, holding a Perspex display case in place. Slowly, silently, he slithered underneath the case, making his way through the tangle of wire securing it to the floor.

When he came out the other side, into the gap between the cases, he paused, listening for any sound of the Englishman. Where had the bastard gone? Kursk darted his head from side to side, cocking his ear, suddenly nervous that the Englishman was nearby. The two men could be centimetres apart. With the darkness, and the noise and smell of the water, they'd never know it. He willed himself to wait, to be patient. This was a matter of who lost their nerve first and made the move that gave away their position.

It was the Englishman who cracked. There was another brief scurry of feet up ahead. Kursk put both hands on his gun and leaned forward into the firing position. He was just about to pull the trigger when the blackness of the tunnel was illuminated by a white-hot ball of flame, a deafening crack of explosive and a sudden blast of air. It picked Kursk up, smashed him against the ceiling of the tunnel, then flung him back down in an avalanche of wire and debris, down through the gaping hole where the metal grating had been, slamming him into the torrent of water and filth down below.

9

Two short cross-tunnels led from the display area of the Galerie Belgrand to the Galerie de Bruneseau, which ran parallel to it. Carver had set the timer-detonator on his packet of C4 putty to five seconds, then hurtled down one of these cross-tunnels, the Avaloir. The flame from the explosion flared down the passage, chasing after Carver, scorching his back as it licked against him.

Now he just had to get back to the surface. But which exit? There were two people on the bike chasing him, so one of them was still up there. Carver wanted him, alive if possible. He tried to put himself in the guy's place. Where would he station himself if he were up top? The smart move would be to find a place where you could cover both exits. On that basis, it made no difference where he came up. The risk would be the same.

There was another factor to consider. The area around the ticket kiosk was an ambusher's paradise. There was cover everywhere and no passers-by to witness what happened. But if Carver's sense of direction was in working order, the other exit must be near the south end of the Alma Bridge. That was much more open, with many more cars and people.

So that was where he'd take his chances.

It took him several minutes to work his way back through the darkness towards the man-made cave where the giant ball was. At last there was a glimmer of light. He dashed towards it with intense relief, running towards the stairs, past the open red door and almost up to the stairwell before he forced himself to stop.

He edged into the stairwell, then looked up, sighting his gun vertically, ready to fire at the slightest movement above him. There was a grille of some kind across the top. He couldn't see any padlock or chain holding it in place. He walked steadily up the circular steel staircase, pausing every few steps to watch and listen for any sign of suspicious activity.

The steps ended at a small platform a couple of feet from the surface. Carver crawled on to it on his belly, keeping himself below the lip of the manhole. He slithered as close as he could get to the side of the hole, then placed his hands on the ground level with his shoulders, the left hand flat, the right bunched around the grip of his gun. Next, he shifted his weight on to his arms, leaning his torso forward and bringing his feet up so that his knees were pressed against his chest.

He sprang forward, throwing himself out of the manhole, keeping his trajectory as low as possible, so that he landed flat on the tarmac pavement. As soon as he hit the ground, he rolled to his left, bringing his hands together in front of him, clasping the gun. He kept his head up, his eyes focused forward, along the line of his arms and his weapon.

He saw nothing. Just a couple of cars crossing the Alma Bridge. There was no sound of gunfire, no smack of a silenced bullet hitting the tarmac beside him.

Carver had rolled through 270 degrees on to his right shoulder when his legs slammed into something hard. He grimaced at the impact of bare metal on his ankle bone. He looked round and saw that he'd come to rest against the dead man's Ducati. The man's helmet was still hanging from one of the handlebars. The sharp, almost nauseating bolt of pain from Carver's ankle had been inflicted by the footrest.

He pulled himself into a sitting position, leaned back against the bike and checked his surroundings again. Still no sign of an enemy. He looked down at his ankle and flexed his foot. It rotated without any trouble, so the bones and ligaments were undamaged and his movement would be unimpaired. He'd certainly have a nasty bruise in the morning, but if he lived long enough to see it, there'd be no reason to complain.

As he sat on the pavement, two young Parisians walked by, a boy and a girl arm in arm. Carver tried to look relaxed and nonchalant, as though it was perfectly normal to be leaning against a motorbike, covered in concrete dust and scorch-marks. He needn't have bothered. The young lovers were far too busy gazing soulfully into each other's eyes to care about anyone else.

He got up and used the kids as cover, following them as they crossed the road at the end of the bridge, walking towards the river-side embankment and the kiosk by the entrance to the sewers. The Honda was still where he had left it. He walked towards it, holding his gun straight down by his side, still sheltered by the two lovebirds in front of him.

There was no sign of the other man. Carver looked at the trees on the river side of the walk – nothing. He scanned the bushes – nothing. To the right of the kiosk ran the Quai d'Orsay, the main road along the Left Bank of the Seine. It led down to the National Assembly and the Musée d'Orsai art museum. Carver walked a few paces down the road.

A bus-shelter stood no more than twenty metres away. It was shaped like a rectangular three-sided box, open to the Quai on the fourth side. A woman, a blonde, was leaning up against the outside of the shelter, looking down the road in Carver's direction. She was wearing a skimpy black singlet, no bra, and a tiny denim mini-skirt. The black nylon strap of the bag on her back crossed her chest diagonally, separating and emphasizing the swell of her breasts.

Carver let his glance linger on her a second longer than it should have done. She felt his appraising look, pulled the bag off her back, held it in front of her chest and replied with a frank, uncompromising stare of her own that said 'Get lost, loser' as surely as if she had shouted it.

He lowered his eyes, like any other guy caught staring. Now he saw the woman's boots. They were heavy, black, calf-length, buckled at the ankle and mid-calf. Motorbike boots. He'd seen them before; he'd seen the black nylon bag before. And why was the blonde looking in his direction? Any bus on this side of the road would be going the other way.

Christ he'd been stupid. He raised his eyes, bringing his gun up from his side and running towards her, flat out, as she reached into the bag, pulled out a silenced Uzi and brought it to bear. Carver slammed into her before she could fire, grabbing her gun and ripping it from her hands. He spun her round and smashed her face-first against the side of the bus-shelter. He kicked the gun away, then he wrapped one arm around the woman's chest, pinning her arms by her side. He held her tight against him, squeezing her between his body and the side of the shelter, making it impossible for her to wriggle free.

He felt the softness of her body against his and caught a trace of her rich, dark scent. For a second, something about it, an unexpected familiarity, distracted him. The hell with that. He stuck his gun against her temple.

'Listen carefully,' he hissed into her ear. 'Your boyfriend is dead. You'll be dead too, unless you do exactly as I say.'

She did not react in any way.

He tried again. 'You speak English?'

No response.

Carver took a pace back, holding his pistol straight ahead. Still keeping his eye on the blonde, he bent his knees and picked up the sub-machine gun, stuffing it into his jacket.

'Turn around.'

She didn't move.

Carver stepped forward and kicked out at her legs, hitting her in the side of the shin. She crumpled to the ground, landing to the left of the bus-shelter. As her knees hit the pavement, Carver stamped his left foot between her shoulder blades, pinning her to the ground. She let out an involuntary grunt as the air was forced from her lungs. Now she was lying along the back of the shelter, hidden from the road.

Carver fired a single shot into the pavement, six inches from the blonde's head. She flinched as the dust and stone fragments hit the side of her face.

'The next one goes through the back of your skull. Now, let's stop pissing about. Do you speak English?'

This time she responded with a nod of her head.

'Good. Now, very slowly, put your arms by your side, palms of your hands facing me.'

She did as she was told.

'Thank you. Now, stay completely still.'

Carver shifted his position, sliding his foot down her back and over her rump, bringing it to rest on the ground between her upper thighs. Then he bent his left knee until it came to rest on the base of her spine. His right foot was flat on the ground. All his weight was bearing down on her lower back. She whimpered in pain.

He unzipped one of the thigh-pockets of his cargo pants and took out a thin strip of plastic that was looped into a figure of eight. The loops were secured by tiny locking boxes through which the plastic strips passed.

'Put your hands side by side in the small of your back.'

Carver placed a plastic loop over each hand, then pulled the loose ends until the plastic was tight around each wrist.

'Roll over on to your back.'

He waited as she obeyed. There was a momentary flash of pure rage in her eyes, in the clenching of her jaws, the pursing of her lips. She looked away, and took in a single short, harsh breath through her nostrils. When she met Carver's eyes again, less than five seconds later, she had regained her self-control. Her face was blank, as if she knew there was more to come. She wasn't going to give him the satisfaction of watching her lose her temper, still less cry or beg for mercy.

'Sit up against the shelter.'

She levered herself upright, then shuffled backwards until she was leaning against the shelter wall, her legs flat on the pavement in front of her. Carver was on his haunches opposite her. Anyone passing by would take him for a boyfriend trying to help a sick or stoned girlfriend. They wouldn't look too closely. They wouldn't want to get involved. They'd pass right by, just like city people always do, in any city, anywhere.

'Why does Max want me dead?'

Still she gave nothing away. But her eyes were more tightly focused on him now, more calculating this time, as if she was waiting to see what he'd got before she made her first move.

Carver wanted to needle her, provoke a reaction. 'Look, I don't blame you for being pissed off. I would be too if I'd screwed up. You shouldn't have tried to take the gun out of the bag, right? You should have just shot through it. So what is it – you're no good at your job? You're out of practice? Maybe it isn't your usual line of work.'

She did react, but not in the way he'd expected. She just looked at him with utter contempt, as if he hadn't got a clue. As if he wasn't even close.

He went back to Plan A. 'You never answered my question. Why does Max want me dead?'

Finally she spoke. 'I don't know anyone called Max.' Her voice was flat, unyielding. She sounded like a suspect in a police interrogation cell who knows the cops can't prove their case. Her accent was American, but spoken by a foreigner. Carver guessed Eastern European.

'OK.'

He got to his feet and took a couple of steps to where the black bag was lying on the ground. Bending down, keeping his gun and his eye on the woman all the while, he picked up the bag, then stepped back to his original position, right by her.

'Let's see what we've got here . . .'

He put his free hand into the bag, pulled out a purse and flicked it open. There were half a dozen credit cards in there arranged in slots, one above the other. Carver slid a couple of them out with his thumb. They bore the name A. Petrova. He took another look at the outside of the purse, checking out the pattern stamped into the leather. Louis Vuitton. He was starting to put the pieces together, but he needed a little more information to be sure.

'What does the "A" stand for?'

She shrugged. 'What "A"?'

'On your credit card. A. Petrova.'

'You mean, like "a" for "asshole"?' This time she let a slight mocking smile play around the corners of her mouth. She'd scored another point.

Carver continued to riffle through the bag. There was a mobile phone. He opened it up and accessed the address book, keeping one eye on the woman. There were lots of Russian names. Some were people; others he guessed were shops, clubs or restaurants. There was nothing under 'Max'. He snapped the phone shut and pocketed it.

Next, his fingers wrapped themselves around a piece of thin card. It was inserted into a small, stiff booklet: an airline ticket in a passport. He pulled them out of the bag. The ticket was an Aeroflot return from Moscow to Paris. The outward segment had already been torn off and used. Now he knew where she'd come from. He knew her full name, too. The passport was Russian. It named her as Alexandra Petrova. According to her date of birth she was almost thirty. She looked younger. Maybe she was. Maybe she'd just assumed an identity older than her own. And maybe he'd arranged her death about three hours ago.

'You've got a Louis Vuitton bag. It contains underwear, a couple of T-shirts, a pair of high-heel shoes and some kind of silky dress. So, what, you were planning to party once you'd finished the job?'

This time he knew he'd got through. She didn't say anything, but she frowned. For the first time, the defiance in her eyes was clouded by uncertainty.

Carver pressed on. 'You left the bag in a one-bed apartment on the Rue St Louis-en-l'Ile. The bag was on the bed. There was a white Chanel carrier bag next to it, with some perfume, lipsticks and a small black box – I'm guessing a watch – inside it. You picked that up at duty free, right? Mixing the hit with a nice bit of shopping. I like it. The feminine touch.'

She wasn't impressed. 'What are you trying to tell me? You're some kind of stalker?'

'No, I'm telling you they planned to kill you too. I've got to admit, it was elegant. They got each set of killers to eliminate the other. See, when Max briefed me, he said the apartment belonged to the target. I was supposed to booby-trap it in case he escaped the hit. But it wasn't the target's apartment, was it?'

She said nothing. Carver let the silence hang between them. He watched Petrova. She wasn't looking at him any more. She was looking down at the ground, thinking, working out the next move. A minute or more went by before she raised her eyes towards Carver again, her hostile glare replaced by a searching examination of his face, as though she were looking for the final clues that would help her reach a decision. Then she made up her mind, nodded to herself and spoke.

'Kursk, the man you say you killed, was given our orders when we arrived in Paris. Someone called him – I don't know if that was this man you call Max. They told us to go to the apartment and wait for further instructions. There were new clothes, boots and helmets there, one set for each of us, weapons and a key. Also a camera, with a big flashgun attached to it.'

'You got changed?'

'Yes.'

'So why were your clothes the only ones in the apartment? What about Kursk's?'

'He threw them away when we left.'

'Why?'

'How should I know? Maybe he likes to travel light. Anyway, about twenty thirty, they called again. We were told to go to Rue Duphot. It's off Rue de Rivoli, near Place Vendôme. When we got there, just before twenty-one hundred, Kursk got another call. We were told our target would be a black Mercedes. We had to follow it and use the camera with the flashgun to scare the people in the car and make them drive faster. After that we had to go back to the apartment, spend the night there and then fly out in the morning. About an hour later Kursk got another call. It seemed to give him great satisfaction.'

Carver nodded. 'It fits. They got you out of the apartment before I arrived. They waited to see that I had completed my work there. Once they knew you would be killed, they called Kursk to deal with me. Like I said, neat. So now we have a new question: why did they want us dead?'

'I don't know. Truly.'

'It must have something to do with the job. Did you see inside the car?'

'Not really. I had my visor down and the flash from the camera was, you know, reflecting off the windows. I think there were four people: two in front, two behind. One of them might have been a woman. I don't know.'

'Where's the camera now?'

'The motorcycle. In the box at the side.'

'Was there film inside it?'

She thought for a moment. 'I don't think so. It just flashed.'

'That makes sense. No photographic evidence.'

She looked at him. 'So now what?'

Carver had been watching her as she spoke. She had a wide mouth, full lips and cool blue eyes. One lid was slightly heavier than the other, one pupil fractionally out of line. Those minuscule asymmetries should have marred her looks, yet the imperfection was mesmerizing, drawing him in. With an averagely pretty, even beautiful girl he'd look once. With this one, it took an effort to drag his gaze away.

'Now we make a decision,' he said. 'I could shoot you, right here and now, and disappear into the night. That has the advantage of simplicity. But I don't want to kill you unless I absolutely have to. So, have you heard the expression "My enemy's enemy is my friend"?'

'Yes, I understand.'

'I think we should work on that basis. We've both been set up by the same people. Our best hope is to get to them before they get to us. So, they're our enemy. I guess that makes us friends.'

She raised her eyebrows, gave a little pout and shrugged her shoulders. 'OK, if you say so, let's talk about that. But first, prove to me that you are a friend. Get me a cigarette. There is a packet in my bag, Marlboro Lights.'

He felt around in the bag, still keeping his eyes on her, until he felt the cigarette pack. He pulled it from the bag, flipped open the top and shook it so that a couple of cigarettes poked further out than the rest. Then he reached over and held the packet close to her mouth.

She leaned forward, feeling for the cigarettes with her lips, using her tongue to separate one from the rest. She slumped back against the bus-shelter wall with the cigarette in her mouth.

'Got a light?'

There was a lighter in the bag. He put the flame to her cigarette. As she breathed in, igniting the tobacco, their eyes met, no more than a foot apart. She didn't say anything, just let him feel the tension as her unflinching, disconcerting gaze held his.

Several seconds went by before Carver realized he'd broken a basic rule. Their heads were so close she could easily have butted him, smashing his nose. He jerked back, as if evading a blow that never came. She didn't move, just kept looking at him.

'Do you still have the helmet?' he asked.

'In the bushes, over there, with the leathers,' she replied, nodding towards a clump of greenery that lay between the bus-shelter and the sewer museum's ticket kiosk.

'Here's what we're going to do, then. First we make them think that they've won. That means getting ourselves killed, the more publicly the better. So . . .'

Carver explained what he intended to do and what Petrova's role would be. She nodded occasionally. Every so often she asked a question or suggested an alternative course of action. The hostility had ebbed, however temporarily, from her voice. Her tone was practical, functional, getting the job done.

At the end he said, 'What do you think?'

'I think we have the same enemy, and I think your plan has a chance of success. Beyond that, I don't bother to think. I have only one more question.'

'Yes?'

'What is your name?'

'Samuel Carver. Most people just call me Carver.'

'Most people call me Alix. And now that we have been introduced, are you going to untie my hands?'

Carver nodded, then pulled a pair of scissors from the same pocket the plastic cuffs had been in. He stepped behind Alix as she shuffled forward, making some space between her back and the shelter. Then he got down on his haunches and forced one blade between the plastic and Alix's left wrist, making her wince as the metal and plastic dug into her even more. Once he'd cut it free, he repeated the process on her other wrist. As he stood up and came round to face her again, she started to rub her lower arms in an effort to restore circulation.

Then she held out a surprisingly dainty hand towards Carver. He reached out and shook it, as if sealing their deal.

'No, you fool,' she said. 'I want you to help me up.'

Carver chuckled edgily, and Alix smiled back. For the first time there was a flicker of warmth, a hint of the woman behind that calculating façade. He pulled her back on to her feet, then picked up her bag and slung it round his shoulder. She let out a pained sigh as she straightened her spine, then felt the small of her back with her hands.

'Sorry about that,' he said. 'You know, just business.'

He regretted the crass words the moment he'd spoken them. There was bitterness in her short, humourless laugh, and when she glanced at him again her eyes had the battered vulnerability of a woman who's no stranger to violence.

'It's never just business,' she said.

Then she picked up her helmet and they walked together towards the Alma Bridge.

10

Nobby Colclough had spent fifteen years as a Metropolitan Police detective before he decided to trade his skills in the private sector. He was used to stake-outs, and now he was sitting in an unmarked Renault Megane parked in the Rue St Louis-en-l'Ile, watching the world go by. And waiting.

It was gone one o'clock in the morning when he got the word from Max telling him the Russians were on their way. He saw them a few minutes later, riding up on a flashy black bike. Jesus Christ! Max hadn't mentioned that one of them was a bird. She was wearing her skirt pulled right up to her waist so that she could straddle the bike, leaving every inch of her thighs exposed to his gaze. She got off, giving him a quick flash of her knickers, then pulled the skirt down over her backside, giving it a little wiggle on the way. Colclough swallowed hard. He wanted to know if the face was as good as the body. Pity the daft tart still had her helmet on.

Now the bloke got off the bike, grabbed the girl's hand and hurried her towards the door. Filthy little monkeys couldn't wait to get at it. Well, sod 'em. They were about to get a blow-job all right.

He watched them go in, then called in to base.

'They've arrived,' he said.

'Stay on the line,' came the voice from the other end. 'I'm betting Carver set his explosives with short-delay fuses. He'll want to get the targets into the apartment before detonation. Shouldn't take long. Are the lights on yet?'

Colclough looked up. 'No. The dirty beggars probably stopped for a quick one on the stairs. Oh, hang on, they've just gone on. Shouldn't be long now.'

Colclough was half right. The place was about to blow, but Carver and Alix had not hung about on the stairs, they'd raced up. Just before they went into the apartment, Carver stopped. He took her black bag off his shoulder, felt inside it for any weapons, then, satisfied, gave it to her.

'You may need this. Remember, we've got exactly sixty seconds, and you've got to look different when we leave. Go straight to the bedroom, get changed, grab what you need and get out. Ready?'

Carver opened the door, walked in, disabled the alarm and turned on all the lights. As Alix ran into the bedroom, he went into the living-room, drew the curtains and took off his helmet, which he placed on the floor in the middle of the room.

Twelve seconds gone.

He strode across to the bookshelves, cut the speaker wires and put the speakers in the fireplace. The Claymores would still go off, creating the explosion he wanted, but the solid brick- and stonework of the chimney-breast would absorb the back-blast and restrict the spread of ball-bearings. The neighbours should survive OK.

Twenty-six seconds.

He retraced his steps back out into the hall, breaking into a run as he crossed into the bedroom. Alix was just slipping on the dress that had been in her case. She had nothing on but a pair of white knickers slung low beneath a smooth, flat, pale-brown stomach. Her breasts were small and neat with perfect rosy-brown nipples.

They rode up her chest as she raised her arms and let the ice-blue dress slither down her body like mercury.

Carver didn't give her a second glance. He went round the far side of the bed, took the Claymore from the wall and shoved it down between the end of the bed and the mattress, with the rear of the mine facing into the mattress, to dissipate its energy.

Thirty-nine seconds.

It took three more seconds to get into the bathroom and another five to rip the bomb out of the cistern, take out the detonator and place both in one of his jacket's side pockets. On the way out, he grabbed Alix's make-up bag and washbag, lobbing them towards her as he went back into the bedroom.

Alix was bending down, slipping on the white sneakers.

'Thought you might need these,' he said with a wry grin as her startled face looked up at him across the bed.

She shoved the cosmetics into her black shoulder-bag, picked it up and dashed from the room, her dress fluttering around her thighs. There were ten seconds left as Carver followed Alix out of the bedroom, down the hall and through the door of the apartment. Carver closed it, and they ran for the stairs.

Five, four, three . . .

Colclough had seen the lights go on. Nothing happened for a while. He wondered if something had gone wrong. He could sense Max's impatience in the silence at the other end of the line. Then the windows of the top-floor apartment exploded outwards, showering wood and glass across the street. There was a sharp pattering sound on the roof and windows of Colclough's car – tiny steel balls raining down like metal hail.

The street was almost empty. The restaurants had all closed, the tourists had all gone off to their hotel beds. There were just two people wending their way home when the blast went off. The woman screamed. The man grabbed her and tried to shield her with his body as the debris rained down around them. They didn't seem to have been seriously hurt, but the woman was weeping helplessly while the man just stared around him, dazed and uncomprehending.

'Bleedin' 'ell!' Colclough shouted. 'Whoever you got to do that job, he doesn't do nothing by half!'

Max didn't seem too excited. 'So, there's been an explosion?'

'Yeah, there bloody has. Hang on a minute, I've got company.'

A woman was running from the front door of the apartment building, a blonde in a blue dress. She ran towards the car, her eyes wide with panic, and pressed her face up against the glass. 'Help! For God's sake, you must help!' she screamed. She spoke English. Sounded like a Yank.

Colclough could hear Max's voice on the speakerphone: 'What's happening?'

'Just some bird got caught up in the blast. Nothing serious. Bit hysterical is all.'

He pressed the button and opened the window. The girl leaned in and started tugging at his sleeve.

'Come quickly, please. It's my mother! She's . . . Oh God, I think she's dead!' she cried.

Colclough did not hear the passenger door open beside him. The first he knew of Samuel Carver's presence was the cold metal of the gun pressing behind his ear and the whispered voice that said, 'Keep talking. I'm not here. Got it?'

The ex-policeman's balding head nodded up and down.

'Now tell the girl to piss off, nice and loud.'

'Er, er, sorry, love,' stammered Colclough. 'Be happy to help. But I'm busy, see? Got things to do.'

Max's voice snapped over the speakerphone: 'Oi, Colclough, get this sorted!'

'You got it, guv'nor,' Colclough replied. 'Listen, love, you heard the man. Naff off.'

Alix smiled and patted his cheek. 'Good boy,' she mouthed, then got into the car herself, sitting behind Colclough.

Carver tapped Colclough's shoulder with his gun to get his attention. With his free hand he pointed at the phone, mounted on the dashboard. Then he pulled his finger across his throat. The meaning was clear: end the conversation.

Colclough turned back towards the phone. 'She's gone,' he said. 'I'm returning to base. Over and out.'

'Right,' said Carver. 'Sit on your right hand. Wedge it under nice and tight. Good. Now put your left hand on the wheel. Don't move.'

'Or what?'

Before Carver could answer, Alix leaned forward and brought her arm round the back of the driver's seat, her fist balled. She gave a gentle squeeze of her hand and a high-carbon stainless-steel blade sprang out from between her thumb and forefinger. She pressed the tip of the blade against Colclough's neck.

'Or I teach you to show a woman respect.'

Having made her point, Alix relaxed back into her seat and snapped the blade back into its handle. Carver looked at her, startled, unable to hide his surprise. He saw a mocking look cross Colclough's face and felt the surprise give way to anger, mostly at his own stupidity.

He reached into one of his pockets, pulled out another plastic cuff-strip and handed it to Colclough.

'Loop one end round the steering wheel. Pass the other end through it. Then pull it tight.'

Colclough did as he was told. One half of the cuff was now attached to the wheel, the other half dangled free.

'Now put your left hand through there,' said Carver, gesturing with his gun at the empty cuff. 'Tighten it with your right hand. Good boy.'

Colclough was now cuffed to the steering wheel. He wasn't leaving the car until Carver cut him loose. Carver patted him down, looking for a weapon.

'Maybe you should have done that to the bird, eh?' Colclough sneered. 'You might've enjoyed it an' all.'

Colclough was balding, maybe twenty pounds overweight. His shirt was white polyester. He was wearing grey suit-trousers, a matching jacket hanging from a hook behind the passenger seat. His shoes were black lace-ups. He wasn't carrying a gun or knife. There was nothing in his jacket.

Carver looked at Colclough with a wry, contemplative smile on his face, then glanced down at his gun. Without warning, he lashed out, smashing the pistol into Colclough's face, cracking his cheekbone and drawing blood. Colclough bent over, holding his face in his uncuffed hand. He prodded his battered cheek with a fingertip and winced.

'What the 'ell did you do that for?'

'You heard the lady,' Carver said. 'Show some respect.'

'My hero,' said Alix, teasingly. She tossed the knife handle up and down in her hand. 'It was in my boot,' she explained, 'then in my hand. From the moment you set me free, I could have killed you any time.'

'Why didn't you?'

'I still might.'

Carver ignored the remark and turned back to Colclough. He took the lump of C4 putty from his pocket and held it out.

'Do you know what this is?'

'I can guess.'

'Good,' said Carver. 'Now, watch.'

He leaned down and stuck the putty underneath the side of the passenger seat, out of Colclough's reach. Then he rummaged through another pocket and pulled out a timer-detonator.

'Max is in town, isn't he?'

Colclough nodded.

'Thought so. An operation like this, he'd have to control it on site. So I'm guessing he's not far from here, right?'

Another nod.

Carver held the detonator in front of Colclough's face. 'I'm setting this to fifteen minutes.You've got that much time to get us to Max. If we get there on time, I pull out the detonator, nothing happens. If we don't get there, I open this door and leave. The lady goes out the back door. You stay locked to the steering wheel.'

He set the timer and skewered it into the putty. The sound of a fire-engine siren echoed in the distance.

'Alternatively,' said Carver, 'I reset it to thirty seconds and we get out now. What's it going to be?'

Colclough didn't say anything. He didn't have to. His laboured breathing and the sheen of sweat breaking out across his forehead told their own story. He turned the ignition, stuck the car in gear and pulled away from the kerb.

'Good man,' said Carver. 'Now, time we had a little chat. Let's not piss about. Tell me where we're going. Describe the place. How many people does Max have? Fourteen and a half minutes left. Talk.'

11

Carver repeated the question. 'How many people?'

'I don't know, all right?' whined Colclough. 'That's the whole point, ain't it? You only know what you need to know. You only see what you need to see.'

'All right, what did you see?'

'It's a big mansion. Old place. Proper flash. You get there and the building comes right up to the pavement, almost like a blank wall facing the street. There's an arch with a driveway through it. That's how you get in.'

'Security?'

'Gates. Metal gates.'

They'd made it back to the river again. Across the water, Carver could see the floodlit towers of Notre Dame. He ignored them, giving all his concentration to Colclough.

'You drive in and there's a little guardroom on the left, inside the arch, yeah? There was definitely an individual there, checking everyone in and out.'

'Cameras?'

'Couple at the front. Didn't see any others. But there might be.'

'All right, then what?'

Colclough thought for a moment. 'A courtyard. There's like an old stables or something on one side they use as car-parking space. The front door's opposite the entrance arch. It's under cover, so you can drive right up, get to the door and you don't get wet. You go in, there's a big, bare hall and a marble staircase right up the middle of the building.'

'That's normal. It's a hotel particular,' Alix interrupted.

Carver turned around in his seat. 'Sorry?'

The girl explained, as if reciting from a guidebook. 'A hotel particular. A classic Paris mansion, probably built in the seventeenth or eighteenth centuries.'

'How do you know about that?' asked Carver.

'Because I was trained to discuss such things.'

'In Russia?'

Alix nodded. 'Of course. It was essential for my job.'

'Which was?'

She broke into one of her non-committal smiles. 'Conversation. So, if this is a typical hotel, all the main reception rooms are on the first floor. Is that where Max is?'

Colclough nodded. 'Yeah, some kind of dining-room. His guv'nor was next door, in some other room.'

Carver frowned. 'What do you mean, "guv'nor"? You're saying Max has a boss? Who is he?'

'How should I know? I never saw him.'

'How do you know he's there, then?'

'Because Max was called into the next room. Went straight through, no argument. So the bloke must've been his boss. I mean, that's logical, yeah?' He looked at Carver with pleading eyes, desperate to be told he was doing all right, that everything would work out OK. His voice cracked. 'Christ, I'm doing my best. I've got a wife, a daughter. I don't wanna die. I mean, what've I ever done to you, for Christ's sake?'

'OK,' said Carver, ignoring Colclough's pleas. 'One on the door. Max. His boss. Who else?'

'I told you, I don't know. Not many. I was told to wait downstairs in some kind of pantry. There was food and coffee there. A couple of other blokes came in and out.'

'Armed?'

'Could've been. In fact, yeah, there was two of them outside the room Max was in, like guards. They had guns, definitely. Anyway, I drank coffee and did the crossword till about eleven. Then I got orders to take up my position. The rest you know.'

'Not quite,' said Carver. 'Where's the pantry, relative to this dining-room Max was in? How did you get there?'

'There was more stairs that went down the back way. You know, like for servants.'

Carver thought. Call it four people to mount proper surveillance of the targets in the hours leading up to the hit. You'd need a couple of them to stay by the accident, monitor what happened and follow the ambulance. That left two, plus the doorman, Max, his guards and his mysterious boss. Seven against one. Not great odds.

He turned round to face Alix again. He'd disarmed her pretty easily at the bus-stop. It wasn't a great sign.

'How much armed combat training have you actually had?'

She shrugged, and pouted. 'Some. Basic self-defence, shooting, nothing special.'

'And knife-work,' said Carver.

'No. That I taught myself. Every girl needs a way to scare off creeps.'

'Bit extreme, isn't it?'

'So were the creeps.'

Colclough spoke. 'Can I ask a question?'

'What?' said Carver.

'Why don't you just get out of here? Trust me, I'll stay schtum. I swear to God, on my girl's life, not a word. Take this car. Head for the nearest airport. Fly as far away as possible.'

Alix nodded. 'Or we could fly to different places. Separately.'

'Yeah, you could,' said Carver, 'if you wanted a pain in the neck from looking over your shoulder for the rest of your short life and an itch in your back, waiting for the first bullet. The people who sent us wanted us dead. They're not going to change their minds on that. So we've got an hour, tops, before the police discover there was no one in that flat and that body gets fished out of the sewers. We've got to assume that Max and his boss are either monitoring police communications or have people inside the force. They'll soon know we're still alive. We've got to hit them before then. And we've got to find out about their organization. I take it Max had some kind of IT/communications set-up?'

'I s'pose so. There was computer screens on the table, but he wasn't letting me anywhere near 'em, so don't ask me what they did.'

'I don't have to. They ran the show. And the computer that ran them has everything we need to know. If we can't get it out of Max, we'll get it from the computer. So, Alix, you in?'

A shrug. 'I guess. But you should know, I'm not a soldier. Attacking a house? I did not get trained to do that.'

'Then just follow me, do exactly what I say, and watch my back. And look on the bright side. Those bastards wanted to kill us. We're going to return the compliment.'

12

Colclough brought the car to a halt. They were in the Marais, directly across the river from the Ile St Louis. Once, aristocrats and courtiers built their mansions there, to be as close as possible to the kings of France in their palace at the Louvre. They filled their homes with paintings, sculptures and furniture of exquisite taste. They dressed in silk and lace. Yet behind the impeccable façades and courtly etiquette raged an unrelenting war for influence, wealth and access to the throne.

When the old order vanished in the revolutionary frenzy of 1789, the Marais went with it. The area was neglected for almost two centuries, only to be revived in recent decades as a Parisian equivalent to New York's SoHo or London's Notting Hill. Now the rich and fashionable rubbed shoulders with the ethnic and exotic: exclusive boutiques next to Jewish delis, gay bars alongside Algerian restaurants. But many of the mansions remained, and one, at least, was still home to conspiracy and intrigue.

'It's just there,' he said, pointing with his free right hand to a gateway about fifty metres ahead of them, on the far side of the road. Then he slumped in his seat and muttered, 'I don't know why I bothered. You're gonna kill me anyway.'

Carver reached across, grabbed the shoulder of Colclough's sweat-sodden shirt and shook him. 'No, I'm not. Not if you do exactly what you're told. If we live, so do you.'

'Aren't you scared I'll talk?'

'Who to? I don't see you going to the police in a hurry. If we're alive, then Max won't be, so you won't be talking to him. And you've already told us, you have no more idea who his boss is than we do. So don't worry. I believed you when you swore you wouldn't blab. But this little chat just wasted thirty seconds. So drive up to the gate, nice and easy. Let the guard open up. And keep your mouth shut.'

Carver pulled a third plastic cuff from his pocket as Colclough started the car again. 'Last in the packet,' he said with a wry smile, handing it to Alix. 'That's for the man on the gate. I'll tell you when.'

The car pulled up in front of the gate. Colclough flashed the headlights. The gates swung open and a man on the far side waved them through. He was holding a gun, another Uzi by the look of it, straight down by his leg, making a token attempt at keeping it out of sight of passers-by.

The man stepped up to the car and motioned to Colclough to open the window. Carver was counting on him doing what all gate-keepers do, bending down and looking inside the car. When he did, he'd see Carver's gun pointing at him. Alix would then get out and cuff the guard. Simple – just so long as Colclough kept his mouth shut.

But the copper lost his nerve. As the metal gates swung shut behind the car and the man leaned down towards the open window, he shouted, 'Watch out! He's got a gun!' The guard stepped back and tried to bring his Uzi to bear. Carver was faster. He raised his pistol and shot twice through the half-open driver's window. He put two bullets, neatly grouped, in the guard's chest, the force of them slamming him up against the brickwork at the side of the entrance arch.

'Big mistake,' Carver muttered, almost to himself.

Colclough was moaning. 'Oh Jesus, I'm sorry, please don't kill me . . .'

Carver ignored him. He threw Alix's gun into her hands. 'Follow me!' he shouted. 'Fast!'

The key principles of close-range urban combat are surprise, speed and controlled violence. Any hope of surprise had just been shattered. That left speed and violence. Carver started running.

Across the cobbles, the main body of the house rose in a block of grey-white stone. As he reloaded his pistol, Carver glanced to the right, where the black bonnet of a 7-Series BMW limousine glinted in the recesses of the old coach-house. Max travelled in style. If Carver got out alive, that would be his getaway vehicle. By the front door he stopped for a second and gestured to Alix to stand on the far side. He took a deep breath, steadied himself, counted to three and kicked the door open, moving in fast, his gun held straight out in front of him. He caught a glimpse of Alix following just behind.

The hallway was tiled in white marble, with little black tiles, like diamonds, on the corners of each white tile. A massive glass lantern, lit by electric candles, hung down the centre of the stairwell. The staircase curved back on itself as it rose up to the first floor. Carver heard a sudden high-pitched warning shout from behind him, then saw a door open to the right of the stairs and a man run out. Carver's reaction was subconscious, automatic. He fired at the man and the back-up who came after him. They both went down. Carver needed to get upstairs, fast. But he never turned his back on a wounded man. He strode ten paces across the marble floor and finished the job: two point-blank head-shots that spattered blood, bone and brain-matter across the marble floor.

Alix whimpered in horror.

'Come on!' Carver shouted as he turned and ran towards the stairs.

Three men down so far, thought Carver, taking the steps two at a time. That left how many – another three, four maybe? He had to get to the next floor before—

The stairs in front of him disintegrated in a clattering blast of sub-machine-gun fire. Carver threw himself down, scrabbling for the cover of the stone balustrade that followed the sweep of the staircase as the last reverberations died away. Then, through the ringing in his ears, he heard a familiar calm, flat voice.

'That's far enough, Carver. Get up. And drop your weapon.'

He craned his neck and gazed up at the top of the staircase. He could see three men. Two of them were big guys, powerfully built but running to fat, with necks wider than their skulls: basic joints of beef from the head down. The third man was standing between them, a tall, thin figure in charcoal-grey suit-trousers, a white shirt – sleeves rolled up his forearms – and frameless designer glasses.

'McCall, bring that man here,' he barked at one of the men. Then he turned to the other guy. 'Harrison, cover him. If he tries anything, shoot him. Shoot McCall too, if you have to.'

The thin man looked down, regarding Carver with a disapproving eye, as if disappointed by what he saw.

'One more time, drop your weapon.'

Carver let the gun fall from his hand. It clattered against the stone step. It struck him that he was alone on the stairs. Alix had vanished. Well, he could hardly blame her for that. She was all right, that girl. He wanted her to get away. And that meant buying her time.

'You must be Max,' he said, getting to his feet.

'If you say so. And now, perhaps you'll tell me what you're doing here.'

McCall reached Carver, pointed his gun at him and waved the barrel upwards. 'Move it,' he said.

'Jesus Christ, Max,' said Carver, moving slowly up the stairs, 'is this the best you can do for staff? Let me give you some advice. If you want top-quality people, it's best not to kill the ones who are actually any good. So tell me, what was it made you want to get rid of me? If I'm going to be executed, you might at least tell me why.'

Max regarded him with the look of contempt that those in the know reserve for the truly ignorant. He opened his mouth to speak. Then he stopped, and tilted his head slightly to one side.

'What's that noise?'

From the courtyard came the sound of a man at the far limits of panic and terror, screaming in desperation. 'Help me! For God's sake, someone, please help me!'

Max frowned at Carver. They were no more than six feet apart now. 'Who's that man?' When he got no response, he turned to the man he'd called Harrison. 'Go and see what that is.'

Harrison hurried down the stairs. They watched him go through the door.

Max refocused his attention on Carver. 'So, you obviously got away—'

The explosion ripped through the courtyard, blowing open the front doors of the building with a blast that echoed round the stone-clad stairwell. McCall moved towards the noise, half crouched, his gun at his shoulder ready to fire, pointing away from Carver. It gave him a fractional opening. He lunged for Max's throat, gripping it with all his force, ignoring the fists with which Max desperately tried to pummel him and the footsteps of the man running up the stairs behind him. The gunstock slammed into Carver's kidneys, sending a shock of pain and nausea charging through his body. He let go of Max's throat and fell retching to the floor.

'Bring him into the dining-room,' said Max.

McCall lifted Carver up by the scruff of his neck, then prodded him again in the back, this time with the gun barrel. 'You heard him. Walk.'

He didn't walk. He staggered into the dining-room through the connecting door, bent over like a chimp. Max had been getting ready to go. There were open cases for a laptop computer, a separate high-speed modem and a 20-inch flat-screen strewn across the table, wires unplugged and wound up, ready to be packed away. Max's suit jacket was draped across the back of a chair. Carver tried to ignore the agony in his back. He wanted to stand up straight, get his dignity back and create the illusion, at least, that he and Max were talking on equal terms.

Max was not impressed. 'Think of yourself as a dead man,' he said, walking round to the table and pulling wires from the back of the computer. 'Do me a favour, Carver, make it easy. Answer my questions. What happened to Kursk?'

'Who the hell is Kursk?'

'The Russian.'

'He's dead.'

'And his partner, the woman?'

'What do you reckon? I'm here. She isn't. Dead.'

'How?'

'I flushed them down the sewers. Like shit. I think you know that.'

Max said nothing for a moment as he slipped the computer into its case, then asked, 'Colclough saw two people return to the apartment. Who were they?'

'I've no idea. I don't know anyone called Colclough. And I'm not going to answer any more of your questions until you answer mine. Why do you want me dead?'

Max sighed as he zipped up the case. 'Please, don't treat me like an idiot. You went back to the apartment. But why? You had no reason to do that. Not unless you wanted me to think that the woman was dead. And the only reason to go to such trouble would be if—'

'I was alive?'

Alix was standing in another doorway at the far side of the room, holding her Uzi, moving it from side to side, trying to cover Max and McCall at the same time. She was carrying the gun properly, high on the shoulder, sighting along the barrel. The gun trembled slightly in her grip, betraying her tension. She looked like a little girl playing with her big brother's toys.

For half a second they all just stood there. Any longer and it would have been too late. If McCall had done nothing, forced Alix to take the initiative, dared her to shoot in cold blood, she might have lost her nerve. But he got cocky, staking his life on her inability to turn the threat of her gun into action. He grabbed Carver with his left hand and threw him to one side, clearing the space to bring up his own weapon. But Alix fired first.

She did it properly, just like a training exercise. She didn't spray bullets all over the place. She fired a three-shot burst into McCall. There was nothing girlish about her now, just a fierce, almost manic concentration in her eyes as she turned towards Max, who was desperately backing away towards the wall. Another burst hit his chest, shoulder and neck – the hits rising as the force of the shots lifted the barrel in Alix's hand. He spun around, blood from a ripped artery spraying in a scarlet arc across the wall. Then he fell to the floor, dead.

Carver got to his feet, wincing, and made his way across the room. The air reeked of cordite and blood. Alix was standing stock-still, her eyes wide open. Then suddenly she turned away from Carver, bent over and started shaking. She was dry-retching, streaming tears and bile and snot. Carver stood next to her, rested a hand on her shoulder and offered her a handkerchief.

'First time?'

Alix nodded.

'You did well,' Carver said. 'You saved my life. Thank you.'

He was seized by a deep, familiar emotion, the comradeship that exists between those who have experienced combat together and survived. Carver had had feelings like this in the Falklands, Iraq and the bandit country of South Armagh. He'd known what it was to have that bond between fighting men. But a blonde Russian woman in a short silk dress, well, that might take a bit of getting used to.

Gradually, her body stopped shaking, her breathing calmed down. Alix stood up, wiping her face. She looked at the two bodies for a second or two. Then she looked at Carver and said, as if seeing her reflection in his eyes, 'Oh my God, I must look terrible.'

Carver gave a clipped, dry laugh. 'Not half as bad as they do. Listen, you'll be fine. But we've got to get out of here. Wipe your prints off the gun. Stick it in Max's hands – the guy with the grey hair. Make it look like they shot each other.'

It would take at least a day for the police forensic lab to work out that all the bullets had come from the same gun. By then, he planned to be long gone.

He turned his attention to the computer in its case on the table. Somewhere inside it was everything he needed to know about the people who'd hired him and everything anyone else would need to know about him. For both reasons, it was coming with him.

So was Max's grey jacket. Carver needed to get out of the clothes he'd been wearing all night, to do something to change his appearance. He looked at the dead men on the floor. Even their trousers were spattered with blood.

Then he struck lucky. Beside the table there was a soft brown leather overnight bag. Max must have had it beside him, ready to leave. Inside there was a fresh white shirt, still in its laundry wrapper. He put it on, then slipped the jacket over the top. It wasn't a great fit, but it would do.

Carver picked up the black nylon computer case. 'Time to go,' he said. But as he walked from the room, he was thinking: if Alix Petrova had never fired a gun in anger before, what the hell had she been doing on this mission?

13

The Pitié-Salpetrière medical complex in south-east Paris dated back to 1656 and the time of the Sun King, Louis XIV. Over the past century it had been modernized and massively increased in size until it became almost a city of its own, devoted to the sick and those who care for them. Tonight its emergency department had turned into a cross between a war zone and a diplomatic cocktail party. The French Minister of the Interior was there, along with the Prefect of Police and the British ambassador. It was past two a.m. when the guest of honour arrived. She was fashionably late, as befitted the world's most famous woman. But she came in an ambulance, rather than the usual limousine.

The operations director was waiting at the hospital. He found himself getting angry with the delay. It was irrational: the more inefficient the Paris ambulance services were, the better it was for him. He wanted the woman dead, after all. More than anything, however, he wanted it all to be over. He turned to the tanned, compact, leather-jacketed man next to him. 'Jesus Christ, Pierre, what took so long?'

Pierre Papin worked in French intelligence. He didn't have a job title. Officially, he didn't have a job. This gave him a certain freedom. Sometimes, for example, he worked on projects even his bosses – the ones he did not officially have – knew nothing about.

'Relax, *mon ami*,' Papin said, pulling a packet of Gitanes from the pocket of his linen jacket. He wore a pristine white T-shirt and a pair of snug-fitting black jeans. He looked like he'd just come from a night out in St Tropez. 'We don't like to rush things in France. You Anglo-Saxons throw trauma-victims into ambulances, drive at a hundred and twenty kilometres an hour and then wonder why your patients are dead on arrival. We prefer to stabilize them at the scene then take them *très doucement* – gently, no? – to the hospital.'

'Well, I hope you explain that to the media. Believe me, they'll sniff a conspiracy in the delay.'

The Frenchman smiled. 'Perhaps that is because there truly is a conspiracy, huh?'

'Not over the bloody ambulance there isn't.'

The operations director's mood was not improved by the trouble he was having getting through to Max. They had not spoken for about an hour, not since Max had called to report that the Russians had been eliminated, exactly according to plan. It wasn't unknown for Max to disappear off the radar from time to time. His obsessive concern for security, secrecy and personal survival saw to that. But it was unlike him to go missing before the operation was complete.

The operations director pressed his speed-dial again. Again he got no answer. He turned back to Papin.

'What's the latest news from the doctors?'

The Frenchman took a long drag on his cigarette. 'The left ventricle vein was ripped from the heart. The poor woman has been pumping blood into her chest.' Papin looked at the operations director. 'This was not a clean operation. The princess will not survive. But a bullet would have been more merciful.'

'Yes, well, that option wasn't available, was it? What are you doing about the autopsy?'

'The pathologist is waiting outside the room, along with all the other vultures.'

'And the formaldehyde?'

'It will be pumped into the body, immediately after the post-mortem. But why is this so important to you?'

'It will create a false positive on any subsequent pregnancy test.'

'So the world will think she was pregnant?'

'So the world will never know for sure.'

Papin frowned. 'Tell me, then, why did she have to die?'

The operations director smiled, but did not answer the question. 'Excuse me one moment.' He turned away from Papin and dialled again. Still no answer from Max. What the bloody hell was going on?

14

There was no way out of Paris at that hour of the morning. Trains weren't running. Carver wasn't going anywhere near an airport. You couldn't hire a car. He could easily steal one, but he never liked to commit minor offences when he was working. They got Al Capone for failing to pay his taxes. They weren't going to bust him for a stolen car.

So they were stuck. They couldn't risk checking into a hotel, even under assumed names. They needed somewhere to go for a few hours, a place that would stay open till dawn, where they could be anonymous. He didn't think that would be too hard to find, not on a Saturday night.

They walked down the main stairs – Carver, carrying the laptop, stopped to pick up his SIG-Sauer – then out the back of the house, through formal gardens to a small door set into the back wall, where Alix had left her bag. They then headed down to the Rue de Rivoli. Carver binned his old T-shirt and jacket on the way. His actions were methodical and unhurried. Nothing about his manner betrayed the intensity of what he had been through that night. Then, without warning, he came to a sudden stop.

He was standing in front of an electronics store. Half a dozen televisions in the front window were tuned to the same channel. A news reporter was standing in the middle of a road talking to camera, though his words were silent, the sets all mute on the far side of the plate-glass. He was standing in front of a police line, surrounded by a scrum of other journalists, photographers and TV cameras. The reporter stepped slightly to one side so that his cameraman could shoot past him.

'Hang on a second,' said Carver, putting out a hand to hold Alix back.

Six images of the Alma Tunnel filled the shop window. The camera zoomed into the tunnel, where an ambulance was parked by the crumpled wreck of a black Mercedes.

Alix stood next to Carver, watching the same images with a look of incomprehension that gave way to shock as their meaning struck her. 'Dear God. Is that the car? The one we—'

'Yeah. That's what I did to it after you and Kursk whipped it in my direction. But what the hell's that doing there?'

'What do you mean?'

'The ambulance. I can't believe anyone got out alive. And if they did, surely they'd be in hospital by now. I mean, the crash was' – he looked at his watch – 'an hour ago. What are they hanging round there for?'

'An hour?' she murmured, half to herself. 'Is that all?'

The pictures had changed. They'd cut back to the studio. A newsreader was sitting behind her desk, a picture of the Princess of Wales inset into the screen. She said a few words, then the picture cut to footage of the princess lounging on a massive yacht, surrounded by smaller boats packed with people trying to get her picture. Carver shook his head. He had nothing against the princess. She'd visited his unit once and charmed every man on the base. When he'd served under an oath of loyalty to the Crown, he'd taken that oath seriously. He'd never had any interest whatever in gossip columns or celebrity tittle-tattle.

'Come on, this isn't going to tell us anything we need to know,' he said, moving on down the road.

He walked to the edge of the pavement and watched the late-night traffic cruising down the Rue de Rivoli.

'We need a cab,' he said.

The impish, cheeky grin that broke across Alix's face brought an unexpected light to her eyes.

'Leave that to me,' she said.

15

Jack Grantham sipped bad coffee from a plastic cup and wondered just how much worse his weekend could possibly get. Still in his thirties, he was one of the highest flyers at the Secret Intelligence Service, or MI6 as it was known to the world outside. But stardom had its drawbacks. He'd been dragged into Whitehall for a crisis meeting at one in the morning, which was bad enough. But there was more, much more. The crisis involved a terrible accident, a beautiful princess and the entire world's media. And then, of course, there were his fellow civil servants.

Looking around the table, Grantham could see some typically unctuous under-secretary from the Foreign Office oozing oily Old Etonian smugness, and next to him the flinty, tight-mouthed, sharp-eyed presence of Dame Agatha Bewley from MI5. So now the infighting would begin. Each department would do its best to avoid the shit-storm that would burst upon them just as soon as the great British public discovered what had happened to their beloved Queen of Hearts, while ensuring they dumped as much crap as possible on everyone else. Well, that would be fun. And just to make life really enjoyable, Ronald bloody Trodd had decided to stick his oar in.

Grantham had more faith in hard facts than Freudian psychology. But he couldn't help thinking of Ron Trodd as the foul-mouthed, unrestrained id that lurked beneath the Prime Minister's bright and shiny ego. He was the ultimate henchman, always ready to do anything, no matter how distasteful, so that his master could keep his lily-white hands clean.

The Foreign Office man spoke first. 'Well, as you know, our ambassador is already at the hospital. The French are fearfully embarrassed, as you can imagine. Not the sort of thing one likes having in one's backyard, as it were. Naturally, we've made it clear we don't hold them responsible. Meanwhile, we're making preparations to get His Royal Highness out to Paris as soon as possible. He's at Balmoral. I gather the young princes have already been informed that their mother has been in an accident.'

'Thank you, Sir Claude,' said Trodd, with a contempt that made the knighthood sound more like an insult than an honour. 'Jack, what has SIS got?'

'Total chaos,' said Grantham, trying to work out how much to reveal, and when. 'Someone's turning Paris into a war zone. There've been reports of muffled explosions coming from somewhere underground, just across the Seine from the scene of the crash. An apartment got blown to smithereens, south of the river. The police are telling the locals it was a gas leak, but a car was seen driving away at high speed. Fifteen minutes later, the same car exploded in the courtyard of a mansion in the Marais district. A team of armed police got inside the house a few minutes ago. They found bodies everywhere. And several of them seem to be British.'

'Bugger!' Trodd slammed the table-top in fury. 'Tell me this isn't a bunch of your lads on some kind of private mission. Have you been pissing about, off the books?'

'No, we have not. We had people in Paris, of course, but it was purely a matter of surveillance. None of them was involved in any dirty work. I can assure you of that.'

'Of course, it's possible that we're acquainted with whoever did do it.' Agatha Bewley's voice was as dry as her appearance.

Trodd frowned in her direction. 'What do you mean by that?'

'Well, we all use outside assistance from time to time. People who do odd jobs. These people may have attacked the princess on their own account. They might have been hired to do it by some other client. The boyfriend might have been the main target. His father had plenty of enemies. Then again, it may indeed just be a terrible accident.'

'Surely that's what one is assuming,' said Sir Claude. 'Is anyone really suggesting that this was some kind of assassination attempt?'

'We don't know, do we?' said Trodd. 'For public consumption, this was an accident. That's the story, and I bloody well hope it happens to be true, because if it isn't, the fallout will screw us all. But if some bastard has taken out the mother of the future King of England, I don't want to wake up one morning and read all about it in the *Sun*. I want to be the first to know.'

'And the Prime Minister?' asked Sir Claude.

'Let me worry about that. For now, I want the Foreign Office to stick to the party line: terrible accident, condolences all round. Stay cosy with the Frogs.'

The diplomat winced. 'Of course, of course . . . but we really must wait until the Foreign Secretary decides how to proceed.'

'The Foreign Secretary will proceed exactly as I bloody well tell him. Now, where was I? Yeah, Jack, I want SIS to find out what really happened in Paris. And Agatha, I want a list of anyone in this country who might have had a motive for taking out the world's most popular woman, and who they'd have used to do it. And by the way,' Trodd leaned forward and looked around the table, 'if you find the bastards who did this, deal with them. Permanently. And keep Number Ten well out of it.'

Trodd got up without another word and stalked out of the room. Sir Claude followed close behind.

Grantham tried to busy himself, putting his notepad and biro away in his briefcase, but he could feel Agatha Bewley's falcon gaze burning into him.

'You have an idea who's behind this, don't you?'

'Come on, Agatha, you know it's not that simple. There are crews all over Europe, half of them right here in London, who could have carried out the operation. And, as you suggested, plenty of people could have commissioned them.'

She held his gaze for a moment, then spoke in a lower, almost confiding tone. 'I think you have people in mind, and I don't like the feeling that I'm being kept out of the loop. I'm sorry, Jack, but I'm not prepared to stay silent for very long. The reputation of my department is at stake.'

'This is no time for us to be fighting among ourselves,' said Grantham, trying to mollify her. 'Besides, if I did, hypothetically, have an idea of who it might be, I don't have anything that even approaches evidence, let alone proof.'

Dame Agatha looked at him silently, pursing her lips in a way that suggested both scepticism and disapproval.

'All right,' acknowledged Grantham, 'I'll admit there are one or two possibilities that come to mind. I'll have a quiet word with Percy Wake. In the old days, before the Wall came down, he helped the service solve a few tricky problems. It was all above my pay-grade, I never sat in on anything, but the legend was that Wake had a genius for seeing ways to get things done. Knowing who to get, predicting how things would play out. He'll deny it, of course, but if there's been any conspiratorial hanky-panky, dear old Percy will have an idea who's responsible.'

'Yes, I'm well aware of his reputation,' said Dame Agatha, coldly. 'I had my own dealings with Wake. I never knew anyone with more influence in Whitehall, whatever the government of the day. And not just there: he had connections in Washington, Moscow, Beijing – the man had an amazing instinct for backing the right men at the right time. But don't forget for a moment that for all the patriotism and principle he displays so proudly, Sir Percy's greatest loyalty is to himself. And Trodd – what are we going to tell him?' she asked, softening her tone just a fraction.

For the first time since he had entered the room, Grantham felt a smile crossing his face. 'Nothing. I think it's time someone showed that saloon-bar bully who really runs the country. Don't you agree?'

Dame Agatha nodded. 'Yes, I rather think I do.'

16

The last time Carver looked, there hadn't been a cab visible anywhere. But no sooner had Alix stepped up to the kerb than a white Peugeot 406 with a TAXI PARISIEN sign on its roof was screeching to a halt beside her. She smiled again, this time at the driver, who beamed back. He looked North African. His head was pumping back and forth to the sound of Arab dance music pounding at top volume from the tiny stereo.

'Rai,' he said, thumbing at the stereo. 'Good music!'

Carver was about to ask him to turn it down, but changed his mind. The noise would make it impossible for the driver to overhear any conversation he might have with Alix.

'Sure,' he said. 'Good music. *Gare de Lyon, s'il vous plaît.*'

The grand old station, with its clock tower that appeared to be a miniature French version of Big Ben, served as the starting-point for trains to the Alps, Switzerland and Italy.

'*Attendez ici un moment,*' Carver told the cabbie when they arrived. He grabbed the computer case, half opened the door, then turned back to Alix. 'Give me your bag, I'll stow it too. Won't be a minute.'

She rummaged in the bag and took out her cigarettes, lip-gloss, a compact and mascara. 'Essential supplies,' she said. 'I must fix my face. And you know, you should do the same. Use the bathroom while you are in there.'

Carver gave her a puzzled shrug, then got out of the car. 'Don't go anywhere,' he said before walking into the station, towards the left-luggage lockers.

Afterwards, as he looked into the men's-room mirror under the harsh neon light, he realized what Alix had meant. His face was streaked with grime and sweat and there was concrete dust in his hair. No wonder Max had been so mocking about his appearance – he looked a total mess. He splashed himself with cold water, ran wet fingers over his scalp, then took another look in the mirror. Big improvement.

Back in the cab, Alix was doing her lipstick. She checked her glossy scarlet mouth in the mirror of her powder compact, then handed all her make-up to Carver with a mock-ingratiating smile. He noticed she had somehow persuaded the driver to turn the music down a fraction.

'OK,' she said as he stuck her make-up in his pockets. 'Where are we going?'

He grinned. 'Good question. Let's see if our man here has any ideas.' He leaned forward and spoke to the cabbie. To Alix's surprise, Carver's French was fluent. He could chat to the driver, even crack a couple of jokes. Between them, they seemed to come up with a satisfactory answer. Carver gave the North African a last encouraging pat on the shoulder and sat back in the seat. 'He says he knows just the place.

'So,' he continued, turning to face her, looking her straight in the eye, 'why did you come back? You know, back at the house. Why didn't you just run away?'

'Where to?'

She glanced at the driver, then leaned towards Carver to make sure she could not be overheard. Her voice was low and urgent. Carver caught a glimpse of the driver's face, looking at them in the rearview mirror, assuming theirs was just another lovers' back-seat conversation.

'When you ran up the stairs, you went so fast I could not keep up,' she explained. 'Then I heard the shots and realized there were people up there. I thought, OK, maybe I can go back out through the gates, but the car was in the way, about to explode. So then I did not know what to do. I guess I was in a panic. I could hear the shouts from outside, then the man running down the stairs. I had to hide, so I just went through the door the other men had come out of. The men you shot . . .'

She paused for a second.

'Anyway, I went through there and I could see some stairs in front of me and I remembered about the place having backstairs. I thought I would take those and find out what had happened to you. If I could help you escape, maybe we would have a chance. And, well, you know about the rest.'

'Well, I'm glad you did, anyway.'

'So am I. I mean . . . that sounds terrible. People are dead. But I am glad. Does that make me a bad person?'

'No worse than the rest of us,' he said.

They were driving up the Boulevard de Sébastopol when Carver saw the green neon sign of an all-night pharmacy and told the driver to stop.

'Sorry,' he said to Alix. 'One last interruption.'

He walked into the store and bought some eyeglasses – the weakest prescription he could find – a pair of scissors and three packs of wash-in hair-dye: black, brunette and red. Alix was going to lose that long blonde mane. It was a pity, but it might just keep her alive.

'What did you get?' she asked him when he got back to the cab. 'A little protection, maybe? In case you get lucky tonight?'

'Protection, yeah, for you.' He showed her his purchases in their paper bag. 'You can be anything you like, but not blonde.'

He said it like a man who expected an argument. But Alix didn't fuss. 'OK. I'm not the same woman I was an hour ago. I'm not wearing the same clothes. Why should I have the same hair?'

They soon reached the destination Carver had negotiated with the cabbie, a club just off Sébastopol. The entrance was underneath a high arch, but there was no name visible anywhere. Two golden statues of women in classical robes held up lanterns on either side of the door. A scrum of people pressed up against the gold-tipped black railings in front of the club, begging to get in. From the looks on their faces, most of them were begging in vain.

'Damn!' muttered Carver. 'Should've thought of that.'

Alix said nothing. She seemed completely unperturbed. She just got out of the cab, smoothed down her dress, tossed back her hair and walked straight through the crowd to the entrance.

There was a bouncer on the door: 250 pounds of West African muscle in a silver-grey suit. He took one look at Alix and unhooked the rope that was keeping the masses at bay. She swept in like a movie star. Carver tried to follow her. The bouncer stopped him. Carver leaned forward and said a few words in French. Then he tucked something into the breast pocket of the bouncer's jacket. The man paused a moment, letting Carver sweat, then waved him in too.

'What were you saying?' asked Alix.

'I told him I was your bodyguard. Then I slipped him a hundred bucks.'

'Hey! It was me who saved your life, remember?'

'Sorry. That bit of the story slipped my mind. Come on, let's eat.'

Within seconds of walking into the club Carver had noted three possible exit routes, he'd spotted two groups of men who might be threats, and he'd discovered there was some kind of restaurant upstairs. Another hundred-dollar bill for the maître d' bought them a corner table with clear sightlines. If anybody came for them, Carver would get plenty of warning. He handed Alix the scissors and dye.

'Go and do, you know, whatever it takes.'

'I could be a while.'

'That's OK. I'm not going anywhere.'

Carver watched Alix disappear towards the ladies' room. Then he summoned a waitress and ordered a double Johnnie Walker Blue Label, no ice. He didn't know how many more drinks he'd get to have. He might as well stick to good ones.

17

The ladies' room looked like the last days of Rome. A couple were screwing in one of the cubicles. Two girls were kissing passionately up against a wall. Another cubicle was being used as a market-stall by a scrawny North African guy in an Iron Maiden T-shirt who was selling wraps of speed, cocaine and smack. Women were chopping powder into lines on the edge of the basin-tops, snorting it, then using their fingers to dab stray dustings of snow from their nostrils on to their tongues. A few more conventional types were peeing, checking their make-up and gossiping about the men they'd left behind in the club.

Alix found a spare basin. She looked at her reflection for a second in the mirror that ran right along the wall. Then she started cutting. A few women looked at her. One of them started talking in French. Alix looked at her and mimed incomprehension.

'You crazy?' the woman repeated in English. 'You cut that beautiful hair, your man, he won't recognize you.'

'Exactly,' said Alix, and smiled.

The woman laughed. 'But *chérie*, there must be an easier way of escaping from him, no?'

'Maybe it's not him I want to escape.'

'OK, a woman of mystery!'

Alix went back to her cutting. She stopped once her hair had been reduced to a neat blonde bob that fell halfway down her neck. She ran her hands through her new cut, tossing her head from side to side to feel how it moved and fell. 'No,' she muttered to herself. 'Too boring.' She picked up the scissors again. A few minutes later she was left with a short, almost boyish crop. She looked at the mirror again, happier this time.

Then she picked up each dye-packet in turn, holding it by her face before coming to a decision. She filled her basin with warm water, bent down and dunked her head. Then she shampooed in the black dye. Now came the boring part: she had to wait twenty minutes for the dye to work properly. So she sat on the edge of her basin, smoked a Marlboro and watched the world go by.

The couple who'd had sex emerged from their cubicle. The woman dashed to the mirror to check her face and hair, while the man scowled at her impatiently. Neither of them seemed too interested in romance. Alix wondered if it had been a professional transaction. She decided probably not. A decent hooker would at least have pretended she'd enjoyed it. That way the john might pay for a second helping.

The dealer's trade slackened off for a few minutes. He tried to persuade Alix to buy, then settled for a broken-English conversation about the difficulties of doing business with clients who were, by definition, screw-ups. Alix sounded like she knew what she was talking about. The dealer was impressed.

'You sell powders too?' he asked.

'No,' she said. 'Something else.'

A pair of blondes walked in, teetering on four-inch stilettos, and for a second the ladies'-room babble fell silent. The two newcomers were identical, but eerily, unnaturally so in their doll-like perfection. They had wide turquoise eyes, perfect little noses and puffed-up, pouty lips. They looked around with blank indifference, as if long since bored by the effect their looks had on the world around them. Either that, thought Alix, or their faces had simply been stuffed with so much Botox they were no longer capable of any expression at all.

The dolls stood next to Alix in front of the mirror, bitching about the man they were with. Bitching in Russian. One of them glanced at Alix in the mirror, and attempted a puzzled frown.

'Ya znayo vas?'

She was asking, 'Do I know you?'

'Sorry,' Alix replied, wide-eyed and clueless, making her accent as all-American as she could manage, 'I don't understand what you said. But I sure love that twin thing you got going.'

The two dolls turned back to their own reflections and swapped a few catty observations about dumb Yankees. They fixed their hair, smoothed down their microscopic frocks and headed back out to the club. As the door swung shut behind them, Alix let out a little laugh, a mix of amusement and sheer relief.

'They were quite a pair, huh?'

Alix looked up to see a fresh-faced, smiling girl, barely out of her teens, wearing jeans and a crop-top. She had clear blue eyes and a dusting of freckles across her lightly tanned face.

'You American?' Alix asked.

'No, Canadian. I come from Winnipeg. My name's Tiffany.'

'Hi, Tiffany, I'm Alexandra. Look, could you do me a little favour? Could you just look outside the door to see if the guy at the corner table is still there?'

'Sure.' Tiffany walked to the door and looked out. 'You mean the cute dark-haired one with, like, a white shirt and a grey jacket?'

Alix smiled. 'Cute' wasn't a word she'd thought of applying to Carver. 'Yeah,' she said. 'That's the one.'

'Hang on, be right back.' Tiffany disappeared through the door. Twenty seconds later she returned. 'You know what? He really is cute. Kinda rough around the edges, but I like that. He's a lot cuter than my date, that's for sure. Anyway, so I asked if he wanted some company. He said he was waiting for someone. I think he really likes you.'

At last, the time was up. Alix rinsed out the dye, then crouched down beneath the hand-dryer and blasted her head with hot air. It only took seconds. That was one big advantage to going so short. She just needed one last touch. She checked out the other women standing next to her. There was a punky-looking rock-chick a couple of basins down with a tub of clear styling gel. That would do. Alix leaned towards her and pointed at the gel. 'Please?' she said. The girl nodded. Alix scooped her right hand into the gel, rubbed her hands together, then started scrubbing her fingers back and forth through her hair, making it look fuller, choppier. Then she stepped back from the mirror and turned her head from side to side to scrutinize every angle before leaving the room.

'That was worth the wait,' said Carver when Alix got back to the table. 'You look amazing.'

'You think so?' asked Alix. 'It feels kind of strange to me, like there's nothing there any more. Still, if you like it, we should drink to my new style.' She summoned a waiter. 'A bottle of Cristal, please.'

A minute later there were two full champagne glasses on their table and a pale, clear bottle sitting beside them in an ice bucket.

'*Na zdorovye!*' Alix said, raising her glass.

For a second she looked at the golden, bubbling liquid, felt the icy chill of the glass against her fingers and caught the sharp scent of the drink in her nostrils. She had never felt more alive, more keenly in tune with her senses. The realization of what she had done that night still horrified her, but the truth remained: she had looked death in the face and survived. She felt possessed by an intense awareness of the fragility of existence. She wanted to squeeze every drop of life she could from every moment that was left to her. And she was going to start right now.

Carver looked at the woman sitting opposite him. The black hair made her seem stronger, more complex. Her blue eyes shone even more brightly against that dark frame, and her bone structure was revealed in all its elegant perfection. He wondered what might have happened if they'd met in anything like normal circumstances. Then he chuckled to himself. A girl like that? She wouldn't have given him a second glance.

He tried to keep things low-key. 'So, you want to eat?'

Alix drained her glass. 'Eat? No way! I want to dance. Come on!' She got up from her chair and tugged at Carver's arm.

He frowned, nervously. 'Did you say dance?' The possibility hadn't occurred to him. So far as he was concerned, the club was just a place to avoid pursuit.

Alix laughed. 'Of course I'm going to dance. And if you won't dance with me, Mr Shy Englishman, I'll find someone who will. And he'll take me in his arms. Our bodies will rub together. We'll—'

'I get the picture,' Carver said. He looked at the dance floor. It was heaving with bodies. If anything, they'd be less conspicuous among the crowd than sitting to one side at an open table.'OK, let's dance.'

18

The manhole cover budged an inch, just enough to shift it out of its housing. For a few seconds, nothing happened. Then it moved again, right out of the hole, and came clattering to a rest on the pavement.

Grigori Kursk winced as the pain shot through his cracked ribs. He breathed heavily. That hurt too. Then he hauled himself out of the manhole and back on to the streets of Paris. He spat on the pavement, trying to get the taste of muck out of his mouth. He'd swallowed half the Paris sewer system. He'd need shots for cholera, dysentery, tetanus – anything the doc could find.

What else? His hearing was gone: the explosion had temporarily deafened him and left his eardrums ringing in angry, shrieking protest. He'd been wearing lightweight body armour, but the blast had still hammered his ribcage and battered his skull. He hadn't had a headache like this since the last days in Kabul, after drinking away the shame of defeat with home-made potato vodka. He felt nauseous, dizzy, spaced out, concussed. Well, screw that. Kursk had been hurt a lot worse than this and kept fighting. He'd probably smelled as bad, too. But it was one thing stinking when you were sat in a foxhole at the arse-end of Afghanistan and everyone else stank just as bad. In the middle of Paris, it wasn't so smart.

Kursk looked around. He was standing on a wide avenue. Up ahead he could see ramps leading up on to an autoroute, but there was barely any traffic. Behind him there were some railway yards, half lit in orange and grey. A few railway workers were wandering between the freight trucks. No one seemed to be doing too much work.

Kursk knew what he had to do. He slumped to the ground, leaning back against a lamp-post by a bus-shelter. Then he waited.

People came by. Three railway workers at the end of their shift, glad to be on their way home, shouted at him, told him to get a job and have a bath. One of them was about to aim a kick in his direction when his pal held him back. 'Hey, Paco, you crazy? You'll never get the smell off your boot!' The men walked off laughing.

Kursk waited.

It took about twenty minutes before he got what he wanted, one guy by himself, about Kursk's size, but flabby. He wouldn't know how to defend himself. Kursk could tell just by looking at him.

As the man walked by, Kursk got up and walked towards him, just another drunken bum begging for a few coins. The man's eyes widened in alarm. He tried to act tough. 'Piss off, tramp!' Kursk grinned and came a few steps closer. The man turned and walked away fast, trying to maintain his dignity, not wanting to run. Kursk caught him in a few steps, grabbed the man's head and twisted it, snapping his neck, then caught him as he fell.

Kursk felt another stab of pain slice through his upper body. It settled into a relentless, grinding ache as he dragged the man's body to the side of the road and dumped it by the railway-yard fence. It hurt Kursk when he pulled off the man's jacket, pants and shirt; it hurt when he got out of his own sodden, stinking, shredded clothes; it hurt when he got dressed again. Everything he did hurt.

He went through the man's wallet and pockets: thirty-five francs in notes and another nine or ten in small change. That was plenty.

Kursk left the man slumped against the fence in his old, sewer-drenched clothes. It would be a while before anyone realized he was dead. No one was going to go too close to a guy like that.

He set off down the avenue, walking under the autoroute. Beyond it, the streets narrowed. They all looked the same: endless apartment blocks, four or five storeys high, occasional bistros, bars and shops. There was a public toilet on one corner. Kursk put a couple of francs into the slot, let the metal door slide open and went in. He washed himself as best he could in the basin, soaping his face and scalp, and rinsing the filth out of the cuts that criss-crossed his shaved head, enjoying the sandpapery abrasion of the stubble against his palm.

When he'd finished, he looked in the mirror. It wasn't too bad. He looked like a tough bastard who'd been in a fight and couldn't give a stuff. Kursk grinned at the thought of all the bourgeois Parisians who might see him and feel a prickle of fear. He took his capacity to intimidate for granted, the same way a beautiful woman assumes she will turn men's heads. A walk down the street was a parade of his powers.

Kursk left the toilet and looked around for a phone-box. He shoved every coin he had into the box and dialled an overseas number. It was a while before someone answered.

'This is Kursk. Get me Yuri. Yeah, I do know what time it is. Just shut up and get me Yuri.'

19

'Can I have one of your filthy cigarettes?'

Papin grinned. 'I thought you did not smoke.'

The operations director grimaced. 'I don't usually. But tonight I think I'll make an exception.'

Papin reached for his Gitanes, then held up his hand for a second, before placing it to his own telephone earpiece. He frowned with concentration as he listened, then spoke briefly into the mike that dangled by his throat. Another nod, a quick goodbye, then he turned off his phone.

'I am afraid I have more bad news,' Papin said, handing over a cigarette, then flicking on his lighter. 'There has been a killing in the Marais. One of the finest hotels in Paris has been turned into a slaughterhouse. An exploded car. A body in the gateway. Two more bodies in the hall. Two more again upstairs. And human remains from the explosion scattered like confetti across the courtyard. The dead men were armed with sub-machine guns. These men were professional killers, who were themselves killed. So I ask myself, why would killers be in Paris tonight?'

'All right, you've made your point.'

'Then follow me.'

They drove to the mansion in the first grey light of the false dawn. Papin flashed a badge at the police officers guarding the gate and keeping back the increasing crowd of rubberneckers attracted by the flashing lights of the vans and squad cars massed in the road outside the gates. Inside, Papin had a brief, angry conversation with a bull-necked man in an ill-fitting suit with sweat patches under the arms.

'That was the detective in charge of the case,' Papin told the operations director, by way of explanation.

'I gathered. What was his problem?'

'He wants to remove the bodies so that they can be examined as soon as possible. I told him he can have them in five minutes. So let's not waste time. Tell me everything.'

They walked up to the first body.

'You know him?' asked Papin.

'Yeah. His name was Whelan, ex-Para. Seems fairly obvious what happened. Someone arrives at the front gate, Whelan goes to take a look, gets shot.'

They walked further in, saw the burned-out shell of the bombed car. The detective was standing by the shattered remnants of the driver's-side door. '*Regardez*,' he said, and pointed inside. The two men looked in and saw the charred steering wheel. There was a plastic restraint clipped to the wheel. A fragment of a severed hand was still inside it. The rest of the body was in pieces all around the courtyard. A crime-scene investigator was photographing each piece.

Papin reached for his cigarettes. He offered the pack to the Englishman.'

'No, I'm all right, thanks. Seen worse.'

They walked into the building and saw the two men sprawled on the floor of the hall, their blood a vivid crimson splash against the black-and-white tiles.

'Nichol, Jarrett, also Paras,' said the operations director. 'They came as a crew with Whelan and two others.'

'Maybe you should think again about your hiring policy,' said Papin.

'Don't worry. We hire the best. That's why these two are dead.'

'You know who did this?'

'I'm pretty certain. I'll know for sure when I see who's upstairs.'

The men went into the dining-room. The operations director winced when he saw Max.

'The one in the jeans is the fourth member of the crew, McCall. I imagine you'll find what's left of the fifth man, Harrison, down in the yard.'

'And the other man, the one I suspect you know well?'

'His name is Max. That's what I called him, anyway. I couldn't tell you what his birth certificate says. We weren't on real-name terms.'

'*Alors*, who is? Have you noticed the interesting variation between the deaths in this room and those downstairs?'

'Of course. Max and McCall were hit by a three-shot burst of automatic fire; the others were killed by separate shots. My guess is your firearms people will find that those came from a SIG-Sauer P226. If they did, the shooter is known to me as Carver. He's the only person who could have done this, except for one minor detail. He's supposed to be dead.'

'Assume he is not. Can you describe him, please?'

'I can't really give you a physical description, but he was wearing a bomber jacket, T-shirt and jeans, all black, and he was riding a Honda XR400 motorbike, also black.'

'You know this because . . .?'

'I paid for them.'

'I see. Did you pay for his accomplice also?'

'No. Carver always works alone.'

'So why are there two weapons?'

'No idea.'

'Please, do not waste my time, huh? Either this man Carver came in with his favourite gun – a gun, you know, with twelve rounds in the magazine – fired four shots, then for some reason decided to pick up a completely different weapon; or there were two different people, firing two different guns. *Alors*, Charlie, what do you think?'

'Seriously, Pierre, I don't know what happened here. I don't even know for sure it was Carver. He was meant to have been disposed of immediately the operation was over. As far as I was concerned, he had been.'

'But if he survived this disposal—'

'Then he would be a very angry man.'

'And he would seek revenge?'

'That would be my assumption, yes.'

'Had he been here before?'

'No.'

'Did he even know of the existence of this place?'

'No.'

'And yet your Mr Carver apparently manages to find this house, out of all the houses in Paris, and kill all the people inside, using two different guns. Then he disappears without a trace. You are right, Charlie. You do hire the best. Maybe that is why you could not dispose of him as easily as—'

'Damn! The computer!'

'*Pardon?*'

'Max had a computer, a laptop.'

'And . . .'

'And look at the table. It's not there. That bastard Carver has got our computer!'

Papin paused to gather his thoughts. Then he spoke with the forced, patronizing calm of a man trying to take the heat out of a situation. 'Perhaps we are rushing to an assumption too easily, huh? Tell me, how did you intend to kill this man Carver?'

When the operations director replied, his emotions were back under control. 'Two Russians, a man and a woman, names of Kursk and Petrova. They work out of Moscow. But they're dead too. We blew their apartment to smithereens.'

'Was this apartment on the Ile St Louis?'

'Yes.'

'Well, it certainly exploded. But there was no one inside. No dead, no wounded. So far as the public and the media are concerned it was just an unfortunate accident, a leaking gas-pipe, nothing to worry about.'

'That can't be right. We had someone watching the apartment. He reported that a man and a woman went into the apartment. Then there was an explosion. Are you sure the people inside weren't just vaporized?'

'No. There was no one inside that apartment when the explosion occurred. So, who were the man and the woman? How did they get out? And where are they now?'

20

They'd danced, they'd drunk champagne, they'd even eaten Thai food from the club's restaurant. Sealed off from the outside, in a world that stretched from their table to the bar to the dance floor, it was almost as if that mad hour of violence and death had never happened. As long as the music played and the drink flowed they were just two regular people, civilians out for a Saturday night. Until Carver realized they'd been made.

'There's a man over there who keeps looking at you,' he told Alix, trying to make himself heard over the thumping din of Eurodisco.

She rolled her eyes dismissively and shouted back, 'Of course there is.'

'No. He's really looking. The fat bloke, with the arm-candy, by the far wall. I think he knows you.'

Carver followed her eyes as she glanced across the dance floor. A big middle-aged guy with buzz-cut hair, a coarse, jowly face, piggy eyes and a shiny golden-brown suit was sitting behind a table. The combination of brutality, self-indulgence and vulgarity was unmistakable. Russian, thought Carver. One of these days he'd meet a rich Muscovite who didn't look like a gangster. But it hadn't happened yet.

He kept watching. The guy's hands were all over two identikit blonde party-girls in glittery microscopic dresses that barely contained their boob-jobs. He was casually pawing their thighs and breasts while the girls giggled and wriggled, pretending to enjoy it. That was their job. But whatever the fat man was doing with his hands, his mind wasn't on the bimbos at all. He was looking at the dance floor.

The Russian gave the girl on his left an elbow in the ribs. That got her full attention. He barked a few words in her ear and nodded his head in Alix's direction. The girl jabbered back at him and he put his hands up in front of his chest to shut her up. She nodded sulkily and shrugged her shoulders, all pretence of sexual attraction gone.

Alix watched the pantomime, then shook her head. 'I don't know him.'

Carver pulled Alix close to him, speaking right into her ear. 'Don't bullshit me. He's Russian. I can tell just by looking at him. Why was he looking at you?'

'I don't know, OK!'

Carver said nothing. Alix sighed heavily.

'All right, the girls were in the ladies' room when I was there. Maybe they're telling him about the crazy chick who cut her hair. How should I know?'

Carver let her go. He glanced across at the Russian, who had a glass in one hand and a girl in the other. He seemed to have lost interest in Alix, but even so, Carver wanted to get out. The question was, how to do it without attracting the fat man's attention?

He was just about to make his move when the lights came up and he finally understood why Max had wanted him dead, why the stakes were far higher than he had ever imagined. It happened without warning. One moment the Eurodisco beats were crashing out, the next there was total silence, the houselights were on and the DJ was delivering a message in French that was being spoken in countless different languages at that exact moment in every corner of the world.

'Ladies and gentlemen, I don't know how to say this,' he began, his voice hesitant and strained. 'I cannot believe it. But the Princess of Wales is dead. She was injured in a terrible car crash, right here in Paris, in the Alma Tunnel. They took her to the hospital of Salpetrière, but the doctors could do nothing. She is dead.' The DJ said nothing for a second or two, then added, 'I'm sorry. I don't know what I can play right now.'

People were standing on the dance floor looking around, as if searching for some clue as to how they should react. Slowly, the murmur of voices grew to a hubbub. There was a rush to the DJ's booth and a desperate clamour for more information, mixed with pleas to come on, stop joking, tell us you're just kidding around. And gradually, through it all came the sound of sobbing as women clung to their partners, weeping, or simply fell to the floor in grief.

Amid the chaos, Carver stood motionless, as stunned as if he had been caught in his own dazzler-beam, unable to grasp the magnitude of what had happened. He felt physically sick, clammy with sweat, his head heavy, blood pounding in his ears. His vision blurred, crackles of light flashing across his eyes, fragmenting the world around him. His mind seemed to be slipping out of his control. Then his survival instinct kicked in, and as he got a grip on his consciousness his pulse slowed and his breathing returned to normal.

He bent almost double, putting his hands on his knees and letting his head hang down. Then he let out his breath in a slow, steady stream and stood upright again, ready to face the truth. It really had happened, and he was the man who'd done it. The evidence was inescapable. The images on those TV screens, cutting from the devastation in the Alma Tunnel to the princess on her holidays, finally made perfect sense.

He thought back to the moment he'd found Alix's bag in the apartment, his conversation with Max, his attempt to justify what he did by targeting those who deserved their fate and trying to spare civilians. Those principles had come to a cataclysmic, bloody end, hadn't they?

In some distant corner of his consciousness, he was aware of Alix standing beside him. Her face was ashen, her eyes a million miles away. She was moaning, wordlessly, no more able than him to articulate the conflict of thoughts and feelings tearing through her.

Carver felt as though every eye in the room was on him, that the mark of Cain was burning on his forehead. He told himself that was crazy: they were all too busy trying to cope with what they had heard to worry about anyone else. And then he realized that his instinct had been correct. He *was* being watched. So was Alix. And the madness was about to begin again.

In the flat, harsh glare of the houselights, Carver saw the Russian. He'd taken his hands off the girls and the drink. Now he was talking into a phone. Every so often he looked in their direction.

'Damn!' spat Carver, under his breath. 'We're getting out of here. Now!'

He did not wait for Alix to reply, just grabbed her arm and pulled her from the dance floor. There was a waitress standing by one of the tables near where Carver and Alix had been sitting. He gave her five hundred bucks, pressing the notes into her hand. *'Pour l'addition. Tenez la monnaie. Alors, où est la cuisine?'*

The waitress did not reply, barely even noticing the money in her hand. There were tears streaming down her face. Carver shook her and asked again where the kitchen was, his urgency forcing her to listen.

'Over there,' she murmured, limply waving an arm towards double doors set into the wall beyond the tables.

'Does it have a staff exit?'

'Yes, but . . .' She stood there motionless, muttering vague protests as Carver and Alix brushed past her.

Just as they reached the swing-doors into the kitchen, Carver glanced back at the table where the fat guy was sitting. He was getting to his feet, gesticulating at two sidekicks who'd suddenly materialized on the floor in front of his table. Carver slipped through the doors and into the noise, the heat and the smells of a working kitchen, the latter a pungent blend of fish, meat, spice and sweat.

He turned to look back through one of the porthole windows in the doors. One of the fat man's underlings was heading downstairs; the other was walking towards the restaurant area, a tall, solidly built guy with pockmarked skin and a ponytail. His suit was an oily blue. His shoes were pale grey. A gold medallion nestled in thick black chest hair, and there was more gold on his wrist and fingers.

Alix was already a few paces ahead of Carver, making her way past the sweaty, food-stained kitchen staff at their stations. A couple of them gave her a whistle and a filthy remark as she went by. Then they saw the look in Carver's eye as he followed and decided that if she belonged to him they'd be well advised to shut up.

Beyond the kitchen more swing-doors opened into a narrow hallway. To the left, it led to a staircase that dropped away to ground level. There were a couple of doors on the far side of the corridor: a store-room, an office. The lights were out. There was no one in either of them.

'Keep moving,' said Carver. 'Go down the stairs. Make a lot of noise. Go!'

He listened to her running along the uncarpeted floorboards, then ducked into the office. The door opened inwards. He stood behind it, holding it almost shut, without letting the catch close completely.

A few seconds later Carver heard the door to the kitchen burst open. He pictured the man with the ponytail standing in the corridor, gun held in front of him, surveying the emptiness in front of him, then hearing the sound of Alix's feet on the stairs.

There were footsteps as the man went by. Carver eased the door open and stepped out into the corridor. He took three quick steps forward. The man heard him on the third step, but it was too late. He couldn't stop, turn and bring his gun to bear before Carver raised his left hand, brushed his right arm away and, in the same cobra-fast movement, jabbed two fingers into his eyes.

The Russian squealed in pain, dropped his gun and lifted his hands to his eyes. Carver kept moving. He shifted his weight on to his right foot, rotated his shoulders and slammed the heel of his right palm into the man's chin. Another shoulder rotation and a shift of weight through the hips brought Carver's left elbow up to crack into the man's cheekbone. Now his right knee piled into the man's defenceless groin. As he doubled up in pain, Carver karate-chopped the back of his neck. The Russian dropped unconscious to the floor. It was the basic five-second knockout – lesson one in the special forces' fighting handbook. Worked every time. Unless the other guy had read the same book.

Carver thought about pulling the man back down the passage by his stupid ponytail, but decided against it and grabbed him under the armpits instead. He dragged the unconscious body into the empty office, then stepped back out into the passage.

Now came the interesting bit. He walked to the top of the stairs and peered down into the stairwell. In the dim light from the passage, he could see a flight of steps, then a small landing, then another flight, which turned back the other way and disappeared beneath him.

'Alix?' he hissed.

He wondered if she'd be there. If she'd run, he knew for certain he was on his own. If she'd stayed, it wasn't so simple. She might be on his side. Or she could be sticking close so she could help someone else.

Alix appeared on the landing. She looked at Carver.

'So, what are we going to do now?'

'The only thing we *can* do for now. Disappear.'

21

The operations director tried to rub the exhaustion from his blood-shot eyes. The job was falling apart around him. He was standing with Papin in the street outside the mansion. It was beginning to get light now. The city would soon be waking up to discover the horrors that had taken place while it was asleep.

'OK,' said Papin, 'let's go through it from the beginning. Forget for the moment whatever happened in the Alma, concentrate on what happened here. No French citizens have been harmed. We will do our best to make it all disappear. But if I am to help you, I must know what happened. And you must deal with any – what do you say? – loose ends. So, to begin. Who owns the house?'

'I don't know. I imagine that when your people start trying to trace the ownership, they will find a mass of shell companies in different tax havens. But I don't know who owns them. And even if I did, I couldn't tell you.'

'How can I help if you play games with me?'

'I'm not playing games. I honestly do not know. And I guarantee that any names I gave you would not appear on any ownership documents anywhere.'

'OK, I understand. Next problem: who did this?'

The operations director thought for a moment. Then he breathed a plume of smoke into the early-morning air and said, 'Carver. It has to be. He knew about the explosives in that flat because he put them there. Kursk had no idea. If he'd gone in, he'd have been killed, and the woman with him.'

Papin nodded. 'OK, so we know a man and a woman went into that apartment. We agree the man must have been Carver. So could the woman be Petrova? Are they working together now? If so, they must have come out together too, because no one died in the explosion. Next question: did they come here? Well, we have evidence of two weapons. The simplest explanation for that is two shooters. Do we have any other suspects? No. Did Carver have any other female accomplice?'

'No.'

'*Eh bien*, let's assume that Carver and Petrova were responsible for the killings here. Clearly, they must be eliminated before they cause any more trouble. We need descriptions. So tell me, Charlie, are you sure you do not know what Carver looks like?'

The operations director ground his cigarette stub under his heel. 'We had him watched on a couple of his early jobs. It was an obvious precaution. He's a shade under six feet tall. Call it a metre eighty, and maybe seventy-five kilos in weight. Dark hair, thin face, intense-looking. Other than that, no distinguishing features that I know of. Actually, there is something else . . .'

'What?'

'Max wasn't wearing his jacket when he died. And it wasn't where he'd left it, the last time I saw him, hanging on the back of his chair. Carver could have dumped the black jacket and taken Max's. It's a grey one, same fabric as the trousers.'

'OK. And the woman?'

'All I know is her reputation. She's meant to be a real blonde-model type.'

Papin raised his eyebrows knowingly. 'Now we have a reason why Carver might want to be with Petrova. But if she was Kursk's partner, what is she doing on the back of a motorbike with the man who killed him? Why is she running in and out of apartments with Carver? Why is she joining him in a gunfight?'

'How the hell would I know? She's a bloody woman. Maybe she fancies him. Maybe she changed her mind.'

'Or maybe she hasn't.' Papin smiled. 'What is it you English say about the female of the species?'

'You mean Kipling? "The female of the species is more deadly than the male." '

'*Alors*, an Englishman who understands women. *Incroyable!*'

22

They were sitting in an all-night bistro, tucked between the sex-shops and tourist traps of Châtelet-les-Halles. It was a quarter past five. Even the local hookers had given up for the night and come inside for a nightcap.

Alix looked exhausted, her adrenalin rush long gone. Carver got her a cappuccino with a double-espresso shot and a *pain au chocolat* to dip into it. It wasn't exactly a healthy diet, but she needed the energy the fat and sugar would provide. Alix ignored the pastry, took a sip of the coffee, then lit a cigarette.

Carver leaned across the table, like a lover. 'Who was he, that man in the club, the one who sent his goons after us? What's his name? What's his interest in you?'

She took another drag on her Marlboro, made a show of blowing a stream of smoke up towards the ceiling, but said nothing.

'Come on, Alix, don't piss me about. You knew him. He certainly knew you. Why? And why did he send his men after us?'

She shrugged. 'His name is Ivan Sergeyevich Platonov. Everyone calls him Platon. He belongs to what you would call the Russian mafia. But the gangs – we say "clans" – are not just

Russian. They come from every race – Chechen, Azeri, Kazak, Ukrainian. They have names, like rock groups or football teams. The Chechens are Tsentralnaya, Ostankinskaya, Avtomobil'naya. The Russians are Solntsevskaya, Pushinskaya, Podolskaya – that is Platon's gang. Every gang hates all the others, but when you are a woman, they are all the same. They all want to fuck you, or beat you, or both. They are all pigs.'

'So how do you know so much about this Platon, then?'

'Everybody knows about him. He is a gangster, but the newspapers talk of him like some kind of superstar: how many houses he has, what new car he has bought, who is his mistress this week. And you must understand, he is not the boss of Podolskaya. There are others, much higher than him. And they have bosses too, men who belong to no gangs, but who control them like, like . . . puppets.'

'So what's Platon doing in Paris?'

'It could be anything. He could be doing a deal for Podolskaya. He could be paying off a French government minister. He could be taking his girlfriends shopping in Paris. You know, I was looking at them in the ladies' room. I couldn't decide: are they twins, or did they just have the same surgery? Platon would like that. Take two girls and turn them into Barbie dolls. He would think it was funny.'

Carver heard the bitterness in her voice. It sounded personal.

'OK, one more time: how do you know him?'

'How do you think? How does any woman ever know a man like Platon?'

Carver thought of the fat man in the nightclub, his body pressing down on Alix. It wasn't a nice image.

'Who was he calling?'

'The man who sent me here.'

'Who is?'

'I don't know. Why should I know? You don't know who sent you. My connection is Kursk.'

'Was. He's dead.'

Alix shook her head, a mirthless smile playing at the corner of her mouth. 'You think? Did you see the body?'

'No.'

'You don't know Kursk. Many people have tried to finish him before now. Some even thought they had succeeded. But he is like Rasputin. You have to kill him again and again before he will die.'

'If you say so. But in my experience, people only die once. You work together all the time?'

'No. Not before tonight, not as partners.'

'What changed?'

Another exhausted, heavy-eyed smile. 'It was like *The Godfather*. He made me an offer I could not refuse.'

'How do you mean?'

'Oh, long story. And I am not going to tell it now.'

Carver looked at his watch, then turned to catch the waitress's eye and made a gesture, as if signing a bill. He turned back to Alix. 'I don't need to hear the story, but I need to know how it ends. I need to know if I can trust you. Whose side are you on now?'

She stubbed out her cigarette. 'Honestly? I don't know. I am trying to decide that myself. It is the same for me, Samuel. I too need to know who to trust. I will be thirty in October. I left home when I was eighteen, so I have lasted twelve years on my own. I am not a drug addict. I am not on the streets, giving myself to drunks for a handful of worthless roubles. I am not raising three children in a rat-infested apartment. Do you understand what I am saying?'

'That you know how to survive?'

'Exactly. I do not take unnecessary risks. So the question I am asking myself when I look at you is, do I trust this man to keep me alive? Or do I go back to Moscow and take my chances with men like Platon?'

'It's not Platon you have to worry about,' Carver pointed out, 'it's whoever planned this job tonight. And if you're even thinking of going back to Moscow, you must believe you've got a connection, someone who might be able to keep you safe.'

'Possibly. But as you say, they "might" be able to keep me safe. If I have guessed right. If they want to help me. You see, that is the calculation I have to make.'

'Is that all it is, a calculation?'

'When you are trying to stay alive, that is all it ever is.'

She was right, of course. Carver knew that. Yet he also knew that he had passed the point where the justifications he gave for her presence weren't much more than a pretence. Sure, they stood a better chance together than apart. He didn't want her running off and telling the world about him. And she might yet give him a lead to the people who'd sent them on their fatal mission. But in the end, he just wanted to be with her. It was as simple as that.

He left money for the bill. 'Come on. The metro starts running soon. That's the safest place for us.'

'And then?'

'Then we're going to take a train, leaving at seven fifteen.'

'Where to?'

'Home,' he said.

The direct line from Châtelet-les-Halles to the Gare de Lyon took exactly three minutes, but Carver went the scenic route, riding all over Paris, switching trains every few stops. It took him more than an hour.

He didn't think that the Russians had picked up their trail after they'd left the nightclub. They'd left the back way; the guy who'd been waiting at the front could not possibly have seen them. But he figured there'd be other goons where the first two came from. There was no point taking chances.

Most of the way, they sat in silence. Then they took the final change, getting on the D-train that would take them down to the Gare de Lyon.

'There are closed-circuit TV cameras at the station,' said Carver, 'so we shouldn't be seen together. When we get there, pick up your bag from your locker. Then check the departure board. There should be a train for Milan leaving at seven fifteen. Get on it. Go to the first-class compartment. I'll meet you there.'

'Why should I come with you?' Alix asked.

Carver couldn't be bothered to come up with a smart reason. 'Because you want to?'

Alix hadn't expected that. This time her smile was genuine, her voice warmer than it had been at any time since they left the club. 'OK. I guess I don't have any better offers right now.'

'Come on, this is our stop.' He handed her a numbered key. 'Your locker. See you on the train.'

Carver let Alix step out of the train ahead of him, then waited on the platform to see if there was a tail following her. When the next train came into the platform, he joined the trickle of passengers who got off and started walking towards the mainline station. He picked up the computer from a separate locker, then went to the ticket office. He was wearing the eyeglasses now, the ones he'd got at the all-night pharmacy. They didn't do much to change his face, but every bit helped. He asked for two first-class seats to Milan and paid cash for the tickets. He then left the ticket office and walked across to an automatic ticket-machine on the concourse outside. Above him, massive cast-iron beams supported a glass roof, making the whole place seem like a gigantic greenhouse.

A few early travellers were breakfasting beneath the white umbrellas of the station café. Behind them, inside the main station building, was the Gare de Lyon's magnificent restaurant Le Train Bleu. It had ornate golden carvings on the ceiling and massive brown-leather banquettes. Compared to the filthy station buffets in England, where surly staff served tasteless plastic slop, Le Train Bleu was a gourmet's paradise. But Carver had no time to enjoy its pleasures now.

He bought a fistful of tickets to different destinations, all for cash. He reached the Milan train twenty minutes after he had last seen Alix. She was asleep, her head slumped against the side of the carriage.

Carver watched her for a few seconds, taking in the contours of her face. All the tension had slipped away from her features, leaving only vulnerability. He took off Max's jacket, folded it neatly on the seat opposite Alix, then reached out a hand and gave her shoulder a brisk shake.

'Wake up,' he said. 'We've got to move.'

Alix came to. She frowned. 'You look different. Older.'

'It's just the glasses.'

'Where are we?'

'We're still in Paris. But we're changing trains. First, though, you've got to make a call.'

She gave him a puzzled look as he took her phone out of one of his pockets and dialled a number. A ringing came from his money-belt. He pulled out a phone of his own and picked up the call. Then he placed the two phones in the luggage rack above their heads.

'Let's go,' he said. 'Follow me.'

Carver picked up Alix's holdall. He had that over one shoulder and the computer case over the other. He left the jacket behind. Carver took Alix's hand and practically dragged her out of the compartment, off the train, across the platform and on to another train. Twenty seconds after they had got on board, the train started moving.

'Where are we going?' asked Alix.

'Aaah,' said Carver. 'That's a surprise.'

23

Two Russians came for Kursk and bundled him into an oversized Japanese 4×4.

'Mother of God, Grigori Mikhailovich,' said the driver, 'you stink like a Chechen shithouse. It'll cost me a fortune to have the car valeted.'

'Shut it, Dimitrov. I need painkillers. Strong ones. Now.'

'Of course, Grigori, whatever you say.'

They took Kursk to a cheap hotel. The owner was expecting them. He was a Russian. He would do as he was told and keep his mouth shut. Dimitrov disappeared. Ten minutes later, he returned. The owner told him Kursk was upstairs in his room, having a shower. When Dimitrov knocked, Kursk opened the door wearing nothing but a towel. His body was covered with vivid black and purple bruises, and slashed by bloody abrasions.

Dimitrov followed Kursk into the room. He held out two pills. 'Demerol,' he said. 'My last ones. I will get more as soon as I can.'

Kursk washed the pills down with neat vodka, wiping the back of his hand across his face when he'd finished. 'OK, now get out of here,' he said. 'I need to get some rest.'

He'd been out for less than an hour when there was another knock on his door. Kursk got up and strode across the room, stark naked. He opened the door.

'I thought I told you not to fucking disturb me.'

Dimitrov held out a phone. 'It's Yuri,' he said.

There were no introductions, just a voice on the other end of the line saying, 'Get on the next train to Milan. Take Dimitrov.'

Kursk rubbed the sleep from his eyes. 'Yeah, sure . . . why?'

'Your partner kept her mobile on. We have tracked it travelling south-east across France. It looks as though she is on a train bound for Milan. The Englishman – his name is Samuel Carver – is almost certainly with her. They were spotted dancing together at some club in Paris. Platon was there with a couple of his latest women. He called me. And I am told that this Carver is carrying a computer that may contain information I do not wish to be made public. I will make sure we have people to meet the train at every stop. If Petrova and Carver get off, they will be followed until you arrive.'

'And then?'

'And then, Kursk, you will kill Carver and get that computer.'

'What about the woman?'

'Bring her back. I will decide what happens to her.'

24

Alix slept most of the way. Carver sat opposite her. He'd crashed out in the plane on the last transatlantic leg of the flight, waking only minutes before they landed in Paris. But even if he'd been tired, he wasn't in any mood to sleep. So he looked out of the window, watching the suburbs of Paris give way to the flat landscape of northern France, then the rich, rolling hills of Burgundy, and finally, past Dijon, through the limestone cliffs and gorges of the Jura to the first foothills of the Alps.

He thought about himself and what he'd done, thought about the girl, tried to figure out what he was going to do. His head was swirling with unanswered questions and unresolved emotions. Carver told himself there was no point fretting about things that were done and beyond recall. The princess was dead. Nothing was going to change that. He had to stick to the rules: concentrate on what he could control. But who was he kidding? He'd chosen to complicate his life by bringing the girl; how much control did he have over her?

He was watching her sleeping, slumped against the side of the carriage, when she slowly opened her eyes, still half asleep, caught him staring and gave him a lazy smile that turned into a yawn.

'What were you thinking?' she murmured, rubbing the sleep from her eyes.

'Oh, I don't know . . .'

She perked up, her eyes now awake, looking directly at his own. 'Were you wondering what it would be like to have sex with me?'

Carver drew in a sharp breath. 'Bloody hell, you don't mince words, do you?'

She laughed, her expression filled with the satisfaction of a woman who looks down upon the single-minded simplicity of men in general, yet is proud to have that power over one man in particular. 'It wasn't so hard to know, the way you were looking at me.'

'You reckon? I wish it were that simple.'

That surprised her. 'What do you mean?'

'I mean, maybe I was thinking about you. But I was also asking why I've put myself in the position where I can have those thoughts. I'm trying to work out just how much of a risk I'm taking, letting you into my life.'

She nodded. 'Hmm, that is a lot of thinking.'

Now it was his turn to smile. 'Well, maybe I'm just more thoughtful than I look.'

'Is that so? Well, I'm too sleepy to worry about your thoughts right now.' She stretched her arms wide, loosened her shoulders and settled back into her seat. 'Wake me up when we get there. Wherever "there" is.'

Carver waited until he was sure Alix was asleep again before rising from his seat and walking down the carriage to the well of empty space between the exit doors. Then he pulled out his spare phone and dialled a London number. A woman answered. She said 'Hello?' in a tired, brittle voice. Carver could hear a baby wailing in the background.

'Hi, Carrie,' he said. 'It's Pablo. Is Bobby about?'

'I'm fine, thank you,' she answered. 'And yes, I'd be delighted to tell you everything I've been up to in the three years since you last bothered to call.'

'I'm sorry, Carrie. You know, I'd really love to talk, but not now. Can I have a word with Bobby?'

'I'll get him for you.'

Carver could hear her shouting 'Darling! Phone for you!' then the click as an extension was picked up. A man's voice went, 'Hang on a second.' Then there was another muffled shout of 'I've got it' and the background sounds of mother and baby were silenced.

'Sorry, that's better,' said the man.

'Hi, Bobby, it's Pablo.'

'Christ! Good to hear from you. What the bloody hell have you been up to? It's been ages.'

'Yeah,' said Carver. 'Look, sorry to be anti-social, but I haven't got much time. Do you have a number for Trench? Need a word with him, and I heard he'd retired.'

Bobby chuckled. 'Retired? Well, he's not the CO any more, but I'm not sure I'd call it retirement. Security consultancies here, company directorships there – the old man's quite a mover and a shaker. So, why do you need him? Looking for a job?'

'Something like that. Listen, do you have the number or not?'

'Oh, sure, absolutely. Hang on a minute.' There was a brief pause, and then, 'OK, here it is . . .'

'Thanks, mate. Look, I know we should, you know, catch up with things. Sounds like you guys have been busy anyway. I'm happy for you. I always thought you'd make a great dad. But I really can't talk now. Speak later, yeah?'

Carver ended the call. He thought about the last time he saw Colonel Quentin Trench, the man who'd been his commanding officer, his friend, even his father-figure. Back then he was Paul 'Pablo' Jackson, recently resigned from the Royal Marines, a former officer and a gentleman turned self-destructive, brawling drunk. He'd spent the night in a cell, courtesy of the Dorset Police. He'd become a regular customer of theirs.

'Hello, Pablo. This isn't very clever,' Trench had said, stepping past the copper at the door and looking around the cell.

'Not very, no,' Carver had replied, ashamed to let Trench see him this way, knowing he'd let the old man down as much as himself.

'Still feeling stroppy, eh?'

'Yeah.'

'Why don't you take it out on someone your own size, then?'

'What do you mean?'

'You could put your talents to better use than scrapping with beer-sodden yobbos. Let me get the word out. You never know, something may come up.'

Three weeks later, the phone had rung. The caller didn't give his name. Nor did he ask for Carver's. 'We can agree on names later,' he said. The man represented a group of rich, powerful, civic-minded individuals based in London. His employers solved certain problems that lay beyond the reach of government agencies, restricted by treaties and laws. 'I was told you might be able to help,' he added. 'You come very highly recommended.'

As the call was ending, the man had said, 'Tell you what, why don't you call me Max?'

'All right, and you can call me Carver.' It was his birth-mother's name. The Jacksons had told him that much soon after his twenty-first birthday. They felt he had a right to know. Later on, when he set about creating an entire new identity for himself, he settled on Samuel for a first name. No particular reason why, he just liked the sound of it.

Now, Carver dialled the number Bobby had given him. Another woman answered the phone, her voice older, with a diction that spoke of finishing schools and debutante balls long ago. Pamela Trench, the colonel's wife, told Carver that her husband had gone grouse-shooting in the Scottish Highlands for the weekend. 'I'm awfully sorry, but he's out of reach of a telephone. Can I take a message?'

'No, don't worry.'

There was a moment's silence, then Mrs Trench spoke again. 'I am glad you called, Paul. It's just that, well, we never had the chance to speak after that poor girl . . .'

The well-meant words blindsided Carver, hitting him like a

body-shot before he had time to steel himself against the memories. 'I know,' he muttered.

'It must have been ghastly for you.'

'Yeah, wasn't too great.'

'Well, I just wanted you to know, we were all thinking of you.'

Carver managed to say thanks before he snapped the phone shut. He struggled to suppress the images that filled his mind: two cars, two accidents, two innocent women dead because of him. He was gripped by a shame that was soul-deep, a stain that could never be erased. And with it came a cold, hard rage, an implacable need for revenge and retribution against those who had sent him, unknowing, to commit an evil act. He would make them pay for the damnation they had visited upon him.

But he couldn't afford to lose his self-control now. His life and that of another woman depended on that. So he sucked in his anger, along with everything else, and walked back to his seat. Alix was still fast asleep.

25

Carver woke Alix just before the train pulled into Lausanne on the north shore of Lake Geneva. They changed trains and arrived in Geneva at ten forty-five, bang on time, then caught a bus through the business district. It crossed the River Rhône, past the Jet d'Eau fountain that sent a plume of water more than 150 feet into the sky. Close to the river, the buildings were faceless modern offices, shops and banks. It could have been any central European city. But behind them rose the hill that led up to the city's cathedral of Saint Pierre. This was the Old Town, the heart of a city that dated back two thousand years. The real Geneva.

'Here's where we get off,' said Carver.

He led Alix uphill along winding streets and through narrow alleyways between looming old apartment buildings.

'They always built tall in Geneva,' Carver commented, seeing Alix gaze upwards, following the rows of shutters towards the distant sky. 'The original town was surrounded by walls. It couldn't spread out. So the only way to go was up.'

'My goodness, a history lesson.'

Carver looked apologetic, almost bashful. 'Sorry, didn't mean to lecture.'

'No, it's fine. I like it. I didn't know you cared about things like that.'

They passed a second-hand bookstore with two arched windows set in a wood-panelled façade. The shop was closed, but there were shelves on the outside, open to the street, filled with old hardbacks and paperbacks. Alix stopped for a second, amazed at the bookseller's confidence.

'But anyone could steal them,' she said.

'Come off it, this is Geneva. We've got UN buildings stuffed with bent officials and banks filled with dollars ripped off from Third World aid. No one bothers to steal books. They steal whole countries here.'

Alix looked at him. 'What are you trying to tell me?'

'Just that there are people cruising round this city with diplomatic plates and fancy suits who make what I do look like charity work. Come on.'

There was a small café next to the bookstore, with a few plastic tables out on the cobbled street and some steps down to a tiny, low-ceilinged room within. Carver walked in. Alix followed, then watched as the owner came out from behind the counter and gave Carver a bear-hug before launching into a torrent of high-speed French. She couldn't follow it, but it sounded as though the man called Carver 'Pablo'. After a while, he disappeared into the kitchen and reappeared carrying a plastic bag filled with provisions. Carver tried to pay. The man wouldn't let him.

The café owner then glanced in Alix's direction and grinned. He looked her up and down, and said something to Carver with a wink and a nudge in the ribs. She didn't need to speak French to know what that was about.

'I'm sorry about Freddy,' said Carver once they'd started walking again. 'He gets a bit over-excited in the presence of an attractive woman. If you saw his wife, you'd know why. Anyway, he's a good bloke.' He held up the bag. 'At least we won't starve.'

They climbed a flight of stone steps that led into a cobbled yard, set against the side of the hill. External staircases and covered passages wound round the buildings that surrounded the yard like the endless stairways of a Maurice Escher drawing.

'Well,' said Carver, 'here we are. I'm afraid I'm on the top floor.'

Alix looked up again, this time with a look of dread. 'Do we have to climb all those stairs? Please, tell me there's an elevator inside.'

'Sorry. The local authorities wouldn't allow it. Said it would ruin the historic character of this fine four-hundred-year-old building. At least it keeps me fit.'

He grinned, and Alix smiled back, enjoying the sense of Carver's deeper nature emerging from beneath his protective mask.

She had no idea what to expect when they got inside Carver's apartment. The killers she'd known in Russia were either total slobs or hygiene freaks. The first group lived in porn-strewn pigsties where the only things that ever got cleaned were the weapons and the only decoration was the inevitable widescreen TV; the second group were anally retentive and emotionally barren, and lived in sterile environments filled with steel, chrome, leather and black marble. The only thing the two groups had in common was the widescreen TV.

There was a third group, of course, the men who gave the killers their orders. They tended to have expensive mistresses and trophy wives. They let the women do the decorating. It kept them occupied during their occasional breaks between shopping expeditions.

Carver did not live like a Russian. He lived like Alix's idea of a proper Englishman. The apartment had exposed beams and wooden floors covered in old, faded, slightly worn Persian rugs. There were bookshelves filled with biographies and works of military history alongside paperback thrillers. There were old vinyl records, CDs by the hundred, and rows of videos. The living-room had a pair of enormous old armchairs and a huge, battered Chesterfield sofa ranged around an open fireplace. Alix imagined herself here in the winter, curled up on one of those chairs like a cat, basking in the warmth of the fire.

Carver had disappeared into the kitchen next door. Alix could hear his voice through the wall: 'I'm just fixing some coffee. Would you like an espresso? Cappuccino?'

'You can make that?'

'Of course. I'm not a total savage. What would you like?'

'Cappuccino, please. No sugar.'

There was a painting above the fireplace, a seaside scene, dated 1887 and painted in a bright, not quite impressionist style. A group of friends were standing at the water's edge. The men had their trousers rolled up; the women were lifting their skirts just enough to be able to dip a toe into the sea.

'It's Lulworth Cove,' said Carver, walking back into the living-room with two cups of coffee in his hands. 'It's on the Dorset coast, just a few miles west of my old base.'

'It's very beautiful.' She smiled. 'What was this base?'

Carver laughed. 'I can't tell you that. You might be a dangerous Russian spy.'

'Oh no,' said Alexandra Petrova. 'I'm not a spy. Not any more.'

Carver looked at her pensively. 'So, are you going to tell me that story? The long one you were talking about?'

She sipped her coffee, and licked a splash of white foam from her top lip.

'OK. But there are things I must do first.'

'What kind of things?'

'Well, all I want to do now is to wash.'

'Fair enough. The bathroom's just down the corridor, on the right. You go and do whatever you've got to do. I'll make us something to eat. And then you can tell me your story.'

26

Papin was making slow progress. There weren't too many photo-fit artists prepared to answer the telephone on the last Sunday morning in August. At last he tracked someone down, but the picture was not ready until past ten a.m. Then he had to find someone willing to put it on air.

On any other day, the threat of an English killer and his sexy blonde accomplice would have led the news bulletins and been splashed on the front page. But this was not an ordinary day. The networks in France, like everywhere else in the world, had only one subject under discussion: the death of the princess. And so, ironically, they relegated the man who had killed her to a brief few seconds and a hastily displayed photo-fit.

Marceline Ducroix, who had served Carver his pastries and coffee in the twenty-four-hour joint in Châtelet-les-Halles, saw the picture on the TV in the back office, where her father and uncle were sitting watching the news. The two men were engaged in a loud argument over whether the car crash was an accident or the result of a typically evil Anglo-Saxon plot. Their conversation distracted her.

The English killer wanted by the authorities sounded like the polite, well-dressed man who had spoken perfect French to her in the bistro that morning. Even so, she wasn't sure it was him. 'Then don't go to the cops,' said her father, when Marceline asked his advice. 'They are all sons of whores. The less you have to do with them, the better.'

Jerome Domenici got home at eight thirty after his night shift at the pharmacy. By then he had already heard about the tragedy in the Alma Tunnel. Everyone who had come into the shop had been talking about it. He caught about ten minutes of the TV news before he fell asleep on his couch.

It was lunchtime when Jerome woke up again. He was fixing himself some bread and cheese, with one eye on his plate and the other on the TV, when he saw the photo-fit. The man looked familiar. He called the number on the TV screen.

Papin was already at the Gare de Lyon when he heard that a man in a grey jacket had been spotted in a pharmacy on the Boulevard de Sébastopol, buying hair-dye and scissors. But he'd been alone. And he'd bought three colours: brunette, red and black. Papin was fairly certain that the woman had used the dye, but which colour?

Meanwhile, there had been multiple sightings of an Englishman answering Carver's description at the Gare de Lyon. Papin had established that the man had bought two tickets to Milan shortly after seven a.m. That meant he must have caught the seven fifteen; but it had already arrived in Milan, the ticket-collector had been interviewed by local police, and he did not recall seeing anyone resembling either photo-fit. On a journey between France and Italy there was no passport control, so there were no border records. There was no way of telling whether Carver had ever got on the train, or with whom. And if he had got on, there was no way of establishing where he'd got on without canvassing every single station along the route.

Before he did that, Papin decided to check the CCTV footage

from the cameras dotted around the station. The coverage was patchy, but Papin did spot a bespectacled man in a grey jacket leaving the ticket office at 7.05. He was carrying a black bag over one shoulder – the computer.

'Is that him?' Papin had asked the operations director.

'It could be. Without the glasses that could easily be Carver.'

'OK. But now look. We have him here at 7.05. The next time we find him he is approaching the gate for the Milan train at 7.09.'

'Yes . . . He bought a ticket, he got on the train. So?'

'So, where has he been? It only takes a few seconds to walk across the concourse. He did something in the meantime. What?'

'I don't know. Maybe he went to the bathroom. Maybe he bought a newspaper.'

'Or maybe he bought another ticket, to a different destination. Carver is good. He must have known he would be spotted at the ticket office, so he used that to create a diversion. Then he got the other tickets at the automatic machines. *Merde!* There is no video footage covering them. Someone will have to check the machines for all the purchases made between 7.05 and 7.09. And meanwhile, I will do something else.'

'What's that?'

'Find the girl.'

27

Alix took a shower. Afterwards she came into the kitchen, where Carver was fixing them both some food. She had one towel wrapped around her body, another around her hair.

'Do you have an old shirt or something I can wear?' she said. 'None of my—'

'Shhh.' Carver held up a hand.

Alix was about to argue. Then she saw that there was a small television on a bracket on the kitchen wall. Carver was watching a satellite news programme.

'It's unbelievable,' he said. 'There are thousands of people outside the gates of Buckingham Palace. There are more of them laying wreaths outside Kensington Palace, where she lived. There's a book of condolence and people are queuing for, I don't know, hundreds of yards to sign it. The Prime Minister's calling her the People's Princess. They've had politicians giving messages from all over the world. There are experts talking about everything from whether paparazzi photographers should be allowed to chase people on powerful bikes, to how the royal princes are going to cope with bereavement. The actual time of death was four a.m., by the way. Like that makes any difference.'

'We didn't know what we were doing.'

'Like that really makes any difference either. Look, do you want some cheese omelette? It's pretty good. This is the place for Swiss cheese, after all. It's just that I've rather lost my appetite.'

'Sure, thanks,' Alix said. 'But I think I should be wearing some clothes when I eat.'

'Of course. Stay right there.'

He was back a few seconds later, holding a grey T-shirt. It said SANDHURST SPECIAL FORCES CHALLENGE 1987 across the front. 'Is that OK? Afraid I've not done much laundry lately, I've been away. It's crazy . . . I was in New Zealand when they contacted me. On my bloody holiday.'

She touched his arm gently, sensing the barely suppressed tension in his voice. 'It's OK. This shirt will do fine.'

'Good. On second thoughts, maybe I will have some of that omelette after all.'

They sat eating and watching the TV for a while. There were cameras at RAF Northolt, west of London. The princess's body was expected at any moment. Finally, Carver got up from the table and switched off the TV.

'You know what? I think I've seen enough of that. They're not going to tell me anything I don't already know. And there's not been anything about our part in it all. Nothing about explosions or gunfights in Paris. Either they don't know, or someone is going to great lengths to cover it all up.'

He walked through to the living-room. 'I thought you were going to tell me your life-story.' He threw himself down on the sofa and waved at the two armchairs. 'Grab a seat. I'm all ears.'

Alix walked into the room. She settled into one of the chairs, pulled her knees up to her chin, then wrapped her arms around her shins in a self-protective embrace. Carver watched her, taking in every detail. He looked at the way the sunlight caught the soft down on her long brown thighs. He looked at the way she ran her hands through her short, damp hair. He was wondering if she would betray him. He thought it might be worth it, just for the chance to have this girl in his apartment, even for a single day. As long as she was there, he could forget about death. Then Alix began to talk.

'Imagine a world without colour. The sky is grey. The buildings are grey, and the people too. The grass is grey. In winter even the snow is dirty grey. No one has any money, and capitalism is the enemy, so there is nothing in the shops, no displays in the shop windows. There are no advertisements in the streets, no bright lights. You queue for bread with your mother and wonder how drunk your father is going to be later, and which of you he is going to hit, if the vodka does not make him unconscious first. That is how I grew up.

'We lived in a city called Perm, maybe twelve hundred kilometres from Moscow. I was a good student. I had lots of time for studying because no boys were interested in me.'

'Oh, come on,' Carver interrupted. 'I don't believe that.'

'No, really. I was not a pretty girl, and my eyes they . . . how do you say it when eyes point in the wrong direction?'

'A squint?'

'Yes, I had a squint.'

'Oh, that explains it.'

'Explains what?'

'Your eyes. There's something just a tiny bit uneven about them.'

Alix started as if someone had slapped her. Carver cursed himself.

'I'm sorry, that was incredibly stupid of me. What I meant was, I think you have amazing eyes. They're beautiful. And they're kind of hypnotic. I can't stop looking at them and, er, now I know why.'

Carver waited to see whether he would be forgiven.

'You were saying . . .'

'I was saying that my squint was not so – what did you say? – hypnotic when I was a lonely little girl. I had to wear spectacles with really ugly thick frames. So the other children made fun of me, the boys and the girls also. Later, I grew up. My body was good, I knew that, but my face, forget it.'

'So how did the ugly duckling turn into a beautiful swan?'

She gave a quick nod of the head that simultaneously acknowledged and dismissed his compliment.

'I belonged to Komsomol, the Young Communists League. I did not love the Party. I did not care about politics. But you had to join, and there were benefits: summer camps, places at better colleges, you know. So, anyway, they had a literary competition. Even under the communists it was important to be *kulturny*.'

'Cultured?'

'Yes, like playing a musical instrument really well, or dancing ballet, or, for me, being able to write a long essay on Chekhov. I said he exposed the decadence and emptiness of the bourgeoisie in Imperialist Russia, proving the need for the revolution. Total bullshit! But it won a trip for me to a big Komsomol convention in Moscow. There were young athletes, scientists, artists and academics. We did not know it, but the state used these conventions to select the best young people to be trained for all the different agencies.'

'Aha!' Carver raised a finger in the air, like some corny old TV detective solving a mystery. 'So this was where they selected you to be a dangerous Soviet spy!' His voice turned more serious: 'What were you, an analyst? Or did you do fieldwork?'

'You could call it that. A woman came up to me at the convention. She went, "Do you mind?" She took off my glasses and looked at me, saying nothing, like someone at a museum who is looking at a painting, trying to decide if she likes it. I did not know what to do. My face went red.

'We went to a small side room. There were two men sitting behind a desk. I had just been reading my essay to the judges of the literary competition. These men looked exactly the same, like they were going to judge me. The woman said, "Take off your clothes, my dear." I was very shy. I had never shown my body to any man. But I also knew I had to obey orders.

'The woman told me not to worry, this was no different to seeing a doctor. I stripped to my underwear and then the three of them started talking about me. It was terrible, so humiliating, like I was a farm animal at market. They were talking about my legs, my breasts, my ass, my mouth, my hair, everything. Then one of the men said, "We will have to do something about the eyes of course." And the other said, "That is no problem, a simple procedure."

'I could not believe it. All my life, the doctors in Perm had said they could do nothing for me. They said my problem was not serious enough to justify the cost of an operation. Anyway, the woman told me to get dressed again. The men talked quietly between themselves for a moment. Then one of them told me I had been selected for a great honour. That September, I would return to Moscow to receive special training at an elite academy. I would learn to undertake duties that would be of great service to the Motherland. If I completed the training satisfactorily, I would be given the finest clothes and my own Moscow apartment. My parents, too, would be granted improved accommodation.

'It was incredible, like a fairy story, like becoming a movie star. When I told my mother, she burst into tears. She was so proud. Even my father cried for joy. That summer, I had my operation at last, carried out by the same doctor who had told me it would be impossible. I threw away my glasses. When I got on the train for Moscow, I was sad to be leaving home. But I was so excited also. I could not believe that fate had picked me out for such great fortune.'

Carver shifted position on the sofa. 'I feel a "but" coming on. What happened when you got to Moscow?'

'My academy was the Feliks Dzerzhinsky University. It was run by the KGB. I was assigned to the Second Chief Directorate, which monitored foreigners within the Soviet Union. I was taught English. I was educated in art, western culture, films, even politics, so that I could hold a conversation with the most sophisticated visitors to our country. And then I discovered what I was really being trained to do. Have you heard of the term "honeytrap"?'

'Sure. A guy meets a pretty girl in a bar. They go back to his place. They have sex. The next day someone shows him the pictures. Either he tells them what they want to know, or wifey sees the snaps. Your lot went for honeytraps in a big way. So, you were one of those girls, huh? The ones westeners who visited the Soviet Union were always warned about?'

'I was the honey in the trap, yes. You want to know the truth? I was a prostitute for the state. When I went to Moscow, I was a virgin. I had not even kissed a boy. By the time I graduated there was nothing I did not know about attracting a man and giving him pleasure. Every trick, every perversion . . . and you know, we were always told to be as dirty as possible because a man will talk much more if he is filmed on his knees being whipped, or taking a dildo up the ass, than if he is simply putting his dick in the mouth of some cheap whore.

'And I was good, you know. When Alexandra Petrova was sent on assignment, all the boys at headquarters would gather round to see the photographs and the videos. And naturally, the senior officers liked to ensure that my work was of the highest quality. So they invited me out to their dachas for the weekend and I . . . I . . . Well, you can imagine what happened.'

She blinked three or four times and looked away.

Carver sat up and held out a handkerchief. 'Hey, come on. Stop beating yourself up. You were a kid. You lived in a dictatorship. You didn't have any choice. I mean, what would have happened if you'd said, "No, I refuse to do this"?'

'If I was lucky I would have been transferred to some small, cold town in Siberia. If not . . . What happens to whores who anger their pimps? They get raped, beaten, killed . . .'

'So it's not your fault.'

She did her best to raise a tired smile. 'So here we are, then, the killer and the whore?'

'That's one way of looking at it, I suppose. But there could be others.'

Alix loosened her arms and stretched her legs. She smoothed the T-shirt down over her thighs. Then she leaned forward and looked Carver straight in the eyes, as if issuing a challenge.

'Perhaps. But I will not know that until I have heard your story, too.'

'Well, I need a drink before I start spilling my guts.' Carver got up and started walking towards his kitchen. 'How about a glass of wine? Let's pretend we're normal, have a nice cold bottle of Pinot Grigio on a summer afternoon.'

She thought for a second. 'Pinot Grigio, an Italian wine. Also known in America as Pinot Gris. Not a classic wine but, as you say, very refreshing.' A smug smile. 'See? I was trained well.'

Carver paused in the doorway. He looked at the beautiful woman in the tatty old T-shirt. 'Yeah,' he said. 'I can believe that.' Then he went to get the wine.

28

The operations director had returned to England. He needed to talk to his boss and decide what they should do. Doubtless they would use their own means to track down their missing operatives. Papin was determined to beat them to it. And then he would take advantage of whatever he discovered.

It amused him to think that no one else in Paris shared his interest in the couple's fate. The TV stations had stopped showing the photo-fits by early afternoon. The death of the princess had become a global tidal-wave, swamping all other news in a mass of grief, speculation and sheer curiosity. The police had been happy to let the other events of the night be swept under the bureaucratic carpet.

So much the better for Papin. He had no competition. Yet he knew Charlie worked for men who would very much like to find Carver, the girl and that precious computer. And all Papin's instincts told him these men would not be alone. Others would also be searching. After all, if his bet was right and Petrova was Carver's new partner, she must have a boss in Russia. He'd be wondering where she'd got to and what she was doing. If Papin could get information that both sides wanted, he could drive the price sky-high. So he commandeered all the tapes from the Gare de Lyon and took them back to his unmarked, unnumbered office. He brewed a large pot of very strong coffee, found a fresh packet of cigarettes and got to work.

His first task was to identify Petrova. The hair-dye Carver had bought must have been intended for her, because he had not used it himself – that much was clear from the CCTV images of him they'd already identified. So Papin's photo-fit of Petrova was already out of date. He decided to start again from scratch. He looked at every person seen walking towards the platform for the Milan train between six forty-five and its departure at seven fifteen. Thankfully, at that hour on a Sunday morning, the station was relatively quiet. He ignored all single males, families with children, anyone who was obviously under eighteen or over forty. All he wanted was single, young, female adults.

Twenty-two fitted the bill, so Papin printed up stills of all of them. Then he started the process of elimination again.

Papin approached the problem logically. Petrova had persuaded a trained assassin to forget all his basic fieldcraft. He should have killed her. Even if he had spent the night with her, he should have killed her afterwards. He could not afford to let a potential witness live. Yet he had done. So clearly this was an exceptional woman.

It took only a few minutes to flick through the pile of stills and, get rid of all the obviously dumpy, plain ones; the backpackers with bulging thighs; the short-sighted, buck-toothed, flat-chested wall-flowers; the anonymous young women whose destiny was always to remain invisible to men. That left seven. Beauty, thought Papin, was indeed a rare commodity. Not that all seven of them were beautiful. But one had to be careful. This woman had been through a tough night. She would be tired, not looking her best. And a closed-circuit camera was not the most flattering lens. Papin looked again, more closely. Four more pictures hit the bin.

Now there were three finalists in Pierre Papin's contest. The first was a pretty little blonde in tight jeans and a lacy white peasant top. Papin smiled to himself. This one would certainly tempt any man. But her golden hair fell to her shoulders. And why had Carver bought dye and scissors if not to get rid of such distinctive locks?

That left two. One was a redhead. Despite the hour and the day, she was smartly dressed, an ambitious young executive, heedless of weekends and holidays. Papin examined her sharp features and the tight, dark slash of her lipsticked mouth. He could imagine what she would be like in bed: fiery, controlling, neurotic. This one would be easy to anger and difficult to control. A man would have to play Petruchio to her shrew. She hardly looked like the seductive model Charlie had described.

The third woman wore a short pale-blue dress. Papin paused to imagine the way it would look as she walked, stretched across her ass but flicking around her slender thighs. He paused to let himself enjoy that thought. It was just business, he told himself. He had to put himself in Carver's shoes. Charlie had said Petrova looked like a model. Well, this girl had the body for it and the fine, haughty features. Even in the blurred, grainy video that much was obvious. Papin looked at her raven-black hair. It was roughly cut, like an urchin's. A coiffure like that could cost a fortune in a smart Parisian salon, or you could get the same effect for free. With a pair of cheap scissors and a bottle of dye from a pharmacy shelf.

Yes, thought Papin, this was the one. It was a gamble to eliminate all the other possibilities, but he was prepared to go all-in. He believed he had found Mademoiselle Petrova.

29

They were both on the sofa now, sitting at either end, with the empty bottle of wine in an ice bucket on the floor beneath them. Carver had showered too. Now he was wearing a loose-fitting white T-shirt and a pair of faded blue linen pants. He looked good. Alix had seen the way he'd been looking at her from the moment they'd first met. She wondered when he'd make his move.

'Your turn,' she said.

'Must I?'

'Yes! I did. And anyway, I want to know how you became who . . . no, *what* you are. I have met lots of people who kill. But I never met one before who made me omelettes, or listened to anything I had to say. I guess I never met a killer with manners.'

'You don't want to be taken in by manners. Having manners doesn't necessarily mean you care about other people. Sometimes it just hides the fact that you couldn't give a damn.'

She looked at him. 'Can you give a damn?'

'About what?'

She said nothing.

'Yes, I give a damn.'

All he had to do was lean towards her, break the invisible wall between them. Her pulse-rate started to rise. Her breathing deepened. Her back arched fractionally. Her lips relaxed, ready to receive his.

But Carver didn't move.

Alix felt like an idiot. Then her temper flashed. How dare he play games with her? How dare he look at her with those cool, assessing eyes?

'You didn't finish your story,' he said.

Alix did not reply.

'Tell me about Kursk. What was the offer he made you? The one you could not refuse.'

'I told you, I have said enough. Now you tell me something.'

'What?'

'I don't care. Anything. Just so long as it is true.'

Carver looked away. He put a hand up to his face. He leaned back and gazed at the ceiling.

'Fair enough, I'll tell you why I didn't kiss you just now.'

Alix was silent, but her eyes narrowed as she looked at him.

'I was scared. I was afraid that if I opened myself up, even that much, I would not stop until I had given myself away, every bit of me. Is that true enough for you?'

'Yes,' Alix whispered.

She had been watching Carver's eyes as he spoke. Something in them had changed, as though a curtain had been drawn aside to reveal a distant view of the man he really was. But now she could see him closing up again. When he spoke again, that other man had vanished.

'So . . . Kursk?'

She wanted to scream at him, 'Forget Kursk!' She longed to get the hidden Samuel Carver back. But she had to find the patience to wait, to let him emerge of his own accord. So she gathered her thoughts and said, 'It was very simple. He blackmailed me.'

'What do you mean?'

She sighed. 'May I smoke?'

She could see him hesitate for an instant. There was a fastidious, disciplined side to Carver. It probably came from his years in the military. All the videos on his shelves were in alphabetical order, all the cooking implements in his kitchen were immaculately arranged. He would not like anyone smoking in his apartment.

As if he knew what Alix was thinking, Carver laughed. 'Sure. Go ahead. Then talk.'

Alix inhaled deep into her lungs, then let out a long, slow stream of smoke that curled and eddied in the shafts of afternoon light that shone through the apartment's deep-set windows.

'I had been in the KGB for less than two years when the Wall came down. Suddenly, all our old allies were rebelling against us, kicking our soldiers out of their countries. It was humiliating. Everything any of us had known was falling apart.

'For a while, we carried on in Moscow as if nothing had happened. In some ways it was easier. More westerners were coming to the city. They thought that the Cold War was over and they had won, so they did not care what girls they screwed, or what they said to us. But then Gorbachev was deposed, Yeltsin took over and suddenly there was no money to pay anyone. The whole country was run by gangsters. However bad it had been before, now it was one hundred times worse. We had nothing. We had to live somehow.'

'You sound like you're expecting me to judge you. I'm in no position to do that.'

'Maybe. Anyway, I was lucky. Because I can speak English I got a job at a hotel, the Marriott, working at the reception desk. I found a good man, a doctor. He was not rich or handsome, but he treated me with respect.

'For a long time, I thought I was OK. Then Kursk started coming to the hotel. He had worked with the girls as a "bodyguard". That was what they called it. The real reason was to make sure we did not do any business for ourselves, or try to run away with a rich foreign client. Kursk liked to remind me that he knew who I was and what I had done. He could expose me at any time. Everything I had worked for would be ruined. I offered him money to go away, but he turned me down. He was happier teasing me, just keeping me like a fish on the end of a line. I knew that sooner or later he would pull on the hook.

'That's what happened. Kursk came to the hotel on Friday morning. He said he needed a partner on a job. He wanted a woman. People would be distracted by her and pay less attention to him. He told me to leave work, tell my supervisor I was feeling sick. If I came with him, he would pay me ten thousand dollars, US. And if I did not . . .'

'Let me guess. He still had some of your old photographs. You would be caught by your own honeytrap.'

Alix nodded.

'So what happened to the doctor?'

'He is still there. He wants to marry me.'

'What do you want?'

'He will give me a home, maybe a family. I will be a respectable woman.'

'But?'

'But I do not love him. I would just be selling myself again.'

'Come here,' said Carver.

He opened his arms, and Alix nestled against his shoulder. He put his arm around her. She could feel him pressing his nose against her hair, breathing in its scent. Then he leaned back against the arm of the sofa and she went with him, relaxing into his lean, muscular embrace.

It took a couple of minutes for Alix to realize that Carver was asleep. She smiled ruefully to herself. She must be losing her touch if men could take her in their arms without being driven mad with lust. But perhaps it was a greater compliment that a man like Carver would let himself sleep. That was the ultimate vulnerability. She could do anything to him now.

Alix slipped out of Carver's arms and got to her feet. She stroked a lock of hair away from his forehead, then gently kissed his brow, like a mother with a child. She picked up the wine bottles, the ice bucket and the glasses and took them through to the kitchen.

She walked along the corridor to Carver's bedroom, smiling as she saw the TV on a plinth at the end of the bed, exactly as she'd predicted. There was a bedside table with a photograph in a silver leather frame showing Carver at the helm of a yacht with a woman hugging him from behind. They were both laughing.

Alix felt a quick, sharp stab of jealousy. Who was this woman making Carver so happy? There was no trace of any feminine presence in the apartment. She wasn't part of his life now. Even so, Alix resented her closeness to Carver and the unforced joy in their laughter.

She told herself she was just being professionally thorough as she looked through Carver's wardrobe, fingering the fabric of his classic English and Italian suits, smiling at his well-worn jeans and baggy jumpers. She thought of his track-pants. Why was it that the older clothes got, the more men seemed to like them?

On the top shelf of the wardrobe, above the hanging suits and shirts, there were a couple of folded blankets and a rolled-up duvet. Alix had to stretch to reach the duvet. She pulled it down, then carried it through to the living-room and draped it over Carver's unconscious body.

So now where was she going to sleep? This was a bachelor apartment. There was only one bed. Alexandra Petrova went to sleep in it.

30

Alone in his office on Sunday night, Pierre Papin pursued the question of Carver, the girl and the train they had taken out of Paris. A check on the ticket-machines at the Gare de Lyon had come up with more than a dozen purchases made during the missing minutes when Carver could have used them. Four of these were for one ticket only. Papin was tempted to dismiss them, but he had to consider the possibility that the Englishman had dropped the girl and continued to a separate destination on his own. Several of the ticket-buyers had used credit cards, none in Carver's name. But that was to be expected. If he had used a card, the name would certainly be that of an alias. So Papin was left with the task of checking twelve separate journeys, involving more than twenty individuals, hoping to track down his two suspects by a process of elimination.

It was a massive task, and it would require a great deal of co-operation. Ideally, Papin should ask for help from other departments, but he had no intention of doing that unless it was absolutely unavoidable. It was a matter of self-preservation.

Papin knew it was said in politics that your opponents are in the other parties, but your enemies are in your own. He operated on that principle. He had a visceral distrust of his colleagues in the various branches of the French security system. He knew they'd happily stab him in the back if it gave their department a moment's advantage. That was the way the game worked in every intelligence community. It wasn't the terrorists, the spies and the other assorted dangers to national security you had to worry about, it was the bastard in the next office.

There had to be another way of tracking his prey. Papin put himself in Carver's position.

OK, he arrives at the station with the girl. They split up in case anyone is looking for a couple. He tells her to go to the Milan train, makes a public show of buying tickets to Milan and lets himself be seen on camera walking towards the appropriate platform. But unless he is engaged in a massive double-bluff, he does not get on that train. He gets on another train, using tickets he has bought from a machine. Yet Carver and the girl do not return to the concourse . . .

Papin had been through the footage. Even if they had hidden their faces from the camera, he would have recognized them by their clothes or the way they walked.

So what does Carver do?

Papin got up from his seat and walked over to the small table where his cafetière was standing, poured out the last dregs into his dirty cup and grimaced at the feel of the cold, gritty liquid on his tongue. He was about to spit it out into his wastepaper bin when the solution suddenly struck him. Of course! Papin's face broke into a triumphant grin. Unless he had led his girl on a mad dash across the railway tracks, Carver must have got on to whatever train was waiting on the platform opposite the one to Milan. Papin reached for a timetable and there it was, departing at thirteen minutes past seven, the express service to Lausanne, Switzerland. Carver and the girl had been on that train, he was absolutely certain of it.

As reluctant as he was to ask for help from any of his rivals in Paris, Papin had no hesitation in making a late-night call to Horst Zietler, of the Swiss Strategischer Nachrichtendienst, or Secret Intelligence Service. Zietler had nothing to gain by screwing him. Papin got straight to the point.

'Horst, I need your help. I'm trying to find two people, a man and a woman. I think they arrived in Lausanne by train from Paris earlier today.'

'Anyone I need to be concerned about?'

'No, they're no danger whatever to Switzerland. But . . .'

'They're an embarrassment to France?'

Papin chuckled wearily. 'Something like that. Let's just say I'd like to know where they went once they arrived in your country.'

'So, what do you need?'

'Cooperation in Lausanne, interviews with any station staff who were on duty yesterday, maybe a look at security footage from, say, ten to twelve hundred hours. But, you understand, this is unofficial, off the record.'

'I'll have a quiet word with the station manager in the morning. I'll tell him you're from the Federal Interior Ministry, following up a possible visa irregularity – purely routine, nothing to worry about. Let's say your name is, I don't know . . . Picard, Michel Picard. You'll need an ID. I'll email a template – work from that.'

'Thanks, I owe you.'

'Certainly, but I'm sure you can find a way of paying me back . . .'

Papin laughed again, this time with genuine amusement. 'Well, now that you mention it, there's a house we've been watching by the Parc Monceau, filled with remarkably beautiful girls. It's attracted some very interesting clients with impressively exotic, imaginative sexual tastes. Perhaps I should send you some of the video footage to see if any Swiss citizens are involved. Purely as a matter of international cooperation, you understand.'

'Of course,' agreed Zietler. 'What other reason could there be? As always, it's a pleasure doing business with you, Pierre. The documentation you need is on its way.'

Papin was on the early-morning flight out of Charles de Gaulle to Geneva. He planned to be in Lausanne by the time the station manager arrived for work.

Monday, 1 September

31

Carver woke just after three in the morning. It took him a second to work out where he was. He was lying on the sofa, still dressed, but someone had draped a duvet over him. He pondered the significance of the gesture. It certainly seemed like a good sign. Faced with a choice between killing him as he slept or making him comfortable and tucking him in, Alix had reached for the bed linen.

So where had she got to now? There was no one in the kitchen, nor in Carver's office. The bathroom was empty, though a pair of women's knickers was drying on the towel-rail. That left only one possibility. Carver opened his bedroom door as quietly as possible and padded across the room. She was in his bed. He could see the outline of her body under the sheet, the shock of her pitch-black hair against the white pillow. One arm was flung out in front of her, half covering her face. As she breathed she let out an occasional soft, barely audible snuffle.

Carver smiled, then shook his head as he recognized a long-forgotten emotion: affection. Fancying a woman was one thing. But when you heard her snore and thought she was cute, well, then you knew it was serious.

It took an effort of will to turn around and leave the room. As he walked back down the corridor, Carver thought about everything Alix had said earlier. He believed the stuff about her joining the KGB. But the very fact that she had been trained to deceive men made him doubt the rest of her story. *She's working behind the desk at a fancy hotel when some thug comes along and says, 'Do a highly dangerous, top-secret mission with me in Paris, or I tell the world you were a hooker?'* No, that just didn't sound credible. On the other hand, it didn't automatically make her his enemy. There were all sorts of reasons why she might want to lie about her real identity and purpose. God knows he did it enough.

He checked his phones and office computer to see if she'd tried to talk to anyone or send any messages while he was asleep. His phones were routed through a sequence of relays that made it impossible for anyone to track where he was. The system also tracked any activity. There had been none at all. He logged on to his ISP mail-server – nothing there either.

That left Max's laptop. It was just conceivable Alix might have used that. The bag was still on the kitchen chair where Carver had left it when they arrived at the flat. It looked untouched. But that meant nothing. She would have been smart enough to leave everything exactly as she'd found it.

Carver opened the padded black nylon case and pulled out the laptop. It was a Hitachi, another grey plastic box just like a million others. Carver opened it, pressed the power button and waited while the Windows 95 operating system rebooted. A box immediately appeared, demanding a password. Carver didn't have a clue what Max had chosen as his personal open-sesame, and he'd bet his bottom dollar Alix didn't either. So no one had sent anything from this computer since the last time Max had used it. Carver closed the Hitachi again. He certainly wasn't any kind of techno-wizard. But the next person who opened up this laptop would be.

He was sure now that Alix had not been able to communicate with anyone since he left her mobile on the Milan train. For now, at least, their presence in Geneva was still secret.

Carver suddenly realized he was starving. He went to a cupboard and pulled out a packet of cornflakes. They were three weeks old, at least, but that was too bad. At least the milk was fresh and cold. He ate the cereal sitting at the kitchen island. After a couple of spoonfuls, he reached for the TV remote control and turned on the set. They were still talking about the princess, showing the same crash-site footage, the same holiday memories. There was a picture of her in a swimsuit that made her look unusually thick around the middle. Some guy on CNN was speculating that she might have been pregnant. Other reporters were commenting on the absence of CCTV footage. Twelve cameras covered the roads between the Ritz Hotel and the Alma Tunnel, but not one of them had produced a single image of the Mercedes at any stage of its journey. He sighed. Whoever had set this up, they had powerful friends. But he had a few friends too.

Carver washed his bowl and put it on the draining board. He wiped the milk and cereal splatters off the worksurface, using these simple domestic chores as a means of clearing his mind. He stood by the phone for a second, his hand hovering over the handset. Finally he picked it up and dialled a number. It rang several times, then there was a grunt of irritation at the other end of the line.

Carver grinned. 'Wakey-wakey. It's Carver.'

'Uhhh . . . what time is it?'

'Half three. Yeah, I know, I'm sorry. But this is urgent. We need to meet. Can you be at Jean-Jacques in twenty minutes?'

There was another grunt, of assent this time, and Carver replaced the handset.

He grabbed the computer, pulled a leather jacket from a peg in the hall and headed out the door. He walked downhill towards the lake, through the commercial district by the shoreline, and on to the Pont des Bergues, a V-shaped bridge whose two arms met by a small island jutting out towards the lake. A walkway linked the bridge and the island, which was planted with trees and illuminated by spotlights. At the far end there was a statue of a man in Roman robes seated on a chair, looking out across the lake with a frowning, thoughtful expression. This was Geneva's most famous son, the eighteenth-century philosopher Jean-Jacques Rousseau.

As Carver reached the statue, he heard a voice from the shadows. ' "Man is born free, but everywhere he is in chains." Well, Monsieur Rousseau, you got that right.'

Carver laughed. 'Now, now, Thor, stop feeling sorry for yourself.'

An extraordinary figure walked into the light. He was well over six feet tall, rake-thin, pale-skinned, blue-eyed and topped with an explosion of blond dreadlocks. He rubbed his face with his hand to emphasize his exhaustion. 'Aww, come on, man,' he said, in a sing-song Scandinavian accent. 'You wake me up in the middle of the night and make me come running like a poodle. How do you expect me to feel?'

'Come and rest your weary limbs on this park bench,' said Carver. 'See if I can make it worth your while getting out of bed.'

He'd met Thor Larsson four years back at a bar where they'd both gone to hear a visiting American blues guitarist. They'd got talking over a couple of beers. By the fifth or sixth round, Carver had discovered that this golden-haired rasta was both a professional software engineer and a former lieutenant in the Norwegian Army's intelligence corps. 'National service,' he'd said, apologetically. 'I didn't have any choice.'

'That's nothing,' Carver had replied. 'I did a dozen years in Her Majesty's Royal Marines. And I bloody volunteered.'

They listened to the blues, talked, drank a lot more beers. Larsson became his tech-man. He never asked precisely why Carver needed untraceable email and telephone accounts, computers that were at least eighteen months ahead of anything available on the open market, and guaranteed penetration of any network, anywhere. He just did the work and accepted the extravagant amounts of cash Carver paid him for his skill and his discretion.

'What's the big deal, then?' the Norwegian asked.

'This,' said Carver, holding up the computer case. 'There's a laptop in here that I need to get into, past all the encryption and password protection. But here's the problem: there are people who want this computer and the information on it. And they want it badly. If they ever discover you've got it, or even that you had it and you know what was on it, they won't piss about. They'll come after you.'

'So what's the good news?'

'I'm going after them, which is why I'd really like to know of any names and addresses listed on this thing.'

'You mean, there are people out there trying to kill you, and you don't even know who they are?'

'I'm working on it.'

'No, apparently *I'm* working on it. So, this laptop, is it gonna be a challenge?'

'Oh yeah. One thing I do know about these guys, they're very well connected. They'll be using military, maybe even NSA-level encryption. Don't ask me about the details, but it's bound to be real high-end stuff.'

Larsson gave a rueful smile. 'Don't say that, man. You know it only tempts me.'

Carver grinned back. 'Well, if you don't think you're up to it, I'll understand . . .'

The Norwegian shook his great shaggy head. 'This is going to cost you, big time.'

'Doesn't it always?'

Carver handed over the case. Larsson turned to leave, but Carver stopped him.

'Seriously, Thor, this could get tricky. Keep your eyes open. If you even suspect that someone's after you, grab the computer and get out. Don't hang around, you understand?'

'Yeah.'

'And if you get anything out of that address book, contact me straight away. It could save both our arses.'

Larsson gave a nod of acknowledgement. They walked together, not speaking, back up the path to the bridge. When they got there, Larsson turned right, towards the more modern side of the city. Carver made his way back to the Old Town, following the familiar winding streets up the hill until he arrived at his building.

Alix was still asleep. It was half past four. Carver got undressed and lay back down on the sofa, obeying one golden rule of military life: never miss a chance to eat, sleep or shit.

The next thing he knew, the apartment was filled with light, a hand was gently shaking his shoulder, and a soft, slightly breathy woman's voice was saying, 'I forgot. Do you take milk and sugar in your coffee, or not?'

32

Carver opened one eye and held up a hand to shut out the morning sun streaming in through the open window. 'Uh, hi,' he mumbled. 'Um, I'll have it strong, just a drop of milk, two sugars, thanks.' A thought struck him out of nowhere and he pulled his hand down to cover his mouth. 'Christ, I haven't brushed my teeth. Hope my morning breath isn't too toxic.'

Alix laughed. 'I think I'll survive.'

She stood there, outlined by a glowing halo of light. She was still wearing his old T-shirt, just that and a pair of knickers, her hair still tousled from bed, not a scrap of make-up on her face. Carver had never seen anything so beautiful.

'Bloody hell, you're gorgeous,' he said. He sounded surprised, as if he couldn't quite believe she was there.

'Silly man,' she said, and ruffled his hair. The touch of her fingers on Carver's scalp sent thrilling shock-waves through his entire body. 'Go and brush your teeth. I'll bring you your coffee.'

Carver didn't know how he was going to get off the couch without revealing just how pleased he was to see her. He grabbed the blanket to cover himself and scuttled from the room, both of them laughing, sharing the knowledge of what was happening.

He dived under the shower, quickly washed with the water as hot as he could take it, then swung the thermostat back the other way and stood for twenty seconds under a blast of water as pure and cold as a waterfall. Now he was properly awake.

He'd brushed his teeth and was dragging a razor over his chin when she walked in, holding a cup of coffee. He caught her eye in the mirror and smiled, just for the pleasure of seeing her there. She walked up to him from behind, handing him the coffee with one hand and running a finger down his spine with the other. He took the cup, placed it on the basin, then turned round and leaned towards her. But she lifted the finger up to his lips, holding him back with the barest touch of her skin against his.

'No,' she murmured, her voice much throatier now. He could see her nipples outlined against the T-shirt's flimsy faded cotton. His skin felt electric, craving the touch of her body, but she gently turned him back to the mirror. 'Finish shaving. Drink some coffee. We have time.'

She continued to stand behind him, leaning up against the wall and watching him with forensic attention as he finished shaving, rinsed his face and dried it with a hand-towel that was hanging next to the basin. He chucked the towel on to the floor beside him, then turned round. Carver stood stock-still, unsmiling, just looking at the girl. Her eyes narrowed, meeting his gaze and matching it, neither one of them backing down.

He crossed the room in two strides and lifted her bodily off the floor, pressing her up against the wall as he kissed her with a passion that had been caged inside him for far too long. She answered his intensity with her own, pushing her mouth against his, wrapping her arms around his neck and gripping his waist with her thighs.

Carver brought his arms round under her and held her up to him, never breaking away from their kiss as he carried her through the door into the bedroom. He put her down on the ground beside the bed, breaking away for just long enough to slide the

T-shirt over her head as she stood with her arms up, arching her back and bringing her breasts up towards him. Then he was running his tongue around a nipple and she was ripping the towel from his waist and they were rolling on to the bed and at last their hunger could be satisfied. Second time around, the frenzy was replaced by tenderness, the urgency by a lazy, indulgent, mutual exploration; getting to know the taste, the smell, the feel of each other; each beginning to learn what worked for the other.

Later, as they were lying together, her head nestled against his shoulder, he felt her body turning. She looked up at him, her chin resting against his chest.

'I had forgotten it could be like that,' she whispered.

He stroked her hair, gently circling a thumb around her temple. 'It's been a long time for me, too.'

'Who is she? The girl in the picture.'

'Her name was Kate. We were going to be married.'

'Did she leave?'

'She died.'

'I'm sorry. I shouldn't have said anything.'

'No, it's time I talked about her. I've spent the past five years trying not to. That hasn't got me very far.'

She nodded. 'All right then, tell me about Kate. In fact, tell me everything. You promised yesterday, remember?'

'I was hoping you'd forgotten.'

'I am a woman. I never forget.'

Carver laughed. 'This KGB training you did, was interrogation part of the curriculum?'

'No, it came naturally.'

He grinned. 'You're great, you know? You're just great.' He ran a hand along her body, relishing every contour. 'And I'm not just saying that because you've got a perfect arse.'

She slapped his hand away in mock annoyance. 'Kate!' she said.

'OK, Kate. Well, I'd been a Marine for, I dunno, ten years or so. Typical soldier-boy – you know, love 'em and leave 'em, nothing serious. But with Kate, I don't know why, but it was much more serious, right from the off. I met her at a party. We started talking and we didn't stop till it was morning. We just sat cuddled up in this big old armchair and told each other pretty much everything about ourselves. By the end of the night I knew she was the woman I was going to marry.'

He looked up at Alix. The light had gone from her eyes.

'I'm sorry,' he said. 'I shouldn't have said so much.'

'No, I asked.'

'I'll stop.'

'No, don't. Tell me everything.'

'There isn't that much more,' he said, as she laid her head on his chest and he stared up at the ceiling. 'I mean, there is, obviously, but what it all boils down to is that we got engaged. I left the service, planning to start a new life. Her dad ran a yacht-charter business and I was going to work with him for a few years before taking it over when he retired. Then . . . then . . . well, then we went out to lunch, and I stayed behind for a minute, just a minute, and she walked across the street alone, and some bastard in a stolen car ran a red light . . . and I wasn't there . . .' He screwed up his eyes for a moment, trying to hold the memories and tears at bay.

He could see the room where they'd had that last meal: him, Kate and Bobby Faulkner, his closest friend since the day they'd both turned up as Marines officer candidates on the same Admiralty Selection Board test. He could hear Bobby telling insulting stories about his past misdeeds, hiding his affection under a smokescreen of mockery.

Then Carver saw the boozed-up wankers by the bar as they were all walking out, felt the jolt against his shoulder as one of them deliberately bumped into him and accused him of spilling his pint, looking to pick a fight. He watched Kate walking out of the door as he said, 'Get the car, this won't take long.'

Then he opened his eyes and said, 'She never stood a chance. Killed instantly. That was a blessing, at least. She never suffered, never even knew what hit her.'

Alix brushed a lock of hair off his forehead. 'But you did suffer?'

'No, I got drunk. I cultivated my rage. Then I made everyone else suffer instead. That's how I got into this business.'

He told her how much his old commanding officer, Quentin Trench, had meant to him, how he'd pulled him out of that police cell and put in the call that had changed his life.

She balled her fist and tapped his shoulder. 'OK, so now you are here and now I am with you. Enough talking. What are we going to do?'

Carver propped himself up on an elbow. 'Follow the money,' he said.

33

Sir Perceval Wake depressed the button on the antiquated intercom that linked his study with his secretary's desk in the hall outside. 'Send him in.'

The apartment in Eaton Square where he lived and worked occupied two floors of a tall, white-fronted house. It stood in a terrace of identical buildings lining a broad boulevard running from the aristocratic playground of Sloane Square to the walls of Buckingham Palace. The government departments of Whitehall were just a five-minute taxi-ride away. This was one of the world's most expensive neighbourhoods. Wake's hunger for money and influence had always been as great as his thirst for knowledge.

For decades, Her Majesty's Government had come to Sir Perceval Wake for advice and paid handsomely for the privilege, as had the chief executives of City institutions and multinational corporations. He'd begun his career as a political history lecturer at Oxford University, but he did not linger long among the city's brilliant but impoverished academics. In 1954, he published a book based on his postgraduate thesis. It was provocatively entitled

Useful Idiots: The Role of Western Intellectuals in the Spread of Communist Dictatorship. At a time when most supposedly progressive, liberal thinkers still believed that the Soviet Union was a force for good in the world, Wake's ideas exploded like a hand grenade in a barrel of fish. He became a hate-figure on the left and an icon on the right.

Within weeks of publication, he was invited to attend a private conference of politicians, financiers and thinkers from Europe and the United States that met at the Hotel Bilderberg in Arnhem, Holland. The organizers aimed to protect western democracy and free markets against the communist tide. That original meeting evolved into an annual event, an institution in its own right. For over forty years, Wake had been an active member of the Bilderberg Group, whose secret meetings, attended by some of the richest and most powerful men on earth, had become the focus of countless conspiracy theories. He regularly attended the World Economic Forum in Davos. He travelled to the 2,700-acre estate of Bohemian Grove in Sonoma County, California, to join the cast of rich, powerful, male Americans parading in torchlight before a giant fake-stone owl – and, the conspiracy theorists insisted, hatching plots for global domination.

To Wake, the accumulation of power and influence was a matter of duty as well as a personal pleasure. He believed that people like him, the ones who truly understood the world, were obliged to save its people from the consequences of their own stupidity. Left to their own devices, the masses made distressingly poor decisions. They elected genocidal maniacs like Hitler. They swore allegiance to tyrannical despots like Stalin and Mao. It was really best for everyone if running the planet was left to the experts.

He rose from his desk to greet his visitor. Wake had taken great care to cultivate his appearance, from the artfully unkempt mane of silver hair that he swept back over his ears to the bespoke tweed jackets, soft cotton shirts and corduroy trousers that signified both his affluence and his status as a free thinker. By contrast, Jack Grantham's drab suit demonstrated that even as a senior officer of

MI6 he was, in the end, just another civil servant. Still, Wake decided, it would be unwise to underestimate him. Grantham did not possess the usual flabby pallor of a desk-bound bureaucrat, and there was a look of measured, sceptical assessment in his cool grey eyes. He had the air, Wake sensed, of a man who had come a long way but still had further to go. His energies had not yet been depleted by the unrelenting grind of the Whitehall machine and there was a toughness about him that was as much mental as physical. He would not be fobbed off by easy options or the countless excuses officialdom found for inaction. Wake had in fact been keeping an eye on Grantham's career for some time. He was curious to see whether his abilities matched his growing reputation.

They exchanged a cordial handshake.

'Jack, my boy, how very good to see you.'

Grantham responded with a single sharp nod of acknowledgement.

'So, how are things down at Vauxhall Cross?' Wake asked, settling back down behind his desk and waving in the direction of a chair to let his guest know that he could sit too.

'Things could be better,' Grantham replied. 'That crash in Paris has stirred things up.'

'I dare say it has. No doubt there will be claims that it could have been prevented, but I can't see that you have any need to be concerned. After all, it was simply an accident. A ghastly, tragic accident, of course, but nothing to worry the Secret Intelligence Service.'

'That depends. We think this might have been a hit. So we're wondering who might have wanted to kill the princess, or her companion, and why.'

'What does that have to do with me?' Wake leaned forward a fraction. His interest had been aroused.

'You've studied every threat to our national security for the past forty years. You've known our leaders and half our enemies' leaders, too. You've been in the room when people have discussed and even planned operations off the books. So you tell me. Why would anyone want to kill the Princess of Wales?'

'Well, now, that's an intriguing question,' said Wake, relaxing back into his chair. 'I imagine you're not the only one asking it. Have the media raised the prospect of foul play?'

The MI6 man shook his head. 'Not yet, but it's only a matter of time. Some of the wilder conspiracy-theory websites are claiming the princess was pregnant. The boyfriend's father swears that the Duke of Edinburgh has been plotting against him. And the princess herself apparently believed the Prince of Wales would have her killed in a car smash. We think she put it all down on tape. God help us if that ever sees the light of day.'

Wake sighed. 'The poor girl, she always had such a desperate need for love, such a strong sense of persecution. Not surprising, I suppose. The parents' divorce was particularly messy. So, was she pregnant?'

'We don't know. We don't think so.'

'Never mind. It's not important. The princess was no longer a member of the royal family, so even if she had given birth her future children would have had no constitutional significance. Nor do I believe for one second that any member of the royal family would have anything whatever to do with an assassination, under any circumstances. The very idea is absurd.'

Grantham paused for a second before he spoke again. When he did so, his voice was quiet, his words impeccably polite, yet there was a steely tone to his voice. 'I'm not suggesting that the palace had any direct involvement, but there may have been others who believed they were acting in the monarchy's or the country's best interests. Let's just suppose – hypothetically – that such people existed. What would be their motive for committing such a crime?'

Wake picked up a pen from the desk in front of him and tapped it a couple of times on the walnut surface, gathering his thoughts.

'I went for a walk yesterday evening, up to the palace,' he said after a short while. 'It was quite extraordinary. Huge crowds were gathered in front of the gates, and there was an anger about them, a feverish intensity quite unlike anything I have ever known in this country. They were hurt, bereft, and they wanted someone to blame. It would only have taken one man on a soap-box to whip them into a frenzy and I swear they would have stormed the gates.'

Grantham seemed about to interrupt, so Wake held up a hand.

'Let me continue,' he said. 'I walked down Constitution Hill, through Hyde Park and into Kensington Gardens. On the grass in front of Kensington Palace, below the princess's apartment, there is a mass, a veritable sea of flowers. Some are magnificent bouquets, some just pathetic little bunches of wilting blooms, but all of them are laid there in tribute. And every minute that passes, more people are bringing more flowers, more messages, more candles. They are talking to one another, weeping, complete strangers collapsing into one another's arms.

'This is something entirely new. All the reserve that has long characterized our nation, all that stiff upper lip and muddling through, has been replaced by an almost wanton hysteria. And yet at the same time it's truly primitive, a return to the cult of the goddess, the mother. Clearly the princess symbolized something extraordinarily powerful. So I can't help but ask myself: if this is the influence she could exert in death, what might have happened had she lived?

'Yesterday, the Prime Minister called her the People's Princess. It was a trite little phrase, but telling all the same. She did indeed have a remarkable hold over the people, and every interview she gave, every picture for which she posed, merely underlined how much more affection and sympathy she commanded than her former husband.

'Of course, that's natural. People will always sympathize with a wronged wife, particularly if she is beautiful and vulnerable. In normal circumstances, that really doesn't matter. But these are far from normal circumstances. The former husband is also the future King of England, and it would be impossible for him to rule effectively, perhaps even to ascend to the throne at all, if there was another, competing court surrounding his former wife. Everything he did would be judged by the degree to which she was seen to approve or disapprove. It would be intolerable.

'Monarchies are by nature monopolistic. They cannot allow competition. So I can, in theory, see why a group or an individual concerned with the preservation of the monarchy might deem it necessary to remove such a threat to the Crown.'

Grantham shrugged. 'But you just said yourself, the death of the princess has plunged the monarchy into crisis. If she really has been killed by some kind of fanatical royalist, then they've got the wrong result.'

'Not necessarily. Only one day has passed since the crash, so it's far too early to tell how its after-effects will play out. A while from now, things might look very different.

'As matters stand, the Prince of Wales cannot possibly marry his mistress, still less make her his queen. The monarchy is at such a low ebb, one can barely imagine it surviving to Her Majesty's Golden Jubilee in five years' time, still less celebrating such an event. But however hysterical they may be now, people will forget the princess eventually. If she fades from their hearts, if the prince is forgiven, if the family survives, well, a dispassionate observer might say that the killing – if such it was – had served its purpose.'

'You sound as though you approve.'

'Not at all. You asked for an objective assessment, and I gave it.'

Grantham nodded. 'Agreed. But that leaves us with another hypothetical. If the crash was not an accident, who was responsible?'

Wake smiled and shook his head. 'Ah, well, there you have me. I'm afraid I haven't the faintest idea. You'll just have to round up the usual suspects, eh?'

'Indeed we will, which is one of the reasons I'm here.'

Wake let out an amused, patronizing chuckle. 'Really? Surely I am not on your list? Has my stock fallen that low?'

Grantham ignored the attempt at humour. 'Let's not waste each other's time. We both know your record. My predecessors weren't exactly scrupulous in their methods. If they wanted a job done off the books, they came to you. No one knew exactly how you made things happen, or who your contacts were. They didn't want to know, of course, because that gave them deniability if anyone started asking inconvenient questions. But *you* knew.'

The old man bristled. 'That was all a long time ago, before the Wall came down. We were at war with an enemy that would stop at nothing. All anyone wants to talk about these days is the Nazis.

Well, they were a danger to this country for six years. Soviet communism was a threat for almost half a century, and I fought that threat. I did my duty. I have no reason to apologize, still less to feel ashamed.'

'I didn't say you had. But if anyone's out there taking people out on the basis of what's supposedly best for this country, or its monarchy, or Christ knows what else, you may just know who they are. So I'm asking you a favour: if you do happen to bump into any of your old associates, pass on a message from me. We want this mess cleaned up. No fuss. No scandal. No one running to the papers saying, "I did it." Tell them to sort it out or we'll stop turning blind eyes and sort them out ourselves. Do I make myself clear?'

'To them, perhaps,' said Wake. 'But you're wasting your time if you think I can help. Still, it's been very interesting to meet you. Perhaps we'll see each other again in less trying circumstances. And now, if you don't mind, I've got work to attend to. Good day to you, Mr Grantham. My secretary will show you out.'

Wake let the other man leave the room before he rose from his desk and walked to one of the tall windows that looked down on Eaton Square. He watched a black cab cruise down the road. He followed a mother chasing her child down the pavement, heard their innocent laughter ringing like bells through the summer air. Then he turned back to the desk, let out a single heavy sigh and started to press the numbers on his telephone keypad.

34

Pierre Papin's taxi pulled up outside the honey-coloured stone façade of Lausanne's main railway station a little after nine o'clock. The manager and his staff were properly Swiss, which is to say as efficient as Germans, as welcoming as Italians and as knowing as any Frenchman.

Within an hour he'd found out everything he needed to know. He followed Carver's trail, taking the train to Geneva, where he walked out of the station into the Place Cornavin, the bustling square whose taxi-ranks and bus-stops were the heart of the city's transportation system. Once he was there it was just a matter of basic old-fashioned police-work, canvassing the drivers to find anyone who'd been around late morning the previous day and showing them the CCTV pictures of Carver and Petrova.

Fifteen minutes in, he struck lucky. One of the taxi drivers, a Turk, remembered the girl. 'How could I forget that one?' he said with a knowing wink, from one red-blooded man to another. 'I watched her all the way from the station, thinking this was my lucky day. I was next in line. The man with her looked like he could afford a taxi, and if I had a woman like that I wouldn't want to share her with the trash who take the bus. But no, he walked right past me, the son of a whore, and stood in line, like a peasant.'

'Did you see which bus they took?'

'Yeah, the number five. It goes over the Pont de l'Ile, past the Old Town to the hospital and back. So, what have they done, these two, huh?'

Papin smiled. 'They're killers. Count yourself lucky they didn't get in your cab.'

He left the cabbie muttering thanks to Allah and then, still posing as Michel Picard from the Federal Interior Ministry, called the control room at Transports Publics Genevois, the organization that ran the city's bus system. Naturally, they were only too happy to supply the names and contact numbers of those drivers who'd worked the number five route leaving the station around eleven o'clock the previous day. There were three of them, and once his memory had been jogged by Papin's photos, one recalled the couple who'd got on at the station. He also remembered looking in his mirror as the girl got off at a stop on Rue de la Croix Rouge, crossed the road behind the bus and started walking up the hill towards the Old Town.

'Some guys have all the luck, right?' he said with a rueful chuckle.

'Don't worry,' Papin reassured him. 'That guy's luck is about to change.'

Twenty minutes later, he was walking the streets of the Old Town. It seemed an unlikely place for an assassin to hide out. In Papin's experience, most killers were little more than crude gangsters, spending their money on tasteless vulgarity and excess. But the beauty of the Old Town was restrained, even austere. The tall buildings seemed to look down like disapproving elders on the people walking the streets. There were few hotels in the area, and it took little time to establish that neither Carver nor Petrova had checked in anywhere within the past twenty-four hours, under those names or any other aliases.

Petrova came from Moscow, so this must be where Carver lived.

And that meant there would be people in the neighbourhood who knew him and his exact address. Papin got out his photographs and started canvassing again.

35

'Well now, there's a surprise.' Carver leaned back, tilting his office chair and putting his hands behind his head. Then he looked back at the computer screen which showed the recent transfers in and out of his Banque Wertmuller-Maier account, and sighed. 'Of course those buggers weren't going to pay. They assumed I'd be dead.' Even so, he had received faxed notification of a $1.5 million deposit from his account manager. He had a loose end. If he could find a way to give it a good pull, the whole conspiracy might just unravel.

He thought for a moment, then got up and wandered into the kitchen where Alix was making herself a late breakfast. The TV was on, still showing news about the crash. He wondered whether anyone in the world was watching anything else.

'Any developments we need to know about?' he asked.

Alix pressed the remote control, lowering the volume, then turned to look at him. 'People are blaming the paparazzi for chasing the car. There are rumours it was going at almost two hundred kilometres an hour when it crashed.'

'Well that's bollocks, for a start. It was one twenty, max.'

'Also they say that blood tests prove the driver was drunk, more than three times over the limit. And there's a survivor, the princess's bodyguard.'

Carver frowned. 'The guy didn't drive like a drunk. And there's a bodyguard? Well, no way would any self-respecting bodyguard let a driver get in a car if he was three times over. The guy would have been completely legless, reeling all over the place, stinking of booze. Christ, you wouldn't let anyone get behind the wheel if he was that far gone.' He slammed his hand against the kitchen work-surface. 'This is bloody amateur hour. They did a rush-job and they've bungled the cover-up. Now every investigative journalist in the world is going to be crawling all over the place, trying to prove it was murder.'

'Well, it was murder.' Alix's voice was quiet, but it cut straight through Carver's bluster. 'We did it. Every time I hear about photographers hounding her to her death, all I can think is, no, that was me. I was flashing the camera, forcing them to go faster.'

'Maybe, but if you hadn't been, someone else would. The real photographers weren't far behind you. And as soon as they got to the crash, did they try to help? No, they started taking photographs.'

A coldness had descended on Carver, the passion of his love-making replaced by impersonal calculation. Alix's voice rose in intensity as she tried to break through his armour.

'How can you just stand there and talk about this as if we weren't involved? Don't you think at all about what you've done?'

'Not if I can help it, no.'

For a moment they fell silent, the only noises in the room the bubbling of the coffee machine and the muted jabber of an ad from the TV set. Then Carver's body relaxed a fraction. He held out a hand and laid it on Alix's shoulder.

'Look, I know how callous that sounds. I'm not a total bastard. But one thing I've learned over the years is not to waste time over people who are already dead. It's the only way to stop yourself going crazy. Am I sorry she died? Of course I am. Do I feel bad that it was me at the end of that tunnel? Just a bit. But where does feeling guilty about that get me, or anyone else? Screw feeling guilty. We were tricked into doing something terrible, and I aim to find the people who did that.'

Carver told Alix what he had in mind. It meant her going undercover, playing a role.

'You've got a lot of experience using fake identities, right? You can fool a man into thinking you're someone you're not?'

'Isn't that what you've been worrying about, that I'm deceiving you?'

'It has crossed my mind, yeah. But forget that for now. I've got another part that might interest you.'

He dialled a local number. When he spoke it was with the guttural bark of an Afrikaner accent. 'Could I speak to Mr Leclerc, please? Thank you . . . Howzit, Mr Leclerc? The name's Dirk Vandervart. I'm what you might call a private security consultant and you've been recommended to me by contacts at the very highest levels. I have a little over two hundred million US dollars looking for a home. I'm hoping you can help me find one . . . Excellent. Well now, I'll be in meetings with clients all day. Why don't we meet at my hotel, the Beau Rivage, at six this evening, *ja*? We will have a drink and discuss my banking requirements. I will give you all the references you need at that time. In the meantime, my personal holding company is called Topográficas, SA, registered in Panama. You're welcome to look it up, though I must say you won't find a great deal if you do . . . *Ja*, absolutely, that is indeed the blessing of Panama! So, are we set, then? Six o'clock, the Beau Rivage, ask for Vandervart. Thank you. And good day to you, too.'

Carver put the phone down with a flourish.

'You sound as though you have done some acting too,' said Alix.

'More than I'd like,' he agreed. 'This business is basically one long game of charades.'

'And that company, with the crazy name. Does it really exist?'

'Mind your own business,' said Carver. He was smiling as he said it, but internally he was making a note to himself. Close down that shelter as soon as this is all over. And hide all the money behind another Panamanian front.

36

In the end, it was just a matter of blind luck. Papin was walking down Grand Rue, the street of art galleries and antique shops at the centre of the Old Town, when he saw a flash of pale blue in the corner of his eye. He turned his head in an automatic reflex and there they were, Carver and Petrova, strolling along the street hand in hand like any other couple, he in jeans and a stone-coloured cotton jacket, she still wearing the same dress in which she'd left Paris the previous day. Papin pumped a fist in triumph. His gamble had paid off!

His first instinct was to duck into a doorway for cover. Then he reminded himself that they had no idea of his identity. He looked into a gallery window and closely examined some Goya prints while his targets walked by on the far side of the road. He let them get fifty metres down the road, then casually ambled after them.

Papin had to smile. The woman wanted to go shopping – *mais naturellement.* She'd arrived from Paris without any luggage, she didn't have a thing to wear, what else would she do? Still, he had to admire her style. She ignored three quarters of all the shops she passed. Then something caught her eye and she went in, found what she wanted, bought it – courtesy of Carver's credit cards, Papin noticed – and moved on. She was doing a thorough job, too, starting with lingerie and working outwards from there. Papin raised an appreciative eyebrow as he watched her pick out a selection of lacy little numbers. Even from across the street and through a shop window he could tell that Carver was in for an entertaining evening.

In the meantime, the Englishman's lust appeared to have addled his brain. To be walking round the streets in broad daylight with a fellow suspect was madness. Either Carver was playing a game so subtle that Papin could not fathom it, or he had concluded that he had no hope of survival and might as well enjoy what little time was left to him.

And then, without warning, Papin lost them. They ducked into a crowded department store down by the river with exits on to four different streets. Papin cursed under his breath. Perhaps Carver was not quite as careless as he had assumed.

He tried to follow them through the busy store, then abandoned that attempt and settled for a foot-patrol around the block, hoping to catch them leaving the building or walking down one of the adjacent streets. But he knew it was futile. One man had almost no chance of maintaining surveillance under those circumstances.

No matter. He might have lost them for now, but he knew where Carver lived to within a matter of three or four blocks. All he had to do was return to the Old Town and start showing his trusty ID card to all the local barkeepers, café owners and apartment-building concierges. Some would refuse to cooperate with anyone in authority as a matter of principle; others, though, would be equally keen to display their credentials as loyal, law-abiding citizens, eager to do their part in maintaining law and order. As any secret policeman knew, it was never hard to find people willing to inform on their neighbours. Papin was sure he would locate Carver's apartment soon enough. But first it was time to open negotiations.

There was a bar across the road that had a Swisscom public telephone on the wall. '*Merde!*' It only took phone-cards, not cash. The barman saw his frustration and gestured across the road at a newspaper kiosk. Papin muttered a curse, then wasted a couple of minutes walking over to the kiosk, paying for a fifty-franc card and returning to the bar. By the time he was standing in front of the phone again his previous good humour had been replaced by gut-tightening tension. He made a conscious effort to summon up an air of confidence, then called the man he knew as Charlie.

'Good news, *mon ami*. I have found your lost property.'

'Really?' replied the operations director. 'That's great news. Where?'

Papin chuckled. 'Nothing would give me greater pleasure than to tell you that right now. But such information is valuable, and I have had to work very hard, at great personal expense, to obtain it. I will require compensation.'

'How much?'

'Five hundred thousand, US, payable in bearer bonds, endorsed to me and given to me in person. I will take you to the property. And just you, Charlie. Don't try any ambush.'

'Wouldn't dream of it, old chap.'

'So, do we have a deal?'

'I don't know. Half a mill sounds like a lot of money.'

'In your situation? I don't think so, Charlie. You have two hours. I will call you again at thirteen thirty Central European Time. If I don't get your guarantee of payment then, I'm going elsewhere. Goodbye.'

Papin ended the call, then thought for a moment. He needed some insurance, but why wait for another two hours? He dialled a London number. He could think of more than one organization that would be glad of his information.

37

The man in the white coat took off his glasses and rubbed a hand across his bearded face. He looked at Carver through tightened eyes, trying to focus.

'So we need to induce a sense of relaxation and empathy, yes?'

'Correct.'

'Then we want sexual arousal.'

'That's right.'

'And finally, we must lower mental defences, maybe create a sense of disorientation.'

'Exactly, Dieter. That's the plan.'

Carver and Alix had concluded the first part of their shopping expedition. She had bought the clothes she needed, and a selection of wigs. He had spent ten minutes getting the Swiss version of a number two clip at a backstreet barber's, which left his scalp bristling with the military buzz-cut a man like Dirk Vandervart might favour; then he bought a designer suit whose shiny silken fabric went perfectly with an oversized gold Rolex to create the defiantly vulgar look of a man with a lot of dirty money to wash. The purchases had been packed in a couple of Gucci overnight bags. Where Carver planned to go, they would need expensive luggage.

Together, he and Alix had taken their costumes to an attic studio above a chocolate shop. It had taken a lot of persuasion and even more money to get the studio's obsessively painstaking Swiss proprietor to compromise his perfectionism and fix them two South African passports on a rush-job. They'd changed into their new gear, posed for photographs, packed away their original clothes, and Carver had put in two phone calls: one to the reservations department of one of Geneva's finest hotels, the other to Thor Larsson. Now he had one last errand to run, but he needed professional advice, and Dr Dieter Schiller was the man to provide it.

'One important detail: the whole thing has got to be soluble. It's going to go into a drink.'

Schiller smiled as he put the spectacles back on. 'You know, Pablo, this is going to be some party. Can I come?'

'Sorry, Dieter, this is strictly professional. And there's one other specification. The dose has got to be packaged so that my associate—'

'Miss . . .?' Schiller raised his eyebrows, waiting for a name.

'Miss none-of-your-damn-business,' Carver replied. 'It's better for everyone that way. My associate needs to be able to deliver the dose easily, without being spotted.'

Schiller shrugged, apparently unbothered by the lack of formal introductions. He was used to the concept of anonymity. In fact, he assumed that none of his clients ever supplied their true names. 'That's no problem. A simple paper wrap will be sufficient. But what to put in it? To start with, for relaxation, I would suggest methylenedioxymethamphetamine – MDMA for short.'

'Ecstasy,' said Alix.

'Ah yes, the drug of choice for modern pleasure-seekers. Makes you feel good, relaxed, full of love for the people around you. Of course, it may also make you psychotic in the long term, but that's not our problem right now. Immediate side-effects can include feeling hot, sweaty, even a little sick. But we can take the edge off that.'

Schiller was sitting at a desk, like any other practitioner taking a consultation. His office was a back room in a private house. There was no brass plaque on the door, though his remarkable, if unorthodox, approach to pharmacology attracted large numbers of wealthy clients who felt the need for personal prescriptions that would never be written by more conventional doctors. Behind him stood a series of wooden cabinets, and above them shelves of glass bottles, plastic containers and small white cardboard boxes.

He swivelled his chair, reached for one of the plastic pill-jars and brought it back to the table. 'Soluble in water, too, so that's no problem. Sadly, though, I can't say the same for Viagra, which many of my older clients like to combine with Ecstasy when entertaining their young ladies. We shall have to be more adventurous with this element of the formula. I would suggest bromocriptine.' Another pill-bottle appeared on the desk. 'Unlike Viagra, it acts on the brain rather than the penis, boosting dopamine – that is a neurotransmitter, you understand – and effectively promoting sexual desire. Strangely, this effect wears off after thirty or forty doses. But again, that is not our problem. Now, this substance is not soluble in water, but it is soluble in alcohol, so please bear that in mind. And the same applies to this . . .'

He turned to the shelves one last time, reached inside a white box and pulled out a rectangular piece of silver-foil with eight clear blisters, each containing a small diamond-shaped pill.

'Flunitrazepam,' Schiller continued. 'Better known as rohypnol, or roofies. As you may know, this sedative, which is a first-rate treatment for anxiety or sleeplessness, has acquired an unsavoury reputation as a so-called "date-rape" drug. It diminishes inhibition and stress while promoting a sense of euphoria. It can also affect short-term memory. We must be careful not to give too high a dose or it will simply knock the patient out. But combined with the other two chemicals it should supply, I would say, a very interesting experience. Now, tell me a little about the person who will consume this cocktail.'

'I've only met him once, and that was four years ago,' Carver replied. 'But he must be mid-forties, I'd say, medium height, quite stocky. Unless he's gone on a diet he'll weigh the best part of two hundred pounds – ninety-odd kilos.'

Schiller reached across his desk and grabbed a pestle and mortar set. 'OK, so a standard dose of each drug will be fine.' He popped three pills into the stone bowl and started grinding them down with the wood-handled pestle. 'Just like an old-fashioned apothecary, huh?' he remarked, looking up at his clients.

He opened one of the small brass-handled drawers in the cabinets behind him and rummaged around until he found a small, clear plastic capsule. He squeezed it between his thumb and forefinger, splitting it in two. Very carefully, he poured the powdered pills from the mortar through a plastic funnel into one half of the capsule, before pressing the other half back on to it.

'There,' said Schiller, handing Carver the completed capsule. 'That will be fifteen hundred Swiss francs.'

'That's a lot for one dose, Dieter.'

Schiller smiled. 'It isn't the dose you're paying for.'

Outside on the street, Alix asked, 'Now what?'

'Now we go and pick up those passports. Then we check into our hotel.'

38

The four directors met around a glass table and sat on plain metal chairs. The table-top was free of paper and writing implements. No minutes were ever taken of the board's meetings. Security was absolute. There were no phones on the table, no pictures on the wall, nowhere to hide any kind of listening device. The air-conditioning vent was plastered directly into the ceiling and could not be unscrewed. The light-fittings were sealed units, fitted with long-life bulbs. The sound- and bulletproof windows were hidden behind blackout blinds. The men had left their phones, wallets, keys and loose change in plastic trays, then passed through a scanner before they entered the room.

The chairman got right down to business. 'Gentlemen, thirty-six hours have passed since the Paris operation. In one important respect, it was a success. The mission's main objective was attained. There are, however, a number of loose ends that need to be tied up.'

'It's a little worse than that, isn't it?'

'I'm sorry, Finance, is there something you'd like to say?'

'Yes there is, actually.' The man's appearance was impeccably tailored, but his voice was tense, teetering on the edge of panic. 'The whole thing's turning into a bloody nightmare. The country's gone mad with grief, the republicans are having a field day and the monarchy's facing the biggest crisis since the Abdication. Meanwhile, we've got an assassin on the loose. He could be anywhere in the world by now. And if he talks, we're done for.'

The chairman sat perfectly still, letting the finance director say his piece. Then he continued as if the words had never been spoken. 'As I was saying, there are a few loose ends. My information suggests that the security services are under extreme pressure to find out what happened. The PM's pet hooligan Trodd has declared that he does not want a newspaper beating him to the truth. This administration is obsessed by headlines, of course—'

A third voice, its accent Australian, entered the conversation. 'Mate, you can hardly blame them. Headlines don't get any bigger than this.'

'Indeed not, Communications. News management will play an extremely important role over the next few days and I'll be looking to you to make sure that we don't see any unwelcome headlines. It's in no one's interests for the actual events or their participants to be made public. I'm sure we can reach some kind of discreet, even anonymous, accommodation with the government. If they are given Carver's name, and a credible assurance that he has already been dealt with, that should keep the wolves from our door. Perhaps the operations director would like to update us on his progress.'

'I've spent the day trying to put a crew together. It hasn't been easy to get people of the calibre we'll need. As you know, we exclusively use freelance operatives, hired at arm's length, and we lost a number of our best contractors over the weekend, but I'm confident that we'll be ready to move within the next twenty-four hours. First we've got to find him, of course.'

'Well, that should be a doddle,' sneered the finance director. 'I'm sure he'll send us a postcard to let us know where he is.'

The chairman frowned at the Consortium's money-man, wondering whether it was time to replace him. He would put his mind to the problem once the Carver issue had been resolved.

He turned back to the operations director. 'Are we any nearer tracking him down?'

'Yes, Chairman, I think we are. He left Paris yesterday morning by train from the Gare de Lyon. He may well have been accompanied by one of the Russians who had, of course, been ordered to kill him – a woman, Alexandra Petrova. If she is indeed with him, it's not clear whether she intends to carry out her assignment or has genuinely defected, as it were. Either way, I'm certain Carver's still in Europe. He bought tickets for Milan but didn't take that route. I'd guess he's somewhere in eastern France, or maybe Switzerland. It doesn't really matter. I don't think he'll try to run. I'd expect him to be much more assertive.'

'By which you mean . . .?'

'That he'll try to get us before we can get him.'

'You don't sound too concerned by this prospect.'

'Well, he doesn't know who we are. And it's going to be very hard for him to find out without alerting us to his presence. Besides, I may have a lead on his precise whereabouts. I have a contact in Paris, name of Pierre Papin, works for French intelligence. He has been tracking Carver and Petrova's movements using railway-station surveillance systems. He says he knows where they went.'

'So why hasn't he told you?'

'He wants money for his information.'

'How much?'

'Half a million US dollars. I think we should go for it.'

'That's ridiculous!' exclaimed the finance director.

'Really?' replied the chairman. 'What makes you say that? Some would call it quite a modest price for keeping us all alive and getting the government off our backs.'

The man in the pinstripe suit took a deep breath and smoothed back his hair, clearly embarrassed by his loss of control. When he spoke again, his voice was calmer, more assured, the voice of a man used to giving orders rather than taking them.

'I simply question whether we can afford to expend many more resources without being certain that the benefits justify the cost.

The Paris operation involved a significant financial downside. Of course, we were able to save a great deal by withholding fees from some of the personnel involved. But even so, there were major logistical outlays, not to mention considerable sums spent purchasing influence within a number of French institutions. We lost a number of men, whose families will have to be compensated and kept quiet. Massive damage was sustained to two properties, which will have to be repaired at great cost. I therefore believe that any further expenditure should be considered very carefully.'

The chairman nodded. Perhaps the finance director was not beyond salvaging after all. 'A very persuasive argument. As you said, Operations, Carver will be obliged to show himself. So make sure that when he emerges from hiding, we are ready and able to deal with him.'

The operations director glared at the money-man who had undermined him, then turned back to his boss. 'But what are we going to do about Papin? If we don't pay him, he'll try to give Carver to someone else. And there's another thing. He's got our computer. It's protected by passwords, encryption and firewalls. There's no way Carver's broken into the files just yet. But he's a resourceful individual. He'll find a way of cracking them eventually. And we can't let that happen.'

'No,' agreed the chairman, 'we certainly can't have that.' He thought for a while, tapping his fingers against the surface of the desk, then continued: 'How are we supposed to make contact again?'

'He's calling at twelve thirty our time.'

'Fine, then have his call patched through to me. I shall persuade our French friend that he has more to gain by keeping us happy in the long term than by making a fast buck now.'

'And if he isn't persuaded?'

'I shall make him pay for his stubbornness.'

39

Bill Selsey, a twenty-two-year veteran at MI6, a man whose chief ambitions were a steady career and a solid pension at the end of it, sidled up to Jack Grantham's glass-fronted office at the far end of one of the open-plan offices that lent MI6 headquarters a deceptive appearance of corporate normality.

'Busy, Jack?'

Grantham looked up from the screen on which he was checking files on the world's professional hitmen and wondering why so many of their whereabouts were listed as 'Unknown'. What was the point of knowing about the bad guys if you didn't have the resources to keep proper tabs on them?

'Nothing urgent. What can I do for you?'

Selsey parked his ample backside on the edge of Grantham's desk, ignoring his colleague's disapproving frown.

'There's an interesting development in the Paris investigation,' he said. 'We just received a call from one of our European partners – Papin, one of the more interesting characters in the French intelligence community. He seems to float around without any formal job title, but he has a habit of popping up in unexpected places.'

'So?'

'So, he says he knows where to find the people responsible for the crash in the Alma Tunnel.'

Grantham sat up in his chair, his mood changing in an instant from polite indifference to total concentration. 'Really? Where does he say they are?'

'Well, that's the catch. He wants us to pay for the information. Says he won't consider anything under half a million dollars.'

'He wants us to pay? Bloody hell, even by French standards that's a bit steep. Whatever happened to inter-service cooperation?'

'He's not doing this for his service, Jack. This one's strictly off the books.'

'Do we trust him?'

'Of course not, he's French. Which means he's self-centred, unscrupulous and couldn't give a monkey's about anything except his own immediate advantage.'

'But is he any good?'

'Not bad, yeah. If he says he knows where these people are, I believe him.'

'All right, but if he thinks we've got half a million dollars to chuck his way, he's obviously not been informed about our budget cuts. Can we get to him for free?'

Selsey's hangdog face brightened. 'Ah, that's the good news. Not only is he working off the books, he's sending his message from a humble pay-phone rather than one of DGSE's secure lines – presumably doesn't want any record of his communications with us and the other bidders appearing on their logs.'

'Bit amateur. We'll have much less trouble tracking that.'

'Perhaps greed is getting the better of him. It's amazing what the prospect of easy money does to people's brains. And he probably underestimates our ability to track him. We only let the Frogs see a fraction of our signals intelligence, after all. Their officers won't necessarily realize just how powerful Echelon and GCHQ really are.'

'Can we find him?'

'Working back to the site of his call is tricky, but not impossible.

We may manage it. But our real chance will come when he calls back. We've got to conduct some sort of negotiation. If we keep him talking, we'll get an exact position.'

'He's not going to be that daft, surely?'

'He stands to make half a mill. He might take a risk for that.'

Grantham frowned. 'I can see why he's not worried about us. Even if we don't shell out any cash, we're hardly going to hurt a fellow professional from a country that's one of our allies.'

'Even if he is French!'

'No, not even then. But there'll be other people out there who are a lot less scrupulous. Papin's got to get his money, take his clients to the killers' location, then get out in one piece himself. Tell you what, Bill, you said this guy's not bad.'

'Yeah?'

'Well, he's going to have to be a hell of a lot better than that to pull this one off.'

40

Alix watched Carver as he worked his way through an enormous helping of venison stew and noodles in the restaurant of the Hotel Beau Rivage, Le Chat-Botté. 'That means Puss-in-Boots,' Carver had said with a cheeky, naughty schoolboy glint in his eye. There was something boyish about the gusto with which he attacked his food, too, as though he didn't have a care in the world, nothing to think about except for the plate in front of him and the glass of red wine to its side. His appetite seemed completely unaffected by the prospect of what they had to do in a few hours' time. Then again, he wasn't the one who'd have to squeeze into a tight-cut skirt.

Even as they went upstairs to his suite, she was still trying to work Carver out, to uncover the true self he kept so carefully hidden – from himself as much as everyone else. So many men she had known had struggled even to be one-dimensional, but not this one. He was so assured in his own world, so uncertain in hers; so cold at some moments, so emotional at others. Yet it sometimes seemed to her as though Carver's emotions were obvious to everyone but him.

She wondered if he knew how powerfully his eyes expressed his feelings. In the short time she had known him she had seen icy rage and aching tenderness, ebullient laughter and exhausted vulnerability. She thought of the books, records and paintings at his apartment, the consideration he could show when he was at ease. Then she thought of him walking into the mansion in Paris, gunning down two men, finishing them off with a shot to the head, and walking away from their bodies without a second glance. She remembered lying on the ground by that bus-stop, her face pressed against the pavement, his knee digging into her spine. How could she reconcile that man with the one who had lain beside her that morning, who was taking her in his arms again this afternoon?

She pulled away a fraction. 'Should we be doing this? I thought we were here on . . .' She tried to find the right words. 'On business.'

'We are,' he replied. 'We have one chance to find out what we need to know. In a few hours, Magnus Leclerc is going to walk into the bar downstairs. You are going to seduce him. I am going to scare him witless. Then I'm going to start asking him questions. Leclerc is our only lead. If we can make him talk, we can find the people who betrayed us. If not, well, it's just a matter of time till they find us, no matter how far or fast we run.'

'So shouldn't we be doing something else? You know, something useful or important?'

'Such as what? This is like any other operation. Most of the time you spend just waiting around. We don't know if the operation's going to work. We don't know if we'll be alive tomorrow. What could be more important than seizing every moment we can?'

She considered what he had said, weighing up the merits of his case. Then she smiled. 'In that case,' she said, 'let's seize the moment.'

41

Pierre Papin was dog-tired. He had worked for almost forty-eight hours, virtually without a break. His eyeballs felt sandpapery and his brain had been coshed. With every passing minute, thought became more of an effort and his tension and uncertainty increased. And yet, for all that, he was making progress.

Some of the locals had been uncooperative, but even dumb insolence provided a form of information. He'd gone into a small café, demanded to see the owner, flashed his ID and shown him the pictures of Carver and the girl. The man had shrugged and said, 'Never seen them before in my life,' but the answer was too quick. He'd not even bothered to examine the photographs. There'd been a small boy in the café, six or seven years old. Papin had got down on his haunches, held up the picture of Carver and put on his most wheedling voice: 'Have you seen this man come into the café?' But before the boy could answer, the café owner had picked him up and stuck a finger in Papin's face, hissing, 'Leave the kid out of this!'

Papin knew he must be getting really close. He knocked on doors, approached women taking dogs for walks or bringing shopping back to their homes, made enquiries with impeccable politeness and a dash of charm. Soon he had discovered Carver's address. But he did not know whether or not his quarry had returned to his apartment while he'd been making his enquiries. The Frenchman needed to answer that question before he made his next move.

He slogged up the endless stairs to the fifth floor of an ancient apartment building and knocked on the door. The sound of an opening lock was followed by the sight of a deeply respectable woman of pensionable age peering round the half-open door with the look of disapproval that was clearly her default expression. Papin showed her his card and, adding an enticing note of intrigue to his voice, explained that he was desolated to disturb madame but there had been reports of an illegal immigrant settling in the apartment level with hers in the building next door. Before taking the appropriate action to rid the neighbourhood of such an undesirable he wished to discover whether the individual in question was currently in occupation.

He produced a device that looked like a doctor's stethoscope attached to a microphone. This seemed to convince the old lady, or at least to arouse her curiosity. She let Papin in, offered him coffee and biscuits (he declined with profuse thanks for her kind hospitality), then watched fascinated as he placed the microphone against several points on the party-wall, listening intently each time. Finally, Papin stepped away from the wall, folded up his listening device and shook his head. 'The individual in question is not in residence, madame,' he said, sounding suitably frustrated. 'But have no fear. I will be maintaining a vigil all day. He will not escape.'

A few minutes later he was standing on the top-floor landing of the building next door, facing a simple dark-blue door. So this was where his quarry hid from the world. Papin was tempted to break in and grab the laptop. It must be in there, he reasoned. Carver hadn't been carrying it when he left that morning. But there were bound to be security measures – Carver was not the type to leave himself unprotected – and even if there were not, Carver would know that someone had been there the moment he stepped through the door, and he'd be off like a startled gazelle. It was far better to keep a low profile. Papin was certain the two of them would be returning to the apartment that day. They'd been walking through town like lovers on a day out, not fugitives on the run – they weren't going anywhere. He'd save them for the highest bidder.

It was time to call Charlie. But when he dialled the number, Papin was put through to another phone and a voice he didn't recognize.

'To whom am I speaking?' he asked.

'That doesn't matter.'

'Then this conversation is over.'

'Wait a moment, Monsieur Papin. I am Charlie's boss. You are talking to me because he does not have the authority to deal with your financial conditions, and I do. I'm afraid that I cannot accept your demand for five hundred thousand dollars.'

Papin had expected some form of negotiation. '*Alors*, monsieur, I am sorry. If you will not pay me the required sum, I will find a client who will.'

'Three hundred. And that is my final offer. Not a penny more.'

'No, I will not lower my price. But I will make you a deal. You pay me two fifty up front, I take you to the location. From there it will be one twenty-five if you find the people, one twenty-five for the computer. You will not pay in full unless you have everything you need. Fair?'

There was silence at the other end of the line while the man considered the offer. Papin wondered what the counter-bid would be. But then came a grunt of assent and the words, 'Fair enough, monsieur. So, what are the arrangements?'

'You will send one man to the front entrance of the St Pierre Cathedral in Geneva, Switzerland. I will be there for precisely five minutes, starting at seventeen hundred hours local time. I will be wearing a dark-blue suit and holding a rolled-up newspaper. I apologize for the cliché, monsieur, but it will suffice. Your representative will say, "Charlie sends his regards." I will reply, "I hope Charlie is well." He will say, "Yes, much better now." He will then hand me the first half of the payment – remember, bearer bonds, endorsed in my name. I will give further instructions at that time. Your man may have back-up for any action that is required, but he will only call for this back-up when I give permission.'

'I understand. Five o'clock this afternoon at the cathedral. I will have someone there. Thank you, Monsieur Papin.'

'On the contrary, m'sieur. Thank you.'

Papin put down the receiver, raised his eyes to the ceiling, then let out a long sigh of relief. He rubbed the back of his neck as he pondered his next move. He had the money in the bag. He didn't need another bidder. But what if there was a way to make more than one deal? He might yet be able to double his money. Yes, that would be something. And if he played it right, he could get the killers and their bosses off his back for good.

42

Deep inside the futuristic, post-modernist ziggurat on the south bank of the River Thames that had been the headquarters of MI6 since 1995 – and which its more cynical inhabitants, unimpressed by the building's expense, vulgarity and sore-thumb prominence, had dubbed 'Ceausescu Towers' – Bill Selsey was sitting by a telephone receiver, waiting for a call. Beside him were other secret service officers wearing headsets, operating digital audio recorders and monitoring the connection between their lines and the tracking equipment at GCHQ. Jack Grantham was sitting at the same table as Selsey, ready to listen in on whatever Pierre Papin had to say.

The phone rang. Selsey paused for the technicians' thumbs-up, then picked up the receiver.

Papin was all apologies. 'I am so sorry, Bill, but I already have a buyer for my information. We are meeting at seventeen hundred hours.'

'Well, I'm sorry too, Pierre. Maybe we could have done some business.'

'Maybe we still can.'

'How would that be?'

'You could buy my buyer.'

Selsey rolled his eyes across the table at Jack Grantham. What was the Frenchman playing at now?

'What do you mean?' he asked.

'Simply that I can now provide you with a complete package: the people who killed your princess and the people who hired them.'

Selsey couldn't help it. He laughed out loud. 'So you shaft the people you've just done a deal with and sell them out to us?'

'Exactly.'

'Bloody hell, Pierre, you've got a nerve! Presumably you'd like to be paid by us too.'

'But of course. The price is the same: five hundred thousand US.'

'Yeah, well, there's just one problem. We don't have that kind of money lying around. You know how it is, endless bloody budget-cuts, every penny has to be justified in triplicate. Probably the same with your lot, right?'

'Yes, it's true. We cannot afford to be extravagant. But this is not extravagance. This is a small outlay for a huge return.'

Across the room a signals tech gestured at Selsey to keep talking. He mouthed the words 'almost got it'. Selsey nodded. He kept talking.

'I agree. If we did get that entire crew it would be good. But to be honest, that's what concerns me. You're planning to deceive a group of known killers. I'm not sure you want to be doing that. In fact, I'd say we're the only people you can trust. We're pros, like you. We're not in the business of harming our allies' agents. So why don't you come in with us? We'll keep an eye on things, cover your back. I mean, even if your clients don't discover you're about to rat them out, they may decide they don't want to pay your money after all. They may try to get it back . . . over your dead body.'

'But it would be no use to them. That is why I demanded endorsed bearer bonds. They can only be cashed by me. No, Bill, your offer is very kind, but I'm sure I can look after myself. And also I would be safer without you. If I do not sell my clients to you, they have no need to harm me. And if I do sell them, and they find out, then I do not think you would be able to save me. So I want money to cover the extra risk, or no deal. What is it to be?'

Selsey looked across at the signals tech and got a thumbs-up. 'Then I'm sorry, Pierre, but it's no deal.'

'I'm sorry too, Bill. Another time.'

And the line went dead.

'Good work,' said Jack Grantham, leaning across the table to give his colleague a supportive pat on the arm. 'So, where is the treacherous little sod?'

'Geneva,' said the signals tech. 'Public phone on the Rue Verdaine, right by the city cathedral.'

'Damn!' muttered Grantham. 'We can't get there in time from here. We'll have to use someone local.' He picked up a phone and dialled an internal number. 'Monica? Jack Grantham. Something urgent's come up in Geneva. Who do we have in the UN mission there? . . . What do you mean one of them's on holiday? It's September, people should be back at work . . . OK, well, get the chap – sorry, the woman, my mistake – get the one who isn't busy lying on a beach and tell her to give me a bell asap, would you? And see what we can rustle up from the embassy at Berne. That's not far from Geneva, right? . . . Excellent. Well, tell them to call me once they're on their way. Coordinate with the girl in Geneva . . . Yes, Monica, I know she's a grown woman, it's just a figure of speech . . . Well, whatever this female is, I want to talk to her. Now.'

He put down the phone with exaggerated care, shook his head silently, then turned to Bill Selsey.

'Right, Bill, this is strictly a surveillance job. I don't want people running round the streets of Geneva firing guns and playing at double-o-seven. I just want every scrap of information we can get on the killers Papin claims to have found. And I want to know about every phone conversation, every email, every text message in and out of Geneva this afternoon. And do me a favour, Bill. Get on to Cheltenham and Menwith Hill. Tell them we need saturation coverage.'

43

Grigori Kursk put down his mobile phone, kicked the hungover blonde out of bed and threw some money after her as she grabbed her clothes and scuttled from the room. He reached for the empty vodka bottle on the bedside table and held it up to the light to see if there were any dregs left at the bottom. He needed something to kick-start his day. He'd been given new orders and was getting back to work.

He called Dimitrov's room, just down the corridor of their two-star hotel in the centre of Milan. 'Wake up, you lazy bastard! Yuri called. We've got a job, Geneva, three hours' time . . . Yeah, I know that's not enough time. That's why you've got to get your arse out of bed and down to the lobby. Tell the others. By the front desk, five minutes. Anyone who isn't there, I will personally ram an Uzi up their arse and blast one right up the nought. Now piss off. I need a shower.'

Five and a half minutes later, Kursk was at the wheel of a BMW 750, forcing his way into the lunchtime traffic on the Via de Larga. He had 330 kilometres between himself and Geneva and the cars around him were moving slower than a legless man in a tar-pit.

He pressed his fist to the horn and kept it there, screaming barrack-room obscenities at every other driver on the road. No one around seemed too impressed; in Milan that passed for everyday behaviour. Kursk slumped back in the driver's seat. 'Fucking Italians. They move fast enough when there's an army after them.'

Finally, the lights ahead turned green, the traffic began to move and they started to make progress. Kursk relaxed a fraction. He took a packet of Balkan Stars from his shirt-pocket, pulled one out of the pack, then reached for the car's lighter. When it was lit he took a deep drag and kept driving, one hand on the wheel, the other holding the cigarette.

Sitting next to him, Dimitrov decided it was safe to risk a question. 'So, what are we doing in Switzerland?'

Kursk blew smoke towards the windscreen. 'We're meeting some French bastard and he's going to take us to that whore Petrova and her English lover-boy.'

'And then?'

'Then we kill the Frenchman and we take the other two back to Yuri. And then, God willing, we kill them too.'

Kursk rolled down the window and yelled down the street, 'Get that useless pile of crap out of my way, you spaghetti-eating son of a whore!'

'Forget it, Grigori Mikhailovich,' said Dimitrov. 'He doesn't understand Russian.'

Kursk pulled his head back inside the car. 'Oh no, Dimitrov, that gutless bastard knows exactly what I'm saying.'

44

Carver had been impressed by the way Alix had gone shopping. On the rare, very rare occasions he'd allowed himself to be dragged along behind a woman on a retail expedition, he'd been bored, exhausted and massively irritated by the endless trail from one crowded, overheated rip-off joint to the next; the constant riffling through rack after rack of clothes that looked identical to him; the relentless questions – 'Does this make me look fat?' 'Which do you prefer?' 'Will this go with those boots we saw?' – to which he could only silently contemplate the same, unchanging answer: 'How the fuck would I know?' But Alix was different. She bought clothes the way he bought munitions. She had a purpose in mind. She knew the effect she wanted to create, and she supplied herself accordingly.

Now she was preparing for her mission with the same professionalism. She showered. She towelled herself down, blow-dried her hair and came back into the bedroom, where Carver was still lying on the bed, draped in a thick towelling hotel robe, waiting for his turn in the bathroom.

Alix got out her underwear and took off her towel. Carver was intoxicated by the intimacy of watching her as she slipped into her knickers and bra. He relished all the sights and sounds that are so normal, even banal, to a woman yet so fascinating to a man: the slither of fabric over skin, the snap of elastic, the little twists and adjustments of her body, the self-absorption as she examined her appearance in a full-length mirror inside the wardrobe door. Yet there was nothing showy about her actions. She seemed indifferent to Carver's eyes washing over her, as if, like a dancer or model, she were so used to being naked in the presence of other people that any modesty or coyness about her body had long since evaporated. Nor was there any vanity in the way she looked herself up and down. Her expression was serious, her self-examination meticulous. She was getting ready for work.

As she stepped away from the mirror, she finally glanced at Carver.

'What do you think?'

'I think you'd better get dressed fast before I lose all self-control.'

'No,' she said. 'Fun is over. Time for business.'

She walked across to the dressing-table which was already dotted with bags of make-up, pots of skin cream, a can of hairspray, brushes, combs and a couple of paper shopping bags. One contained a skullcap made of some kind of nylon that looked like thick pantyhose. She put it on, pushing her hair underneath it until every strand had disappeared. As she worked, she caught Carver's eye in the dressing-table mirror.

'So, were you always rich?' she asked.

He looked at her with eyebrows raised, taken by surprise by her question. 'Rich, me? Christ, no! Far from it.'

'But you were an officer. I thought in England only the upper classes became officers.'

Now he smiled. 'Is that what they told you in KGB school?'

'You can tease me, but it's true. The rich lead the poor. It's like that everywhere.'

'Maybe, but I didn't become an officer because I was rich. I became an officer because I was adopted.'

Now it was her turn to be surprised. She stopped her handiwork and turned her body to face him.

'How do you mean?'

'My mum gave me away. She was just a kid who got pregnant. She came from the kind of family where abortion wasn't an option, but they weren't going to have a teenage daughter pushing a pram around, either. So they sent her to a nursing home, told everyone she was visiting relatives abroad, and then got shot of the baby as soon as they could.'

Alix had turned back to the table and was rummaging through her make-up as she listened to Carver's story. Now she looked into the mirror again, frowning this time.

'Who raised you, then?'

'A middle-aged couple. They'd never had children of their own. They were nice enough and they meant well, but they couldn't cope. By the time they realized that they wanted a quiet life more than a child they'd got a stroppy little toe-rag running round the place, making a racket all day. So they sent me off to boarding-school. They felt it was the best thing for me.'

'Did they love you?' She was powdering her face.

'I don't know. They never said so, not out loud. But I think they cared for me. You know, in their own way.'

'And what about you? Did you love them?'

Carver sighed. He got up off the bed and walked over to a chair, near to the dressing-table. 'Well, I didn't dislike them,' he said as he sat down. 'And I was grateful to them. I knew they were making sacrifices for me, I appreciated that. But I don't think I really knew how to love, not from the heart. I mean, why would I? If you don't get that from your mother, you never find out about love until much, much later, and then, suddenly, it's like, oh . . . right . . . so that's what they were talking about. Comes as quite a shock.'

'And then you lost her, too.'

'Yeah. Not so good, that.'

Alix twirled her mascara brush through her eyelashes.

'So, how old were you when you went away to school?'

'Eight.'

'*Bozhe moi!* And the English think they are civilized!'

'You don't know the half of it. The school was in this ancient country house, miles from anywhere. The first morning, we all got woken up at seven o'clock. We got dressed and the dormitory captain led us downstairs to the lawn at the back of the school. And we did drill, proper military drill. Quick march! Left turn, right turn, stand to attention, stand a-a-a-t . . . h'ease! It makes me laugh now, it was so bloody mad.'

'Yet you became a soldier?'

'Well, schools like that have been churning out upmarket cannon-fodder for centuries. They were specifically designed to produce reasonably intelligent, physically fit, emotionally screwed-up young men who'd travel to the world's hottest, nastiest places, do their duty and lay down their lives when required.'

'And you are one of these people?'

'When I'm working.'

'And when you're not working?'

'I don't know. That's what I'm trying to sort out.'

For a few moments they were silent. Alix concentrated on her lipstick. With her newly painted face, done in a style unlike anything Carver had seen on her before, her bald head and her half-naked body, she look oddly impersonal, like a showroom dummy waiting for its costume. Then she reached for the other bag and took out her wig. She pulled it over the skullcap, brushed it and sprayed it, and suddenly Carver was looking at a completely different woman.

He expected her to get straight up and cross the room to the closet where her clothes were hanging. Instead she sat there hesitantly, her eyes vague and unfocused, as if her concentration had been broken by some inner uncertainty.

'There was something I didn't tell you yesterday, about my past,' she said.

Carver sat back in his chair. 'Go on.'

'I said everything about it was bad. But that's not true. I had special privileges because of what I did for the state. At home in Perm, women wore horrible, shapeless sacks. They ate stale food that tasted of nothing. They worked so hard. When my mother was only forty she was already old, like a woman of sixty in the west. But in Moscow I was dressing in Armani, Versace, Chanel. I had never before owned more than two pairs of shoes, always made of plastic. Now I had a closet filled with shoes from Paris and Milan. Sometimes I would take men back to my apartment. There were beautiful Italian sheets on my bed. There was Scotch whisky in the drinks cabinet. You cannot imagine. No one in Russia lived like that – no one outside the highest levels of the Party. I loved those things. It did not matter what I had to do, I would never have given them up. I sold my soul.'

Carver leaned forward. 'Did you like my flat?'

'I'm sorry?'

'Did you like my flat? I mean, it's nice, isn't it? You haven't seen my car, but that's pretty nice too. So's the boat I keep on the lake. And I think you know how I paid for them.'

'So what are you saying, that you are as bad as me?'

'I guess. But who's to say what's good or bad? People get on their high horses. They sit in their comfortable, safe little lives and they talk about moral standards. But any idiot can come out with this week's socially acceptable bullshit when they don't have to face any consequences or get their hands dirty. I spent years watching good friends get blown to pieces, spilling their guts for politicians who lied through their teeth. I know there are bad guys out there, and I know what they can do. That changes your perspective, big-time.' Carver grimaced. 'Sorry, got a bit carried away.'

'No,' she said, 'I understand. And I like it when you get passionate. I like seeing who you really are.'

'Christ, do you think that's the real me?'

She was about to reply when there was a knock at the door. Carver went to answer it, picking up his gun from the bedside table along the way. He opened the door a couple of inches and then relaxed when he realized who was on the other side.

'Thor! Good to see you. Come in.'

Larsson's tall, gangly figure – all arms, legs and hair – ambled into the room. He was carrying two large nylon kit-bags, suspended from his shoulders. He saw Alix getting up from her make-up table and stopped.

'Oh, I'm sorry. I had no idea.' A shy smile spread across his face and his blue eyes creased in private amusement. 'Am I interrupting?'

'Not at all,' said Carver, 'we were just getting ready. So, Thor Larsson, this is Alexandra Petrova.'

'Call me Alix,' she said, standing on tiptoe to give Larsson a peck on the cheek.

'Uh, yeah . . . call me Thor,' he answered, as his face flushed beneath his freckles.

Her smile gently teased Larsson for his embarrassment, yet welcomed him as a friend.

'OK, Thor, please excuse me. I think I should get dressed.'

The two men stood watching her for a second as she flitted across to her clothes. It took an effort of will for Carver to drag his eyes and his thoughts away from Alix and force himself to concentrate on the gear Larsson had carted to the hotel room in his bags.

'Right,' Carver said, 'assume that this room is the command centre. I'll be here, in the first phase at least, monitoring communications. Then we need a wire on Alix, hand-held remote video that you'll have to control, and a complete sound-and-vision set-up for the other room, the one where Alix will take the guy we're going for.'

'No problem,' said Larsson. 'I've got everything you'll need.' He rummaged in one of the bags and pulled out a couple of cigarette packets. 'These should do the trick.'

Carver looked unconvinced. 'Are you sure? I can't afford for this to go wrong. It's the only chance I've got.'

'Relax,' said Larsson, patting Carver's shoulder. 'Have faith. I know what I'm doing. And by the way . . .' He bent down till his face was right by Carver's, and murmured, 'I want to talk about that other job you asked me to do, the decryption. Call me later tonight. We need to speak. Alone.'

45

Papin stood at the foot of the steps in front of the ancient cathedral. It was four minutes past five, and no one had arrived. Or perhaps they had. Perhaps he'd been set up and they were watching him now, waiting to see where he went next, trying to get their hands on the goods for free.

He gazed across the square. He didn't see the man with the shaven head, holding a metal briefcase, walk out of the cathedral's main door and come down towards him. He didn't know the man was there until he felt the crushing weight of his hand on his shoulder and heard a voice behind him growl 'Charlie sends his regards' in a Russian accent that made it sound like 'Chully syends his rigards'.

Papin gave a twitch of surprise and turned around to face his contact. He had been expecting an Englishman, or perhaps a Swiss, at any rate someone with whom he could conduct business in a civilized fashion. But this Russian just stood there, massive and brutish, gazing at Papin with blank implacability.

A few seconds passed in silence, then the Russian said, 'OK, wrong man,' and took a step back up the steps.

'No! No! Right man!' Papin exclaimed, suddenly panicked. 'I hope Charlie is well!'

Grigori Kursk looked at him, shook his head, spat on the ground, then grunted, 'Yeah, much byetter now.'

Papin glanced down at the case. 'Do you have the money?'

Kursk gave a single nod.

'Give me the first instalment.'

'Don't understand.'

'The money, two hundred and fifty thousand dollars. Give it to me.'

'Not here. Everyone see. In car. We go to car.'

Kursk walked away. Papin waited a couple of seconds, then followed him over to a black BMW parked on the uphill side of the square. There were three men inside, crammed on to the back seat.

'I said no back-up. Just me and you. No one else,' Papin insisted.

Kursk opened the passenger door. 'In!' he commanded.

The Frenchman knew now that it had all gone wrong. There would be no money in the case. The only issue now was his own survival. If he tried to run, he had no doubt the Russian would follow him and kill him. But he still had the information they needed. As long as he could keep it from them, that would be his edge.

Kursk glared at him. 'OK. Now, where to go?'

Papin said nothing.

Kursk kept his left hand draped on the wheel. But the right reached out, gripped Papin round the neck and started squeezing. Papin writhed in his seat, trying to escape the Russian's grasp. But it made no difference. He could not break free, and the effort just made him suffocate even faster. Surely the man had to stop. Surely he couldn't kill him now. Papin was desperate for breath, the blood pounding in his ears, his eyes popping, vision blurring. Still the fist closed round his neck. He could feel his voicebox being crushed by the pressure. When his resistance finally gave way he could only croak, 'OK . . . OK . . . I'll tell you.' At last the hand relaxed. Papin's chest heaved as he dragged air into his lungs, each breath burning like poison gas as it passed through his ravaged throat. 'Go to the end of the road, turn right.' He gestured feebly to show what he meant. Kursk started the car and began to drive.

They turned right across a small square and weaved their way along a series of narrow, intersecting cobbled streets. Finally, Papin pointed to the side of the road. There was a parking-space. 'Pull up behind that red car,' he said. The BMW came to a halt at the kerbside.

Papin turned his head towards Kursk. The Russian regarded him with the cloudy, dead-fish stare of a man incapable of remorse.

'Across the road,' Papin said. 'You see the alley? It's through there. He has the top apartment.'

'Are they in apartment?'

'No.'

'They come back?'

'Yes, I think so. Tonight, maybe.'

'Is only one way in?'

'I think so.'

Papin slumped back in his seat. The exhaustion that had weighed on him all day seemed to be dragging him down, robbing him of any energy or will. When Kursk reached out again, both hands this time, Pierre Papin hardly moved a muscle as his life ebbed away.

When it was over, Kursk got out of the car. He stood on the cobbles, leaning on the BMW's bodywork as he lit a cigarette and looked up and down the street. It was deserted. He gazed up at the buildings around him. There were no faces at any windows, no sign that he was being observed, just some kids playing in front of a café back down the street.

He knocked on the rear window and waited as it rolled down.

'OK,' he said to the men in the back seat. 'Time you did some work.'

In the passenger seat of a car parked at the end of the little side street a man was looking through the hefty telephoto lens of a high-spec digital camera. His finger was pressed to the trigger. The camera was on a sports setting, the shutter whirring, firing off several shots a second. Next to him a woman spoke into a mobile phone. 'Two of them have crossed the street. They're going up to an apartment building; I think they just forced the front door. I can see the Frenchman in the front seat of the car, but he's not moving. I'm pretty sure they've killed him.'

Grantham shook his head and sighed. 'That stupid, greedy bastard. Well, he can't say he wasn't told.'

'What do you want us to do, sir?'

'Nothing. Just keep watching. We offered Papin our help and he wouldn't take it. That's his problem. Our priority remains what it always was. We keep watching.'

'Yes, sir. I understand.'

'Good. Keep me informed of any further developments.'

'Absolutely.'

Jennifer Stock hung up and put the phone back in her handbag.

'Just spoken to the boss,' she said to the photographer. 'He says forget the Frenchman. Get those shots through to London. Then carry on as you were. Wait and watch.'

Stock wriggled in discomfort. It was hot inside the car. Her blouse and skirt were getting creased against the seat. She cursed under her breath. If she'd known she was going to spend half the day on a stake-out she'd have worn a T-shirt and trousers.

46

Magnus Leclerc did check on the Panamanian Mercantile Registry, on which all offshore companies had to be registered. Sure enough, Topográficas, SA was there, as were three nominated directors, none of whom was Mr Vandervart. That was no surprise: why have a Panamanian company at all if not to be invisible? Nor were there any published accounts. There wouldn't be: the lack of any requirement to keep books or records of any kind was another advantage of Panamanian corporate law. So he knew no more than he had done before, but then, he hadn't expected to. It was hardly unusual for his clients to wish to cover their tracks, and the possibility of wasting an hour in a bar seemed a small price to pay for the chance of landing a nine-figure account.

He arrived at the Hotel Beau Rivage shortly after six, asked for Vandervart at the reception desk, and was informed by the receptionist that his host apologized profusely but he was tied up in a meeting and would be a few minutes late. In the meantime, if monsieur would care to make his way just across the atrium to the bar, M. Vandervart would join him there soon.

It was a perfect example of an upmarket European watering-hole:

ornate plasterwork on the walls, gathered green silk blinds over the windows, reproduction antique chairs grouped around white-clothed tables. Leclerc walked to the bar and ordered a vodka-martini from the grey-haired man behind the counter. He collected his drink and walked across to a corner table. The only other customers were an elderly American couple. The man was already ordering his second bourbon; his wife was pursing her lips. It looked like the start of a long night of marital hell.

He knew all about that. Leclerc took a sip of his martini and contemplated the ritual display of martyrdom and resentment that awaited him when he got home. Marthe would depict herself as shattered after her long day of doing precisely nothing apart from playing tennis, spending his money and undertaking the minimal amount of childcare required for two independent-minded teenagers. He had warned her he might be late home and told her not to worry about his supper, but that wouldn't count for much. She'd make a point of wearing the most shapeless, unappealing tracksuit she could find. She'd sigh theatrically, roll her eyes and tell him the food was ruined. She'd—

Mon Dieu!

A woman had just walked into the bar. She was tall, with a beautiful face framed in a brunette bob. She was wearing a softly cut white blouse over a tight dark-blue skirt. Her long legs were tanned. Her high heels exactly matched her skirt, as did her elegant little shoulder-bag. She looked absolutely respectable yet totally desirable. Leclerc spotted the ancient American ogling the girl as she cast her eyes around the bar, evidently looking for someone. The American's wife hissed and slapped the back of a mottled, ring-burdened hand across the sleeve of his jacket, redirecting his attention back to her.

Then the brunette caught Leclerc's eye. Her face suddenly lit up with a smile, letting him know she'd recognized him and that nothing at all could have made her happier. She walked across to him and stopped beside his table.

'Monsieur Leclerc?' She held out elegant fingers whose smooth, unblemished skin was a delightful contrast to the gnarled claw of the old harridan, who was now casting poisonous looks in their direction. 'I'm Natasha St Clair, Mr Vandervart's assistant. He's still tied up, I'm afraid.'

'*Enchanté*, mademoiselle,' replied Leclerc. 'I am Magnus Leclerc. But please, Natasha, call me Magnus. Can I persuade you to join me, while we wait for M'sieur Vandervart?'

'Are you sure? I mean, if you think it's all right . . .'

'But of course, I insist.'

'Thank you, that would be very nice. I just hope I haven't intruded on you.'

She blushed a little as she sat down opposite him, smoothing her skirt over her perfect thighs. She then gave a regretful little shake of her head and a frown of concern.

'You know, Mr Vandervart is a wonderful man, but I really think he should take it easier. It's not my place to say anything, of course, but men like him work too hard. Of course, they want to do the best for their families, but sometimes they should think more about themselves. Don't you agree?'

Magnus Leclerc would happily have agreed with any proposal the girl cared to put to him. 'Absolutely,' he said, with an enthusiastic nod.

The girl smiled, as if grateful for his approval. She placed her elbows on the table and leaned forward a fraction, letting her scent waft across the table and accidentally giving Leclerc the tiniest glimpse of cleavage as her breasts were squeezed between her upper arms.

'Mmm,' she purred, 'that martini looks so tempting. It's very naughty of me to have a drink while I'm still supposed to be working, but could you get one for me, too? Is that all right?'

'But of course, I'd be delighted,' said the banker.

As he got up from the table and walked towards the bar, he realized that his pulse was racing. He ordered a drink and adjusted his tie in the mirror behind the bar. When the martini arrived, the barman raised an eyebrow in a gesture of wry acknowledgement, one man to another: you got lucky there. Leclerc smiled back, gave the barman a friendly slap on the arm and left him a ten-franc tip.

Then he turned round and carried the drink back towards the girl.

She didn't like to admit it, but Alix was enjoying herself. She'd felt eyes following her as she crossed the foyer – the lust of the bellhop and the concierge; the envy of the plain receptionist; the considered, competitive assessment of the pretty one. When she walked into the bar she'd had to suppress a smile at the comic spat between the old man and his wife. Then she'd watched the banker trying not to gawp at her like a goggle-eyed sixteen-year-old virgin, and had known this was going to be easy.

From then on, she'd worked by the manual: the smile, the eye contact, the gestures that would both arouse a man's interest and signal her availability, the conversational gambits that ended in a question, inviting the man to agree. Ask any top-class pick-up artist, if you start the other person off saying 'yes' they don't stop, all the way to the bedroom.

She'd been tempted to see if she could work her magic without any chemical assistance, but seducing Leclerc was just a means to an end. They had to get him talking as well. So when he went up to the bar she'd reached into her bag and taken out her cigarettes and lighter. Anyone watching would have seen that. They wouldn't have noticed the little capsule she palmed, nor seen her snap it in two and deposit its contents into Leclerc's glass as she reached across and idly toyed with the olive on its black plastic stick. The powder settled on the surface of the martini, but disappeared with a couple of stirs of the stick. Leclerc returned to the table to find Alix looking up at him with a guilty look on her face, saying, 'Oops! You caught me! I was just about to steal your olive. I'm sorry. I can't resist them!'

He tried to give her his smoothest smile. 'Well, here's one of your very own.'

Alix took the olive from the glass Leclerc had placed in front of her and slipped it into her mouth, between her glossy red lips. 'Mmm, delicious!' she said, then playfully ran her tongue along her upper lip. Then she told herself to stop fooling around. If she were too obvious, too easy, Leclerc might get suspicious. Time to be a bit more respectable.

She looked at him slightly wide-eyed, like an eager, respectful pupil sitting at her favourite professor's feet. 'I've always been fascinated by Swiss banks. They sound so powerful and mysterious. You must tell me all about your work. I'd really like to know.'

The barman's name was Marcel. He'd spent more than thirty years serving drinks, watching the games that play out when men, women and alcohol collide. He thought of himself as a connoisseur of the arts of seduction. So the moment the girl stepped into his domain, then shone her smile at the man in the corner, Marcel's interest was aroused.

He was reasonably certain that this was some kind of con. The man was a mark, and she was playing him. After the second martini, she'd discreetly switched to sparkling water, but the man had stayed with his liquor. Marcel chuckled to himself and looked forward to the evening's entertainment.

The bar was beginning to fill up now. A group of businessmen had come in, each in turn checking out the brunette and smirking to one another as they ordered their drinks. Then a bizarre figure strode up and perched on one of the long-legged chairs by the glossy wooden counter-top. He was almost two metres tall, dressed in battered, patched jeans and a T-shirt printed in lurid shades of yellow and purple. He had hair like a black man, except it was a pale, sandy colour, and his eyes were Nordic blue.

Marcel sighed, sadly, bemoaning the loss of proper standards. Nowadays it was impossible to tell the difference between beggars and millionaires. A man in tatty denims could be a rock star, an actor or one of those American computer tycoons people kept talking about. Maybe he was the hippy son of a wealthy family. When he ordered a Heineken, he gave the number of a Junior Suite. His watch was a Breitling Navitimer – an expensive chronograph, but also a serious, functional one. He had good manners, too. Businessmen tended to place their orders brusquely, without a please or a thank you, but this white rastaman took the trouble to converse a little in a calm, easy-going voice. He showed respect for Marcel's job and his dignity. Maybe the clothes could be forgiven.

'Would you like some matches, m'sieur?' Marcel said, nodding at the Camel cigarettes on the counter, next to the beer glass.

The man smiled. 'No thank you, I'm trying to give up. Keeping them there is like a test. If I can have a couple of beers without smoking a cigarette, I'll know I'm getting somewhere.'

He glanced across to the corner of the room, turned back to Marcel and said, 'Have you seen the couple in the corner? She just stroked his face. Then he took her hand and kissed it. Isn't love great?'

Marcel winked. '*L'amour, toujours l'amour . . .*'

In the earpiece hidden beneath his dreadlocks, Thor Larsson could hear Carver's voice.

'Yeah, I saw it. It's almost scary how good she is at this.'

Inside the Camel packet there was a miniaturized video camera pointing through a pin-size aperture, with a signal transmitter linked to a video monitor and recorder in Carver's room. A microphone and an audio transmitter were hidden in Alix's bag. Everything she and the banker did, every word they said, it was all going down on tape.

'I wonder what she's like in bed,' mused Larsson, apparently for the barman's benefit.

Carver laughed. 'Well don't expect me to tell you.'

'If only I could hear what they're talking about.'

'Don't worry. I'm getting the audio feed from Alix, clear as a bell.'

'Could you get me another beer, please? And some nuts, if you've got them. I think I'll stick around.'

47

Grigori Kursk was a patient man. He'd learned that lesson in Afghanistan. Too many of his comrades had rushed into combat, hoping to overwhelm the mujahidin guerrillas with sheer weight of firepower, only to be outsmarted, ambushed and sent straight to hell. Kursk could wait for hours, days, as long as it took to make the other man move first and expose his position. Only then would he strike. So he did not care whether it took Carver all night or all week to return to his apartment. He would be ready for him whenever he came.

The two men he'd sent up to the apartment had reported that the door was steel-framed and secured with deadbolts to the top and bottom as well as the side. The hinges were reinforced. The only way to force entry would be with a bomb or a bazooka. Kursk himself had examined the windows through his field-glasses. The glass was extra thick, almost certainly bulletproof.

It was no more than he had expected. Carver was no fool; he was bound to take precautions against men just like himself. In the meantime, Kursk needed to take some safety measures of his own.

A call to Moscow gave him the contact number he needed, a Swiss-registered mobile.

'I work for Yuri,' he said. 'I need to dispose of a car, a BMW 750 saloon. It has something in it. That has to go too, you understand? . . . Right then, I'll send a man with the car. Also, I want a van, like a phone company or a delivery van, something like that. My guy will pick it up. Twenty minutes. You'd better have what we need. You don't want Yuri to hear you let me down.'

Kursk sent Dimitrov away with the car. Papin was still in the passenger seat, kept upright by a tightly strapped seat-belt. Now Kursk was alone in the street. It was quiet, respectable, a place where he stuck out like a bear in a tea-shop. He needed to escape the prying eyes that lurked behind all those flower baskets and net curtains. A sign caught his eye a little way up the road: Malone's Irish Pub. Perfect.

He took his beer and a whisky chaser to a seat by the window where he had an unobstructed view down the street. No one could get in or out of Carver's building without him seeing. Kursk savoured his drink and looked around the pub. He'd known places just like this in Moscow. He guessed there were a million just like it, right around the world. But it was OK. Compared to some of the places he'd sat and waited, this one was a palace.

Jennifer Stock had left the car and gone for a little walk, looking in shop windows, stopping for an early-evening cup of coffee and spotting Kursk and all three of his men. There were, she reflected, tremendous advantages to being female, if only because the instinctive male refusal to take one seriously was impervious to any amount of supposed sexual equality. You could wander up and down and they just thought you were a silly woman who had no sense of direction or couldn't decide where to go. You could poke your nose into nooks and crannies and they just put it down to feminine curiosity.

It was far easier to talk to people, too. The nicest man could arouse a certain amount of suspicion or even fear when he approached a stranger. Children were taught to shy away from men they did not know. But anyone of any age or gender would talk to a woman. In fact, it was the big-eyed, squiffy-haired son of the local café owner who'd told her all about the Frenchman who'd been asking his papa questions that morning, and the funny men in baggy coats who'd got out of the big black car.

'Oh yes, I saw them,' she said, ruffling the little boy's hair. 'They were funny, weren't they?'

It was while she was sitting in the café, drinking her double espresso, that Stock took the call from London. It was Bill Selsey.

'Hi, Jen, just got a hit on that BMW with the Italian plates you were asking about. Turns out it's registered to a company called Pelicce Marinovski. They supposedly import furs from Russia.'

'Really? The men in that car didn't look much like furriers.'

'Yes, well, Pelicce whatever-it-is doesn't look much like a legitimate import-export company, either. Can't find any proper accounts anywhere, no premises, no evidence of any sales.'

Stock frowned. 'Is this some sort of front for the Russian mafia?'

'Possibly, so be careful, all right? These are not nice people to do business with.'

'My orders are to watch from a distance and not to interfere. That's what I intend to do.'

'Good girl, that's the spirit.'

48

Magnus Leclerc felt suffused by warmth. For some reason, the bar had become much hotter. He'd taken off his jacket and tie, but he was still sweating like a pig. He hoped Natasha hadn't noticed. Aaaah, Natasha! She was amazing. She understood him. It was incredible. He'd hardly known her for an hour, but already he felt this amazing connection to her, a profound empathy, as though she could see right into his soul, and he into hers.

He'd told her about Marthe, the bitch, how hurt he was by her constant bickering, her petty criticisms and her rejection of his sexual needs. He'd been afraid Natasha would laugh at him. But she didn't. She sympathized. This beautiful girl took his hand in hers. Then, very gently, she ran her perfect fingers down his cheek. Leclerc almost cried at her consoling gesture. It had been so long since he'd felt that kind of comfort.

So long, too, since he'd been this turned on. Maybe that was why he felt so hot – he was burning up with lust. He wanted to screw her so badly. He gazed at her, mentally stripping away her clothes, speculating on the body beneath. For a second, he didn't even realize she was talking to him.

'Sorry,' he said, 'did you say something, *chérie*?'

'I was just saying that maybe we should try to find Mr Vandervart. I don't know what's happened to him. I think he must still be up in his suite. Do you think we should go upstairs?'

A pathetically grateful smile broke over Leclerc's face. 'Upstairs? Oh yes, I think that's where we should go.'

When he stood up, he was uncomfortably aware that the floor wasn't quite as steady as he would have liked. Natasha skipped to his side, picked up his discarded coat and tie and took his arm in hers, helping him find his balance as he walked out of the bar. He couldn't work it out. He'd only had, what, four martinis, maybe five? He shouldn't be affected like this. Then he felt her hip against his and the soft weight of her breast as it brushed against his arm, and a big, happy smile crossed Magnus Leclerc's face. He didn't care how drunk he was. He felt absolutely great.

Alix led the molten, drooling banker down the corridor and up to the door of the suite. She knocked, pressed her ear to the door, then turned to Leclerc. 'He doesn't seem to be there. I'm sure he won't be long. We could wait in my suite if you like. I'm just next door.'

Not giving him a chance to reply, she stepped up to the next door, inserted her key and let them in. 'This isn't very cosy, I'm afraid,' she said, leading him past the formal, stiff-backed antique furniture in the living-room through to the bedroom with its king-size bed covered in a sky-blue quilt. Directly opposite the bed was a cabinet containing a TV set. It was a no-smoking room, but some-one had left a packet of cigarettes in an ashtray next to the TV.

'This is a bit more comfortable,' said Alix, putting down her handbag on a bedside table. 'Why don't you take it easy? Sit down on the bed and I'll fix you a drink from the minibar. Another martini?'

'No,' he said, grabbing her arm. 'Don't worry about drinks. Stay with me here.'

He patted the bed beside him. Alix sat down. She let him run a hand up her thigh, stopping him only when he tried to reach beneath her skirt. 'Hold on,' she said, running her other hand playfully through his hair. 'What would Marthe think if she could see us now?'

'Oh screw Marthe!' said Leclerc. Then he burst out giggling. 'No, on second thoughts, I'd much rather screw you!'

He dived at Alix, grabbing her shoulders and trying to force her flat on the bed. She laughed, and squirmed out from under him.

'Not so fast,' she said. 'If you want to have me, you must do exactly as I say.'

'Anything!' leered Leclerc.

'Stand up, opposite me.'

He obeyed at once.

'Remove your shirt.'

Again, he did as he was told.

'Now, take off your trousers and then stand perfectly still.'

When he had finished, he watched open-mouthed as Alix undid the buttons of her blouse, discarding it in a flutter of creamy silk. She then unzipped her skirt and let it slide to the floor before stepping out of the ring of crumpled fabric. Alix was wearing white lace lingerie from La Perla that accentuated the lithe, athletic curves of her body. She still had her high heels on. Opposite her, Leclerc was in a pair of baggy Y-fronts, their waistband lost in his doughy flesh. He was still wearing his grey woollen socks.

'Lie on the bed, right back against the headboard,' she told him.

Leclerc scuttled backwards, fell on the bed and propped himself up against the pillows.

'Soon, very soon, you will have your way with me. But first I am going to have my way with you. Stay there, don't move a muscle, and don't say a word!'

Alix strode around the bed to a chest of drawers. She bent down to open a drawer, making Leclerc groan with pleasure at the view, and pulled out three long, narrow, black silk scarves.

'What—' Leclerc began.

'Shh . . .'

She walked back to the bed, laid the scarves along the bedspread and knelt astride Leclerc's chest. Then she reached for his right wrist, expertly knotted one end of the first scarf around it and tied the other end to the top of the bedpost. Leclerc now had one arm dangling helplessly in mid-air, but he seemed less concerned by that than his desperate attempts to get his face up to Alix's breasts as she leaned across him. She ignored him, wordlessly grabbing his other wrist and repeating the procedure with the second scarf.

When both arms were secure she leaned back and ran a hand through Leclerc's chest hair, idly toying with his nipples as she said, 'Do I look good to you?'

'Oh God, yes,' he groaned.

'OK then, take a good long look and remember what you see. Because now you see me, and now' – she picked up the final scarf and whipped it around the banker's head, covering his eyes – 'you don't. You're helpless now, at my mercy. So I ask myself, what am I going to do?'

She placed her forefinger against his lips, teasing him as he desperately tried to suck it. Then she lay flat on top of him and started wriggling downwards, down and down until her head was directly above his underpants.

'Mmm, what have we here?' she said.

She raised herself up on to her haunches again and started to pull the underpants from his waist.

'Please, please!' he moaned, trying to lift his arse off the bed to make the job easier.

Alix bent forward over Leclerc, lower and lower, till her head was only millimetres above him, and—

'Thank you, Miss St Clair, that will be all.' The voice was a harsh, guttural Afrikaans.

Alix climbed off the bed and glared furiously at Carver. 'You took your time!' she mouthed at him.

'I'm sorry,' he mouthed back, holding his hands out, palms down, in the universal gesture of pacification.

'Who are you? What's happening?' squealed Leclerc, writhing on the bed.

Carver slapped him once, very hard, on the side of the face.

'Shut up, Mr Leclerc,' Carver snapped. 'If you value your life and your reputation, shut up and listen. Here, let me help you.'

Carver pulled a handkerchief from his pocket and shoved it in the other man's mouth, gagging him. He took the belt from the trousers lying on the floor and tied it tight around Leclerc's ankles, rendering him entirely helpless.

'My name is Dirk Vandervart. I am about to ask you a series of simple questions and you are going to give me honest answers. There are two reasons why you are going to do this. The first is that we have been following your evening with Miss St Clair. In fact, we have recorded all the most interesting moments on tape. I don't think your wife would like to hear all the things you said about her, do you? Particularly when she watches you seducing a young woman and letting her tie you to her bed. Wouldn't reflect well on you, your marriage or your bank, eh? Right then, refuse to talk, attempt to mislead us or reveal anything of what happened in this room this evening and those tapes will be made very, very public.

'The other reason why you will talk is simple: I will cause you very great pain if you do not. Please be in no doubt about this, Mr Leclerc. For example . . .'

Carver took hold of Leclerc's left hand and started bending back the little finger. Leclerc shook his head from side to side.

'Hurts, doesn't it? If I keep going, just a little bit more, the bone will snap like a twig. Then the finger will swell like a sausage grilling on a braai. Ach, man, let me tell you, that hurts so much, you'll wish I'd just cut it right off.'

Leclerc's whole body was jerking now as if jolted by electric shocks. Carver appeared not to notice, and just kept talking.

'And once I've done one finger, I'll do all the rest as well. And your toes. And you don't even want to think about the rest of your body. So, would you like to talk?'

Leclerc nodded frantically.

'Very sensible decision. Here, let's make you a little bit more comfortable. Perhaps you could help me, Miss St Clair?'

Together, they dragged Leclerc upwards, so that his back was resting against the headboard.

Alix leaned forward and murmured in his ear, 'I'm sorry, Magnus. Just tell Mr Vandervart exactly what he wants and you can go home to Marthe. You love her really, don't you, Magnus?'

Another desperate nod.

'OK, then.' Alix pulled the gag from his mouth.

Carver spoke, still in character as Vandervart. 'I want to know about one of the accounts you control. It's number 4443717168.'

'But I control hundreds of accounts. How can I remember them all?' Leclerc's blindfolded head turned from side to side in blind supplication.

'You'll remember this one. On Saturday morning, you acknowledged receipt of one and a half million US dollars into the account and sent a fax to that effect to the account holder. But by Sunday afternoon, you'd made the money disappear. How did you do that? And who gave you the orders? Because I don't think you'd steal all that money for yourself . . .'

'No! No!'

'So what happened?'

'I can't tell you. I can't! They'd kill me!' His voice was high-pitched, begging for an understanding he knew he would never receive.

'Who are "they", Magnus?'

'I can't tell you!'

'Because they'd kill you.'

'Yes!'

'What makes you think that I won't kill you first? Open your mouth.'

Carver reached round to the small of his back and pulled his SIG-Sauer from the waistband. He jammed the silencer between Leclerc's teeth.

'Can you guess what that is? Correct, it's a nine-millimetre pistol. Believe me, I won't hesitate to pull the trigger. It's what I do. But I can do something else, too. I can keep secrets. And no one will ever know anything about this evening, ever, if you just tell me what happened to that account.'

'Nothing happened.'

Carver slapped Leclerc a second time. 'I thought we had an understanding here.'

Leclerc moaned. 'No, really, nothing happened. No money ever went into that account. None came out. The receipt for the deposit was a fake.'

'So who gave the orders for it to be issued?'

'I can't tell you . . . I can't!'

Carver sighed. He stuffed the gag back into Leclerc's mouth, then picked up his hand again. 'This little piggy went to market,' he said, giving the index finger a sudden, sharp tug. He moved along the hand. 'This little piggy stayed at home. This little piggy had roast beef. And this little piggy . . .'

There was a muffled howl behind the handkerchief. Carver held Leclerc's little finger for a few seconds longer, forcing it back, letting the pain intensify, then took out the handkerchief.

'Did you want to say something? Or do you want me to prove how serious I am?'

'No, please, I beg you . . .'

'Then tell me. The orders – where did they come from?'

'From Malgrave and Company. That's a bank in the City of London.'

'Who sent them? I need a name.'

'I do not know, but I think they must have come from the very top, from someone with great influence. It could not have happened unless my own company president had agreed.'

'So, who runs Malgrave and Company? Who's the boss?'

Leclerc attempted a pained smile. 'You don't need me to tell you that. It's a family company. The current chairman is Lord Crispin Malgrave.'

'Thank you, Mr Leclerc. You've been very helpful. You'll be out of here in a moment. Tomorrow morning you will receive an email. Photographs will be attached to it, stills from our videotapes. I hope they will serve as reminders to you to keep quiet. I would not wish any further unpleasantness.

'Now, Miss St Clair, perhaps you would be so good as to get dressed again and help me tidy this room.'

Carver then turned towards the pack of cigarettes, with its hidden camera, and delivered a message to Thor Larsson, watching the monitor in the other suite. 'You can pack up and get out of there too.'

49

Alix stood in the shower trying to scrub away the memory of Leclerc's hands on her body and the smell as her lips hovered over him. The hotel provided two plastic bottles of mint-flavoured mouthwash. She used them both up. They had not even kissed, let alone had sex, but still she felt defiled. By the time she walked back into the bedroom, Carver was silently packing away the video gear. Leclerc was sitting on the side of the bed, slumped and deflated.

Alix collected her own possessions, then helped Carver as he untied and dressed Leclerc, though the blindfold stayed on. The banker was led out into the corridor, down the emergency staircase and out through a door at the rear of the building. Thor Larsson was waiting to greet them in his battered Volvo.

'Got everything?' asked Carver, still in character as Vandervart.

'Sure,' said Larsson. 'And don't worry. The sound and picture quality is superb.'

Ten minutes later, Leclerc was bundled from the car in a quiet side street. By the time he'd untied the blindfold, the Volvo had rounded a corner and was out of sight.

Larsson dropped Carver and Alix on the Pont des Bergues, leaving them to walk up to the Old Town while he returned to his own apartment. Within minutes of getting there, he'd gone online and started hacking into the hotel mainframe. He wanted to erase any sign of their presence. It took half an hour and all of Larsson's expertise, but finally it was as if Mr Vandervart, Miss St Clair and Mr Sjoberg had never reserved a room or crossed the threshold of the building.

As they walked back across the river, arm in arm, Alix asked Carver, 'Would you really have hurt Leclerc?'

'If I had to. If that was the only way of making him talk.'

'It's scary seeing you like that. It seems so natural to you.'

'Not really, I was just getting the job done. And if you think I'm a natural, you should see yourself. I was pretty freaked out sitting in front of the video watching you and him. Made me wonder what someone would think watching us.'

They were on the far bank of the river now, and they walked for a while in companionable silence, still carrying the overnight bags they'd taken to the hotel in their spare hands. Then Carver spoke again.

'Why did you really go to Paris?'

There was no aggression in his voice, none of the menace he'd directed at Leclerc. He was asking a straight question, just as if he were curious.

'It was like I told you,' Alix replied, just as straightforwardly. 'Kursk wanted a woman to help him on a job and he was willing to pay ten thousand dollars.'

'But there's no doctor, is there, no respectable fiancé?'

Alix opened her mouth to speak, then seemed to think better of it. She sighed and looked away.

Carver's voice hardened a fraction. 'No, and I don't see you working at a hotel reception desk, either. People like you and me don't hold down normal jobs. We've been out of that world too long to handle nine-to-five. So, what have you really been doing?'

Alix pulled her arm away and stopped walking. 'For God's sake, isn't it obvious? The same thing I always did. My clients were Russian, very rich, very powerful. Sometimes I was more like a girlfriend, staying with the same man for months at a time.'

Carver wanted to stop. He knew there was nothing to be gained from digging deeper. But he couldn't help himself. 'Like that guy in the club, with the two blondes?' he added, and now there was an edge to the question.

Alix looked at him with an acid contempt he had not seen since that first night in Paris. 'Yes, like Platon. Before those girls it was me sitting next to him in clubs, laughing at his jokes, letting his hands grab my tits, going down on him, fucking him. OK? Are you satisfied now? Or would you like me to be humiliated a little more?'

'No, I get the picture.'

'Do you? Do you understand what it is to be a woman in Moscow today? There is no law, no security. The choice is not between a good life or a bad one, it is between surviving or dying. I did what it took to, as you say, get the job done. Then Kursk came to me, talking about a job in Paris, saying he needed a woman. I thought maybe there was a chance to escape and start again. A new life.'

'Why didn't you tell me this before?'

There was real pain on her face now, anger giving way to resignation. 'How could I tell you the whole truth? I invented my respectable lover and my respectable job because I hoped maybe you would respect me a bit more. But I lied. I am not respectable. Are you happy now?'

Carver took her shoulders in his hands. 'Alix, I don't give a damn whether you're "respectable". Of all the people in the world, I've got the least right to judge you. I just want to know what's true.'

She looked up at him. 'Does it matter? Can it ever be any different to this, between you and me?'

They were all talked out now, nothing left to say as they walked up the hill and turned the corner into the street where Carver lived, lost in their own thoughts.

*

In the rearview mirror of the Swisscom van where he had spent the past two hours, Grigori Kursk saw them coming. Alexandra Petrova was wearing a brown wig and clothes he'd never seen on her before, but it made no difference. He'd seen her in so many wigs, so many disguises, he could see right past them and recognize her from the set of her body and the way she walked.

He smiled when he saw the man next to her. The Englishman had hurt Kursk's body and his pride alike. He had let himself get suckered into a high-explosive trap, and though he hadn't let a hint of discomfort or vulnerability show to his men, every breath he took sent a sharp pain stabbing into his cracked and bruised ribs. Now he was going to enjoy his revenge.

He called Dimitrov, who'd taken his place in the Irish pub, and the two other men he'd left near Carver's apartment. His message was the same: 'They're here. Be ready for action. And remember, we take them both alive.'

50

A door opened a fraction, throwing a sliver of blue-white neon light across the charcoal-grey cobblestones.

'Psst! Pablo! Come inside!'

Carver was dragged from his introspection like a man being woken from a deep sleep. He looked around and saw the source of the voice.

'Not tonight, Freddy. Sorry, mate, we're not in the mood.'

'Just come inside. This is serious!'

The urgency in Freddy's voice made Carver stop and look at him. He glanced at Alix, too, but saw no response in her, one way or the other.

They walked past a couple of outside tables into the little, low-ceilinged café. There was one other person in the place, an old man hunched over a bowl of minestrone. Carver nodded in his direction and said, '*Bonsoir, Karl, ça va?*' The old man grunted a non-committal reply and returned to his soup. 'He's in here every evening, last customer of the night, always a bowl of minestrone,' Carver explained, though Alix wasn't paying any attention.

He turned back to Freddy. 'What's the problem?'

Freddy gave the serving-counter a flick with the cloth he kept tucked into his white apron. 'No problem, not yet. But later, I don't know. There are people looking for you, Pablo. First a Frenchman: he came here this morning saying he was working for the Federal Interior Ministry. That was obviously a lie. He was a cop of some kind, I'm sure. Then an Englishwoman, very polite, charming, but asking questions.'

'Describe her.'

'Typical English, you know. Not so chic, not elegant, but quite attractive.'

'Hair? Clothes?'

'Er, let me see . . .' Freddy frowned. 'OK. She had pale-brown hair, like a mouse. And she was wearing a skirt with some kind of pattern on it, flowers maybe.'

Carver nodded. 'She's sitting about fifty metres back down the road in a mid-blue Opel Vectra. There's a man with her. When we walked by she grabbed his hand and looked in his eyes, like they were pretending to be lovers or something. What did she want to know?'

'She spoke to Jean-Louis when my back was turned. He told her about the other men, too.'

'What other men?'

'I don't know. I did not see them. But Jean-Louis saw some men get out of a black car this afternoon. Then the car went away but not all of the men were in it. They may still be around.'

'How many men were there?'

'I don't know. Wait a moment.' He walked to one side of the room, opened a door and poked his head through. 'Jean-Louis!'

A child's voice came from an upstairs room.'Yes, Papa?'

'Come here, son.'

There was a scurrying of footsteps down a staircase, then a small bundle of energy rocketed into the room, saw Carver and shrieked, 'Pablo!'

His father glowered at him, trying to look stern. 'Tell Monsieur Pablo what you saw this afternoon. You know, the funny men.'

'The ones the English lady asked me about?'

'Yes, them.'

'There were three of them, or maybe four. They looked funny. They had big coats on, even though it was nice and warm outside.'

Carver got down on his haunches to look Jean-Louis in the eye. 'Could you see if they were carrying anything under their coats?'

'No, they were all buttoned up. They must have been boiling.'

'Yes, they must. But thank you, that's very useful. Now, did you see where they went?'

The child nodded. 'Yes. Some went towards your house. But some didn't. I don't know what happened to them. I had to come in because Maman said it was time for my dinner.'

'Well, don't you worry. You did very well. I think you could become a famous detective one day. Don't you agree, Freddy?'

Freddy looked shocked. 'My son? A *flic*? That's not funny, Pablo.' He crossed himself in mock horror, then turned to his son. 'OK, now, back up to bed. Come on, up you go. I'll be up soon to read you a story. Go!'

Carver watched the boy scamper from the room, then turned back to Freddy.

'There's a Swisscom van up the street, on the other side of the road. How long has that been here?'

Freddy gave an exasperated sigh. '*Merde!* How would I know that? Truly, Pablo, you are no better than a cop yourself.'

'I'm sorry, but this could be important. Just try to remember back earlier in the day, when you went out to serve people at the tables. Was the van there this morning? Were there telephone engineers doing work anywhere?'

Freddy thought for a moment, his eyes closed. 'No, there was no van there, no engineers. It must have arrived late in the day.'

'So either there's been some last-minute phone crisis, or it's got nothing to do with Swisscom. We've got to assume it's the latter. So now we've got the Frenchman, the Englishwoman and her pal in the car, and a gang of men in big coats who used to have a black car that's now disappeared and a van's arrived. And it doesn't look like any of them have got anything to do with the others. Jesus . . .'

Alix looked at him. 'So now what?'

'You stay here, while I go and work out what the bloody hell's going on.'

'Oh, you're going to leave me, the helpless woman?'

'No, I just don't want to fight anyone else if I'm busy fighting with you at the same time. That would be a distraction. So I'm going to find out who's out there, deal with them, then we can carry on with whatever it is we're doing. If that's what you want.'

Freddy rolled his eyes and left the room. 'I'll just go and, er, finish cleaning up the kitchen,' he said over his departing shoulder.

Carver and Alix glowered at each other for a moment, neither wanting to give way. Then she gave a quick shrug of concession.

'Go. Freddy can look after me.'

Carver said nothing, just looked at her. Then he turned and walked towards the kitchen.

'Hey, Freddy!' he called out. 'Is there a back way out of this place?'

51

Carver went the long way round the block, walking round three streets until he worked his way up to the far end of the street. Now he was looking back down the road towards the van, the café and the blue Opel. Malone's pub was just in front of him. If anyone had been asking questions in the café, chances were they'd gone in there too. He might as well do the same.

Carver pushed open the door and walked into a reek of cigarettes and old Guinness. They had the usual crowd in, office workers from the UN and the local banks trying to prove they were flesh-and-blood humans beneath their anonymous suits. Carver gave a quick wave of recognition to the hefty man in a green Ireland rugby shirt standing behind the bar, then looked casually round the room, just like any other punter, checking out the evening's action.

It didn't take much effort to spot the man in the coat. He was perched on a stool by the window, looking straight at Carver and jabbering into a phone. That was a giveaway to start with. He snapped the phone shut the moment he caught Carver's eye. That was the clincher. Carver walked up to the bar, shaking his head at the idiocy of a man who didn't even have the brains to feign a lack of interest.

'Pint please, Stu.'

The man in the rugby shirt replied, 'No worries, mate,' in a broad Aussie accent and stood by the pump as the foaming, creamy beer slowly settled and darkened in the half-litre glass in front of him.

Carver leaned on the counter. 'That bloke by the window, the ugly bugger in the black coat, he been here long?'

Stu looked across the room. 'Dunno, couple of hours, maybe. Hasn't drunk much, the tight bastard. Had a mate in earlier, but the other bloke left.'

Carver paid for his drink. He was about to carry it away when he seemed to be struck by a sudden thought.

'Tell you what, Stu, you might want to ring for a doctor. I've got a premonition. There might be a bit of an accident.'

'Strewth, Pablo, I don't want any fighting in here. Take it outside if you want to have a ruck.'

Carver patted him on the shoulder. 'Don't you worry. It won't take a second.'

He strolled back across the pub to the seats by the window, nice and casual, exchanging smiles with pretty girls he bumped into along the way. The Russian was only a few feet away now, watching him, uncertain how to react to his target approaching him as if he didn't have a care in the world.

Between Carver and the Russian, three young office-babes were clustered around a bottle of wine, swapping giggly, high-pitched gossip. One of them had left her handbag on the floor. The women flicked glances at Carver as he walked by. He turned his head and grinned cheekily back at them, giving the prettiest of the trio a saucy wink.

He wasn't paying attention to where he was going. That's why he tripped on the handbag and fell forward, his glass jerking backwards and sending a spray of Guinness arcing through the air towards the girls, who shrieked and leapt out of the way as the foaming black liquid splashed across their clothes. Carver's hands flailed for something to grab on to, and they landed on the man in the coat, who staggered backwards as Carver ploughed into him. Chairs were knocked across the floor, the excited, outraged squeals of the women echoed round the room, and no one noticed the way Carver's fists tightened their grip on the fabric of the man's coat, or the sudden jerk of the neck that sent Carver's forehead smashing into the bridge of his nose as the two men fell helplessly to the floor.

Within a couple of seconds, the chaos had subsided. Carver pulled himself to his feet with a dazed expression on his face and looked down in anguish at the bloodstained wreck lying unconscious on the floor. 'Oh God! I'm so sorry! Are you all right?' he said, helplessly. He looked around at the gawping drinkers. 'Someone call an ambulance, quick!' There was a pause, then his eyes widened. 'Where's the men's room?' he gasped. 'I think I'm going to be sick.' He bent over, put his hands to his mouth and puffed out his cheeks, staggering towards the back of the pub as nervous drinkers stepped back to let him pass.

It wasn't until he was through the swing-door, down the corridor beyond it and into the men's room that Carver straightened up, wiped a trace of blood off his forehead and permitted himself a smile. That was one down. But how many more still to go?

Then the door behind him opened. He looked in the mirror. And he got an answer.

Grigori Kursk had a decision to make. He'd hoped Carver and Petrova would return to the apartment. He'd planned to capture them and the computer there, but now it looked like they'd split up. Dimitrov had spotted Carver in the pub, but he was alone. Petrova was nowhere in sight. She must still be in the café. Kursk sent his other two men down to reinforce Dimitrov. But now, should he join them, or should he go after the girl?

He considered the situation. Carver was good, there was no doubt about that. But Kursk trusted his men. They might not be rocket scientists, but they were ex-Spetsnatz troopers, trained in one of the world's toughest special forces regimes. He, meanwhile, could deal with Petrova alone. He knew where to find her. He'd bet money Carver had played it the same way he would have done: keep the bitch safely out of the way then do a man's job by himself.

He got out of the van, stretched his back, ridding his spine of the stiffness brought on by two hours cooped up in a car seat, and walked down the road towards the café.

MI6 agent number D/813318, Grade 5 Officer Tom Johnsen was using his time on surveillance to get to know Jennifer Stock a little better. She hadn't struck him as anything special at first glance. Her face was handsome, rather than pretty. Her manner was friendly, but businesslike, designed to underline the fact that, during working hours at least, she was an agent first and a woman second. He respected that, and he liked the fact that she hadn't let a desire to be taken seriously kill her sense of humour. The longer he spent in the car with Jennifer Stock, the more interested Johnsen became in the woman, rather than the agent.

He was intrigued by the way she underplayed her attraction. She wore no make-up that he could see, and her hair was cut for convenience rather than glamour. She also seemed oblivious of her figure. That might be why it had taken him longer than usual to notice that she had amazing legs and fantastic breasts – not too big, but so round and pert and generally pleased-to-see-you that it was all he could do to look her in the eye. She'd given him a bit of stick about that, but he reckoned he'd got away with it. And it had been Jennifer's idea to act like lovebirds if anyone started looking suspiciously at two people sitting in a car. That had to be encouraging.

They were swapping horror-stories about trying to find a decent home in Switzerland on a measly MI6 allowance when Johnsen saw a man get out of the Swisscom van and head towards the café.

'Hang on a minute, we've got company,' he said, reaching for his camera and firing off a few frames.

'I know that man,' said Jennifer. 'He was hanging around this afternoon, but he was driving a black BMW then. Oh, now this could be interesting . . .'

They watched as he went into the café.

'The other two are still in there, right?' asked Johnsen. 'So, do we follow him in, try to get a closer look?'

Jennifer shook her head. 'That could be tricky. It's tiny in there. If I go in, the guy who runs it's bound to recognize me. And if there's any trouble, we'd have a hard time staying out of the way.'

'Yeah, but we're supposed to find out what's going on with these clowns. And whatever's happening, it's happening in there. Tell you what, I'll take a little recce. Just stand at the door, cast an eye inside. Then I'll come back here, tell you what they're up to, and we'll decide our next move. OK?'

Johnsen already had his hand on the door-handle. By the time she said OK back to him, he'd already thrown his camera carelessly on to the back seat and was out of the car, walking towards the café.

52

They walked into the narrow men's room one at a time. The first man had spiked dyed-red hair, with a straggle of rats' tails, like a punk mullet, flopping on the collar of his black overcoat. He must have pushed the door open with his back because he was spinning round as he came in and there was a MAC-10 sub-machine gun in his hands, another being held by the man behind him. The guns were fitted with Sionics noise-suppressors that would make them virtually silent and far more accurate than the regular short-barrelled MAC. That was the first thing Carver noticed, right about the time he was reaching into his jacket for his SIG. By the time he had his pistol out in front of him, swinging from one man to the next, he'd noticed something else: they weren't firing at him.

If this had been a hit, they'd have come in blasting and he'd have been blown to smithereens long before he'd had a chance to draw. But they were just standing there, looking professionally mean and surly, but also pissed off, like they'd really have enjoyed the opportunity to kill him but were being prevented from doing so. That made sense. Whoever had sent these bozos needed Carver alive. As long as Alix and the computer were out there, it wasn't enough just to take him out. They needed thc full set.

So now Carver had another piece of information to factor into his calculations. He wasn't going to die within the next few seconds. They might be pointing guns at him, but no one was going to start shooting just yet. But if he let them take him, he was in for some hardcore interrogation. Then there was Alix to consider. How long would she be safe at Freddy's place?

The bozos didn't seem to speak English. They just stood there, glowering. The redhead kept blinking. He had a speed-freak's dilated pupils and grey-white pallor, the flesh of his face burned away till his cheekbones, brow and Adam's apple stood out in unnatural relief. Carver could almost hear the humming of his over-stimulated nerve-endings and feel the effort it was taking him to maintain even the semblance of restraint or rationality.

Nothing happened for a few seconds, no onc knowing what the next move should be. Carver had no intention of making any provocative movements, not when a cranked-up crazy with a gun was standing six feet away. Then the other gunman started to move along the gap between the urinals on one wall and the basins on the other. He eased by Carver, staying just out of reach, and took up a position beyond him, making sure Carver couldn't cover both men with just one gun.

The man pointed at Carver's gun and flicked his finger as if to say, 'Hand it over.' Carver looked at him dumbly. The man had a fleshy face, as smooth and stolid as a potato, with small eyes and a bully's full, sulky lips. He gestured again, this time more force-fully, with a greater degree of irritation. 'Oh,' said Carver, all wide-eyed and innocent, 'you want my gun? Well, here it is.'

He threw the SIG-Sauer hard at the potato-man's feet, sending it clattering on to the tiled floor and skittering into his ankles. The piggy eyes looked down for a fraction of a second, and that was long enough for Carver to swivel on his left foot and send his right crash-ing into the man's fleshy jaw. He staggered backwards, absorbing the blow, and Carver moved with him, grabbing the man's right arm and using it as a lever to swing him round, like a dancer twirling his partner, sending him careering across the floor towards his pal with the red hair.

As the two men collided, Carver grabbed the suppressor of the potato-man's MAC and ripped it from his grasp. He pivoted round to face the two men. The redhead hesitated for a fraction of a second, wondering whether to fire, and that brief pause was all Carver needed. He took a single pace forward, holding the gun barrel like a baseball bat, and swung it hard, backhanded, slamming the handle into one round head before his left elbow jerked back the other way, into the speed-freak's face. That movement set Carver up for another backhander with the gun. He put all his strength into the swing, connecting with a crack that shattered bone and sent a spume of snot and blood flying across the room before the man with the punky red hair collapsed unconscious to the ground, right next to his pal.

Carver took a moment to collect his breath. He checked his reflection in the mirror, smoothed down his hair and straightened his clothes. Then he picked his pistol up from the floor, tucked it away and walked back out of the men's room.

When he got back into the pub, Stu the barman was waiting for him.

'You all right, mate? You looked like you were about to chunder.'

Carver smiled ruefully and wiped his hand across his mouth. 'Yeah, I'm fine. But you'd better tell the customers not to go in there for a while. There's a bit of mess on the floor.'

'Anything to do with those two blokes who went in there right after you?'

Carver shrugged. 'Two guys? No, don't think I saw them.'

The Australian grinned. 'Jeez, mate, I'm glad you never picked an argument with me. Listen, the doc's on his way and so are the cops. A couple of the punters insisted on calling 'em. Law-abiding bastards, these Swiss.'

'I'll be off, then.'

'Yeah, that might be an idea. And you'd best drink your Guinness somewhere else for a while, too.'

53

Petrova had spotted him coming into the café and had tried to rise from the table where she'd been hunched over a cup of coffee, feeling sorry for herself. Kursk had seen her like that plenty of times before, filled with self-pity and bemoaning her situation, like every other ungrateful whore. Before she'd even got to her feet he'd wrapped an arm around her throat and was holding her tight enough to choke. She struck out with her arms and heels, but the blows just bounced off Kursk. He didn't even notice them.

There were two men in the room, an old geezer slurping soup at another table and a balding, middle-aged man wearing a white apron behind the serving-counter. Kursk pointed his gun at him, gesturing for him to come out from behind the bar. The man started moving, never taking his eyes off Kursk. When he reached the middle of the room, Kursk gestured again, pointing at the floor. The man got down on his knees, and Kursk stepped over, dragging Alix as easily as a child with a cuddly toy, and stamped on the man's back, forcing him face-down on the ground.

The old geezer hadn't moved. Kursk figured he must be senile. There was no point trying to communicate with him, so he just swung a foot at the man's chair, knocking it out from under him and sending the old boy crashing to the floor. Then Kursk kicked him in the head, just to reinforce the message, and fired a bullet into the floor between the two men. They lay there, the older one moaning incoherently as Kursk put his gun to Alix's head and hissed in her ear.

'You're coming with me, you treacherous bitch. Yuri wants you alive, but just try anything clever and I'll put a bullet through your jaw and smash your pretty face to pieces. You'll live all right, but you'll wish you hadn't. Now, move!'

They started towards the exit, and that was when Tom Johnsen walked up to the doorway. He stopped there for a moment, trying to make sense of what he could see: two men lying on the floor, a third man holding a woman he was threatening with a gun. A coward would have done the smart thing and got the hell out of there. But Johnsen was not a coward. He was a trained agent. He was also a brave man faced with a felon abducting a woman. So he reached for his weapon.

Kursk put two rounds into Johnsen's upper body before he'd even got a hand on his gun, the impact sending him sprawling backwards into the street. Then the Russian turned back to the men on the floor, men who had just become eye-witnesses to a homicide, and shot them point-blank in the back of their skulls, the bullets ripping half their faces off as they exited into the floor.

Alix turned her head and spat in Kursk's face. 'You bastard,' she croaked, gasping for the air to force her words out. 'You didn't have to do that.'

He pounded the pistol into her head, leaving her dazed and barely conscious as he pulled her out of the café. He didn't have to do that, either. But it felt good anyway.

As she watched Tom Johnsen walk up to the café, Jennifer Stock had been thinking about the weird ways in which life threw men and women together. When she got up that morning, she'd had no more expectation of meeting someone new than she'd had of spending the day cooped up in cars doing surveillance. But that was how the day had gone, and that was how she'd found this man.

She liked him, that much was certain. She liked the way he'd smiled when he first opened his car door and let her in. She liked the way the sun had caught the golden hairs on his strong, muscular forearms when he held the steering wheel, his sleeves rolled up as he drove. She liked the way he'd tried and failed not to stare at her breasts, and his guilty-schoolboy look when she'd caught him at it. 'Sorry,' he'd said, shamefacedly. Then he'd perked up and added, 'Still, you look so great it would be rude not to.' She'd tried to be cross, but she'd actually felt ridiculously pleased.

She sighed to herself, knowing where all this would lead and wondering whether the pleasures would be worth the inevitable complications that arose from a relationship with someone else in the service. Then she told herself to stop acting like a silly schoolgirl and start paying attention to her job. And that was when she saw the look of surprise on Tom's face and the two steps he took as he staggered backwards, as if hit by some invisible blow to his body, collapsed and then just lay there motionless in the middle of the street.

What she'd just seen was so far removed from what she'd been thinking that it took Jennifer a couple of seconds to make sense of it all. Then, understanding and horror collided in her brain and she was throwing open the car door, pulling out her gun and racing up the street, crying out the name of the lover she'd never have, concentrating so hard on his dead body that she did not at first register the presence of the other, far bigger man, nor the woman in his grasp.

Then they were standing opposite each other, Jennifer and the killer, and immediately she knew that even though they were both armed, it really made no difference. During her small-arms training, Jennifer had been told that during the Second World War 85 per cent of soldiers never fired their weapons in anger, even when their own lives were threatened. Normal, non-psychotic human beings are overwhelmingly inclined not to kill one another. So the most important psychological element in military training is to overcome that inclination and turn decent people into killers. But in the case of Jennifer Stock, that training hadn't worked. She knew she had to shoot the man in front of her or she herself would be shot, but she just couldn't do it. He knew it, too. She could see it in his eyes, in the tiny twitch of a smile at one corner of his mouth.

Their whole encounter could be counted in seconds on the fingers of one hand, yet it seemed to stretch for hours as the smile spread and his finger tightened on the trigger and the muzzle of his gun flashed and then Jennifer felt herself being picked up by a force stronger than gravity and thrown through the air just like Tom had been. And then she felt nothing at all.

Kursk paused for a moment to be sure that the woman was dead, then continued on his way. When he got to the van he yanked the rear cargo-doors open, picked up Alix and threw her in, locking the doors behind her.

As he walked round towards the driver's door, a flash of movement caught Kursk's eye. He looked across to the far side of the street, up at the end of the road, and saw a man leave the Irish pub. It was Carver.

He spotted Kursk at the same time, and started to run down the street towards him, keeping his head down, his body covered by the line of parked cars as Kursk fired in his direction.

Kursk sheltered behind the van door for a second, waiting to see if any of his men would follow Carver out of the pub. But there was no sign of them. Carver must have taken them out. Now they were one on one again, just like they had been in those Parisian sewers. Kursk didn't like those odds. But he could see another way of getting at the Englishman: the woman lying helpless in his cargo-bay.

Kursk fired two more shots in Carver's direction, just to keep his head down, then leapt into his cab and fired up the engine, flooring the accelerator as he engaged the transmission. He could see Carver ahead of him, running into the street and standing there in the firing position, legs apart, arms outstretched in front of him. But Kursk ignored the bullets as they shattered the windscreen in front of him and ripped into the bodywork at his side. He aimed the van straight at Carver, forcing him to dive out of the way and sideswiping a row of parked cars. The van careered back across the road, but then Kursk regained control of the wheel, sat up in his seat and drove off into the night.

Carver could not catch him now. And if he wanted the woman back, he was going to have to beg.

54

The moment he'd seen the tall, massively built figure standing by the Swisscom van, Carver had known it was Grigori Kursk and realized that he'd made a terrible mistake. He should never have left Alix. Her place of safety had turned out to be a trap.

Now he could do nothing to help her. He dared not fire on the van as it hurtled away. Any shot through the side panelling or rear door could easily hit Alix. He couldn't even aim to blow out the tyres. She was unprotected and unsecured. At the speed Kursk was now driving her body would be battered like a pinball round the vehicle's interior. Carver, of all people, did not need telling that sudden deceleration could be fatal to a passenger.

So what had happened at the café? Carver ran back down the pavement, forcing his way through the knots of people who were already emerging on to the street. Their faces were filled with an anxiety that was rapidly giving way to a greater curiosity, that insatiable desire of human survivors to cast eyes on those who have died. The respectable citizens that Carver shoved out of his path looked like spectators who'd turned up late for a public hanging and felt cheated to have missed out on the big moment.

A dozen or so rubberneckers stood in a circle around two bodies in the street, a man and a woman. Carver recognized them as the couple he'd seen in the blue Vectra. Christ, what had happened here?

Then he heard a single word cried out in a child's high, keening voice: 'Papa-a-a!' Carver forced his way into the café and saw Jean-Louis on his knees, his father's blood splashed all over his Winnie the Pooh pyjamas, shaking Freddy's dead body and crying, 'Wake up, Papa, wake up!'

Carver stepped over to the little boy and picked him up, hugging him to his chest. Suddenly it was all too much. He felt surrounded by death, overwhelmed by loss and racked with guilt for the destruction which seemed to surround him like a contagious disease, afflicting anyone he touched. He felt his chest heave, his breath catch, and then he was staggering to a wall, leaning his back against it and sliding to the floor, the boy still in his arms.

He did not know how long he stayed like that, but the next thing Carver knew, Jean-Louis was being pulled from his grasp. He felt a sharp pain in the side of his leg and dimly realized someone was kicking him and a female voice was screaming, 'How dare you? How dare you hold my son when his father is dead because of you?' Carver opened his eyes and saw Freddy's wife, now his widow, Marianne. He caught a glimpse of a face battered by loss, but eyes within them burning with rage. She bent down and slapped him hard in the face. 'Get up! Get up, you pathetic, useless excuse for a man. My man is dead. Your woman has been taken. Why don't you get up and do something?'

Carver looked up at Marianne, unable to find words to apologize for what he had done. Then he got to his feet and looked down at the blood that covered Dirk Vandervart's shiny suit and his flashy designer shirt. He walked across the room and picked up the bag he'd left there fewer than fifteen minutes earlier, when Freddy had had nothing to fear, when Jean-Louis had still thought his daddy was immortal.

'Anywhere I can get changed? The cops'll be here any moment.'

Marianne opened the door to the stairway, no trace of forgiveness in her face, her voice still harsh and unrelenting. 'Up there,' she said. 'Leave the dirty clothes. I'll get rid of them.' As Carver walked by her, she grabbed his arm. 'You want me to think about forgiving you? Well, find the people who did this and kill them. Kill them all!'

By the time he'd washed the blood from his hands and face and got back into his regular clothes, the police had arrived downstairs and were questioning Marianne and Jean-Louis. Carver wanted to get out, but he needed a hat, something to cover his hair and shade his face. He ransacked Freddy and Marianne's bedroom, searching through chests of drawers and wardrobes until he found an old blue cap emblazoned with the dark red badge of Servette, Geneva's football club, abandoned on a closet floor. He beat it against his thigh to knock out the dust, shoved it on his head, then climbed out of a bedroom window and down a drainpipe into the yard at the rear of the building. Now it was just a matter of acting nice and casual.

He made his way back to the street. There were three police cars and a couple of ambulances jamming the road outside the café. A forensics man was taking pictures of the two bodies. A few feet away there were two other men, having some sort of an argument. They were talking French, but as Carver walked by, he realized one of them was speaking with a pronounced English accent.

'I must insist on being allowed to inspect the bodies,' the man was saying. 'I represent Her Majesty's Government. These were my colleagues. They may be carrying official documents which I must retrieve.'

I bet you must, thought Carver. The only government officials who went on stake-outs in foreign countries were MI6 agents. They'd moved faster than he'd expected. Now he'd have to move faster still.

At the end of the road he stopped by his own car, an Audi RS6 saloon. It looked like a perfectly normal example of Audi's solid, ultra-reliable mid-range model, but appearances were deceptive. Beneath its bland steel-grey exterior lay a 4.2-litre V8 engine that would rocket it up to 60 miles per hour in a shade over four seconds. It had four-wheel drive that clung to the road like iron filings on a magnet. There wasn't a police vehicle in Europe whose driver would give it a second glance; but if any cop ever tried to chase it, he'd discover he couldn't get within glancing distance anyway.

Carver slipped behind the wheel and got the hell out of town.

55

Yuri Sergeyevich Zhukovski did not conform to Carver's image of the stereotypical Russian. He did not look like a gangster. He was physically unimpressive, no more than medium height, with a narrow face, his short, greying hair starting to thin on top. His charcoal suit, white shirt and nondescript patterned tie suggested a man who had no interest whatever in looking fashionable, or making a show of his wealth. He could easily be taken for an intellectual of some kind, an academic, perhaps, or a scientist. His voice was quiet and unassuming. But the steely chill of his grey eyes and the directness of his gaze revealed the truth about his ruthlessness, his ambition and his will to power. If the former Colonel Yuri Zhukovski of the KGB spoke quietly, it was not because he was too meek to shout. It was because he had absolute confidence that his merest whisper would instantly be obeyed.

His day had begun with an eight a.m. meeting in Moscow, discussing the purchase of the last aluminium smelter in Russia that was not yet in his hands. His negotiating tactics were very simple: he named a purchase price, then informed the vendors that if they did not accept it they would be dead within the week. That was the way business worked in the frontier economy of the new Wild East, and it suited Zhukovski very well. Not all his business interests, however, were proceeding quite so smoothly. Not all his partners were quite so open to intimidation.

In the Challenger jet that had flown him to Switzerland that afternoon, Zhukovski had taken a call from an African president. He was an old comrade from communist days, who'd been KGB-tutored in Kiev like so many members of Africa's late-twentieth-century ruling class. But there was nothing comradely about him now. He was trying to renege on a $100 million order. And it wasn't for aluminium.

'My dear Yuri,' intoned the raddled despot, whose holdings in Zurich precisely matched the aid that had poured into his country over the past three decades, down to the last billion, 'as I have explained to you many times in recent weeks, this isn't personal. This is politics. We just can't be seen to be purchasing the type of product you are proposing to sell us.'

He spoke English in a voice that combined the rich musicality of African speech with the languid self-confidence of an English gentleman. After Kiev, he had completed his studies at the London School of Economics. That, too, was typical of his caste.

'I am not proposing anything, Mr President, I am honouring the contract we both signed,' Zhukovski said, patiently.

'A contract signed in very different circumstances, when a very different mood prevailed in western governments. The simple fact is, we have been under intense pressure to alter certain aspects of our defence procurement and strategy. People have even threatened to withhold the aid my people need so desperately.'

Zhukovski's eyes closed in mute frustration as he made his reply. 'Please, Mr President, spare me the heartfelt speeches. We made a deal. I'd be obliged if your nation would stick to it.'

'I'm afraid that will be impossible,' said the president. 'But don't blame me. Blame that damn woman, parading herself in front of all those television cameras.'

'That damn woman is now dead. She won't be in any position to influence anyone any more, and the only cameras she'll be parading in front of will be the ones at her funeral. Everything will soon go back to normal.'

'Well, I hope it does. And if it does, I'll be only too happy to buy your products again, Yuri. But until then, our deal must be postponed. And don't act so outraged. I doubt I'm the only one of your clients who's decided to rethink his plans.'

Zhukovski remained outwardly calm, his voice betraying none of his frustration, let alone his anger. 'As you know, Mr President, my dealings with my clients are always completely confidential.'

'Quite so. Well, send my regards to Irina.'

'And mine to Thandie. Goodbye, Mr President.'

'Goodbye, Mr Zhukovski.'

He closed his eyes and slowed his breathing, calming his mind. He had two more calls to make. One was to a government minister in Moscow, assuring him that his monthly payment would arrive in full and on time. The other was to the senior partner of a Monte Carlo law firm. He represented the family whose patronage had been responsible for Zhukovski's rise from a mid-ranking officer to a multi-billionaire; the family who had allowed and even bankrolled his purchase of State-owned assets at knock-down prices; the family who were still his secret masters. They would need to be reassured that their assets were still secured. They would not hesitate to find another front-man if such assurance was nor forthcoming.

Zhukovski's Bentley had met him at the private airport east of Lake Geneva and whisked him off to the mountain estate just outside Gstaad. He'd been there for almost four hours when he got the message from Kursk. Carver had escaped again, but then Kursk revealed, scarcely able to keep the sadistic glee from his voice, that he'd captured Alexandra Petrova.

Zhukovski could imagine what Kursk would do to Petrova if he were ever given the chance. That time might yet come. But when Kursk pulled up outside the palatial chalet – the Swisscom van absurdly out of place on a driveway intended for supercars and limousines – Yuri Zhukovski had not yet decided what to do with his lovely runaway.

'Alexandra, what a pleasure to see you,' he said as she was led into his study, looking bedraggled and exhausted, and barely able to stand. 'I was wondering when we'd meet again. You look tired. Sit down.' He glanced at a butler hovering at the far side of the room. 'Get her something to eat and drink.' Then he focused his attention back on the woman in the dirty blouse and torn blue skirt, her head bowed, a hand rubbing the bruise at the back of her scalp. 'Now, Alexandra, tell me what you've been up to. Tell me . . . everything.'

Zhukovski's tone could not have been more charming, nor his concern more genuine. But the menace behind the sweetly spoken words was as sharp as a naked blade.

Tuesday, 2 September

56

Carver spent what was left of the night in a Novotel outside Mâcon, eighty-odd miles inside the French border. He'd driven all the way on side roads, staying away from autoroutes, tollbooths and prying official eyes. Along the way, he'd considered what to do next. Every minute that passed put Alix in greater danger. So far as Kursk was concerned, she had betrayed him. His boss would certainly feel the same way. The longer she stayed in their hands, the further away they could take her and the more harm they could do.

Yet he could not afford to take stupid risks. If he wanted to get to Alix, he first had to reach London in one piece, confront Lord Crispin Malgrave and uncover the men behind the Paris conspiracy. But it looked like both the Russian mafia and British intelligence were on to him. By now his description would have been posted at airports, docks and train stations. If he was caught along the way, he'd never get to her at all.

He woke at half past seven and put in a call to Bobby Faulkner. It was an hour earlier in London, but he'd never yet met anyone with small children who slept much beyond dawn. His friend picked up the phone with a sleepy 'Uh, hello?'

Carver got straight to the point. 'Is your line secure?'

Faulkner let out a tired chuckle. 'Morning, Pablo. Two calls in three days, that is an honour. What do you mean, is my line secure?'

'Are you bugged, tapped, under any kind of surveillance?'

'I'm an estate agent these days, Pablo. You'd know that if you'd bothered to stay in touch. So unless the competition are trying to find out if any tasteful three-bed properties in need of minor refurbishment are coming on to the market, no, I'm not bloody bugged. Why do you ask?'

'I need a favour, a big favour. You know, brother-officer kind of thing.'

'The sort I have to do for you on account of all those years we spent fighting side by side, saving each other's arses, getting pissed—'

'Yeah, that kind.'

'You've got a nerve, haven't you? But then, you always did. So, tell me about this favour. I'll make a cup of very strong coffee and try to wake up.'

'OK,' Carver said. 'Do you still have that boat?'

'Ye-e-s,' said Faulkner, cautiously.

'Where do you keep it?'

'Poole, just like the old days. And it's "her" not "it", you should know that. Come on, Pablo, what's this all about?'

'I need to get across the Channel and I don't want to go through any check-ins, customs or passport controls. So that leaves sailing across. And you're the only bloke I know with a thirty-six-foot yacht. So I need you to come and get me. If you're in Poole, I reckon Cherbourg would be the best bet.'

There was a long sigh on the other end of the line, then the clatter of a china mug on a marble worksurface. 'Let me get this straight. You want me to sail solo a minimum of, what, nine hours, assuming the wind and tide are feeling kind, pick you up at Cherbourg, and then spend another nine hours bringing you back? Christ, Pablo, if you're going to be in Cherbourg anyway, take the ferry like any normal human being.'

'No, Bobby, I really can't. And you won't be sailing solo on the way back. I'll be crewing for you.'

'God almighty . . . When's this crossing supposed to take place?'

'Tonight. You'd have to get over there today, and I need to get back under cover of darkness.'

There was a long pause on the other end of the line. Carver heard water being poured into a cup, the rattle of a spoon, then the slurp of a man taking that first hot sip of morning coffee.

'OK, Pablo, what's the story? What kind of trouble are you in?'

'I'm afraid I can't tell you that.'

'Well, you're going to have to. Listen, I'm a married man. I've got a family to think about. I can't go risking my neck just because you call up and ask me for a favour. I have the right to know just how much trouble I'm getting into.'

'Yes,' agreed Carver, 'you have that right. But you really don't want to know what's going on here. If you take me across, I'll say goodbye the moment we get to dry land and I won't get back in touch until this is all over.'

'Until *what* is all over?'

'Until I've sorted out a little personal problem.' Carver thought for a moment, trying to work out how much he could say. 'Listen, Bobby, I've met a girl, the first since Kate who's meant anything to me. I think she might be someone really important in my life.'

Faulkner laughed. 'And you need to get into the country without her husband finding out?'

'I wish. No, she's been kidnapped. Someone grabbed her last night, a Russian. But I don't know where he's taken her and I don't know who he's working for.'

'Where was she when this Russian took her?'

'Geneva.'

Another sip of coffee, then, 'I don't get it. Why do you need to come here?'

'Because the people who gave this bloke his orders, or know who did, are in London. But I don't want them to know I'm on the way. So no credit cards, no customs, no passports.'

There was silence at the far end of the line.

'Well, you in?' asked Carver.

'I think I feel a touch of flu coming on,' said Faulkner.

'Are you saying you're not well enough to help?'

'No, I'm saying I'll call in sick at work. Can you get to the yacht-basin at Cherbourg by nine this evening, local time?'

'Yeah.'

'Great. See you there, then.'

'Thanks, Bobby, I owe you.'

'Oh yeah, you do.'

Bobby Faulkner didn't enjoy telling his wife he was disappearing for the next twenty-four hours, minimum, leaving her to cope with the baby while he did a favour for a man neither of them had seen for three years. Wives did not, by and large, believe that a husband's loyalty to the men he'd served with should exceed his loyalty to his women and children. Bobby could see that Carrie had a point, a bloody big point, but he also knew that the honour codes that bound brother-officers were unbreakable.

It was perfectly obvious that Pablo Jackson was in serious, possibly criminal, trouble, but that made no difference. Faulkner had known old comrades who'd ended up in jail before now. You turned up at court to give them moral support, kept an eye on their families while they were inside and threw a bloody great party when they got out. And you did it because you knew that if the positions were ever reversed they'd do the same for you.

So he gritted his teeth and endured Carrie's anger, her tears, and then her icy silence. But he did at least promise her that he wouldn't set off on Pablo's hare-brained scheme alone. So he put in a call of his own.

'Hello, Quentin,' he said when he was put through.

'Bobby, dear boy, what can I do for you?'

'I just had a call from Pablo Jackson. Did he get through to you the other day? I gave him your number.'

'No. Pamela said he'd rung the house, but I never heard from him.'

'I think he's in a bit of bother.'

Faulkner explained the situation, and ended with a request for help. 'I'd be bloody grateful for a hand on the boat. It would make the crossing a lot easier.'

Trench laughed. 'So we'd reverse our old positions, eh? You'll be my skipper and I your humble crew.'

'I wouldn't put it like that, QT.'

'Don't worry, just pulling your leg. I've got a couple of meetings today, but nothing my secretary can't reschedule. Where do you need me?'

'Poole Yacht Club, ten o'clock. My boat's the *Tamarisk*, a Rustler 36. I'll be onboard. Just step on deck and we'll be off.'

'Well, then, no time to waste talking. See you there.'

Carver hadn't eaten since lunch the previous day. He did some serious damage to the Novotel's breakfast buffet, paid his bill in cash, then stopped at a petrol station and filled the Audi's tank to the brim. He had a little over twelve hours to drive from the eastern edge of France to its north-west coast. On the autoroutes that would have been a breeze, but he had to stick to minor roads clogged with traffic and interrupted by countless small provincial towns. His car's performance wouldn't be much help if he was stuck behind tractors, trucks and old Citroëns. He needed to be on his way.

57

'Have you made the calls?'

Bill Selsey looked at his colleague with sympathy in his eyes – sympathy and an intense gratitude that he'd not been the one who'd had to do every senior officer's least favourite job.

'Yeah.' Jack Grantham looked drained of his usual air of purpose. 'She was an only child, you know. Her parents' pride and joy. A First at Cambridge, a glittering career. All that was missing was the husband and children. The worst thing is, the parents have no idea what their kid's really been up to. At least if your boy's in the army you know there's always the chance of bad news. But these people were sitting there thinking their little girl had a safe diplomatic job in Switzerland. And who the hell ever gets killed in Switzerland?'

'How did you explain it? Car crash?'

'Yeah, the usual: a hit-and-run, tragic accident, death was instantaneous, she didn't suffer. All that bollocks.'

'I got you a coffee.'

Selsey handed over a white plastic cup filled with an indeterminate brown liquid. Grantham took a drink and grimaced.

'Bloody hell, that's awful.'

'Some things don't change,' said Selsey. 'New HQ, same old rubbish coffee.'

Grantham managed a bitter laugh. He drank some more, then shook his head.

'It wasn't meant to be like this. I told them, just watch, don't get involved.'

'I know,' agreed Selsey. 'I said the same thing. Told her to be careful. Are we sure yet, how it all happened?'

'Pretty much. Murcheson, the other lad from Berne, spent all night with the Geneva police. He's seen all their forensic evidence, read the witness statements. Johnsen was taking photographs right up to the moment he decided to get involved. It seems pretty clear that our Russian friend from the black BMW, the one we think killed Papin, had managed to swap vehicles. He'd got hold of a telephone company van and was using it to watch one of the properties on the street. Presumably it was the place Papin had led him to, where the Paris crew were hiding out. So he's watching that and we're watching him and everything's tickety-bloody-boo until for no good reason anyone can work out, the Russian decides on a change of plan and goes into this café.'

'Maybe he just fancied a decent cup of coffee?'

'Well, I can sympathize with him there. But there must have been more to it than that because Johnsen took it upon himself to go up to the café himself, and by the time he got there the Russian had grabbed a young woman – identity unknown, by the way – and was dragging her out the door. Then Johnsen decides to do his knight in shining armour act and gets shot for his pains. So then the Russian starts shooting witnesses, two in the café and Stock, who'd come rushing up the road when she saw her partner go down.'

'What a bloodbath. Still, one can't help wondering about this mystery woman, the one who got abducted. The Russian must have wanted her very badly if he was prepared to kill four people without blinking. And he didn't kill *her*, you'll note.'

'Not yet, no.'

'So she's the key to it.'

'Well, she's part of the key, certainly. Because there's something else.' Grantham was picking up speed now, finding new reserves of energy. 'At almost exactly the same time as the Russian was shooting people left, right and centre at the café, there was another fight going on up the road at an Irish pub.'

'Good grief. Sounds more like Dodge City than Geneva.'

'I know, but here's the interesting thing. There were three victims of this pub brawl and they were all Russian, all carrying diplomatic passports. They wouldn't say a dickie-bird about what happened. But they were all armed with sub-machine guns and they were all taken out by one man, before they could fire a shot.'

Selsey gave a whistle of admiration. 'Sounds like an impressive chap.'

'Yes, and this same mystery man was next seen running down the street shooting a pistol of his own. And guess what his target was?'

'Don't tell me, the Russian?'

'You got it. The Russian, driving away in his van, presumably with the woman stuck in the back. So what does that tell you?'

'That the mystery man and the mystery woman were both being chased by the same bunch of Russians.'

'And the Russians got their information from Pierre Papin, who was trying to flog us a lead to the people who killed the princess. Which means . . .'

Selsey had no trouble finishing the sentence: 'That if we find the mystery duo, we've got our killers.'

'Exactly.'

'Maybe those poor bloody kids didn't die entirely in vain.'

'Somehow, Bill, I don't think that will bring much comfort to their parents.'

Neither man knew what to say next. Before either could think of anything, the phone rang. Grantham picked it up. He listened to the voice on the other end of the line for a few seconds, frowning at what he heard. Then he said, 'Hang on a second,' and gestured at Bill Selsey, pointing at something on his desk. 'Pass me that pad, quick, and a biro.' Selsey handed them over and Grantham started writing, his phone pressed between his shoulder and his ear.

Finally he put the ballpoint down and transferred the phone to his hand. 'Thanks, Percy, I really appreciate this. As you may know, this all got personal for us last night. Anyway, well done. You've come up trumps once again.'

Grantham put the phone down and suddenly his face, so miserable a few minutes earlier, was wreathed in a beaming grin. 'We've got them! Percy Wake seems to have persuaded his contacts that they need to be a bit more helpful. They've handed over two names. Surprise, surprise, it's a man and a woman. And I'm going to have them if it's the last thing I do.'

58

'Bugger!'

Bobby Faulkner stood helplessly in the cockpit of the 36-foot yacht the *Tamarisk*, his hand on the starter-button of its Yanmar diesel engine, listening to the spluttering cough of a motor that didn't want to start. A mocking jeer came from his crewman, Samuel Carver, standing at the bow of the boat, a line in his hand, waiting to cast off.

'Don't tell me you forgot to fill her up!'

It felt like old times to Carver, going off on a mission with Bobby and QT. He'd spent all day with nothing to drag his mind away from Alix, driving himself crazy trying to work out what had happened to her, trying not to dwell too long on what her captors might be doing to her.

Along the way, he'd put in a call to Thor Larsson, received a one-word progress report on the computer decryption – 'slow' – and asked him for a final piece of technical assistance. 'I want to ruin their day,' he'd said. Now he was back in a familiar routine, using banter and mockery to push fear to one side, finding comfort in the unspoken affection that underpins male friendships.

Faulkner called back, 'Piss off! The tank's full, there's just a bit of sludge in the fuel-line. Should clear all right. It always does.'

Another, older voice spoke up from the stern of the boat, three or four feet behind Faulkner: 'Fear not. It was just as feeble when we left Poole. But we got underway eventually.'

Carver grinned at the sound of his old commanding officer's voice, feeling reassured by his presence, happy that for once someone else was looking out for him. The old man must be in his late fifties by now, but he still looked pretty much as Carver remembered him: quite short, stockily built but brimming with bullish energy. There were probably a few more pounds round Trench's waist, and the lines on his ruddy face were etched a bit deeper, but time would do that to any man. There were dark smudges round his eyes, too, but Trench had explained them away soon enough: 'I was off shooting in Scotland over the weekend with some old chums. We swore we wouldn't stay up drinking and talking all night. Told one another we were getting too old to go to bed at three and be out on the moor by eight. And then we did it all over again. Typical!'

Faulkner disappeared into the bowels of the boat to fiddle about with the engine. The other two men returned to the boat's open cockpit. They sat down opposite each other on the cushioned benches that curled around its sides, interrupted only by the hatch on the forward side that opened on to a ladder down into the boat's cabin.

Trench leaned forward, his elbows resting on his thighs. 'So,' he began, with the look of an affectionate uncle amused by his nephew's latest scrapes, 'Bobby tells me you've got yourself a sexy new mail-order bride.'

Carver hadn't been expecting that. 'Sorry?'

Trench chuckled. 'Forgive me, dear boy. Inappropriate comment. You must be under terrible pressure, with this Russian girl of yours going missing. I was just trying to bring a touch of levity to the situation, a little joke about the way most ladies from her neck of the woods find a chap in the west. Wrong move, obviously.' He cleared his throat, then tried again. 'So, tell me about this girl. I gather she's the real thing.'

Carver grimaced. He didn't feel in the mood for a heart-to-heart conversation.

'Maybe . . . but you never know, do you?'

'I should have thought that was the whole point. You know instantly. I did, when I met Pamela. Took one look at her and thought, "Bloody hell, she's a cracker." '

'OK, yeah, that's part of it. But it's not that simple. You feel a certain way, but you can't necessarily trust that feeling. You can't be sure what she's thinking. You don't know what she wants, or what's going to happen between you. Can't be sure of anything, basically.'

The older man sighed. 'Goodness me, that's not the dashing young officer I used to know. You were always decisive, confident, absolutely sure of yourself and your men. You didn't sit around worrying all day. You just got on with the job in hand.'

'That's because I knew what the job was. I had orders, I knew my targets and there was a specific definition of success. That stuff was easy. This stuff isn't.'

Trench nodded. 'Then let's stick to specifics. What's this female's name? Age? Description?'

'Alexandra Petrova; just about to turn thirty; maybe five-eight tall; weighs around a hundred and thirty pounds; blonde hair, blue eyes.'

'Bloody hell,' repeated Trench, 'she is a cracker.'

'Yeah, but there's a lot more to it than that.'

'How do you mean?'

'She just gets it. And I think I get her. We've got a lot in common, stuff most people wouldn't understand.'

'Such as?'

'Such as things that are private and none of anyone else's business.'

The older man nodded again. 'Touché. Quite right. That sort of thing is best kept private, eh?'

Faulkner emerged through the hatch with a determined look on his face. He glanced at the two other men.

'Not interrupting, am I?'

'It's fine,' said Carver. 'We're done. So, is this boat any closer to moving?'

'Absolutely,' said Faulkner, with a triumphant smile. 'Like a rocket. Gentlemen, return to your positions, if you please.'

He waited while the two men went to either end of the boat and picked up their lines, then pressed the starter again. The engine coughed, spluttered, gave a couple of encouraging chugs, then died away again. 'Damn!' muttered Faulkner. He pressed again, and again. On the fourth attempt, the engine finally sprang into life. The lines were cast off, Carver and Trench returned to the cockpit, and the boat moved away from the finger pontoon to which it had been tied.

Slowly, Faulkner picked his way down a narrow channel between the bobbing hulls and gently swaying masts of the other yachts moored at the thousand berths of Port Chantereyne, Cherbourg's yacht marina, the largest on the entire French coastline. Within a few minutes they'd reached the relatively open water of the Petite Rade, Cherbourg's inner harbour.

Faulkner pointed back towards the shore. 'See over there, near that bloody great ferry? That's the ocean-liner quay. The *Titanic* tied up there, just before she set off to meet that iceberg.'

He pushed open the throttle and took the engine up to full speed as they passed a huge circular fortification and moved into the outer harbour, the Grande Rade. The harbours were enclosed by giant sea-walls, and another castle guarded the final opening into the English Channel.

'Get to work, chaps,' said Faulkner. 'Time to get our sails rigged.'

Soon, the two great white triangles of the mainsail and the jib were outlined against the darkening sky, and for a few moments Carver was lost in the glorious freedom of a yacht meeting the open sea, heeling away from the breeze. Faulkner turned off the engine, and now the only noise came from the flapping of the sails, the gentle creaking of lines under pressure and the rush of water and air. Away to the north, black clouds were massing on the horizon. Carver tapped Faulkner on the shoulder and pointed towards them.

'That doesn't look too friendly,' he said.

'Cold front coming down from the Arctic,' Faulkner replied. 'It's due to hit us some time in the next two or three hours. The wind's westerly now, force four. It's going to veer to the north and freshen to five or six, maybe seven at times. Pretty blowy, but don't worry, the Rustler can handle it, and the tides are in our favour most of the way. Still, there's rain forecast too, so it won't be pleasant. I've got a spare pair of waterproofs stowed under the bed in the bow-cabin. You can use those. Might as well get them on now, while you've got the chance.'

Carver went below. He made his way through the Rustler's cramped main cabin, squeezing past the galley and on between a wooden table and a seating area till he came to a plain wooden door. It opened into an even tighter space, most of which was occupied by a sleeping area shaped like a mutilated triangle, squeezed into the bow of the boat. The mattresses were hinged by the hull of the boat and lifted up to reveal storage spaces below. Carver rummaged around until he found a pair of orangey-red waterproof trousers and a matching windcheater jacket. The jacket was built to keep out a hurricane, with a collar that zipped all the way to Carver's chin, and wristbands fastened by Velcro.

As he tightened them up, he thought about the two other men on the boat, how the apparently casual, even amateurish appearance both presented to the world hid huge reserves of courage, competence and, when necessary, ruthlessness. He thought back to all the times they had given, taken and passed on instructions, about the precision with which they were trained to recall and repeat what was said to them. They all knew the devastating effect even tiny misunderstandings could create in times of war.

Carver went back over all that had been said and he knew that he had been betrayed. He wondered whether both of his old comrades had been in this together. One of them he knew now was an enemy; the other might yet be an innocent dupe. So what did that make him? A dupe, certainly, but hardly innocent. The pieces of a puzzle that had been jumbled in his mind began to fall into place, and a picture emerged. It was a portrait of himself, but it was hardly flattering. It showed a man who had been fooled, not once but repeatedly; a man who had extended his trust to a tiny handful of people and chosen the wrong ones every time. One of these days, if he lived that long, he would go back over it all in his mind and work out, not where he had gone wrong – that was now obvious – but why. These men had been his friends, his brothers-in-arms. Once they had been willing to risk their lives for him. What had he done since then to make them want to betray him? Perhaps you didn't have to do anything. His mother had given him up just for being born.

He'd dealt with that. He could deal with this.

So, where would the battle take place? A yacht in a storm was a lousy place for a fight. It was cramped, it was constantly pitching and rolling in all three dimensions, and everyone onboard was wearing wet, bulky clothing. Sticking a gun in a set of waterproofs was no problem. Getting it out in a hurry was a lot trickier. And standing steady enough to take an accurate shot would be damn near impossible.

The key point was the hatch and the ladder between the cockpit up on deck and the cabin down below. Anyone caught there would be a sitting duck. The next few hours would consist of an unacknowledged jockeying for position in which two, maybe all three of the men onboard would silently compete to be in the right place when the moment finally came for one of them to show his hand. Meanwhile, Carver intended to stack the odds in his favour.

Stashed away in the same storage space as the weatherproof clothing Carver found what he'd need later. For now, though, he was going to keep things nice and civil, as if he still thought they were all good friends. Them against the world, just like the good old days.

He walked back to the cockpit hatch and stuck his head through. 'Anyone fancy a cup of coffee?'

He took the orders and put the kettle on the galley's gas-stove. He filled three mugs, added milk and sugar, and went back up on deck. Now there was one last task.

The yacht's mast was supported by ropes, or shrouds, that

stretched up to its top from the side of the hull. They were kept taut, away from the side of the mast, by two horizontal spars, or spreaders. A white plastic pot, about eighteen inches high, had been hoisted up to the port-side spreader. The pot was a radar-reflector, designed to ensure that the yacht's position was known to passing vessels. It was secured by a line tied to a cleat at the bottom of the mast.

Carver made his way over to the cleat. He loosened the line, held it in his hand and called back to the cockpit, 'Sorry, Bobby, this has got to go.'

'What are you talking about?' shouted Faulkner.

'I can't be on anyone's radar screen.'

'Have you gone totally mad? We're about to do a night crossing of one of the world's busiest shipping lanes. Five hundred ships sail along or across the Channel every day, and if any one of them so much as touches us it'll be like an elephant stepping on a matchbox. We'll sink. And then you'll never enter the bloody country at all. Nor will the rest of us.'

An affable, who-cares grin broke over Carver's face. 'Then we'll just have to keep our eyes open, won't we?'

59

Alix was alone in the darkness. They had treated her well enough so far. The first night, Yuri had let her sleep in peace. That had surprised her. It wasn't his usual technique. During the day that followed, the questions were insistent but polite, even civilized. How did she meet the man? Why did she go with him? Why hadn't she killed him? Had she even tried? Since she had let him live, what had she learned from him? Where was the computer? And what had she given away?

Only that last question had been asked with any undercurrent, Yuri barely bothering to disguise the implication that more than information was at stake. Still, she had not been mistreated. The chalet staff had treated her with a distant familiarity, more like an occasional guest than a prisoner. She had been served the same food as everyone else, been allowed to drink the same wine.

But all the while she'd known it couldn't stay this way for ever. Sooner or later, Yuri Zhukovski's patience would run out. He'd want answers to darker, deeper questions and he wouldn't care how much he had to do to her to get them. Sooner or later, he would grow bored of simple conversation and resort to the physical methods that would tell him what he needed to know.

Yuri was operating under intense pressure, that much was obvious. A crisis was brewing somewhere in the vast web of corporations that formed his business empire. He had spent hours shut away in his study calling his most senior associates and negotiating with clients, while Alix was left under Kursk's icy supervision, his eyes following her every movement with an unbroken, implacable hatred, not just for her personally (though that was enough) but everything she represented. Whenever Yuri emerged to continue his interrogation, she could see the stress that gripped him in the grinding tension of his jaw and the obsessive clenching and releasing of his fists. She would pay for that tension, she was certain. He would let it loose on her.

Eventually she had been ordered upstairs and left by herself in a heavily shuttered room until he was ready to deal with her. She had little idea how long she had spent trying to prepare for what was bound to come. It might have been one hour, it might just as easily have been three. Time seemed to move at a different speed in that velvety darkness.

And then she heard footsteps in the corridor outside. She knew what they meant. She took a deep breath, forcing herself to stay calm, focusing on her pounding heart and slowing her pulse as she let her breath go. She must stay still now, stay silent. There would be screaming enough in the hours to come.

60

Magnus Leclerc had been given a number to call in case of emergency. He'd been told it was very unlikely that anyone would complain about the phoney money transfer. But just in case, there were people who'd want to know about it. And they'd be very grateful for the information.

It wasn't easy to summon up the courage. He'd had a lot to think about.

If he were exposed, as Vandervart had threatened, it would destroy his marriage. The more he thought about it, the less that looked like a problem. He'd be rid of Marthe for good, and the only thing he felt about that was relief. He'd lose his job, too, of course, and the status that came with it. There'd be a certain amount of humiliation, even mockery, to be endured. But underneath, he knew, plenty of his banking peers would be thinking that they'd have liked a crack at the sexbomb in the white lingerie. They'd say old Magnus was a sly old dog, didn't know he had it in him. He'd be back in business within months.

Or maybe not. Maybe he'd just stick a finger up at all of them and fly away to the Cayman Islands. He'd spent years quietly saving, skimming and pocketing money. He could spend the rest of his life on a beach if he felt like it.

Put it like that, and there didn't seem much to be lost by talking. But what if he kept his mouth shut?

There was a reason Vandervart had wanted Malgrave's number. He obviously wanted his money, by any means necessary. That was going to cause big, big trouble. Sooner or later, people would work out that Leclerc had been the root cause of that trouble. And they wouldn't be happy. He did not like to think how they would react. Then again, he did not believe for one moment that Vandervart would stop at sending a few videos to the media if he felt he had been betrayed.

The possibilities spun round and round in Leclerc's head in spiralling permutations. He spent a sleepless night in the spare room, then went into work still unsure of his next move. Finally, he came to a conclusion. He dialled two numbers. One was the number Malgrave had given him.

A woman's voice answered. 'Consortium. How can I help you?'

He was put through to a man who spoke in a courtly English accent. The man thanked Leclerc profusely for his information, then asked him where he could be contacted, later in the day, 'just in case we need to ask you any further questions, check the details of what this man Vandervart was after, that sort of thing'. Leclerc was eager to be as helpful as possible. He provided his phone numbers and his home address. He wanted the man to appreciate how sorry he was about the Vandervart problem. He did everything he could to make up for his carelessness. The man was most understanding. 'I sympathize with you, monsieur,' he said. 'You have been through a terrible ordeal. Anyone would have reacted the same way.'

When he put down the phone, Leclerc was sweating. He wiped his forehead and loosened his tie. Then he called a second number. It belonged to a travel agent. He asked for the earliest flight to Miami. The agent booked him first class on the next morning's British Airways flight to London, Heathrow, connecting there with the lunchtime departure for Miami. Leclerc used his company credit card.

He went home that evening after work and tried to act normally. The arguments were no worse than usual, the silences between them no more deafening. They were sitting in the lounge after dinner, Leclerc lying back in his leather recliner watching a badly dubbed American cop show on the TV, when the doorbell rang. He grabbed the remote control and turned the sound down on the TV. The bell rang three more times, harder and more insistently. 'Go and answer it,' he ordered Serge, a sullen, gangly boy of seventeen who was the younger of his two children. The kid remained motionless in his chair, letting everyone know how much he resented this intrusion into his busy schedule of sitting around, before hauling himself to his feet. He slammed the door as he left the room and stalked into the entrance hall.

Leclerc craned his head in the direction of the front door. He heard it open. He heard his son say 'Who . . . ?' and then he heard a cracking sound like a cross between a bat hitting a ball and an eggshell cracking against a bowl. Then came the muffled thud of something heavy flopping down on to the floor.

Marthe was the first to react. She leapt from her seat and was halfway to the door into the hallway when it opened and two men walked into the room. They had pump-action shotguns in their hands. There was blood on the butt of one of the guns.

The first man through the door had fiery, spiky orange-red hair. He almost collided with Marthe in the middle of the living-room floor, barely breaking stride as he swung his knee into her midriff. Marthe bent double, soundlessly, the air knocked out of her, and he shoved her backwards, sending her skittering into the wall. Leclerc's daughter Amelie, a thin, plain young woman of nineteen, screamed. The second man, round-faced and full-lipped, punched her in the mouth to shut her up then threw her across the room. She ended up in a heap next to her mother.

No more than five seconds had passed since the men entered the room. Leclerc was still stuck in his recliner, watching helplessly as his womenfolk were attacked. He struggled to his feet, his eyes widening as one of the men swung his shotgun round until it was pointing at his guts. The other had his weapon aimed at the two women, huddled together against the far wall.

The two men glanced at each other. The red-haired man gave a quick, commanding jerk of his head. And then they both started firing.

Wednesday, 3 September

61

The cold front hit just after midnight, the weather changing as suddenly as the channels on a TV. One moment they were sailing smoothly towards their destination with a fresh, mild wind blowing on a beam reach from the west, directly across their northerly course; the next, the air was 10 degrees colder and the wind had shifted 45 degrees to the north, picked up speed and filled with stinging rain that beat down with an incessant intensity. The angry new wind picked fights with everything it met. It drove into a sea that was flowing down the Channel on an ebb tide, piling the rolling swell into shorter, steeper waves that crashed into the boat, tossing it, bouncing it, dropping it like a toy.

There was no point in all three of them staying on deck, so they agreed a roster of two-hour watches. The course was set by auto-helm. Whoever was topside simply had to keep an eye out, ready to override the system and take the helm if the need arose. Carver went first; Trench volunteered to go second. That way, Faulkner could take an uninterrupted break till it was time for his watch. He needed the rest. He'd spent well over twelve hours at the helm. By the time his watch was over it would almost be dawn. They'd all get up then.

Carver didn't expect any trouble during his time on duty. When he was standing in the cockpit, anyone wanting to attack him would have to climb up a ladder and through the hatch, coming out of the light into the darkness. Unless he fell asleep at the tiller, no one was going to overpower him that way. He'd be vulnerable only when he went back down below deck.

At the end of his watch, Carver stepped up to the hatch, gripped the top then swung his legs through, missing the ladder completely and jumping straight down into the cabin. He landed in a crouch on the heaving floor. Trench was sitting on the edge of the main table in the centre of the cabin.

'Bloody hell,' he said coolly. 'That was a bit dramatic.' There was a mug in his hand. 'Hot toddy,' he said, holding it up appreciatively. 'You should try some. We left some for you in a Thermos. It's in the galley.' Trench then nodded to his left, where Bobby Faulkner was stretched out on a settee. 'Fast asleep. Poor chap was absolutely shattered.'

'Think I'll crash too,' said Carver. 'Anyway . . . your turn. Good luck. It's bloody cold and wet up there.'

Trench grimaced and said, 'Great,' just like any man about to go out into foul weather. He made his way past Carver and put his mug in the galley sink. He showed no outward signs of tension or even alertness, yet he never completely turned his back as he scuttled up the ladder and out into the cockpit, pulling the hatch closed behind him as he went.

Carver let him go. Trench might just have been inviting an attack. And there was no guarantee Faulkner was really asleep. He didn't want to find himself fighting both men at once.

He picked up the Thermos and poured himself a mug of toddy, savouring the steamy fumes of brandy, honey, lemon and tea. But just as he was about to take the first sip he was distracted by a clack of hard plastic from the cabin floor. There were two mugs down there, knocking into each other. Faulkner must have had a drink too.

And now he was lying unconscious, passed out on the settee. Carver went over and shook him hard, but there was no response.

Well, that settled one thing. It would be a straight fight, Trench against Carver, master against pupil. And by the time Bobby Faulkner awoke from his drugged stupor only one of them would be alive to greet him.

62

The *Scandwave Adventurer* was longer than three football fields laid end to end. It weighed around 100,000 tons and it could carry over six thousand standard shipping containers at a speed of more than 25 knots. That made it around fourteen thousand times heavier than Faulkner's yacht and a little over three times as fast. The combination of size, weight and speed also made it about as manoeuvrable as a runaway steamroller.

Knowing all this, its designers had given their vessel every possible assistance. It had state-of-the-art radar, satellite tracking and telecoms equipment. The skipper knew the precise position of his ship on the surface of the globe. He could track every other ship for miles around. In shallow waters he could map the precise contours of the ocean-floor beneath him, making it virtually impossible to run aground. As the men who managed the Scandwave Shipping Corporation regularly told themselves, no one needed experienced crew these days. The technology sailed the damn boat all by itself.

So when the wind changed that night and the cold, biting rain came in from the north, the watchman posted on the exposed, narrow deck, high up in the icy air beside the bridge, did not stand up proud and tall, exposing himself to the bitter blast, because that was his duty and he was proud to do it. No, he sat right down, with his back against the deck's low steel wall, cupped his hands to make a tiny shelter from the wind, and lit a cigarette. He was damned if he was going to get cold and wet on the pittance they were paying him, when the rain was so heavy he could barely see the bow of his own ship, let alone anything further out to sea. And besides, there was a guy sat by the radar screen. Let him watch out for passing traffic.

And so it was that the *Scandwave Adventurer*, bound from Rotterdam to Baltimore, sailed west down the English Channel with its load of six thousand containers. Meanwhile, the yacht *Tamarisk*, bound from Cherbourg to Poole, sailed due north, across the English Channel, with its load of three tired men. And neither had the faintest idea of the other's existence.

63

Part of Carver wanted to front up to Trench and ask him what had really happened, why he'd acted the way he had. But even if the old bastard told the truth, he wouldn't say anything Carver couldn't work out for himself. Whoever had been hiring Carver for the past few years must have already put Trench on the payroll while he was still commanding the service. It made sense. He was the perfect recruiting officer and Carver had been the perfect candidate for an assassin's job: capable, well trained and sufficiently angry and disillusioned to get his hands dirty for the right price.

There was no point feeling sorry for himself. He'd been bought and paid for. Once he'd outlived his usefulness, Trench had planned to dispose of him, just like any other redundant piece of kit. It wouldn't be the first time Trench had sent men on suicide missions. Any commanding officer had to be willing to sacrifice lives for the greater good. Carver could moan all he liked about betrayal, he could play the wounded child wondering why Daddy was being so beastly to him, but Trench hadn't asked to be his surrogate father even if he'd been happy to exploit the feelings Carver projected on to him.

In any case, Carver concluded, he'd spent his entire working life being paid to kill people. He wasn't in any position to complain if someone wanted to kill him.

But he didn't have to let them get away with it.

There was a deep pocket in Carver's waterproof jacket. It was sealed by a vertical zip, and it ran right down the left side of his chest. In it were two plastic tubes a little less than a foot long. They were coloured red at their base, then lightened via an orange band to a yellow top decorated with a silhouette of an archer standing on top of a logo that read IKAROS. At the bottom of the tube there was a red plastic tag.

Carver took one out and moved to the side of the ladder. He reached up and pulled the hatch open with one hand, letting in a blast of spray-soaked air and the crashing, pounding noise of the storm. Then he lifted up his other hand, holding the tube horizontally, level with the deck outside. He pulled the tag. There was a sudden propulsive 'Whoosh!' like a firework being launched, then a man's shout of alarm, the scrabble of ricochets on the sides of the cockpit as the tube shot to and fro, and finally, less than a second later, the explosion of a distress-flare.

As thick red smoke roiled through the open hatch, Carver hurled himself up the ladder, through the opening and into the hellish scarlet fog. Ahead of him he could just make out the outline of a man. He saw his arm being raised, then came the flame of muzzle-flashes and the crackle of small-arms fire as Trench fired into the smoke, towards the hatch. Three rounds slammed into the wooden door-frame, somehow missing Carver on their way, and then Carver crashed into Trench's midriff, pushing him backwards on to the bench at the back of the cockpit.

Carver drove his right fist as hard as he could into Trench's groin. His left hand reached out for Trench's right, driving it against the side of the cockpit in a desperate attempt to knock the pistol from his grasp. The two men were fighting the smoke as much as each other, almost as if they were underwater, unable to breathe, desperate for oxygen, lost in a primal struggle for survival.

At last, Carver felt Trench's grip slacken on his gun. Ignoring

Trench's desperate attempts to hit him with his free hand, and the swiping of the older man's legs, he forced his right hand between Trench's fingers and the handle of his gun. He caught hold of one of the loosened fingers and bent it back, making Trench cry out in agony as the lowest joint was dislocated. The gun fell to the deck and skittered away across the bucking, rain-slick surface.

Carver scrambled to his feet, his chest heaving and eyes streaming with tears. Trench was sitting in front of him, holding his wounded hand, coughing and gasping for breath. The older man tried to get up, but Carver hit him twice, left and right to the face, putting the full power of his shoulders behind each punch. Then he grabbed a handful of Trench's grey hair and smashed his head against the wooden rim that ran round the top edge of the cockpit's perimeter, three savage blows that left Trench semi-conscious and bleeding.

Carver grabbed the front of Trench's jacket and hauled him into an upright position on the bench.

'Sit on your hands,' he commanded.

Wincing with pain, Trench forced his hands under his thighs.

The flare was still spewing out smoke, though the relentless gale was now blowing it away in a billowing red plume. For a second, the air around Carver cleared and he was able to drag some pure, clean sea-air into his burning lungs.

'Where is she?' he snarled.

Trench looked at him through bleary, unfocused eyes. 'Where's who?'

Carver slapped him once, hard, to the side of the face.

'Alexandra Petrova, that Russian girl of mine you were going on about. Big mistake, that. Gave yourself away. Now, where is she?'

'Christ, her . . . I haven't a clue.'

This time Carver caught him with a backhander.

'I mean it,' Trench insisted. 'I knew nothing about the Russians. They weren't my idea.'

'So who's idea were they?'

A weary, battered smile appeared on Trench's face. He was

leaning slightly forward, his mouth hanging open, still struggling for breath.

'I taught you everything you know about resisting interrogation, dear boy. Do you seriously think you're going to make me talk now?'

Carver looked Trench in the eye. 'No,' he said. 'I don't.'

'So now what are you going to do?'

The question took Carver aback. He realized he did not have an answer. And in that fraction of a second's indecision Trench struck, drawing his knees up to his chest and then driving his legs forward into Carver's body, catapulting him across the deck.

At that moment a wave hit the *Tamarisk* amidships, spraying the two men with foaming water and bucking the deck upwards and sideways. As he staggered backwards, Carver lost his footing and fell helplessly to the deck.

His head landed by a small black object lying on the cold, wet wood. As the boat lurched again, he realized that it was Trench's gun and it was sliding past him, back across the deck, back to the man who wanted to kill him.

Carver's old commander – his teacher, his role model – picked up the gun with his one good hand and swung his arm round to take his shot. His eyes glittered with fierce, gleeful triumph, then widened in a momentary flicker of shocked surprise as Carver fired the second emergency flare.

The rocket hit Quentin Trench in the face, the plastic tube driving up through his palate into his brain and sending him sliding across the narrow stern-deck and over the side of the boat before the flare itself detonated, blowing his skull apart in a starburst of blood, brain, searing light and bubbling smoke.

And as the flare cast its gory light across the water, illuminating everything in its path, Samuel Carver saw the gigantic bow of the *Scandwave Adventurer* bearing down on him, an unstoppable wall of black steel, as vast and irresistible as an avalanche.

64

The 100,000-ton container ship was no more than two hundred metres away, its hull looming high over the top of *Tamarisk*'s mast, its superstructure lost to sight in the teeming rain, far beyond the glow from the flare. The ship was moving as fast as the weather would allow, forcing through the waves as if they were no bigger than ripples on a pond. Carver knew at once that even if the blazing flares had alerted the ship's crew to the presence of the yacht sailing directly across their path, it was far too late for them to change course or speed.

He had around twenty seconds before the *Scandwave Adventurer* smashed into the side of the yacht. Carver gathered his senses. It wasn't too late. If he could start the engine and loosen the sails, he could steer straight into the wind, maintain his speed and twist away from the onrushing mass. The two boats would end up side by side, the container ship overtaking him like a juggernaut passing a moped. Even a glancing blow from the container ship would still be fatal, but at least there was a chance it might miss.

He dashed to the engine's starter-button. He pressed it. The engine coughed, spluttered and died. He pressed again. Nothing.

Five seconds had elapsed. The boat was still sailing directly towards its gigantic executioner.

Samuel Carver was not a yachtsman. But he was an ex-Marine. He'd spent years studying, planning and executing waterborne operations. He'd attended the military sail-training courses with which the British armed forces, steeped in the nautical traditions of an island race, were obsessed. Now he prayed he could remember everything he'd ever been taught.

Carver disengaged the auto-helm and crouched by *Tamarisk*'s tiller, the wind in his face, sea-spray foaming around him, the rain beating against him so hard he had to screw his eyes into slits to maintain any vision at all. The massive hull was no more than a hundred metres away now, still travelling just as fast, still on course, still oblivious of the yacht's existence. He could now see flecks of rust on its hull, the white depth markings running down from its plimsoll line.

He breathed hard and pushed the tiller away from his body, directly towards the *Scandwave Adventurer*. For a long, endless, agonizing second nothing happened. Then the bow of the yacht turned into the wind, began to swing round, and the boom bearing the mainsail rushed across the boat, over Carver's head. The jib at the front was jammed tight against the mast. The wind was pushing it over to the far, port side of the boat. But the sail was held back by the taut rope holding it in its previous position to starboard.

Moment by moment, the *Tamarisk* shifted its course. It slewed anticlockwise in the water, turning three quarters of the way round the dial, till it was no longer running broadsides to the container ship but pointing almost directly at the vast black-painted behemoth. And then the turning stopped and the *Tamarisk* lay there, dead in the water.

The container ship was now no more than fifty metres away. As the *Tamarisk* had completed its tack, Carver had frantically worked the rope holding the jib sail, fighting against the tension generated by the wind in the sail. The line loosened and the jib flapped helplessly in the wind. The boat would not move again until

Carver reversed the procedure. He had fewer than five seconds till impact.

He dashed to the jib-winch on the port side of the boat, frantically turning the handle to tighten the line and heave the jib round the mast to the point where it could once again catch the wind that would power the *Tamarisk*. The *Adventurer* was now so close that Carver could not even see the top of its hull, which loomed over the yacht, twice as high as its mast. Every second brought it another ten yards closer. There was no time left, nothing more he could do. And then, somehow, the jib caught a gust of wind, filled for a moment, and gave the *Tamarisk* a little push – no more than a few feet of movement, but just enough to bring the boat round a fraction.

Then Carver felt the craft being gripped by a far mightier force. Below the waterline of the container ship, the bow flared out in a great, round, bulbous protrusion, like the head of an oversize whale. It was designed to push water away from the ship in such a way that it minimized the wake left behind it. It was so effective that the *Adventurer*, like most modern mega-ships, generated less of a wake than a 40-foot cabin cruiser. The water was displaced in a huge, rolling swell that picked up the *Tamarisk* and flung it up and away from the container ship.

Now Carver was in the lee of the *Adventurer*, which put a block of steel as high as a church steeple and as long as a suburban street between the wind and his yacht. It was like sailing into the eye of a hurricane. The air stilled. His sails flapped emptily. He was completely helpless once again, bobbing on the water like a rubber duck in a bath. To his left, the huge hull of the container ship went by for ten, twenty, thirty seconds, as if it filled the entire ocean, one vast ship that never seemed to end.

Suddenly the current of the bow-wave took hold once again, swinging back towards the ship's hull and taking the *Tamarisk* with it. Now the yacht was propelled directly towards the flank of the ship, which came closer and closer, looming higher and higher until Carver could almost stretch out his left arm and touch the cold, wet steel.

Then the current swung again, flinging the yacht back out to sea. The container vessel was passing by fifty metres away, and Carver could see the giant capital letters that spelled out its name emblazoned on its stern like a giant farewell as it powered on into the distance. The words grew smaller and less distinct until the ship was swallowed up by the darkness and the rain.

There was no sign of the flare now, no indication of where Trench's body was floating. Carver briefly considered looking for it, but the wind, waves and current would already have washed the charred corpse away from its original position. He had no searchlights to sweep across the surface of the water, no engine to carry *Tamarisk* back and forth. He could waste hours without finding anything. When morning came, the body would be spotted and hauled onboard whatever ship had discovered it. The coastguard would be called, an investigation begun. That would inevitably lead to the *Tamarisk* and Bobby Faulkner.

So now another clock was ticking. All Carver could do was press on. His back and legs were aching. The sweat was chilling against his skin. Fatigue washed over him like the waves that surrounded the boat.

He was still slumped over the tiller two hours later, when he heard a coughing sound over the howl of the wind and the beating of the rain. He looked up and saw Bobby Faulkner's head and shoulders emerge through the hatch. He looked around, sleepily.

'Where's Quentin? What's the daft old bugger got up to now?'

He paused, and gave Carver a ragged, doped-up smile.

'Have I missed all the fun?'

65

It took Bobby Faulkner a couple of minutes to get his drugged head round the fact that Quentin Trench was dead. Then he spent another couple shouting at Carver, his voice slurred, his thoughts disordered, blaming him for what had happened, calling him a murderer. He said his wife had been right. He said he should have stayed at home and gone to work. 'Brother-officer my bloody arse!' he ranted. 'You're nothing but bloody trouble. Should've left you in France. Let you sort your own sodding problems out, none of my business. Now Quentin's dead, best commander a man ever had. And it's all your bloody fault.'

Carver let Faulkner say his piece. He considered his options as the other man ranted. He could either suck it up and say nothing, or he could rip right back at him. He thought about going for the strong, silent option. It would probably be the more mature response. But he couldn't be sure Faulkner wouldn't try something stupid as long as he saw Carver as a murderer and Trench as the innocent victim. Plus, he was tired and hacked off and he'd taken about as much as he could stand tonight – and the night before, and the ones before that. So he grabbed Faulkner by the neck and hauled him close till his face was just a few inches away. Carver stared into eyes still bleary with chemicals.

'Listen,' he said. 'Listen very hard, because I'm only going to say this once. Quentin Trench was a lying, treacherous bastard who tried to kill me and would have killed you next. He stuck something in that hot bloody toddy you guys made, knocked you out. For God's sake, you're a big boy, you must know you've been drugged. And it couldn't have been me, could it? I was up on deck, on watch.'

Faulkner shrugged non-committally, unable to argue but unwilling to agree.

'He shot at me,' Carver continued, 'but he missed. Look.' He pointed to the frame of the hatch. 'There are the bloody holes. And none of this would have happened if you hadn't got him on this boat in the first place.'

Carver let Faulkner go and moved across to the tiller, steering the boat north, waiting for the first faint glimmer of the dawn.

'Why would Quentin want to kill you?' Faulkner asked. 'He loved you like a son. Told me so himself.'

'He sent me on a mission I wasn't supposed to survive. And when I did, he wanted me dead. Look, I've spent the past five years working off-the-books black ops, jobs that never happened. I never knew who gave me the work. I didn't think they knew who I was, either. Better that way, for both our sakes. Turns out I was wrong. One of my bosses knew exactly who I was, because he was Quentin. I've been working for him all along, I just didn't know it.'

Faulkner frowned. 'Hang on. It was you that called me first about Quentin. That's why I thought of him when you called again about the boat.'

'That's right. I thought he could help me. Pretty stupid, right?'

'So how did you find out he was out to get you?'

'Because he made some stupid crack about Alix, the girl I told you about, being a Russian mail-order bride. How did he know she was Russian? I didn't tell you that. He had to be on the inside. All I needed to know then was whether you were in on it too. And I knew you were in the clear once I saw you lying there unconscious.'

Faulkner was trying to work it all out, struggling against the numbed synapses in his brain.

'How do I know you're telling the truth, Pablo? How do I know you're not going to kill me too?'

'Because I would have done it already. You've been unconscious or incapable for hours. I could have tipped you over the side any time. Anyway, you know the truth yourself. What was the last thing you remember before you went out?'

Carver watched Faulkner screw up his eyes, trying to create a picture in his head. He took a couple of deep breaths, expelling the air through his nose. He muttered to himself. Then his eyes opened and he shook his head sorrowfully. 'You're right. It must have been him. We were down there. I was sitting down, thinking about getting some rest. He came over. There was a mug of something in his hand . . . I don't remember anything after that.'

'He knocked you out. Then he came after me. But he forgot how good I am at my job. So he died.'

Faulkner leaned forward. 'What, precisely, is your job, Pablo?'

Carver said nothing.

'Come on,' Faulkner insisted. 'You turned my boat into a battlefield. I've got a right to know.'

'I told you already,' said Carver. 'Black ops, accidents. Like, say, a veteran Marine officer with years of experience at sea who runs into a storm on a night crossing of the Channel and gets fatally wounded by a distress flare. It goes off too early while he's trying to warn an oncoming container ship of his presence and blows him overboard. That kind of thing.'

'So what was this job Trench sent you on, the one where you met this girl? The one you weren't meant to survive.'

'Don't ask,' replied Carver. 'We'll both be happier if we drop the subject right now. So, take the tiller for a while. I'm going down to the cabin to check a couple of things out. Do you want a cup of coffee to help you wake up?'

He went below. The ship's radio was mounted on the wall of the cabin by the chart table a couple of steps away. Carver ripped the radio from its mounting and smashed it against the side of the table.

'What's going on down there?' Faulkner called down from the cockpit.

'Sorry,' said Carver. 'Think I might have knocked something. Don't worry. No harm done.'

He made the coffees and took them back up to the cockpit.

Carver stood with his mug in his hand looking at the southern shore of the Isle of Wight, which lay straight ahead of them a few miles off, a black outline against a dark-grey sky, the bottoms of the clouds streaked by the first orange rays of the rising sun.

'What was that all about?' asked Faulkner.

'I was putting your radio out of action. When we get to shore you're going to need a reason why you didn't radio for help when you discovered your two crewmates were missing.'

'There's only one lost.'

'I'll come to that. Here's what you're going to do. The moment you get ashore, get the harbourmaster to call the coastguard. Then tell the truth. You were drugged. You'll still have traces in your bloodstream. The mug Trench used will still be rolling round the cabin somewhere. When you woke up, you clambered up on deck and both your crew members, Trench and Jackson, were missing. So was the ship's dinghy – don't worry, it will be. Naturally, your first instinct was to call mayday, but the radio was kaput. They're not going to know when that happened. Now you're frantic because two of your oldest friends have disappeared overboard and you haven't got a clue what happened. You certainly haven't got a clue why there are bullet-holes all over your boat. I mean, there's no gun anywhere, is there? Now, think you can manage that?'

Faulkner thought for a while, then answered, almost reluctantly, 'Yes, I suppose so.'

They weren't far from the English coastline now. Poole lay on the far side of the Solent, north-west of the Isle of Wight, to the left as they were looking. There was just a chance Trench had ordered a welcoming committee to greet them, in case he hadn't got the job done at sea. Carver turned his head right, to the north-east, gazing at the horizon. Then he turned back to Faulkner.

'Change course,' he said. 'We need another harbour.'

66

Yuri Zhukovski told his people to give Alix breakfast. He'd gone at her for hours. Now he was satisfied that she had nothing more to tell him. He just had to decide what to do with her next. He would use her to get what he needed. It was simply a matter of how.

The servant said nothing as she went into the room, but her presence was enough to wake Alix from a fitful sleep that was really nothing more than a semi-conscious doze. She winced as she propped herself up and watched the servant carry the tray towards her. The restraints that had tied her were gone, but the bruises showed up inky blue against the skin on her wrists and ankles. There'd been violence, too, and the memories of what he'd done to her were as vivid as the welts on her body.

She looked at the servant, another Russian, as she placed the tray on the table beside the bed. The woman's face was masked in the mute, dead-eyed blankness that had disguised the true feelings of a thousand generations of serfs. But Alix could still feel the contempt radiating off her.

She collapsed back on the bed. She knew she had to eat, she just didn't have enough strength left to lift the food to her mouth. Later, she thought. Later, maybe she'd try again.

67

Jack Grantham met Dame Agatha Bewley for an inter-agency breakfast in the Coffee Room at the Travellers' Club in Pall Mall, London. Housed in Charles Barry's 1832 pastiche of an Italian renaissance palace, it had long been the traditional London meeting-place for diplomats, ambassadors and visiting dignitaries.

As an MI6 officer, Grantham was, in theory, an employee of the British diplomatic service, the Foreign and Commonwealth Office. His Travellers' membership made a useful addition to that cover, but he was not by nature a club man and he despised the atmosphere of entrenched, inherited privilege that hung over the gentlemen's clubs of Pall Mall like an old London fog. He had to admit, though, that the place came in handy. He didn't have to worry about finding restaurants or booking tables. He simply ate at the Travellers'. That saved time, avoided wastage and increased efficiency. And those were principles Grantham liked.

'I was sorry to hear about your two people in Geneva,' said Dame Agatha, breaking a piece off her croissant and covering it in thick, dark marmalade. 'It's never easy to lose staff like that, particularly when they're young. No children involved, I gather. That's a blessing, at least.'

Grantham stuck his fork into a sausage. He'd gone for the full English breakfast, same as always.

'I suppose so,' he agreed. 'Anyway, something good may have come of it all. We're starting to get names and faces. We're just not sure how they all fit together.'

Dame Agatha was a fastidious woman. She chewed carefully, swallowed, and then, having made sure her mouth was empty, asked, 'Anything you'd like to share with us?'

Grantham had just filled his face with fried egg and bacon. 'Mmm,' he managed, with a nod.

Dame Agatha put down her knife and ignored her food. She then sat very still, looking at Grantham over the top of her glasses.

'Go on,' she prompted.

'You seem sceptical,' Grantham said. 'Don't be. I'm not trying to dump you in it.'

'So what do you have so far?'

'Two names: an English male called Samuel Carver and a Russian female, Alexandra Petrova.'

'Where do these names come from?'

'Let's just say Percy Wake pulled a few strings, called in some old favours. I asked him, he delivered. At this point, I don't care how.'

Dame Agatha gave him a look that suggested she'd noted Grantham's response but had yet to accept it.

'Carver and Petrova – what do we know about them?' she asked.

'Not a lot. Carver has to be an alias. There is no record of any UK passport in his name – not a genuine one, anyway. He has no credit cards, he appears on no airline databases and we can't find any bank accounts. Petrova used to be a low-ranking KGB agent, Moscow-based. She started work just before the Wall came down. They used her for honeytraps.'

He took out a brown manila envelope, opened it and passed a couple of black-and-white pictures across the table.

'Pretty girl, isn't she?' said Dame Agatha.

'She certainly was when those were taken, seven years ago. She didn't snare any of our agents, but a couple of businessmen said more than they should have done.'

Dame Agatha raised an eyebrow. 'Men are such simple creatures.'

'Plenty of women have fallen for that sort of thing,' Grantham retorted. 'All it took was some handsome Stasi agent saying "I love you" and half the female staff in the West German government were happily passing secrets to the East.'

Dame Agatha sipped her tea, thoughtfully. 'I suppose you're right. Human weaknesses are universal.'

'Good thing too, or we'd never find out anything. Anyway, this Petrova woman disappeared off the radar five or six years ago. She still lives in Moscow, so far as we know. But she's not been up to any espionage activity and she doesn't have a criminal record.'

'She sounds like a most unlikely assassin,' Dame Agatha observed.

'Either that or a seriously good one, because she's stayed right out of the limelight.'

'Seems unlikely, though, doesn't it? One minute she's sleeping with her targets, the next she's killing them. I suppose both acts require the same detachment, a callousness towards the other person. But the training required would be quite different. What makes you think she's involved? Apart from the leak of her name, of course.'

Grantham swallowed a final mouthful of sausage, mushroom and baked beans.

'Two days ago we received a message from a French intelligence agent, off the record. He said he knew where to find the people we were looking for and he'd tell us in return for half a million dollars.'

Dame Agatha laughed. 'One really has to admire the French. There's something majestic about their complete lack of scruple.'

'Yes, that's what we thought too. We told him to get lost, of course. Then we traced his phone and set a team of agents on to him. He was in Geneva.'

'Aaahh . . .'

'Well, anyway, our people followed the Frenchman. He met a man carrying a briefcase.'

'Containing half a million dollars?'

'I don't know, the case was never opened. But the Frenchman must have thought the cash was there because he went off with his contact, which was a big mistake. They got into a black BMW, registered to a Russian fur-importing business in Milan. There were three other men in the car. They drove to a street in the Old Town. The Frenchman was then killed. Cut a long story short, the Russians hung around the neighbourhood till about nine p.m. local time, when all hell broke loose. The first Russian, the one who'd met the Frenchman, kidnapped a woman from a café, killing the owner, a customer and both our agents in the process.'

'My God . . .' murmured Dame Agatha.

'I know, a total bloodbath. Anyway, we believe Petrova was the woman who was kidnapped. Meanwhile, the other three Russians were getting beaten to a pulp in a pub-fight just up the road. Witnesses said they heard the man who whipped all three of them talking at the bar. They said he sounded British.'

'Is this our Mr Carver?'

'That's what we reckon.'

'So the girl was kidnapped at the same time as this Carver fellow was getting into his fight. That sounds like someone was after them both. Sounds like a clean-up operation.'

'Exactly. But how did all these Russians get involved? Everybody's assumed the events in Paris were planned by a British organization. I can't yet make the connection with Moscow.'

'Do you know anything about the kidnapper?'

'Yes. He's called Grigori Kursk. The Moscow police know him well. He's been arrested on countless charges of assault, a couple of murders, too. But the charges never stick. Citizen Kursk has powerful friends.'

'So Kursk kidnaps Petrova,' said Dame Agatha. 'His men go after Carver. But Carver escapes. Where does he go next?'

'Where would you go?'

Dame Agatha smiled. 'As far away as possible.'

'That would be logical,' Grantham agreed. 'But look at it from Carver's perspective. He's spent the best part of two days in the company of a woman whose only known talent is seduction.

There's a chance she's got her hooks into him pretty deep. What if he wants to get her back?'

'Then he goes after the Russians.'

'Maybe he doesn't know who they are. Maybe he's as confused as we are, because he got his orders from London. So if he wants to find out who's got the girl . . .'

'He has to come back here.'

'Precisely,' said Grantham. 'Which is why MI5 may need to become involved.'

Dame Agatha was about to reply when one of the club servants sidled up to Grantham's chair, coughed discreetly to attract his attention and whispered something in his ear. Grantham nodded and dismissed the man, then said, 'Excuse me, Agatha, I won't be a moment,' before following the servant out of the room.

He returned fewer than five minutes later. His mood seemed greatly improved as he sat down and poured himself a fresh cup of coffee from a silver pot.

'That was the office,' Grantham said. 'We've just had some more information from Moscow. One of our people there thought Petrova looked vaguely familiar. So she stopped trawling through police databases and had a look at some newspaper cuttings. It turns out that Grigori Kursk isn't the only one with powerful friends.'

68

Half a mile from the mouth of Chichester Harbour, on the West Sussex coast, Carver lowered *Tamarisk*'s inflatable rubber dinghy. He powered up the outboard – that, at least, started first time – and made his way to the shore. The harbour was a natural inlet whose four main channels cut miles inland, creating a great expanse of sheltered water that was a yachtsman's paradise. Sailing clubs and marinas had sprung up at half a dozen villages scattered around the bay. At eight o'clock on a damp September morning it was no trouble for Carver to find a jetty, tie up his dinghy alongside a dozen others and stroll ashore without attracting any attention at all.

He got a bus into Chichester where he bought a cup of coffee and a sandwich, and a train ticket to London. In the station café he read a morning paper. The royals were getting it in the neck. Apparently they weren't displaying a sufficient quantity of grief. Meanwhile people were building little altars outside Kensington Palace, complete with photographs, candles and flowers.

Carver felt like a foreigner in his own land. The whole place had gone crazy. There was an atmosphere of barely suppressed hysteria in the air, a pent-up frenzy.

He kept reading. Some actor he'd never heard of believed the tabloid press should be held accountable for the death. A politician thought something had to be done to stop the press being so aggressive. A pop diva swore that everyone had blood on their hands.

'No, love, just me,' muttered Carver, under his breath.

He was finding it hard to focus on the words in front of him. He'd been up all night. The night before that he'd got no more than four hours' sleep. There was a point where the effects of fatigue on the brain became almost indistinguishable from those of alcohol. Reactions were slowed, judgement impaired, temper harder to control. He was getting there fast.

His train pulled in and he got on board. The journey took ten minutes shy of two hours, and he crashed all the way – just enough rest to take the edge off his exhaustion without really refreshing him. It was just after eleven, and by now, Carver knew, Faulkner would have talked to the authorities. Even if Trench's body had not been found, mariners up and down the English Channel would have been alerted to look out for it. So long as Faulkner stuck to the script and did not give him away, there was no reason for Carver to be worried. But his time was running out, and so was Alix's. She'd been in Grigori Kursk's hands for more than thirty-six hours. Carver didn't want to think about what that meant.

Leclerc had told him the instructions for his phoney bank transfer had come from Lord Malgrave. Under normal circumstances, Carver would have tracked him for days, getting used to his routines before choosing the perfect time and method to make his move. But that wasn't an option now. He had to confront the banker straight away.

The bank's head office address was in the London phone book. Carver called and asked for the chairman. He was told that Lord Malgrave would be in meetings all morning. That was all he needed to know.

He took the Underground. It was hot, crowded and dirty, but faster than a cab. Before long, he emerged into the heart of the City of London, a financial district whose global power and importance was equalled only by Wall Street. Soaring glass and steel towers were superimposed over a maze of narrow winding streets, home to institutions dating back more than a thousand years.

The administrative headquarters of Malgrave and Company were located behind a glossy black front door flanked by stone columns and surmounted by a carved family crest. The great stone building exuded confidence and security. Carver guessed it dated back to the early days of the century, the era of global trade and national prosperity that flourished before its illusions of unstoppable progress were shattered in the slaughterhouse of the First World War.

He walked around the block, checking out the service entrance that opened on to an even narrower side street at the back. He thought about going in that way, trying to get up the backstairs to the chairman's office. But he didn't know where that office was, and he didn't have time to search for plans or recce the building. There was nothing else for it, he had to walk in through the front door. And that meant looking the part.

He found a barber's and had a shave. Twenty minutes in a gentleman's outfitters provided him with a charcoal-grey pinstripe suit, double-vented in the classic City style; a pink-striped Egyptian cotton shirt, gaudier than any New York banker would wear but perfectly acceptable in London; dark-blue tie, plain gold cufflinks and a pair of black lace-up Derby shoes. He bought a Mont Blanc pen and an elegant black briefcase. Into the case went his money-belt and his gun: he didn't want to ruin the line of his jacket.

He stopped in a stationery store for a pad of letter-writing paper and a packet of envelopes, then drank another coffee while he took out the Mont Blanc and wrote a short note: 'Carver is dead. Trench likewise. Circumstances as yet unknown. All communications have been compromised (UK govt suspected) – telephone and email silence essential. Request immediate meeting to relay emergency instructions in person.'

There was just one other thing he'd need: a small, easily portable video recorder. He got himself a new Sony digital model that recorded on to a PC-compatible disc.

That was the shopping done. The props had been chosen, the script written. The curtain was about to go up.

He passed through the open front door and gave a curt nod to the uniformed commissionaire, who immediately straightened his back and nodded back, instinctively acknowledging an officer's presence. At the reception desk, Carver flashed a brief, agreeable smile at the immaculately groomed brunette behind the desk and handed her the envelope with the words, 'Please have this conveyed at once to Lord Malgrave. It is extremely urgent.'

The receptionist dialled a number and had a short urgent conversation. A couple of times she glanced back at Carver, trying to judge his respectability. Then she held her hand over the receiver and said, 'I'm very sorry, sir, but Lord Malgrave is in a meeting.'

Carver remained unruffled. 'I quite understand,' he said, not sounding offended in the slightest by this rebuff. 'I know he's very busy this morning. But I'd like to speak directly to his lordship's personal assistant, please.'

The fine lines of the receptionist's neatly tweezered eyebrows crumpled into a brief frown. 'Of course, sir,' she said, giving him the handset.

'Thank you,' said Carver. He spoke to the chairman's PA. 'My name is Jackson. I have an urgent message for Lord Malgrave. It concerns our transactions in Paris, and I absolutely assure you he will be grateful to read it. If he doesn't think it's worth pursuing, I'll be gone before you know it.' He paused to hear what the PA had to say, then uttered a reassuring 'Absolutely' followed by an enthusiastic 'Excellent!' Then he handed the phone back to the receptionist. This time his smile was broad. 'Thank you so much for your help. They're expecting me on the sixth floor. Could you tell me, please, where can I find a lift?'

Lord Crispin Malgrave did not cut an impressive figure. He wore a double-breasted suit and an old school tie, and he had the oiled salt-and-pepper hair and the ruddy complexion – redolent of hunting-fields, shooting parties and salmon streams – of the British ruling class. But the façade was cracking, the arrogance peeling away to reveal the raw fear beneath.

Carver had been shown into Malgrave's private office. The chairman's PA was an elegant woman in her fifties, brisk, efficient and bossy. The man was running a bank, and still he had a nanny. She watched over Carver until her master arrived, as if worried he might steal a paperweight if left to his own devices.

Malgrave had scurried into the room, sweating panic from every pore. He dropped like a loosely packed sandbag into the leather-backed seat behind his mahogany desk, said, 'Thank you, Maureen,' and barely waited till she'd left the room before blurting out, 'Trench is dead? Are you sure? How do you know?'

Carver leaned towards the desk and stuck out his right hand.

'Hello,' he said. 'My name is Samuel Carver.'

Malgrave did not move. He seemed to need all his energy just to stop his mouth flapping around like a freshly caught fish. Eventually, he managed to get some words out.

'But you told my secretary—'

'I lied.'

'What about Trench?'

'He's dead. That bit was true.'

Malgrave did the maths. He worked out who was next. Then he leaned forward in his chair, his eyes pleading, hands held out in supplication. 'Oh God, no, please don't. I'll do anything!' He thought for a second. 'I owe you money. Of course! I'll pay you in full. Three million dollars. Plus interest!'

Carver let him burble on, his silence only making Malgrave all the more effusive.

'Look at me,' he said, once Malgrave had finally shut up.

The banker looked puzzled.

'Look at me,' Carver repeated. 'Just shut up, look at me and pay attention. I don't want your blood-money. And I'm not going to kill you. I'm a soldier, not a psychopath. I take life when there's no alternative. You have an alternative. You can tell me about the Russians.'

'What Russians?'

'The ones in Paris. The ones you sent to kill me.'

Malgrave shook his head. 'I don't know anything about them, I swear to you.'

Carver was inclined to believe him. Malgrave didn't have the nerve to be an accomplished liar. And his ignorance about the Russians tallied with Trench's.

'OK,' said Carver, 'so what do you know?'

Malgrave wiped a silk handkerchief across his sweaty brow. 'The chairman told me that he was planning to . . . you know . . . the princess operation. I mean, I didn't like it, didn't approve at all, argued strongly against the whole plan, in fact. But he said it was vital for the preservation of the monarchy, and besides, he'd committed the Consortium; that we were being funded externally, millions of pounds from a foreign backer. The money was wired from Zurich, anonymous of course. I had no idea who'd sent it. So you're saying it was Russians . . .'

Malgrave frowned, his panic subsiding a little as he considered the possibility. 'But why would Russians . . . ? I mean, what possible interest could they have in killing her?'

'I don't know,' said Carver. 'When I find them, I'll be sure to ask. Meantime, since no one else has a clue who these Russians are, why don't you call your chairman and arrange a meeting? Now.'

'But that would be impossible.'

Carver opened his case and took out his gun. 'Here's the alternative. So call him. Say you need to see him, in person, immediately. If he asks why, tell him you can't talk about it on the phone. Make something up. Then tell your chauffeur you need your car. We're going for a drive. Got that?'

Malgrave nodded.

'Right,' said Carver. 'Start dialling.'

69

Dame Agatha Bewley was back in MI5's headquarters at Thames House, on the north bank of the River Thames. It wasn't excitingly new. It wasn't impressively old. It wasn't provocatively ugly or inspiring in its beauty. It was just there, a Department of Works project from 1929. Millions of people drove to and fro in front of it along a crowded riverside route. Not one in a thousand ever wasted their time even looking at it. As a home for domestic spies, it really couldn't have been better.

After her breakfast at the Travellers' Club, she had been driven to work in her official black Jaguar, and on the way she'd thought about Sir Perceval Wake. Now that his services were not so regularly required by his country, had he gone into business on his own account? What was it Grantham had said in that meeting, straight after news of the crash had come through? Something about Wake's genius for black operations, his instinct for their execution and consequences. Wake had always disturbed her. She didn't feel comfortable with a man whose desire for influence was so apparent, but whose sexual and emotional needs were so well masked.

Wake was a lifelong bachelor, with no known lovers of either gender. He'd been around so long, the chances were he hadn't been security-vetted in decades. He could be hiding some secret shame that would leave him open to blackmail. He might equally well be asexual, of course, repelled by the thought of bodily contact. But a repressed sexuality was almost as dangerous as a perverted one.

So, what had he been doing for kicks? Dame Agatha knew she'd have to be careful. Wake was still connected all the way to the top. If he caught wind of any investigation, all hell would break loose. So she kept it discreet. A team had been dispatched to keep an eye on Wake's home, his movements and any contacts he made. She'd been summoned to the room where the operation was being controlled at around half past twelve; now she was leaning over a workstation, one hand on the table-top, the other on the back of a chair. One of her agents was sitting there, running the communications system.

A voice came over the speakerphone:

'We have two males entering the building, both white, smartly dressed. One looks to be in his fifties, grey hair, florid complexion. The other is younger, probably late thirties, short-cropped hair, carrying a briefcase. We have pictures. Mark's just setting up the link now, should be sending them through to you any second.'

Two grainy photographs, shot long-distance through a telephoto lens, appeared on the computer screen at the centre of the workstation.

'I know one of them,' said Dame Agatha. 'Lord Crispin Malgrave, the chairman and major shareholder of Malgrave and Company. He's a steward of the Jockey Club, receives regular invitations to the royal box at Ascot and has donated at least five million to the Conservative Party.'

'You're very well informed, Agatha,' said her deputy, Pearson Chalmers, who was standing next to her, watching the same screen.

'I should be,' she replied. 'The last time Lord Malgrave joined the royal family at Ascot, he had lunch beforehand in Windsor Castle. I was sitting next to him.'

'My, you do move in high circles.'

'Not often. But Lord Crispin lives in them. Now, who's the man with him?'

'A bodyguard?' suggested Chalmers. 'He has that military look.'

'Possibly.' Dame Agatha cast a sceptical eye over the figure on the screen. 'But would a bodyguard carry a briefcase? Put him through the system. See if his face jogs the computer's memory.'

She pressed a button on the workstation and said into a microphone, 'Keep watching. Await further orders. Good work so far.'

Dame Agatha cut short the conversation with her field agents. She was thinking about the military man standing at Wake's front door. Was this the killer Grantham had mentioned, coming back to England on the trail of his lost girl? It was a very long shot indeed, but if Wake really was involved, then the killer would certainly want to talk to him. But where did Lord Malgrave fit in? Dame Agatha decided to wait a while and see if she could get to the mystery man without offending too many senior members of the British establishment.

She turned back to Pearson Chalmers. 'You'd better call Jack Grantham at SIS. Tell him we may have something for him. If there's an interrogation, he'll want to sit in.'

Chalmers raised an eyebrow. 'I'm all for inter-service co-operation, but isn't that taking it a bit far?'

Dame Agatha smiled. 'No. We've both got our necks on the line. This time, for once, we'd better stick together.'

She pressed the button again and spoke to her agents in the field. 'When Sir Perceval Wake's visitors leave I want a tail put on Lord Malgrave. But make it discreet. As for the other man, lift him and bring him back here. I'd like a word with our mystery guest.'

70

The first things Carver noticed were the photographs. On the bookshelves, on the mantelpiece, a couple on the desk itself – everywhere pictures of the man whose room this was. He was sharing a joke with Ronald Reagan and Mikhail Gorbachev, standing in a dinner jacket next to an evening-gowned Margaret Thatcher; he was drinking cocktails with JFK and Jackie by the pool at Hyannisport, admiring the steaks on the Bush barbecue at Kennebunkport. There were dedications to 'My good friend Percy' from Richard Nixon, and 'Mon cher Percéval' from General Charles de Gaulle. There was even a greeting in Cyrillic script on a picture of the old Soviet leader Leonid Brezhnev.

This man didn't name-drop. He name-bombed.

Then Carver spotted a picture on a cabinet behind the desk. It must have been taken at a royal gala. The old man was standing in a reception line. He was talking to the guest of honour. She was wearing a long, blue dress and had a diamond tiara pinned to her feathered blonde hair. The inscription at the bottom, written in a rounded, girlish hand, read: 'Thank you so much for those wise words of advice!' The 'so' had been underlined. Twice.

Unbelievable. The old boy had just had the princess killed, but he still wanted the world to know that they'd been pals.

Perhaps he thought they still were. Sir Perceval Wake struck Carver as the kind of man who believes that reality is whatever he says it is, whose lies are convincing because he genuinely believes them to be true. For example, he still thought he could call the shots. His tame commander was bobbing about in the Channel with his head blown away. His troops were filling up the morgues of Paris. The Russians clearly reckoned they had him under control. But in Wake's mind, he was the chairman and he was still the boss.

It still worked, for some people. When they'd arrived, a secretary had told Malgrave that the chairman wanted to see Carver alone. He'd been asked to wait outside the office. Malgrave had obeyed at once. If anything, he'd looked relieved.

Carver was asked to leave his case and gun with the secretary. He complied, then went into the office.

'You've got a nerve coming here, Carver,' Wake said, as if his arrogance alone was enough to keep a killer at bay.

'Who's the Russian?' asked Carver.

'Which particular Russian did you have in mind? As you can see' – Wake waved an arm airily at the walls – 'I've known quite a few.'

'Really?' said Carver, walking up to a bookshelf and peering at the pictures in the silver, wood and leather frames. 'Which ones are the Russians, then?'

'Well,' said Wake, 'let's see now.' He rose from behind the desk and came over to where Carver was standing. He searched among the rows of happy snaps. 'Ah yes, that's Nikita Khrush—'

Carver swung round to face Wake and jabbed the first and middle fingers of his right hand into the old man's eyes, as hard and fast as the fangs of a snake. The old man yelped and bent double, his head in his hands. Carver then grabbed Wake's jaw and pulled it upwards till their eyes met. He kept his grip tight and repeated, 'Who's the Russian?'

Wake looked up at him, blinking back tears. 'Can't tell you,' he said. 'Just can't . . .'

Carver didn't have time to waste. He wrapped his right arm around Wake's neck, standing behind him, his mouth by Wake's right ear, the two men clasped together in a warped intimacy. Then he started tightening.

'Who's . . . the . . . Russian?' he hissed.

Wake's hands flapped helplessly. His head rocked back and forth and his chest heaved as he fought for air. It occurred to Carver that he might be going too far. The old man's heart might give out before he could talk. When he heard a croaking sound in Wake's throat, he eased his arm a fraction. Wake took a ragged breath.

'Zhukovski,' he gasped. 'Yuri Zhukovski.'

'Who's he?'

'One of the oligarchs, the men who own Russia. He's got paper mills, aluminium smelters, armaments factories, assets everywhere.'

Carver frowned. 'I thought the state still controlled all weapons manufacturing.'

'It does. But Zhukovski is a middle-man. He finds buyers, collects payments in dollars and passes it on to the Kremlin in roubles, taking a cut along the way.'

'Nice business.'

'That's not all,' said Wake, relishing the small sense of control that his knowledge provided. 'Back in Soviet times, many factories had parallel, black-market production lines, controlled by local party chiefs and gangsters. Those lines still exist. The armaments industry is no exception.'

'And oligarchs like Zhukovski have taken over from the gangsters?'

Wake attempted a bloodied smile. 'Do you seriously think there's a difference?'

'But what's his interest in the princess?'

'You're a bright young man. You work that out. But he was prepared to pay millions to get rid of her. It was all his idea.'

'And you agreed. Why?'

'Long story, goes right back to the old days . . . I had no choice . . .'

Carver pulled his arm away from Wake's throat, then shoved him back against the bookcase, pinning him there. 'What exactly did Zhukovski do in the old days, then?' he asked.

'He worked for the state.'

'Everyone worked for the state. That's what communism meant. What part of the state?'

Wake grimaced. 'Dzerzhinsky Square.'

Carver understood. Dzerzhinsky Square was the headquarters of the KGB. So Zhukovski's power over Wake went all the way back to the Cold War days. The old bastard had probably been playing for the other side, just another one of Britain's band of upper-class traitors. Zhukovski would have known and used the information as leverage. But that was ancient history. Carver had more important issues to deal with in the here and now.

'Has he got the girl?'

'I believe so.'

'Well, get on the phone and call him for me, then.'

Carver stepped back. Wake pushed himself away from the bookcase. It took him a second or two to find his balance, then he staggered back to his desk. He collapsed into his chair.

'You don't believe in social niceties, do you?' Wake said.

'Not when I'm working. Not when there are lives at stake.'

'You think you can actually save that girl? Ha!' The laugh came out as a bitter croak. 'You don't know who you're dealing with.'

'Nor does he. Get dialling.'

Wake picked up his telephone and spoke to his secretary, trying to keep his breathing even and the pain out of his voice. 'Please get me Mr Zhukovski. I suggest you try his mobile number first.'

A few seconds later, the telephone rang. Wake answered it. From the outset he put on a fine performance. Well, thought Carver, the chairman was hardly going to let this paymaster know that his whole operation was falling apart.

'Yuri, my dear chap . . . Yes, it's good to speak to you too. I have someone here who wants to talk to you. His name is Samuel Carver.'

Wake held out the phone. Carver grabbed it.

'Have you got her?'

There was silence for a moment on the other end of the line.

'Good afternoon, Mr Carver. My name is Yuri Zhukovski.'

'You know my name,' said Carver. 'Now prove that she's still alive.'

'Of course,' said Zhukovski.

Carver heard the sound of scuffled footsteps on a floor, then Zhukovski said, 'As you requested . . .' and he heard an unmistakable voice cry, 'Carver! Don't—' Then there was a slap, a muffled female cry of pain and more scuffling as she was dragged away.

Zhukovski returned to the phone as if nothing had happened, his tone as even as before. 'So, Miss Petrova is in my hands. To be frank, I had expected you to contact me sooner. I know all about your adventures with Monsieur Leclerc in Geneva.' He let out a contemplative sigh. 'I hope you enjoyed watching Petrova at work. I always used to. In any case, I take it you want her.'

'Of course.'

'Very well, what will you offer me in exchange? Please bear in mind that I require a high price. My men wish to let her know what they think of her treachery. I need hardly describe what that will entail. If you want the woman, you must give me a very good reason for denying them their amusement.'

'The computer,' said Carver. 'I have the laptop on which Saturday night's operation was planned and controlled. The firewalls are down. The files have been decrypted. And the man who had it was very efficient. He kept records of every order, every transaction, every detail of the project.'

He was trying to work out how far to take the bluff. He had nothing in his hand, but he didn't have an option. He had to go all-in.

'This man did some digging of his own,' Carver continued. 'He must have had a suspicious nature. Two people he'd never heard of were dumped on him. He wanted to know who they were, where they were getting their orders. He followed the trail all the way back to Moscow. Trust me, Zhukovski, you need that computer. You certainly don't want me to keep it.'

'What's to stop you copying the hard disk?' the Russian asked.

'What's to stop you killing the girl and taking the computer anyway?' Carver retorted. 'But you want to get on with your business, I want to get on with my life. Neither of us has any interest in seeing any of this go public. Let's just do the trade and have done.'

'Very well. Be at the main entrance of the Palace Hotel, Gstaad, Switzerland at nineteen hundred hours this evening, with your precious computer.'

'That's less than five hours from now,' snapped Carver.

'Yes,' the Russian agreed, 'it is a tight schedule. But if you start now and do not waste time – for example, by trying to double-cross me in any way – it should be possible for you to make it. And of course, you will come alone and unarmed. I do not need to explain what will happen if you break either of those conditions. Beyond that, I make no promises. If you can persuade me that you have something to offer, perhaps I will let you take the girl. If not, well, my people feel as strongly about you as they do about her.'

The line went dead. Carver handed the phone back to Wake.

'Call your secretary,' he said. 'I need to get on an afternoon flight to Zurich or Geneva. Now.'

There was only one flight that could possibly get him to Switzerland in time to make the deadline, and even that would be a close-run thing. The plane left Gatwick airport, roughly thirty miles away to the south of London, at 14.50. He should be checking in now. It got in at 17.20, local time, which would leave him an hour and forty minutes to get through passport and customs control, meet up with Thor Larsson, pick up the computer and drive 150 klicks to Gstaad.

By any rational analysis, Carver didn't stand a chance. But if he ran flat-out to Victoria station and caught the next airport express; if there were no delays in London's notoriously inefficient train system; if he could pick up his ticket and dash to the gate; if the plane was on schedule and the customs quick; if Larsson's Volvo had full tanks and the roads were clear . . . well, maybe he could make it. Just.

He put the handset back on the receiver. Wake was still sitting, unmoving, behind his desk, drained of animation.

'I suppose you're going to kill me now,' he said.

'I'd love to, old boy,' said Samuel Carver. 'But I really haven't got the time.'

71

They caught Carver as he sprinted down Ecclestone Street, just outside an Italian restaurant. He was going at full pelt, jinking between pedestrians like a rugby player evading tackles, his concentration focused on getting his exhausted body the best part of a mile through a crowded city in seven minutes flat. The only other thought on his mind, the one that was giving him the energy to keep going, was the nagging fear of what was happening to Alix, and what might be done to her if he did not make that evening deadline.

So he didn't notice the black Ford Mondeo that dropped one passenger behind him, sped up the street and deposited another two some fifty yards ahead before coming to rest double-parked by the kerb. The first he knew of any of it was when a heavily built man in a black donkey jacket stepped sideways right into his path, body-checking him.

Carver was sent sprawling on to the pavement, the breath knocked from his lungs. Instantly, the other two men joined their pal in the donkey jacket, picked Carver up, dragged him to the car and threw him into the back. By the time he woke up to what was happening, the doors on both sides of him had been closed, there were guns pointed at him left and right, and a tough-looking bastard in a Chelsea Football Club sweatshirt was holding out a pair of cuffs.

Carver cursed his carelessness, his stupidity and the fatigue that had caused both failings. The lift had been made with practised precision. But no matter how good the people who'd grabbed him had been, he should have been paying attention, he should have seen them coming.

He wondered whether Percy Wake had sold him out, but he couldn't work out why. The old man must have known that if Carver went down, he'd be dragged down too. Maybe his Whitehall connections were so strong he thought he couldn't be touched.

Or was there another possibility? Maybe this had nothing to do with Wake. Carver looked at the two men sitting next to him in the back of the Mondeo, and the other two in the front. They were calm. They hadn't said a word apart from a quick radio message, indicating that they'd got their man and they'd be back within five minutes. They didn't act like criminals of any kind. They didn't look tense, and they weren't screaming threats or smacking him about unnecessarily.

Carver thought about the organizations based within five minutes of the Vauxhall Bridge Road that had well-trained men capable of seizing a dangerous man in broad daylight, right in the middle of London. There were three possibilities. It was just a matter of where the driver went next.

He didn't make the early left that would take them to New Scotland Yard. So it wasn't the cops. When they made their way down towards the River Thames, he didn't go straight over Vauxhall Bridge, so that eliminated MI6. Instead, he turned left on to Millbank and drove along the river till he arrived at the big pale-grey building with its cast-iron ornamental lamps and decorative statues dotting the bland façade like hopeful dabs of make-up on the face of an unattractive woman.

Now Carver knew who'd taken him.

72

It was hardly a formal interrogation. They were in a regular office rather than an interview room. There was no tape machine or video camera. This wasn't a conversation anyone wanted on record.

'What a very complicated man you are,' said Dame Agatha Bewley, casting an eye over several leaves of paper and a series of photographs bundled in a plain brown folder. 'Your adoptive parents raised you as Paul Jackson – their surname, and the one under which you served in the Royal Marines and Special Boat Squadron. You were awarded a Military Cross and three Queen's Commendations for Bravery as well as numerous minor awards and campaign honours. A very distinguished career – I congratulate you.

'Your birth-name was Carver. That, of course, is your professional identity today. The passports found in your possession, however, make no reference to Jackson or Carver. They name you as a South African called Vandervart, a Canadian called Erikson and a New Zealander, James Conway Murray. That's odd, because not one of these gentlemen has entered the United Kingdom at any time in the past month. Yet, here you are, large as life. And here' –

she picked up a sheet of fax paper from the table in front of her – 'is a reservation on the fourteen fifty flight from Gatwick airport to Geneva in the name of Mr Murray. Interesting. Do you go to Geneva a lot? Were you there on Monday? Do you, perhaps, own property there?'

'I'd love to help, but I've got a plane to catch,' said Carver, trying not to display the anxiety and tension ripping through his guts and grasping at his throat. There was a clock on the wall. It had a red second hand that swept round the dial, pulling Alix further away from him with every completed rotation.

'Dashing off to rescue your Russian girlfriend, are you? The KGB tart.' It was Grantham speaking, without any of Dame Agatha's pretence of polite, civilized enquiry. He was playing the bad cop.

Looking at him, Carver wondered whether it was really his style. Grantham could handle himself, that much was obvious. But he didn't have the oppressive reek of excess testosterone that oozes like rank body odour from the kind of man who likes to throw his weight around. Grantham's natural instinct would always be to use a stiletto rather than an axe, a sniper's rifle rather than a blunderbuss. He didn't convince as a bully.

'Miss Petrova,' Grantham went on, 'let's talk about her. Let's discuss what the two of you were doing in Paris on Saturday night.'

'I don't know what you're talking about,' said Carver.

'I'm talking about the murder of the Princess of Wales.'

'Murder? It said on the news it was an accident. The driver was drunk. He was driving too fast. An accident.'

Grantham got up from his seat, walked round to where Carver was sitting and bent down till his mouth was right by Carver's ear.

'Don't piss me about, Carver. You're just a squalid, loathsome murderer. You don't care about anyone. If the money's right, you'll kill them in cold blood.'

Carver looked at him and smiled. 'That's a nice pen you've got in your jacket pocket,' he said, as if he were paying a compliment.

Grantham looked down, puzzled. His jacket was hanging open.

There was a gold-capped Waterman in the right-hand inside chest pocket.

'You've seen my service record,' Carver continued. 'Stuff the handcuffs, I could have stuck that pen in your throat, straight through the carotid artery, at any time during your moving little speech.' He waited a beat, then added wearily, 'But I didn't, did I?'

Grantham stood up, straightened his neck and buttoned his jacket. He looked down at Carver, opened his mouth to say something, then changed his mind and stalked back round the table to his chair.

The second hand swept past the twelve once again.

'Now . . .' Carver looked across the table at Dame Agatha. 'You operate according to the laws of the United Kingdom.'

It was a statement of fact, not a question. She nodded in agreement.

'So a man is innocent until he is proven guilty beyond a reasonable doubt. That proof requires evidence – witnesses, forensics, a weapon. Is there any evidence whatever linking me to the death of the princess?'

This time it was Dame Agatha's turn to stay silent.

'I thought not,' said Carver. 'And even if there was, there's never going to be a trial, not of me or anyone else. No one wants it. Everyone's happy with the accident story. So there's just one thing I want to say. I swore an oath to serve Her Majesty the Queen when I joined the Royal Marines. I took that oath seriously. I consider myself bound by it still. Do you understand me?'

Dame Agatha assessed the man in front of her through shrewd, narrowed eyes, then said, 'Yes, I believe I do.'

'Does the chimp?' asked Carver.

Grantham was breathing heavily. His anger wasn't an act any more. He was barely in control of his temper. Dame Agatha laid a hand on his arm. 'Don't let him provoke you,' she said, almost maternally, as if preventing a fight between two squabbling sons.

Then she spoke to Carver. 'As you say, you have been very well trained. You are familiar with covert operations. Let us imagine, purely for the sake of argument, that the tragic events in Paris were not an accident. Suppose foul play were involved. Why don't you tell me, purely hypothetically, what you think might have happened?'

Carver shrugged. Fighting these people hadn't achieved much. The only remote hope he had of getting out of this interview room any time soon was to cooperate, as fully and quickly as possible.

'Well, if I were planning that operation, I'd want someone really good to do the job. Problem: no one reputable would knowingly accept it. Only a psycho would get a kick out of killing the world's best-loved woman. But a nutter like that would be too unreliable. 'To get someone good you'd need misdirection. You'd feed them a pile of crap about taking out a car carrying, say, a radical Islamic terrorist planning a major atrocity. Because that would seem like a job worth doing.'

'Yes,' said Dame Agatha, 'I can see that.'

'Now you've got another problem. If this professional ever finds out what he's really done, he's going to be seriously pissed off. No one likes being lied to, right? So you've got to kill him before he knows what's really happened.'

'A double cut-out,' said Grantham. 'Eliminate your own operative.'

'You got it,' said Carver. 'But if the man's any good, he might get away. He might do serious damage to the people who've been after him. And he might protect himself by, say, taking a computer that has details of the entire operation stored on it and putting that computer somewhere safe, so that if any harm befalls him, the computer's contents can be made public.

'That's the sort of thing that might happen. You know, hypothetically. Now, can I catch my plane?'

'Not yet,' said Grantham. 'There's something else. I lost two of my agents in Geneva.'

'I'm sorry about that. But I had nothing to do with their deaths.'

'I know,' said Grantham.

'So you'll also know that the man who did kill them was a

Russian called Grigori Kursk. He was working for another Russian, Yuri Zhukovski. And on Zhukovski's orders, he abducted what you called "the KGB tart". Her name is Alexandra Petrova. And yes, she's the reason I'm flying to Switzerland.'

'How do you plan to get her back?' asked Dame Agatha.

'An exchange: her life for my computer.' He smiled. 'My hypothetical computer.'

'And you trust this man?' Grantham did not bother to keep the disbelief out of his voice.

'Of course not,' said Carver. 'But I trust myself. I can cope.'

'That's not all, though, is it?' said Dame Agatha, thoughtfully. 'You took a woman's life, whether you intended to or not. Let's not pretend otherwise. Now you want to save another woman's life, even if you lose yours in the process. Some sort of redemption, isn't that it?'

'If you say so. I'd rather think of it as a standard recovery mission. But I can't complete it unless I catch my plane.'

'Don't worry about that,' said Dame Agatha. 'It can always develop engine problems and leave a little bit late. Happens all the time.'

Carver looked from one spy to the other. 'So you're letting me go. Why?'

Dame Agatha spoke first. 'As you said, MI5 operates by the laws of the land. And you're quite right, no one wants a trial. We could kill you, of course, outside the law. But that would be problematic. These things are hard to keep under wraps. Sooner or later, someone always talks. So we're prepared to be accommodating . . . if you do a favour in return.'

'Such as?'

'Tell us what you know about the people who planned the assassination.'

'Were you watching Percy Wake's house?'

'Yes.'

'Well then, you saw me go in there with Lord Malgrave. Start with them. Ask yourself how a former KGB agent like Zhukovski ever knew a British intelligence asset like Wake, how he had enough power over him to order a job like this. And call the coastguard. Check if they've found a body floating in the Channel – a bloke with a great big smoking hole in his face. He used to be Lieutenant-Colonel Quentin Trench, once of the Royal Marines. He ran the operational side of the group.'

Dame Agatha jotted down a couple of notes on a leather-bound pad. Then she asked, 'So what was the reason for Paris?'

'Wake told his people it was vital to preserve the monarchy.'

'Yes, he said the same to me, at length,' said Grantham. His manner was calmer now, his self-control restored. But there was still an edge of hostility to his voice.

'That's not why he ordered the hit, though,' Carver continued. 'The whole thing was bought and paid for by Zhukovski. Does he give a toss about the fate of the British monarchy? I don't think so.'

Grantham frowned. 'So what was his motive?'

'Well, I reckon Zhukovski paid the Consortium several million pounds. He's a businessman. He must have thought he could turn a profit.'

'How?'

'Look at the guy's interests. Zhukovski's a player in the Russian arms trade. Well, I'm not big on the royals. But even I saw the princess on TV, talking to all those kids with their arms and legs blown off.'

'What are you getting at?' Grantham asked.

'Landmines. Russia's one of the world's major producers of landmines, and mines are one of the world's most tradeable commodities. They're tiny, weigh sod-all and they're made of plastic. You can shift them as easily as cigarette packets and everybody wants them. Governments, terrorists, good guys, bad guys – everyone needs landmines. And what do they cost to produce – fifty quid each?'

'More like twenty-five,' said Grantham.

'And they sell for . . . ?

'Black market, around two hundred pounds.'

'Well then,' said Carver. 'There's your motive. Landmines are a billion-dollar business. But they're also evil little buggers. So plenty of people want the business shut down. They start anti-mine campaigns.'

'I know, I've got the files on them,' murmured Dame Agatha, wryly.

'But those campaigns never got anywhere because politicians don't care about mutilated kids in Africa or Kosovo,' Carver went on. 'Not until the world's most photogenic female turns up and starts cuddling babies. Then they take one look at the opinion polls and suddenly everyone's drafting international treaties against landmines. That's very bad for a man who sells the bloody things. Suddenly people don't want to buy his products. All those billions are disappearing right in front of his eyes. So what does Zhukovski do? We know he has no problem with taking human lives. He wouldn't make landmines if he did. So he spends a few million to make the problem go away. You could call it a motive. To him, it's just a sensible investment.'

Dame Agatha tapped her pen against the table-top. 'Yes, that's a theory.'

'Can you think of a better one?' asked Carver.

'No,' said Dame Agatha. 'But I don't have to. I can say it was an accident.'

'OK, then, anything else? I need to be on my way.'

'Yes,' said Grantham. 'If we let you walk out of this building, don't think you've got away with anything. Dame Agatha may have her scruples, but I'm not so bothered by the idea of an execution. I'd shoot you right now and not think twice about it.'

'Why don't you then?'

'Because I'd rather own you. You have a debt against your name. A debt that can never be repaid. What you did cannot be undone. But you can make . . . let's call them reparations. You can do things for me, for your country. If you get killed along the way, tough luck, I couldn't care less. If you succeed, well, you've done some good to set against the harm. So there it is. I have you taken out to some landfill site, shot in the back of the head and buried under several thousand tons of garbage, or you go to work.'

Grantham paused, looked Carver in the eye. Then, quite quietly, with just a twist of irony in his voice, he added, 'Now who's the chimp?'

Carver nodded, taking the shot. He'd started the pissing contest, Grantham was entitled to piss back. And he seemed like a decent bloke, underneath. Carver wondered what their professional relationship might have been if he'd stayed in the SBS – the soldier and the spook, both on the same side, both roughly the same age and with comparable ranks. They'd have worked pretty well together. It would be very different now.

'OK,' he said. 'Suppose I accept these terms. What's the first job?'

'Zhukovski, obviously, but not because I care about you rushing off to rescue Moscow's very own Mata Hari. You don't strike me as a knight in shining armour. All you really care about is getting the Russian before he gets you. So get him. And get his sidekick Kursk. You'll be doing us a favour.'

'Don't suppose I get any back-up,' said Carver.

'You must be joking.'

'Didn't think so. What if I succeed?'

'Then you live to fight another day. Under the same terms as before. There's no shortage of landfills.'

There was silence in the room. Then Grantham spoke again, a new note of conciliation in his voice: 'Look, you used to be a good man, Carver. You did good work. This is your chance to do good work again. It won't be public. There won't be any medals. But you'll know . . .'

Carver weighed up Grantham's words. He was offering him a chance of redemption, just as Dame Agatha had done. Looked like there'd be a lot of redeeming going on. That was probably just as well, all things considered.

'Don't bother calling the airport,' he told Dame Agatha. 'That plane can leave without me.'

She looked surprised. 'Are you declining our offer?'

'No, but I need a flight that gets me there faster. So, if it doesn't sound too much like back-up, I need to use your phone.'

Dame Agatha pushed it across the table. Carver dialled the operator.

'Get me Platinum Private Aviation. They're at Biggin Hill . . .'

He held a hand over the mouthpiece and said to Dame Agatha, 'Also, I need my case back and everything in it: the gun, the passports, the video camera and the money. Don't worry, I won't shoot.'

Grantham drew a gun from his own shoulder-holster and pointed it at Carver. 'Just in case you change your mind.'

Dame Agatha stepped outside the office. A moment later the door opened and she returned, accompanied by a secretary carrying the case. Carver gestured at her to bring it over. He was already talking to the jet-charter company.

'You're in luck,' said a friendly, efficient voice on the other end of the line. In British aviation, as in British medicine, it was amazing how much more helpful people became the moment you decided to go private. 'We've got a Lear 45 inbound from Nice. The crew overnighted in France, so they can still get you to Switzerland and back within their time limit for the day. I'd suggest flying into Sion. It's a much smaller field than Geneva or Zurich, but closer to Gstaad, just a fifteen-minute helicopter ride across the mountains. Don't worry, we'll sort that out for you. Meanwhile, we'll get the plane refuelled, flight-planned and ready to leave as soon as we can. Should have you on the ground at Sion in a little under three hours.'

'Great,' said Carver.

'Happy to help,' said the voice. 'That will be £5,546, inclusive of all taxes and the helicopter charter at Sion. Can you give me a credit card?'

'Yes,' said Carver. 'It's an Amex, name of James C. Murray . . .'

After completing the booking, Carver told the two spies, 'Right, I'll be on my way.'

Dame Agatha watched him leave the room, then turned to her colleague from MI6.

'You didn't tell him about the girl.'

Grantham put his gun away. 'No.'

'I think you're wrong about his feelings for her, you know.'

'Well, in that case he's wasting his time.'

She frowned. 'How do you think he will react when he finds out?'

'He'll be filled with rage. He'll want to lash out. He'll be even more inclined to kill Zhukovski, or die trying.'

'So we win, whatever happens,' said Dame Agatha.

'Yes,' said Grantham matter-of-factly. 'That's the general idea.'

It was now 2.40 p.m. in London, an hour later in Switzerland. There were just under five hundred miles between London and Gstaad, and Carver had two hundred minutes in which to complete them. Up on the wall, the clock continued its measured, relentless progress.

73

Sion airport was laid out lengthways along a valley between two lines of mountains. The valley was narrow and the runway shared the space with an autoroute, the two strips of tarmac running dead straight, side by side, barely two hundred metres apart. As he watched Carver's Learjet come in to land, Thor Larsson wondered how many times pilots had got the two surfaces muddled up and landed on the A9.

When Carver got off the plane, Larsson was waiting for him with the computer.

'Here it is,' he said. 'The, er, special adaptation has been made as you requested. And, aah . . .'

Larsson looked away, his eyes fixed on the distant mountaintops.

'What is it?' Carver asked.

'I finally managed to open some of the files,' he said. 'I know what all this is about, what you did.'

Carver nodded. 'OK. Did you also find out what they *told* me I was doing? Does the name Ramzi Hakim Narwaz mean anything to you?'

A diffident smile crossed Larsson's face. 'Yeah, I know about him.'

'And?'

'And I don't blame you for what happened. You were double-crossed. So, anyway . . . you need to know the password. There are eight characters: T r 2 z l o t G. The first "T" and the last "G" are capital letters. This is very important. The password is case-sensitive.'

'How the hell am I going to remember that?' asked Carver.

'Simple. I have created an image for you, like in a picture book. There r 2 zebras lying on the Grass. Capital "T", capital "G". Do you get it?'

Carver gave an impatient snort, but Larsson persisted. 'Come on, repeat after me. There r 2 zebras lying on the Grass.'

'Jesus wept, I haven't got time. I can't afford to be late.'

'You can't afford to forget this, either. The system gives you three chances to get the password right. If you fail, a virus is released that wipes the entire hard-drive. There'll be nothing left at all.'

Carver did as he was told – five repetitions. Larsson handed over the laptop in its case, which Carver slung across his chest, from one shoulder to the opposite hip.

'Thanks,' he said. 'My chopper's across the airfield. Walk with me. We can talk on the way.'

It was just after half past six, local time, and the sun was beginning to dip behind the highest of the peaks to the west, casting jagged black shadows diagonally across the valley as Carver strode across the apron to the helicopter pad. He had a little under thirty minutes to get to the Palace Hotel. The weather looked clear. Allow five minutes to take off, fifteen to get to Gstaad, and another five to get from the chopper to the rendezvous at the other end. Yes, it should just be possible.

'How much did you manage to retrieve?' he asked Larsson.

'Only a small proportion of what's on there, but enough to know that Max had logged every detail of that operation, and a lot more besides. It looks like he was making himself a safety-net in case anything went wrong.'

'Anything about the Russians?'

'Kursk and Alix are mentioned in a couple of emails. But nothing to link them to Zhukovski yet.'

'Damn!' Carver thought for a moment. 'Never mind. That's not necessarily a deal-breaker. Anyone with proper investigative powers would be able to find a link. The point is, Zhukovski can't afford to have those leads out in the open. You've taken a copy, right?'

'Of course.'

'Good, that's part of *my* safety-net. Here's the other.' He reached into his briefcase and took out the video camera. 'I taped my confession on the flight over. How I was recruited, how they tapped me up for this job, the way the hit went down, all the names, what happened afterwards. It's got everything.' Carver smiled ruefully. 'Well, almost everything. I kept Alix out of it.'

Larsson laughed out loud. 'You old romantic!'

Carver cleared his throat gruffly. 'Yeah, well . . . Anyway, if I don't contact you by nine a.m. tomorrow, get the computer files and the confession out to every news agency and every website anywhere you can think of. I want it everywhere.'

'You got it,' said Larsson. 'But don't worry, you'll make it. You always do, right?'

'I don't know this time,' said Carver.

They were getting near the helicopter pad now. The machine was sitting there silently, waiting to start up and go.

'It's crazy,' Carver added. 'I'm doing this all wrong, breaking every rule. I've not planned anything, not even my way out. But for some reason I don't care.' He looked beyond the helicopter at the mountainous horizon. 'It's like I've handed myself over to fate. I'm about to be judged. I'll be found innocent or guilty. I'll make it or I won't.'

'I understand,' Larsson said.

The pilot started up his engines. Now Carver had to shout over the rhythmic whomping of the rotors. He handed Larsson his briefcase.

'Take this. It's no use to me now. There's a bunch of money

inside. If I don't make it, the money's yours. Don't argue. It's the least I owe you.'

Carver gave Larsson a slap on the shoulder.

'OK,' he said, 'gotta go. Cheers.'

Larsson watched the helicopter rise into the sky then curve away towards the north and the mountain passes that would take it through to the wealthy ski resort of Gstaad. By air, you could cut straight across from one valley to the next; by road, you had to go the long way – round the mountains, not over them – and it took a little over an hour. Larsson jogged towards his car, the briefcase in his hand. Carver might not have planned a way out, but he was going to do his damnedest to make up for that.

74

Carver felt as though the film of his life had started to run backwards. Five days ago he had flown through mountains in a helicopter and got into a jet. Now here he was, on the other side of the world, flying back through mountains in a helicopter having just got off a jet. Then the sun had been rising, now it was setting. Then he'd been about to kill. Would he, now, soon be killed?

The pilot tapped him on the shoulder and pointed down a lush green valley to a huge white tower rising from the valley floor like a castle keep, complete with pointy-topped turrets at each corner.

'The Palace Hotel!' the pilot shouted. 'Impressive, huh?'

Carver bobbed his head in agreement. Next to the tower was a great white wall, pierced by the windows of the hotel's bedrooms and suites. Huge chalets were arrayed in a protective circle around the main building, on the fringes of grounds spotted with the dusty brownish-pink of tennis courts and the piercing turquoise of an outdoor pool.

The helicopter put down on the hotel's own pad. Carver got out. He had a standard deal with the helicopter company: the pilot would wait for an hour and take him back at no extra cost, but at minute sixty-one, he was taking off come what may.

'See ya!' shouted the pilot.

'Hope so!' Carver yelled back. Then he walked towards the looming castle tower.

It was like an old friends' reunion. There was Kursk with his bogus Swisscom van, and next to him were his three stooges, each decorated with their personalized assortment of stitches, plasters and bandages. They stood there glowering at Carver, fizzing with thoughts of vengeance. Right now they were being restrained by their orders, but the slightest provocation could send them over the edge. He decided not to give them any excuse. He did not react as the Smurfs surrounded him, one on either side, the third directly behind him.

'You speak English?' he said to Kursk.

'Little,' the giant Russian grunted.

'OK, then. I have a meeting with your boss, Mr Zhukovski. He said be here at nineteen hundred hours. I'm here. Let's go.'

Kursk just looked at him, his eyes as dead as the glass balls in a stuffed moose.

'Fuck you,' he snarled.

Carver felt a sharp, excruciating crack at the back of his skull. The computer case was ripped from his hand. And then came oblivion.

He regained consciousness in the back of the van. His head ached, and there was a sharp throbbing pain just behind his right ear. Carver knew he was in the van because he could hear the sound of the engine and the tyres on the tarmac, and he lurched with the vehicle when it turned right or left. He couldn't see anything, though, because there was something over his head. It felt close over his face and constricting around his neck, like a drawstring bag that had been pulled over him and then tightened.

He tried to reach up to touch it, but he couldn't. His wrists were cuffed. His ankles were imprisoned in leg-irons. The cuffs and irons had been clamped as tight as possible, pinching his skin and cutting off the blood supply to his hands and feet. They were linked by a short vertical chain, so he could not raise his hands more than a few degrees above waist height. There was something tight around his midriff, too, like a wide belt. At the back of the belt a hard square box dug into him when he leaned against the side of the van.

He could also feel the metal panelling, hard and cold against his thighs, buttocks and back. His hands were gloved with padded mittens, like soft boxing gloves, that made it impossible to feel anything, so he couldn't actually touch his bare skin. But he didn't have to. He knew perfectly well that he was stark naked.

The van seemed to be driving uphill. But then it turned sharply, slowed down and started to descend. Carver heard the sound of the exhaust change, echoing as the van was driven indoors before dying away completely. There was a metallic rattling in his right ear and the clatter of an opening door, then Carver felt a sharp tug on the chain by his wrists and he was desperately scrabbling for some kind of purchase as he was dragged right out of the van and dumped with a bone-cracking thump on the floor.

There was another tug on the rope and he was pulled to his feet, the cuffs digging even deeper into his wrists. Then he was led, blind and half crippled, shuffling across the garage, through a door and down a passage. He heard another door being opened. A few more shuffles, then he got a shove in the back that sent him skimming across the floor until finally he lost his balance and crashed helpless to the ground again. Behind him he heard the slamming of bolts.

So, judgement had been passed down. He had been found guilty. Now it was just a matter of hearing the sentence.

75

Carver did not know how long he was kept alone in the darkness. He tried to get some idea of the dimensions of his cell by getting to his feet and stumbling in one direction until he hit the nearest wall. Then he made his way around the perimeter of the room. It felt square, maybe twenty of his chained, restricted paces on each side. He ended up huddled in a corner, shivering as the chill from the concrete floor seeped into his bones and stiffened his muscles.

It was pretty uncomfortable, but nothing out of the ordinary. The techniques they'd used so far had been pretty crude: basic sensory deprivation – the room was dead silent; it must have been fully soundproofed – mixed with the physical and sexual degradation of enforced nudity. If this was the best they could do, he could handle it. But given Zhukovski's KGB training, he suspected it was only the start. They were giving him plenty of time alone to sit and imagine what might be next. They wanted his fear to make their job easier.

Carver told himself to clear his mind of apprehension. Stay positive. Focus on his own agenda.

An age seemed to pass before he heard the bolts being drawn

back and the sound of footsteps and harsh Russian voices. He was dragged back to his feet and led by the chain again. They left the room and made their way back down the corridor. Then he felt hands on his shoulders turning him around 180 degrees, and he was pulled forward again.

His toes stubbed against something hard, which made him cry out in pain and surprise. There was laughter around him. Then Carver received a sharp kick in the backside and he felt his arms being pulled upwards. He heard just one word in English: 'Stairs.'

He lifted his right foot as high as the leg-irons would allow and was just able to get a grip on the rough concrete corner of the first step. He brought his left leg up to meet it. It was a slow, degrading process, and Carver was sent on his way by regular slaps and kicks, each accompanied by his jailers' raucous laughs.

Finally he reached the top. Soon the floor was smooth, first with cool stone tiles, then with warmer planking, before he felt the softness of carpeting underfoot. He went down a series of shallow steps, stumbling and almost falling at the bottom before a tug on the chain brought him upright again.

There was another one-word command: 'Stop!'

Carver stood still. Someone grabbed his wrists and removed the mitts from his hands. Next came fingers at his throat, a sharp tug, and suddenly the hood was pulled from his head and he was blinking his eyes against the light. Gradually his vision cleared.

He was standing in the den area at one end of an open-plan living-space. He could feel the warmth of flames against his bare back. There was a fire behind him, open on all four sides. The steps down which he had tripped were set beside the stone fire-surround. In front of him a rich Persian rug covered the floor. To his left a long chocolate-leather settee in the shape of a shallow U was set against the wall, facing a massive widescreen TV on the other wall. Kursk's stooges were sitting on the couch. One of them, the redhead, held what looked like a basic old-fashioned TV remote control. Kursk himself was standing next to Carver, saying nothing, just watching.

Carver's eyes were fixed on the figure in the matching leather armchair, sitting directly in his line of sight, wearing a drab formal suit. The man looked him up and down with the detached objectivity of a police surgeon inspecting a corpse on the mortuary slab. There was something profoundly disturbing about this studied examination. For the first time Carver felt shamed by his nakedness and his captive status. He had to force himself to keep his head up and his gaze steady.

'Good evening,' the man said. 'I am Yuri Zhukovksi. Let me explain your situation. The first thing you must understand is that you have no hope of escape. Even assuming that you could somehow free yourself, like Houdini, from your shackles, you can be disabled in an instant.

'You will notice that there is a black nylon belt around your waist. This is a REACT belt, short for remote electronically activated technology. It has a power-pack secured at the back, out of your reach, that is capable of sending a fifty-thousand-volt charge through your body – activated, as its name suggests, by a remote-control unit.'

Now Carver knew what the man on the couch was holding.

'This belt is used by American authorities to restrain violent prisoners,' Zhukovski continued, 'but has recently been condemned as a torture device by those feeble-minded liberals at Amnesty International. They object to the total physical incapacity induced by such a massive shock, along with agonizing pain, brain trauma and even incontinence. For my purposes, those all seem like recommendations.'

Carver looked down at the black band that encircled him. 'Ouch,' he said, drily. 'I'm sure it hurts. But here's something *you* should know. I have taken a copy of the computer hard disk, just as you anticipated. I have also recorded a full video confession, admitting to my part in the death of the Princess of Wales. You have a starring role. And if I'm not safe and sound tomorrow morning, every major media outlet in the western world is going to get copies of both.'

Zhukovksi frowned, as if genuinely puzzled by such misguided threats. 'And this, you think, will protect you? Please, use your intelligence. How many fake confessions do you suppose have flooded into TV stations and newspapers over the past few days? Every crank in the world wants his moment of glory. As for computer disks and conspiracy theories, there are already hundreds of those. No one will pay any attention. They will simply throw your disk and your video confession into the trash, along with all the rest.

'OK, we have dealt with that, I think. Now let me introduce you to my staff. They will, I hope, be making your short stay here as uncomfortable as possible. Mr Kursk, of course, you have met. So, now . . .' Like a lead singer introducing his less important bandmates, Zhukovski pointed to the emaciated figure with the punky red hair. 'That is Mr Titov. I must say, you made a very great mess of his face. He has the control for your belt, as you may have noticed.' The round-faced man with the sullen lips, his nose now hidden beneath bandages, came next. 'Mr Rutsev,' said Zhukovski. 'And finally' – he gestured towards a tough-looking, short-cropped man whose crude features had not been improved by being headbutted in a Geneva bar – 'Mr Dimitrov.'

The man gave an ironic bow. Carver nodded back.

'And, of course,' Zhukovski continued, 'I have saved the best till last.'

He looked up at the one person Carver had been trying to will away, the lovely figure perched on the arm of Zhukovski's chair, running her shiny crimson fingernails through his hair and sighing with satisfaction as he ran his hand down her bare thigh.

Yuri Zhukovski smiled at Samuel Carver and said, 'I believe you've met my mistress.'

76

Alix looked as though she had been sprayed with money. Her hair had been restored to a honey-blonde mane that tumbled around her bare shoulders. Her skin seemed to glow golden-brown. Her lips were a liquid red. There were diamonds glittering on her ears and in the bangles round her wrists. Her high-heeled black boots clung to her calves as tightly and smoothly as stockings.

The dress she was wearing was little more than a sliver of glittering, semi-transparent material, like featherlight chainmail, that hung from her neck and fell to a point between her upper thighs. The firelight sparkled off the shimmering fabric as it stroked her breasts and stomach, making it plain that she had nothing on underneath. When she half turned to whisper and giggle in Zhukovski's ear, giving a quick, mocking glance in Carver's direction as she bent down, her eyes flicking up and down his body like a lion-tamer's whip, he could see that the dress left her back completely bare before flirting with her naked buttocks in a whisper of silver.

So this, at last, was the true Alexandra Petrova, a professional courtesan, a valuable possession to be pampered, petted and then used by her owner exactly as he desired. Carver's throat tightened as he choked on his humiliation. The last pillar of his faith had been kicked away. There was nothing left now. The love that was supposed to redeem him had been revealed as a hollow sham.

He should have been angry. He wished he could be. Fury would at least give him energy. But as he stood before her, stripped of all dignity, the emotion that filled him was forgiveness. Some last vestige of self-delusion forbade him from blaming Alix. It told him that this was not her fault, that the haughty prostitute who stood before him was not the real woman he had loved, but a false identity. He tried to give himself reasons not to believe the evidence of his own eyes and ears. And as he did so, he understood, for the first time in his life, what it meant to give oneself utterly to another human being, to lose one's own identity in theirs.

Be that as it may, he wasn't going to give her the satisfaction of seeing him grovel. He pulled back his shoulders, lifted his head and asked Zhukovski, 'How's the landmine business? Sold any more since Sunday?'

Zhukovski nodded. 'So, you worked it out. Now, I have a request to make of you.'

He leaned forward in his chair.

'Apologize, please.'

'Oh yeah?' said Carver. 'Why should I do that?'

'You have caused me a great deal of trouble. But we can come to that later. First, I insist that you apologize to Miss Petrova. You forced her to endure your crude attempts at making love. Even worse, you bored her. Now you should say sorry.' He turned his head to look at Alix. 'Don't you agree, my dear?'

'Absolutely,' she said, then closed her eyes and gave a shiver of disgust that made her dress sparkle with every tremor.

Carver looked at her sadly. 'You're better than that,' he said. 'I know you are.'

For a fraction of a second he thought he saw a shadow of remorse – or was it pity? – cloud her eyes. Then she blinked, and when her eyes opened they were stony again, communicating nothing but disdain.

'Make him apologize,' she said. 'I would like that very much.'

Carver did not move.

Zhukovski nodded.

Titov smirked at Carver, then pressed a round white button on the black box in his hands. Suddenly, 50,000 volts surged through Carver's body, the shock making every nerve scream in pain, jerking his body like an epileptic marionette, rocking his head from side to side and ripping an animal howl of pain from his throat.

Titov kept his thumb on the button. One second ... two ... three ...

Unable to maintain his balance or control his limbs, Carver dropped forward to the floor, his fall barely broken by his tethered hands. He lay there writhing helplessly, his wrists and ankles tugging and scraping against their shackles, drawing blood. He was utterly controlled by the electric commands ripping through his central nervous system. His body was slippery with sweat. His heart was pounding. He was about to black out.

Then, at last, Zhukovski nodded again and Titov lifted his thumb from the button. The current stopped flowing, and Carver's body flopped into blissful immobility.

Gradually, his pulse slowed. Carver lay immobile for a full minute while his Russian audience compared notes on his involuntary performance, the men jigging about on the couch and hooting with laughter as they mimicked him thrashing about. Then he gathered his breath and slowly, painfully, pulled his knees up behind him, so that he was sitting on his haunches, with his head on the ground, like a Chinese peasant prostrate before an emperor. It took him a few more seconds to gather enough strength to raise himself up until he was kneeling upright.

His fall had brought him closer to Zhukovski and Alix. They were only a few feet away now. His eyes were almost level with her breasts. With every breath he was bathed in her heady, spicy scent. His eyes were filled with the silver light dancing across her body. Even now, after everything that had happened, he was overwhelmed by desire, torn apart by longing for her.

'Apologize,' said Zhukovski. 'Kiss her feet and beg for forgiveness.'

Carver looked up, searching Alix's eyes for some sign of hope, some recognition that he had not been utterly deceived.

'You don't want this,' he said.

'Yes I do,' she replied. Her voice was steady and cool, leaving no room for doubt.

He barely heard when Zhukovski repeated the single word, 'Apologize,' or noticed when he nodded again to Titov.

As he endured that second electric whipping, it seemed to Carver that it was another voice to his that screamed so loudly, another body that flopped and twisted so spastically. When the current stopped and he opened his eyes, he saw he was lying right at Alix's feet. He did not need to get to his knees again. Once the power to move had returned, he could wriggle forward on his stomach, his pulse still racing, his chest heaving as he gasped for air, the sweat dripping from his body. He could stretch his neck so that his lips kissed the shining black leather as he whispered, 'I'm sorry.' But whether he was apologizing to her or simply to himself he really could not tell.

Alix gave a flick of her foot, kicking his face away from her. Carver lay motionless, face-down on the rug, the gross physicality of his naked body a stark contrast to the intricate delicacy of the rug's swirling, intersecting patterns.

Then she said a few words in Russian to Zhukovski. The Russian got off his chair, settled on his haunches and grabbed Carver's face, lifting it so that the two men were looking into each other's eyes.

'Let me translate,' said Zhukovski. 'Alexandra says you disgust her. She says she wishes to leave the room before the sight of you makes her physically sick.'

He paused for a moment as Alix turned on a four-inch heel and stalked from the room.

'Take a good look, Mr Carver. You will never see her again.'

'I won't be missing much,' he croaked. His mouth was parchment-dry, his throat scoured by the force of his screams.

Zhukovski let go of his head, which flopped back down against the carpet. 'Come now, you don't really mean that. Even now, after she has reduced you to this pitiful state, you would crawl after her if you could, begging her to take you back.'

Carver didn't reply. He was too busy trying to get back up on his feet. Paying painstaking attention to every movement, he made his way from his belly to his knees. He put one foot flat on the floor, then the other. He drew himself up until he was standing to attention in front of Zhukovski, who had returned to his chair and was watching the spectacle with amused interest. Carver swayed slightly, grinding his teeth as he struggled for his balance and some semblance of dignity. His cuffed hands were held down in front of him, pathetically preserving his modesty.

Zhukovski gave three slow, deliberate claps.

'Congratulations,' he said. 'That was done like a true soldier. But my point remains. The woman has destroyed you. You fought my best man, Kursk, to a standstill. You overcame three of his subordinates – look at the mess you made of Titov here. You killed Trench and most of his men. But Alexandra brought you to your knees.'

Still Carver said nothing. It was taking all his concentration just to remain upright. Zhukovski watched his striving, then spoke a few words to Titov, who at once picked up an ornately carved wooden chair, heavily decorated with gold leaf, and placed it behind Carver.

'Sit down,' said Zhukovski. 'Relax. I would be interested to hear your side of the story.'

He issued another order to Titov, who walked round to Zhukovski's chair and handed his master the small black box.

Carver found himself staring at the omnipotent white button. Zhukovski caught his eye. Carver's guts tightened as his system flooded with cortisol, the stress hormone, the anticipator of pain and bringer of fear. He swallowed hard. His armpits prickled.

Zhukovski smiled, then pressed the button, holding it for a single second, just enough to power another jolt through Carver's body that picked him right off the chair yelping like a wounded dog and set him back down again with an impact that almost sent him toppling backwards to the floor. Titov gave a gleeful cackle of delight and directed a sharp volley of Russian profanities in his direction. Zhukovski simply nodded contentedly.

'Well, we've established that this keeps you under control,' he said. 'We can now talk alone, just the two of us.'

His men were dismissed with a wave of Zhukovski's hand. On his way from the room, Titov stopped by Carver's chair, looked at him for a second and sent a haymaking right-hander smack into the side of Carver's face.

The punch wasn't as powerful as it might have been. Titov had to hit downwards to reach his seated target, and Carver was able to twist his head, which deflected some of the impact. So he was stunned, rather than knocked out cold; his jaw-bone was cracked, not shattered. But the pain was just as bad. As Titov left the room, happily rubbing his bruised knuckles, Carver twisted and rotated his head, trying to clear his brain. His mouth was filled with blood from his shredded cheek and battered gums. His tongue gingerly probed his teeth. A couple of molars felt as loose as baby-teeth.

Suddenly, without any warning, his body shook with a tremor that seized him from head to toe – an unwanted reminder of his earlier convulsions, like the aftershock that follows an earthquake.

'Titov has never had much self-control,' mused Zhukovski, ignoring Carver as he squirmed and shivered. 'So far as he is concerned, that is just an opening skirmish. He will want a lot more satisfaction before his score is settled. And I agree with him. I too have not finished with you. I want you to understand about Alexandra, that you never meant anything whatever to her. So let me tell you about the real woman, not your fantasy lover.'

He got up from his chair and moved to a sideboard on which bottles and glasses were arrayed. There he poured himself a glass of vodka, neat, and returned to his chair.

'It was my wife Olga who discovered her, you know, at a Komsomol gathering. She was just a slip of a girl from the provinces – Kirov, if I recall—'

'Not Kirov,' said Carver. 'It was . . .' He frowned. He knew where Alix had lived as a child. The name was on the tip of his tongue. But for the life of him he couldn't recall it.

Zhukovski shrugged indifferently. 'I do not really care where it was. What was obvious from the moment Olga brought her to my attention was that this was a girl of astonishing capacities. Her eyes were crazy, of course—'

'She told me,' said Carver. That much he did remember.

'Her teeth, too, did she tell you that? We had to fix those. But the rest was all Alexandra.'

He put his vodka on a side table to the right of his chair, taking the time to marshal his thoughts.

'It was her hunger that struck me most,' Zhukovski continued. 'She was hungry for a better life, hungry for experience and, yes, hungry for sex. Every atom of that girl was female, yet she had a masculine desire for sexual conquest. There was no form of pleasure she would not explore. And then, as the duckling turned into the swan and for the first time in her life she became aware of her powers of attraction, she acquired a hunger for power. Perhaps she wished for revenge on all the boys who had spurned and mocked her – who can say? But she used her power over men like an empress. Some girls had to be persuaded, even forced, to put their bodies at the service of the motherland. Not Alexandra. She gloried in it.'

'What did she do afterwards, when the Wall came down?' Carver asked. He was starting to gather his senses now, the pain of his electrocution was fading, his body was back under control. He could sit still in his chair without twitching like an impatient schoolboy.

'You see,' Zhukovski said with a smile, nodding in satisfaction that he had been proved right, 'you could not resist. You still want to know everything about her. Well, I will tell you. I left the Committee for State Security – what you would call the KGB – preferring to pursue my interests in private enterprise. Alexandra came with me.'

'You were her pimp?'

'Is that what she told you? I will have words with her about that.

No, I kept her for my own use. As I have already told you, she is my mistress.'

'So why would you send your little pet on a suicide mission to Paris?'

'Because it was not a suicide mission. My orders to Wake were clear. His chosen assassin had to die. That was you, of course. I could not trust a man I did not know. But I had no intention of losing two of my most valued people. It was the English who decided to kill them as well.'

Carver grimaced. 'But Alix . . . why send her?'

Zhukovski shrugged. 'Because she was bored. She had started complaining that she had nothing to do all day except shop, eat lunch and go to beauty salons. I told her that every other woman in Russia would kill to have her life. But she was not convinced. She said she wanted to work in my organization.'

'And you believed her?'

'I believed that she was bored. And I knew that a woman who feels like that will soon cause trouble. She gets drunk in public, or she screws her tennis coach. So I thought, OK, this is a simple job. All she has to do is sit on a motorcycle and flash a camera. If it works, then maybe I can think of further assignments.'

Carver could imagine Alix being driven crazy by a life that required nothing of her except a futile fight against time. She was approaching thirty. Zhukovski might start looking elsewhere. She would see other, younger girls examining her, waiting for the first wrinkle, the slightest thickening of her waist or drooping of her breasts, the first sign that her power was waning. She was smart enough to plan another life. But would that life have to be within Zhukovski's organization, or had she been telling the truth when she talked of wanting to escape?

Stupid question. She'd made her feelings perfectly clear on that score. A boot in the face wasn't exactly a subtle hint. Forget her, she didn't want to be rescued. If she wanted to be part of Zhukovski's crew, she could go to hell with the rest of them. He could still turn things around.

He measured the distance between him and Zhukovski. He

could cover the gap in a single leap, he was sure. Zhukovski would be hampered, being in a soft armchair. He'd find it tougher to get to his feet.

Carver let his head sag on his shoulders, then mumbled, 'It's over, isn't it?'

'Yes,' said Zhukovski. 'For you it is.'

The Russian relaxed, confident that Carver was a broken man. He reached his right arm out towards the vodka sitting on the table beside the chair, turning his head towards the glass as he did so. And in that moment of vulnerability, Carver leapt.

He had already tensed his feet against the ground, pressed his toes into the carpet, bunched the muscles on his upper thighs and sucked in his stomach. Then he'd pushed up and away from the chair with every remaining ounce of his strength, aiming to smash head-first into Zhukovski's face.

He stopped dead in mid-air as 50,000 volts jack-knifed his body for the fourth time, crashing him down to the carpet, leaving him grovelling in agony once again.

'Did you really think I would be that careless?' asked Zhukovski, getting up from his chair. He stood over Carver. 'Well, did you?' he repeated. Then he kicked Carver in the guts, doubling him up. 'Don't you understand who I am?' Zhukovski had not raised his voice so much as refrigerated it, delivering every word with a frozen, deliberate matter-of-factness. 'I was a colonel in the KGB. I made dissidents watch as their entire families were burned alive – wives, children, mothers, fathers, everyone. I made prisoners place their hands in boiling water, then peeled their skin off like a tomato. Do you want me to do that to you?'

'No,' groaned Carver. 'Please. I beg you. I'll help you. I can do that. I know the password to the Consortium's computer. I have the key to decrypt all the files. I'll tell you. Just, please . . . just stop hurting me.'

'Well now . . .' Zhukovski was almost whispering to himself. He was walking round Carver, circling his body. 'Why would I want to do that?'

He kicked Carver again, this time at the base of his spine,

making him arch backwards as the wounded muscles went into spasm. As Zhukovski kept moving around him, Carver shrank into a fetal curl. He was dry-retching, unable to speak. Then Zhukovski stamped on his ankles.

'I'm not impressed,' he said. 'I had expected a former member of the Special Boat Service to have a greater resistance to physical pain. Perhaps you have gone soft. Or perhaps you are merely pretending to give in. What do you say?'

Carver's face was lying to one side on the floor. He was resting the weight of his head on the undamaged side of his jaw. Zhukovski could clearly see the angry red swelling that marked the area where Titov's punch had connected, so he ground his heel into the centre of the bruising, gradually increasing the pressure on Carver's face, pinning his battered head while his body writhed helplessly. Carver let out a muffled howl of pain.

'No, that was not pretence,' said Zhukovski. 'But still, you might have set a trap for me. For a man of your skills it would be no problem to booby-trap a computer. Replace the battery with explosive, and one strike of a single key would set it off. I have used that method of assassination myself. Perhaps we will finally discover what secrets are hidden in this ridiculous machine. But if it really is a trap, you will be the one who dies.'

77

When Alix had said that the sight of Carver was making her physically sick, she was telling the truth. As he lay naked and defeated at her feet, slobbering over her Versace boots, it was all she could do not to retch. She had to kick him away before she vomited right over him.

But she was not nauseated because she held Carver in contempt, she was sickened with herself. She had delivered the only man who truly loved her into the hands of a monster. She had played one game too many, told one too many lies. And now Carver was paying the price for her treachery.

She had been furious with him, that last night in Geneva. At first it had just been the sulky irritation that follows a lovers' tiff. That had given way to sullen frustration at his refusal to take her with him when he went to investigate what was happening. She felt patronized, the little woman left behind while the big strong man went off to work. And then, when Kursk appeared and turned the peaceful café into an abattoir, she had felt the helpless rage that comes with fear and abandonment. She blamed Carver for her seizure and she stoked up her anger against him in order to fortify her for what she had to do next.

She would die, she knew, if Yuri Zhukovski ever suspected that her relationship with Carver had been anything other than a professional deceit. Her survival depended on persuading him that she had simply gone back to what she did best: using her powers of emotional and sexual manipulation against a helpless man. So she'd laced her account of the previous three days with sneering mockery. She'd portrayed Carver as a deluded fool, capable enough at combat or sabotage, but a fumbling amateur when he held a woman, rather than a gun, in his hands.

There was a certain truth in that, of course. But that was why she'd liked him so much, why she knew now that she could have loved him, if only she'd let herself. It was Carver's unexpected emotional vulnerability that made him a complex, lovable human being, not just a killing machine.

She'd told herself that as long as she was alive there was always hope that somehow she might be reunited with Carver. She did not know how or when, but she felt sure he would try to find a way to get her back. Until then, all she could do was convince Yuri that he had nothing whatever to worry about. So she'd turned off her true feelings and given herself to him, letting him use her as he wished, paying her penance by prostituting herself more utterly than ever before in her life.

Finally, she had done one last service, the one she really could not forgive herself for. When Carver had called, shortly after lunch – fewer than twelve hours ago, though it seemed like a different age – she played the part of the helpless kidnap victim, crying out to him and squealing in fake pain when Yuri pretended to slap her. When the bogus negotiations were over and Carver had been set on his way, Yuri had grabbed her by both arms and looked directly into her eyes as if searching for any last sign that she had betrayed him. He had not appeared to find any.

'You are a good girl,' he'd said. 'I always had faith in you and you did not give me cause to regret it. That was very sensible. I should have hated to have to punish you. But now' – his face cleared and his mood lifted – 'now you deserve a reward. Go into town – one of the men will drive you – and buy whatever you like. Make yourself beautiful again.' He ruffled the short black hair with almost fatherly affection. For once there was a trace of warmth, even affection, in his voice. 'I miss my pretty golden girl.'

Alix did as she was told. She spent hours trying on the shortest skirts, the highest heels and the sparkliest jewels the boutiques of Gstaad – a town well used to expensive women – had to offer. But that was just the start. Her body was massaged. She had manicures and pedicures. Her face was caked with masks then soothed with creams. Her hair was lengthened with extensions ('From Russian women, just like you!' the hairdresser had squealed, thinking this would make her happy rather than deepen her self-loathing), then dyed back to blonde, then artfully styled and sprayed. Finally, after her face and limbs had been painted to the absurdly artificial beauty-queen perfection a man like Zhukovski would understand best, she was ready to be delivered into his presence again. The girl in the salon had barely raised an eyebrow at the marks on her skin. She had long since stopped being shocked or even surprised by her clients' personal habits.

Alix had teetered into the chalet's vast living area in her stiletto-heeled boots and Stella McCartney micro-dress to be faced by the hungry, lascivious stares of Kursk and his crew of deadbeat psychopaths. Yuri had greeted her with the flicker of a smile and the words, 'Alexandra, my dear, you look magnificent. I cannot wait to see the look on Mr Carver's face when he sees you!'

She had been unable to keep the falseness from her laugh.

'Don't worry,' Yuri had said, taking her reaction as a sign that she wanted nothing to do with the Englishman. 'I know how you had to suffer, and I am going to make him pay. We will have dinner first, and then he will be brought to us. And then we will be entertained.'

Alix was sitting opposite Yuri in the dining-room when she heard the van arrive. It drove past the front door and down the drive that spiralled around the chalet to the basement garage. There was a slamming of doors and a scuffling of feet, somewhere down below them in the bowels of the house. When the servants brought in the food, she could not taste it. The vintage champagne seemed flat and stale on her tongue.

At last, Yuri told the butler, maid and cook that they could return to their homes in the village. He waited until they had left the building, then rose from the table, took Alix's arm and walked her back to the living-room. He placed himself in a chair by the fire and patted one of its overstuffed arms, indicating that she should perch there. Alix obeyed. She even forced herself to tell him, 'I'm looking forward to this.'

She had expected Carver to walk into the room tall and proud, ready to negotiate with Yuri man to man. When he was led in like an animal, his body exposed, his head shrouded in black, it was all she could do not to weep. She forced herself to remain cold and aloof as he suffered the agonies that destroyed his body from within and crushed his spirit before her eyes. And then, at last, she'd been able to escape.

Alix had kept her composure until she was out of the room. She stifled her sobs until she reached the marble sanctuary of her bathroom, with the door locked behind her. Only then did she weep for her man, for herself, and for the love that had been thrown away.

She ran a bath, partly to cover the sound of her crying, but also as an excuse for her absence. Men took it for granted that women had an almost infinite need to soak themselves in bubbles and scented oils. Besides, she knew that Yuri would have forgotten her by now. She had seen the venom in his eyes when he looked at Carver and had known what that meant.

Alix lay in the bath, breathing the Chanel-scented steam, watching her limbs turn lobster-pink in the hot water. By the time she rose to her feet, letting the bubbles slide from her body as she reached for her soft, heavy cotton towel, she knew what she had to do. Whatever it cost.

78

Zhukovski spoke into a telephone. A few seconds later, Kursk, Titov and Rutsev reappeared. Carver was placed in the middle of a five-man procession. Kursk led the way, carrying a gun, a Beretta 92. He walked side-on, pointing the gun behind him at Carver, whose left arm was held in Rutsev's fierce, vindictive grip. Titov came next, holding the belt's remote control. Zhukovski made up the rear. Only Dimitrov was missing.

The line of men went through the living area and into the hall. Kursk signalled Carver to stop. Then he walked to the far end of the hall, furthest away from the front entrance, to what looked like a standard wooden door, set into an alcove under the main stairs. But the everyday domestic appearance was misleading. When Kursk opened it, his grunt of effort suggested a far heavier, more solid construction – something designed as a barrier to people and sound alike. Another sign from Kursk told Rutsev to lead Carver towards him. Once again, Carver was covered twice over: the gun in front of him, the belt control behind.

The door had opened on to a set of bare concrete steps that led down to the basement of the chalet. Kursk went ahead, got to the bottom, turned to face back up the stairs and shouted, 'OK!' The other men then started to walk down into the basement. The stairs opened into a narrow corridor lit by the harsh flickering of a bare fluorescent tube.

Carver recognized the feel of the concrete beneath his feet. He could smell stale exhaust fumes. The garage where he had first arrived at the chalet must be down here. But that was not his destination. Instead, Kursk led the group through a thick steel door into a completely bare, windowless room, roughly twenty feet square. The walls were a brilliant chalk-white, as were the floor, the ceiling and the inside of the door. He caught a familiar whiff of new paint. This was the place where he had been left before, blindfolded.

He looked around and realized he had missed some of its salient features. A closed-circuit TV camera at one corner of the ceiling was focused on the room's only furniture, a single high-backed metal chair, right in the middle of the room. It was bolted to the floor and set at right angles to the door. Leather straps had been attached to the back, the arms and the legs of the chair, ensuring that anyone sitting in it could be totally restrained. A black wire snaked from a socket on the wall to a pair of headphones resting on a hook attached to the back of the chair. A second hook held a roll of silver tape. There were more fluorescent lights on the ceiling. On the wall directly opposite the chair a large, shallow box, maybe four feet wide and three high, had been fixed. It had a black frame, but the biggest surface, facing the chair, was clear. The interior was white and fitted with yet more lights. They had not yet been switched on.

The room was no warmer than it had been before. Carver could feel the sweat chilling on his skin. He felt dazed, his mind fried by successive electric shocks. His face throbbed. His back and ankles were painfully tender. He longed for a sip of water to ease his raging thirst. But he wanted to take a piss just as badly. It had taken all his concentration not to wet or soil himself when the shocks had ripped through him. Now his bladder was sending stabbing reminders through his guts. He had to hold out. He would not let Zhukovski see him dirty himself now.

Rutsev pulled Carver over to the chair and shoved him into it. Then he strapped him down, securing his chest, waist and thighs. The straps' buckles were fastened behind and underneath the chair. With his hands still cuffed, Carver had no hope of reaching them. His head, however, was left free. Rutsev had to remove Carver's leg-irons in order to bind his ankles to the chair-legs. Carver longed to kick the fat-faced Russian, just for the pleasure of causing him pain. But the stun-belt was still round his waist, its control still safely in Titov's hands, and Kursk had his gun on them all the time. There was no purpose to taking the risk. He had more important things to do.

Rutsev was wearing a watch. It told Carver the time was 12.12. That was good to know.

Dimitrov came into the room, carrying the computer case. He unzipped it and removed the laptop, handing it to Zhukovski. The case was left on the floor a few feet from Carver's chair, impossible for him to reach. Now the whole gang was in the room except Alix. Carver supposed she must be upstairs, getting herself ready for a long, hard, sweaty night screwing the boss.

Zhukovski turned to Carver. 'I will give you the computer,' he said. 'You will not open it, or start it up, or do anything until my men and I have left the room and the door has been closed. If you try anything that even looks suspicious you will be shot. We will be in another room, watching you through that camera.' Zhukovski gestured at the CCTV that peered down from the ceiling. 'When you have opened and started the computer and successfully entered the password, raise your hands.'

Kursk moved to the door and stood there, his Beretta pointing at Carver, while the other men filed out of the room. Then he too slipped through the door, walking backwards, keeping the gun on Carver until the last possible second. The door slammed shut. Carver heard the scrape of metal on metal and then two sharp impacts as a pair of bolts were slid into place. He was alone. He had the laptop. Now he could start to fight back.

First, though, he had to open the damn thing. With his hands cuffed together, he couldn't keep the Hitachi still with one hand and press the catch with the other. He ended up holding it almost vertically, jammed against the strap across his thighs. It flopped open, and that movement was almost enough to send it crashing off his lap. Carver slammed his linked fists down on the open keyboard, stopping it just in time. Then he sat back, to let the adrenalin subside and to allow his pulse to slow down. He took a couple of deep, calming breaths, then pressed the power button and waited for the password box to appear.

His mind was blank. He hadn't got a clue what should go in that narrow strip of pure-white screen. Those repeated bursts of electroshock must have battered his brain as thoroughly as a pummelling from a heavyweight. His circuits were fried. His short-term memory had been burned away. No wonder he hadn't been able to remember where Alix grew up.

Carver tried not to panic. He fought against the tightening in his throat, the fluttering in his stomach and the desperate sensation that his mind was skidding out of control. He had to dig deep into the furthest recesses of his consciousness. The information was there, somewhere, if only he could find it.

There was a word-image, he knew that, a way of making sense of the letters and digits. Something about zebras. But how many sodding zebras? Two? Four? No, two, definitely two. What had they been doing? Lying? Dozing? Or was it sleeping?

He collected his thoughts. The sentence had to be eight words long. He closed his eyes and tried out the various possibilities. He felt like a child doing a spelling test. OK. He was pretty certain he had it now. His linked hands hovered over the keyboard as he rehearsed the sentence: I see two zebras sleeping on the grass. That was it.

But what if he was wrong? Larsson had been adamant: he had only three chances to get it right or the hard-drive would be wiped – that much he could remember. Well, no point waiting all night. His right index finger hovered over the keyboard, then started tapping.

I . . . c . . . 2 . . . z . . . s . . . o . . . t . . . G

A message appeared on the screen: 'Password failed. Remaining attempts: 2'.

No! The fear and tension gripped Carver again, even tighter than before. Where had he gone wrong? 'I'm sure there are two zebras on the sodding grass,' he muttered. And then he realized he'd solved the problem: not 'I see' but 'There are'. Yes, that was it.

T . . . r . . . 2 . . . z . . . s . . . o . . . t . . . G

There was something crushing about the computer's immediate response: 'Password failed. Remaining attempts: 1'. He was almost sick with nerves.

'Think, you stupid bastard, think!' He was talking out loud now, nodding his head, jerking his upper body against the restraints. 'The zebras, two of them, on the grass . . . aren't they sleeping? They can't be. So what the hell are they doing? Dozing, lying . . . lying, dozing . . . Lying. They're definitely bloody lying.'

One last deep breath. One final hover of his index finger over the keyboard. Then he went for it.

T . . . r . . . 2 . . . z . . . l . . . o . . . t . . . G

Nothing happened. For an endless, heart-stopping second the screen was completely blank. Frantically, Carver hit the space-bar again and again. Then the familiar Windows desktop appeared, and the screen was dotted with icons. And hidden away within the grey plastic box a tiny transmitter beamed a single signal.

Zhukovski was right. It was a booby-trap. But the computer was not where the danger lay. Slipped within the padded sides of the carrying-case were two sheets of C4 explosive and thermite incendiary accelerant, linked to a radio-operated timer-detonator. That timer had just been activated by the space-bar – thirty minutes' delay for each strike of the bar. In precisely four hours it would set off a firebomb that would instantly incinerate anyone in its vicinity and reduce the chalet to ashes and cinders.

Carver raised his head to the ceiling, then punched the air with his fists.

He remained on his own for a couple of minutes. He guessed Zhukovski would wait a while to make sure there was no detonation. Then the white door opened and four of the Russians filed back in. Kursk had his gun out, as always. Rutsev alone was missing from the gang.

Zhukovski walked across to the chair and picked the Hitachi off Carver's lap. 'Thank you, Mr Carver,' he said. 'You have done me a favour and provided rich entertainment. I was greatly amused by your ridiculous little aide-memoire, trying to remember how many zebras were – what was it? – lying on the grass.'

Carver fought the temptation to tell Zhukovski that the joke would soon be on him. The bomb would detonate at a time when the chalet's inhabitants would be fast asleep with their bodies shut down and their minds least capable of swift response, even if they awoke. By then, either Carver would have found a way out of his captivity, or the Russians would have destroyed him. The odds were heavily against him, but he hadn't given up yet. He felt a strange mix of profound mortal terror, knowing that he had only hours to live, and equally deep elation. At least he'd go down fighting. At least he'd make them pay.

'Why don't you let me help you?' Carver pleaded. 'I can get into the files.'

Zhukovski looked at him with an expression of pity at his boundless stupidity. 'I don't give a damn about the files,' he said. 'And if curiosity should strike me, well, Moscow has the finest cryptographers in the world. If you truly have found someone able to crack these codes, which I doubt, be assured that I will have no problem doing the same.'

He bent down by the chair, his hands on his knees, so that his face was level with Carver's.

'Let me tell you what *does* matter to me,' Zhukovski said. 'I want to see you suffer. I want you to die as slowly and painfully as possible. You fucked my woman. It does not matter how or why. If word should spread that you did this and escaped with your life, both my friends and my enemies – many of whom are the same people – would see that as a sign of weakness on my part. But if stories of your torture spread across Russia, if men sitting over bottles of vodka tell horrific tales of what happened to the man who tried to cross me, if they see that my woman is more slavishly devoted to me than ever . . . well, then they will know that Yuri Zhukovski is not a man to be trifled with.'

He turned to Titov and issued a series of instructions that prompted another leering grin to break across his henchman's emaciated death's-head face. Titov put the stun-belt control in the back pocket of his trousers, then stepped up to the chair and pushed Carver's head against its solid metal back, hard. He placed a strap across his forehead and tightened it so that the leather seemed to dig into his skull. A second strap was forced across his mouth, then yanked tight so that it both gagged him and tugged against his loosened teeth and cracked jaw. Agonizing pain now accompanied each of the tiny movements of which Carver was still capable.

Carver was frightened now, really frightened. When he'd tried to jump Zhukovski, he'd known it wouldn't work. He was just trying to engineer a situation in which he could play the part of a beaten man, begging for his one chance of salvation – the computer. He'd been prepared to take whatever punishment Zhukovski could hand out, for the end justified the means. But now he was not play-acting. His terror was entirely genuine.

Carver had seen a TV show once about a British prisoner-of-war who pretended to go crazy so that the Germans would hand him over to the Red Cross. But by the time he was finally free, the pretence had become reality. He had truly gone mad. Carver was like that prisoner. When the cuffs were taken from his wrists he made no attempt whatever to resist as his hands were secured to the arms of the chair. He did not want to give Zhukovski or his men the slightest excuse to press the white button that had so completely enslaved and unmanned him. Just the thought of what it would be like to squirm and jerk against his restraints, the imagined pain that would cause, was enough to leave him in a muck sweat. The final straps were tightened without any further bolts of electricity. He almost wept with gratitude.

There was a smooth efficiency to Titov's actions. His normal twitchiness had been replaced by the calmness of a man who took deep comfort and satisfaction from his labours. But he had not finished his handiwork. First, he reached behind the chair and picked up the headphones, which he placed over Carver's ears. There was no sound, simply a muffling of the world around him, as if he had stuck his fingers in his ears. Next, Titov grabbed the roll of tape. He pulled out a strip about four inches long and tore it off with his teeth. Then he leaned forward and pulled on Carver's eyelids, forcing them down.

As soon as Carver realized what Titov was doing, he immediately closed his eyes. He wanted his captor to know that he was co-operating. He was doing everything he possibly could to be good.

Carver felt the sticky grip of tape on his right eyelid, then a jerk as it was pulled upwards, and a second grip as Titov smoothed the other end of the strip on to his forehead. His eye was open now, wide open. And he could not blink.

Once Titov had done the same thing to his other eye, he took a step back from the chair, placed himself directly in Carver's eyeline and took the dreadful black box out of his trouser pocket. He held it up next to his grinning face in his left hand. He stretched his right arm out in front of him and raised his index finger. He looked at the box. Then he turned his head and looked at the finger. And then he winked.

Carver heard the muffled sound of laughter. At the edge of his vision he could just see Dimitrov doubled over. But Carver didn't care about them. His full concentration was on Titov's finger as it slowly, ostentatiously rotated in the air, swooping from one side of his body to the other, closing in until it was just inches from the black box and its gleaming white button.

Carver's taped eyes widened even further. His gagged mouth emitted a pathetic, wordless whimpering. His sweat was slick against the back of the metal chair. Titov let him suffer, relishing every second of Carver's terror. Then he put the box back in his pocket and turned away.

He was leaving the room! The torment was over!

Carver saw Titov walk out of his field of vision. He saw Dimitrov pick up the black computer case and take it with him as he, too, departed. He heard the slamming of the door and the clicking of the bolts. For a few moments Carver just sat there, naked, cold and immobile in the silent solitude of his gleaming cell.

Then, without warning, the white box on the wall opposite him burst into blazing light, a white-hot glare that burned into his defenceless, wide-open eyes. At the same time, the headphones came to life and his ears were pounded with a deafening burst of white noise, like the static of an untuned radio. The noise exploded in his skull, filling his brain with a random roar that had no structure or meaning, nothing that his mind could grasp or comprehend. Meanwhile, the light attacked him like a blowtorch. And there was absolutely nothing he could do.

Samuel Carver was trapped in hell. The noise and the light would go on for ever, and he could not turn them off. He could not close his eyes. He could not block his ears. He could not move any part of his body. He could not even hear himself when he screamed.

79

Gstaad was the St Tropez of ski resorts, a beautiful old home for crass new money, a place where age and cash met youth and beauty then made a deal that suited both parties. Back in the seventies and eighties, Arabs awash with petrodollars swapped sand for snow and rushed to Gstaad. Now it was the Russians' turn.

The very smartest hoteliers, desperate to preserve at least the illusion of class and exclusivity, had tried to exclude Moscow's oligarchs and mafiosi, wringing their hands, bowing apologetically and explaining that the best suites in high season were booked up months, even years in advance. But someone had to buy the jeroboams of vintage Cristal champagne at 7,500 Swiss francs a pop, down in the Green Go Club beneath the Palace Hotel. Someone had to send their sable-coated lovers teetering round the jewellery and antique shops. And no one did that quite as willingly, exuberantly and downright flagrantly as the winners in Russia's new gangster economy.

Even the Russians, however, tended to go elsewhere in September. Many hotels closed down for a three-month break between the end of the Alpine summer and the first heavy snowfalls of winter. No one came to Gstaad to see the leaves turn red. So Zhukovksi's arrival had not gone unnoticed.

His name was not in any telephone directory or on any property register. But Thor Larsson had sat down in only his second bar of the evening when a big bearded German Swiss in an immaculately clean and well-pressed pair of workman's overalls overheard his question to the barman and growled, 'Zhukovski? That Russian? He's got a big place in Oberport, right out on the edge of town, up there in the forest, heading out towards Turbach.'

That had been three hours ago. Now Larsson was sitting in his Volvo, looking down at the shadowy bulk of the chalet. It looked like a Heidi-house on steroids, a four-storey mansion dressed up like a wee mountain farmhouse. The fantasy came complete with carved wooden balconies, wooden cladding on the upper floors and wooden trusses supporting the deep overhang of the roof. But for all the careful display of dead tree, it was still a steel-and-concrete construction underneath.

The house was set on the side of a steep hill, with the main entrance at the back of the property, up by the tree-line. That made sense, Larsson thought. You'd walk through the chalet to the main reception rooms at the front, with spectacular views down the mountainside, looking right across the whole valley in which Gstaad lay.

There was a large circular drop-off and parking area by the door. To the left of the property, a drive made its way downhill, curled round and then led to a garage directly underneath the ground floor. So a chauffeur could leave his employers by the main entrance then drive on to take the cars out of sight. And that, Larsson felt sure, was the way Carver had been brought in. It didn't seem too likely that there'd been a butler waiting to greet him at the door. Carver wouldn't be leaving by the front exit, either – he and Alix saying a polite farewell to Yuri Zhukovski, then heading on their way. When you looked at it like that, it was obvious this meeting was always going to turn sour.

Even so, Larsson had great faith in Carver's powers of survival. He clung to the image of him dashing from the chalet, guns blazing and in need of a quick getaway. When that happened, he'd be waiting, engine running.

It was past midnight and he was sitting alone in the darkness, waiting for something to happen, though he didn't know what or when. The Grateful Dead were playing on the stereo. He had a stone-cold slice of pizza and an even more frigid cup of black coffee. All things considered, it was just like being at home.

80

Yuri Zhukovski took his time. Some three hours passed before Alix heard his footsteps coming up the stairs then striding down the corridor. She'd been listening to the men drinking downstairs, bragging to one another and singing the filthy barrack-room songs they'd learned back in the old Soviet days. At one point the partying stopped, there was a tramp of footsteps across the flagstoned hall and then, a little later, a muffled crackle coming from somewhere deep in the belly of the building. Was that gunfire? Alix tried to pretend that there might be some other explanation, but she could not escape the obvious conclusion: Carver had been shot. She closed her eyes and prayed.

Please, God, let him live. Don't take him from me now.

The men had returned to the living-room, the brays of their boastful laughter even louder than before. Finally, the party had broken up. A few moments later, the door to the bedroom slammed open and there was Yuri, silhouetted against the light from the corridor, one hand holding the computer case.

Alix patted the bedspread next to her. She was arrayed there for his pleasure, on top of the bed, leaning against a pile of snow-white pillows in a short satin nightdress the colour of café-au-lait, trimmed with lace and cut high on the thigh. She had one knee up, the other leg stretched out in front of her, revealing a pair of tiny matching knickers.

'Come here, my darling,' she purred. 'I've been missing you.'

Yuri placed the black bag on the floor, took a few steps into the room, then stood quite still in the middle of the carpet. She knew he must have been drinking with his men, but his voice betrayed no trace whatever of drunkenness as he replied, 'No. You come here and prove how much you've missed me. Prove it on your knees.'

Afterwards, she helped him out of his clothes, nuzzling against him, dutifully arousing him as she led him to the bed. But now that Yuri's immediate physical needs had been satisfied, he seemed more interested in discussing the pain he'd inflicted on Carver.

'We let him stay there for an hour or so,' he was saying as they slipped under the covers. 'Then Kursk and his boys burst into the room and dragged him out of his chair. He was totally disoriented. It was obvious that he was completely unable to see – he'd been looking into that light for so long. He was waving his arms around in front of him like a blind beggar.'

Somehow Alix managed to give a little titter, as if amused by Carver's degradation. Yuri seemed encouraged by her appreciation.

'They led him out of the room, into the garage. Then they put him up against a wall and he stood there, cowering like a whipped dog, looking around with his pathetic staring eyes, still taped wide open. I must say, it made me feel quite nostalgic. Just like the old days. And the fascinating thing was, his hands were free. He could have taken the tape off his eyes, closed them for a bit, but he just couldn't work it out. I was glad. I wanted him to see what was happening. I wanted him to know.'

'I want him to know too,' said Alix, nibbling Yuri's ear and wrapping her thighs around his.

'Still, after a while I ordered Titov to tear off the tape, to see what would happen. Carver blinked a few times and shut his eyes. When he opened them again, he was crying, weeping quite pitifully. Kursk slapped him a few times, and that seemed to wake him up. He seemed suddenly to realize where he was: standing up against a wall with four men pointing guns at him. And then, then – and I must say, this was perhaps the most satisfying moment of all – he tried to stand up straight, die like a man . . . but he couldn't. He fell over. One of the men had to go over and drag him up again, just prop him against the wall . . .'

Alix had been trying not to listen. It was just too painful. So it took her a few seconds to comprehend what Yuri was saying. He was describing Carver's death. Her prayer had gone unanswered. It felt like a knife to her heart. She couldn't breathe. She gasped for air.

'Are you all right?' asked Yuri.

She nodded, and smiled apologetically. 'Sorry. I'm fine. Tell me the rest of the story.'

He took one of her breasts in his hand and gave the nipple a contemplative stroke with his thumb, his eyes fixed on her face, his expression impassive as she let out a little gasp.

'So, as I was saying,' he went on. 'The men were all armed with their guns. But the guns were loaded with blanks. So they fired a volley at Carver and he was huddled up against the wall and it took him a second to realize that he was still alive. And then he wet himself all over the floor, like an animal. So naturally I made him get down on his knees and crawl through his own urine. It was really quite satisfying.'

Carver was alive! It was all Alix could do to stop herself rolling off Yuri and simply flopping on the bed, overwhelmed by relief. Yet that joy was mixed with a bitter shot of anger and shame at the ordeal he was enduring on her account.

'Where is he now?' she asked, raising her head from Yuri's chest.

'Back in his favourite comfy chair,' Yuri replied.

Alix knew what that meant. Yuri had taken her to see the basement torture chamber the day before, when it was being prepared. It was a test of her loyalty and a warning against betrayal. The unspoken message was clear: you too could end up in that chair.

She tried to keep her voice calm. 'Will he survive the night?'

Suddenly Yuri's eyes turned hard and suspicious, with a new intensity that seemed to cut through the semi-darkness of the bedroom.

'Why do you ask? You seem very concerned for his safety.'

Somehow, Alix forced a laugh. 'Of course I am! I do not want him to die just yet. I want a long, deep sleep. Maybe in the morning I will have a little breakfast in bed. Then I will have a bath, get dressed . . .' She lay back down again so that she was whispering into Yuri's ear. 'In my sexiest new clothes . . .' She paused again. 'And then I want to go downstairs and watch him die with my own eyes, right in front of me. And I want him to suffer.'

Yuri gave a sharp, almost cackling laugh and slapped Alix hard on the rump.

'You are a bad, bad woman!' he shouted. 'That must be why you make me so hard!'

Hating herself for her complicity, Alix let him screw her and pretended to enjoy it. Then she remained motionless and silent until he fell asleep. She was tempted, oh so tempted, to kill Yuri there and then, press a pillow against his smug face until he suffocated. But there was just a chance he might wake up and fight back, and she could not afford to be defeated now.

There was a gun in the bedside table, on Yuri's side of the bed. Slowly, hardly daring to breathe, agonizingly aware of every sound, Alix slid open the drawer and removed the pistol. It was a SIG-Sauer, like the one Carver had used. The two men in her life had that in common, at least.

The glowing red numbers of the digital clock on the table gave the time as 04:01.

The master bedroom suite had his-and-hers walk-in closets. In Yuri's, she found a pair of jeans and a belt and stuffed them into a laundry bag which she hung over her left shoulder. The trousers would just about fit Carver – he and Yuri were about the same height, though Carver's build was leaner. But would he be in any fit state, mentally or physically, to get dressed and make a run for it? Could he fight his way out if they were discovered? Alix longed to see and hold him again. But that ache of anticipation was undermined by an equally powerful fear of what she might find. Part of her wished she could just run away and hide from the strain of multiple deceptions and the pummelling of repressed emotions. But there was no point trying to close her eyes and wish all this away. Life was as it was. She just had to deal with it.

She pulled on a robe and tiptoed barefoot back across the bedroom to the door. She turned the handle with painstaking care, never taking her eyes off the bed, then opened the door a few inches, just enough to see into the corridor.

It seemed clear. The men would be upstairs, Kursk in his own small room, the others in an attic dormitory. They would not believe that Carver could possibly escape. Even so, knowing Kursk, there was bound to be a man standing guard somewhere. For all his crude brutality, Kursk was very seldom inefficient and never, ever careless.

The ground floor was completely unoccupied, though the air was still heavy with the stench of stale smoke and spilled alcohol. If there was a guard, he would be downstairs, in the cramped control room next door to the main chamber. A panel of dials and switches ran the light and sound effects available to an interrogator, and a TV monitor showed the feed from the camera high on the torture-room wall.

Standing by the heavy door that led down to the basement, Alix thought back to her side-arm training, almost a decade ago. She checked the magazine of the SIG and made sure a round was chambered. Then she disengaged the safety and stepped down the stairs, holding the gun out in front of her, clasped in both hands, ready to fire at any moment.

There was no one in the basement corridor. She stepped noiselessly across the bare concrete floor to the door of the control room. Now she held the gun in her right hand, behind her back. With her left, she eased the door open. If there was anyone inside, she planned to tell him she wanted to see the Englishman suffering. The men all knew she was back in Yuri's good books. They would want to indulge her for fear of angering him.

The door swung into the room. Alix slipped in after it, side-on, trying to conceal her handgun. She needn't have worried. There was a guard in the room, Rutsev, but his piggy round head was slumped against his chest and the only sound in the room was the slow, even snuffle of his breathing. In the quiet room, with no reason to believe that anything could happen, he had succumbed to the effects of all the gut-rot vodka he had consumed that night.

Alix wondered what to do next. She could not allow Rutsev to wake up and sound the alarm. But there didn't seem anything in the room that she could use to tie him up or gag him. There was no alternative. She would have to shoot him as he slept.

She held out the gun barely a hand's breadth from his head, trying to keep it from trembling, trying to summon up the will to kill another human being in cold blood. She thought of all the times his lecherous eyes had played across her body, the hands he had let slide oh so accidentally across her arse and breasts. It wasn't enough. And then, for the first time since she had entered the room, her eyes were caught by the glow of the TV monitor.

She turned her head and saw Carver, his limbs and body bound, his mouth and eyes forced open, the earphones clamped to his head. It was the absolute silence and stillness that shocked her most of all. He must have been undergoing agonies beyond all comprehension, yet there was no sign whatever of his suffering. Even the ability to communicate his pain had been denied him.

Alix couldn't take her eyes off the screen. For all the horror, there was something mesmerizing about the sight of such pure, unrelieved torment. For ten long seconds she stood there, unmoving, then she tore her gaze from the monitor, spun round and put two bullets into Rutsev's skull without an instant's hesitation. It blew apart like a ripe watermelon. A stew of blood, brain, bone and hair sprayed against the bare grey wall behind him, heavy drops of thick red matter clinging to the rough surface of the concrete before they spattered on to the floor.

Once again, Alix had killed a man. But this time she did not double over in shock. This time she barely even looked at the remains of the man she had just killed as she left the room. Her mind was on another man. Seconds later, she was sliding open the bolts on the white cell-door.

81

The main problem with torture lies in the human beings on whom it is inflicted, for they have a limited capacity for pain. Even the toughest, best-trained soldiers and agents will reach a point where they will say absolutely anything to relieve their suffering, rendering intelligence gathered by means of torture virtually worthless.

Sometimes, of course, intelligence-gathering is not the real aim. Sometimes torture is inflicted for its own sake, either as punishment or for the torturer's pleasure. But then another problem rears its head. If the body is punished beyond a certain point, it simply shuts down, either through unconsciousness or death. It takes real skill, even artistry, to keep the pain and injury at just the right level – not too gentle that they serve no purpose, yet not so harsh that they become counter-productive.

The mind, too, reacts just like the body. Many torture techniques rely on psychological rather than physical stimuli. The victim is humiliated, degraded, made to feel less than human. He (or she) is deprived of sleep, bombarded with noise and light, or, conversely, denied any sensory stimuli whatever: no sound, no light, no touch, no smell. Again, the torturer must aim for that

Goldilocks balance. You want your victim to be disoriented, demoralized, bereft of hope, unaware of the passage of time, so that seconds feel like minutes and days pass by in a flash; but you don't want to induce full-scale psychosis. Not too soon, at any rate.

Again, though, the question of shutdown arises. A mind that can no longer make sense of the world around it or order the information it receives into any coherent meaning will eventually abandon the attempt and retreat into itself. Hallucination takes the place of reality. Memory fails. A person's very identity starts to slip away.

Samuel Carver was exhausted and hungry before he even reached Gstaad. Since then, the successive traumas he'd suffered had weakened him to the point of collapse. He'd made no attempt to resist when they led him back to the cell and strapped him back on the torture chair. When Titov hit him with a final blast from the stun-belt, just for the sheer pleasure of hurting him, there was something strangely lifeless about the spasms that had racked his body, as if he were no longer aware of the pain.

Carver didn't feel the teeth being wrenched from his jaw as his head fought against its straps. When the headphones and lightbox were switched back on, his overloaded brain rejected the barrage of incoherent stimuli and Carver drifted into a sort of dream-state. His dazzled, dessicated eyes were still wide open, but the blazing whiteness had been replaced by images from his subconscious, long-hidden recollections of people and places fused into a new world of their own.

There were two golden women – at least he thought there were two; sometimes they seemed to meld into one and their bodies and faces were never quite the same from one moment to the next. These women seemed to like him. He sensed their bodies close to him. But when he went to touch them, they drifted away out of reach and he couldn't make sense of what they were saying, though their faces seemed kind and their smiles let him know how happy they were to see him. He wanted to talk to them, to tell them he felt the same way. But he couldn't speak. No matter how hard he tried, he could not say a word. His mouth just would not move.

He walked through his old school corridors and then straight into the officers' mess at Poole. All his friends were there. There was an older man – what was he called? Carver loved him very much, but then the older man seemed to be angry with him and Carver was suddenly very frightened, just like he'd been during those first terms at boarding-school when the teachers got cross with him and he was all alone, far from home, with no one to comfort him.

And he was standing in a tunnel, with a car coming towards him, its dazzling headlights filling his eyes, and his eyeballs seemed to burn as if they'd been set on fire and he longed to be somewhere safe and dark, and as he spiralled back through his psyche he came to a place that was absolutely secure. He was floating in water, only it wasn't ordinary water because it was rich and sweet. But now he was being pulled from this warm, safe place and being dragged out into the cold. He fought and kicked but it made no difference. He was ripped out into the open. He screamed and yelled, and for a moment everything was all right again. He was cradled in two warm arms and his head was pressed against something deliciously soft and safe and his mouth was filling again with sweetness. But that too was lost, because other hands were grabbing him and taking him away and he was crying again because he wanted to keep feeling that softness and tasting that sweetness.

Next he became aware, as if watching from the far end of an impossibly long corridor, that something new was happening to him. A blissful darkness had descended and he could feel gentle hands, warm hands touching his face, stroking his forehead and cheeks. These hands seemed different to the ones in his dream. They were somehow more substantial, more real. And it struck him that his mouth seemed to be moving again and he wondered if he could talk.

'Who are you?' he croaked. 'Who's there?'

82

Andrei Dimitrov was dragged from his deep, vodka-soaked oblivion by the distant sound of gunfire. He propped himself up on his thin horsehair mattress and rubbed a hand across his aching head. He could have sworn he'd heard a pistol being fired, somewhere off in the distance. But now there was nothing but the silence of the early hours.

And then a thought struck him, making his guts swoop like a thrill-seeker on a rollercoaster ride. What was the time? He scrabbled for his watch and tried to make sense of the luminous dial. Ten past four. He was supposed to take over watch duty from Vasili Rutsev at four. If Vasha got pissed off and told Kursk, he'd be dead meat.

Dimitrov tumbled from his bed and scrabbled around on the floor for his clothes and shoes, trying not to wake Titov, who was snoring and farting in the next-door bed. His MAC was in a metal cabinet next to the bed. He got it out and stubbed his big toe against the bedstead, adding one more pain to the grim effects of a desperate hangover. Dimitrov groaned, under his breath. He was getting too old to drink this much.

He crept past Kursk's bedroom and made it down to the ground floor without getting caught. Still bleary-eyed and aching, he shoved open the door to the basement and headed downstairs.

It was the smell that hit him first, the unmistakable acrid bitterness of a fired gun and the sweet sickliness of spilled blood. Dimitrov woke up fast as the adrenalin hit his bloodstream – the ultimate natural hangover cure. He crept down to the basement corridor.

'Rutsev!' he shouted. 'Vasha!'

There was no reply.

Dimitrov made his way to the control room. The door was ajar. He kicked it open, holding the MAC at his shoulder, ready to fire. Then he let the gun fall to his side as he saw the bloody mess that had once been his comrade's face. God knows, Rutsev had been a sadistic bastard and his friendship with Igor Titov got sicker with every day that passed, but they'd fought together in Afghanistan and Chechnya, and on the streets of Moscow. Who'd have thought he'd get blown away in a luxury chalet in the Swiss Alps?

But who'd shot him? Dimitrov racked his brain, trying to recall whether there'd been any signs of forced entry anywhere in the house. He'd swear not. But no one in the house could have done it. The boss was upstairs screwing that stuck-up tart Petrova, Titov was out cold, and Kursk had no reason whatever to attack Rutsev. There'd been no arguments, let alone fights, during the course of the evening.

That just left the Englishman. But he was in no state to kill anyone. And anyway, he was strapped to a chair in a locked room.

Wasn't he?

Andrei Dimitrov looked at the monitor that showed the interrogation room. Then he looked again, and his blood ran cold.

The chair was empty.

83

Alix had been weeping as she stuffed her gun in her shoulder-bag and ran across the chilly white room to the hellish tableau at its heart. She could barely see through her tears as she loosened the tape from Carver's eyes and brushed her hand over his face to close his eyelids. She pulled the headphones off his head and then set about undoing the straps that tied him to the chair.

She worked her way down from his head, starting where the suffering was worse. The leather binding that had gagged his mouth had wreaked havoc. As she pulled it away a mass of clotted blood came with it; a single tooth, like some obscene decoration, was stuck to the surface of the clot. Alix had to look away for a moment to ease the heaving in her throat before she returned to her task.

The stun-belt round his waist was padlocked shut, but the battery packs that powered it could be removed, and with them its power to inflict any more pain. By the time she'd finished she was kneeling at his feet. She kissed the bleeding flesh where the straps and shackles had bitten into his skin – an echo of his own kiss, all those hours ago. It felt like a kind of atonement.

Carver made no response, and when she got to her feet he was still frozen, eyes and mouth wide open, so motionless that for a moment she feared he might be dead. But no, his flesh was warm, his chest still rising and falling with quick, shallow breaths. Alix leaned forward and took him in her arms.

When Carver finally spoke in that cracked, quavering voice, confessing his blind helplessness, Alix broke down, sobbing against his shoulder. She had never experienced true compassion before. When men had broken down in her arms she had counted it a victory. Now she felt a sense of limitless giving, a longing to care for the man in her arms, to nurse him and restore him, no matter how long it took.

First, though, she had to get him out of the chair, away from the blazing glare of the lightbox. She spoke into his ear: 'Help me, Carver. We must move you. And I need you to help me.'

For the first time, he turned his head to look at her. He blinked several times, trying to restore his vision, then screwed up his eyes and peered at her face, searching it for clues.

'It's me,' she said. 'Alix. I came back for you. I'm so sorry, my darling. I was so cruel to you. But I never meant it. You must believe me. I love you. Now, please, please try to walk . . . do you understand?'

Another frown, more blinks, and then Carver gave a slow, deliberate nod.

'Can you walk?'

A dry, inarticulate croak emerged from the wreckage of Carver's mouth. Then his arms and legs quivered, summoning up the energy and will for a massive physical effort. Alix took a step back to give Carver room as he lifted his hands on to the arms of the chair, then pushed with all his might. Slowly, inch by inch, his face grimacing with strain and concentration, he raised himself until he was upright. Then he collapsed into Alix's arms.

She tried again. 'Come on, my darling, walk for me. One step . . . just one step.'

Carver nodded again, then stuck out his right leg, with all the stiffness of a man trying out an artificial limb. He shifted his weight forward.

'Well done, that was great. Now, another step.'

He took another stiff-legged pace, moving on to his left foot. Then he gave a brusque shake of his arm, brushing Alix away, and took two more ungainly strides before falling once more into her waiting arms.

'Anxsch,' he mumbled. He closed his eyes, thought for a moment, then tried again. 'Thanxsch.' He squeezed out the word past his swollen, lacerated tongue and through his loosened teeth.

Alix laughed, and blinked away her tears. 'You're welcome. Now, come with me, into this corner, away from the light.'

She led him slowly into the corner under the camera and propped him like a broomstick against the wall.

'You OK?' she said, taking her hands off his shoulders and letting them hover right by him, ready to catch him if he fell again.

'Uh-huh.'

She brushed a quick butterfly kiss against his parched, cracked lips. Then she reached into her bag for the clothes. As she pulled the jeans out, the SIG-Sauer came with them. It crashed on to the floor.

'Gun . . .' said Carver, looking at the weapon, but not making any move to pick it up. He nodded to himself. 'Good. Need a gun . . .'

Alix ignored it. She was busy easing the jeans over Carver's feet and pulling them up his thighs and over the vile band of black nylon until, at last, he had a shred of dignity again. There was one last important job to do, but now she felt weirdly shy. Alix couldn't understand it. After all the things she'd done, all the men she'd been with, she was nervous about zipping up Carver's trousers. Why should this seem so much more intimate?

He sensed her unease, and smiled again. For the first time she saw a faint glimmer in his eyes, the merest hint that the real Samuel Carver was coming back to her.

'I can do tha',' he mumbled.

She had to help his fingers find the zip. He gave a tug and got it about halfway up. She shook her head at her own foolishness and finished the job.

'You love me?' he asked her, as if this were a new idea to him.

Alix nodded, biting her top lip.

'Promise?'

'Yes,' she whispered, so softly that she could barely hear the word herself. Then, fractionally louder, she repeated, 'Yes, I promise.'

He nodded. 'Tha's good . . .'

She took him in her arms again. 'It's all right, my darling. Everything's going to be all right.'

The next thing she knew, Carver had grabbed her with unexpected strength and flung her to the ground as the sound of gunfire blasted around the room.

84

Carver's vision was still blurred and dotted with dancing lights. He saw the world like a film that's been partly burned away, a picture scorched with white shafts of pure light. Gradually, though, he was beginning to get some faint sense of connection to the world outside.

He knew now that the woman with him was called Alix, and he was sure that she was one of the beautiful women with golden hair he'd been trying to talk to, the ones who'd kept drifting away. She seemed very upset, as though she'd done him harm, and as he thought about it, he did remember a terrible hurt, a pain in his heart, but he couldn't remember when or why that had been. It didn't matter, though, because she said she loved him and everything was going to be all right. She'd promised.

And then he'd seen Dimitrov come through the door. He'd known at once that this was a very bad man, one of the men who'd tried to hurt him, and this bad man was holding a gun. He was aiming it at the two of them. Carver did not want the man to shoot Alix, and a deep, untrammelled, all-consuming rage rose within him, sweeping through his consciousness and blowing all the rubble of Samuel Carver's identity away.

He entered some kind of fugue state in which another unknown identity took over, as if someone else's spirit had inhabited his body and run away with his mind. It was this other persona that threw Alix to the ground, then tumbled forward, ignoring the bullets spewing from Dimitrov's MAC-10, picking up the SIG as it went before rolling into a crouched firing position and putting three bullets into the Russian's chest.

Without saying a word, Carver got to his feet, walked across to Alix and brusquely pulled her upright. She looked into his eyes, startled by his sudden roughness, and was shocked to find no sign of recognition.

'Godda get out,' he said. 'Garage. Car.'

He took Alix's hand and dragged her from the room with a power and determination that made no sense to her. He bore no relation to the shattered man she had been tending to just seconds earlier.

They ran down the corridor towards the garage.

Upstairs, in Yuri Zhukovski's bedroom, the red numerals on his bedside clock clicked over to 04:15, and then the clock was obliterated as the bomb in the computer case exploded, creating a fireball that expanded at supersonic speed and generating a pressure-wave that smashed everything in its path before the vacuum that had been left behind sucked it back to its point of origin again. Zhukovski, too, was blasted into smithereens and his remains incinerated. One second he was a billionaire oligarch with thousands of workers under his command, but by the end of that same second he had simply ceased to exist.

The bomb was a small one. The explosion caused little structural damage outside the confines of the master bedroom suite. But the fire it started was soon blazing out of control.

Down in the basement, Carver stopped at the sound of the explosion and a grin of pure inhuman triumph spread across his face.

'Go'cha!' he hissed.

Alix was staring at him as if uncertain what or who she was looking at.

'Bomb,' he announced. 'Nasty accident. Serve him righ'.' He looked up, cocking an ear for any sound of further explosions. 'Godda geddout,' he repeated. 'Now!'

They hurtled down the corridor and into the garage. Carver looked around for the control that would open the door.

'It's OK,' shouted Alix, 'I know how to do it.'

She pressed a button on the wall and the great metal door swung up and then back, coming to rest under the ceiling.

Outside, they looked back at the chalet. Flames were already reaching out of the gaping holes where the master bedroom's windows had been and licking the night sky. Smoke was billowing across the hillside, and the ground beneath them was covered in glass.

Carver started to run up the tarmac drive that curved round to the main entrance to the chalet. Alix hesitated for a moment, then followed him. As bizarre as Carver's behaviour had become, he was still her best chance of safety.

As he came round the side of the house, Carver left the drive and melted into the undergrowth. Alix almost fell over him, as he'd crouched behind a large bush. He waved a hand angrily at her, ordering her to get back. Carver then turned his head and scowled at Alix, holding a finger to his mouth and shushing her before returning to his position. He was watching the front door, waiting for the remaining inhabitants of the house to appear.

Kursk was first. He emerged from the chalet, gave three or four hacking coughs, expelling the smoke from his lungs, then stood up and looked around him. He was unarmed, Carver noticed, baring his teeth like a predator spotting prey.

A few seconds later, Titov came out. He had rescued his submachine gun from the fire, but the smoke had affected him more than Kursk. Titov was bent double, his hands on his knees, hacking and wheezing. Kursk gestured at him angrily, wanting him to hand over the gun. Titov seemed unwilling to obey.

Carver rose to his feet and made his way stealthily through the undergrowth. He emerged at the edge of the circular parking-zone in front of the house and walked towards the two men, the left half of his body painted in tones of red and orange by the conflagration raging beside him.

The two Russians were too involved in their own arguments and discomforts to notice Carver until he was no more than five metres away. He was standing quite still, and he waited until Grigori Kursk saw him, recognized him and acknowledged the gun in his hand. Then he put two bullets into him, stomach and crotch. Carver didn't want a quick, efficient killing. He was shooting to cause pain.

Kursk shrieked, a high-pitched wail that seemed utterly incongruous coming from his massive frame. He was curled up on the ground, his hands grabbing at his torn entrails.

Titov had looked up at the sound of Carver's gun. The third shot blew the MAC-10 from his hands; the fourth shattered his left knee. Now he was down and howling too.

Alix looked on, appalled by a sadism she'd never seen in Carver before. He was repeating the torture he himself had suffered.

He stood over Titov and put another bullet into his thigh, sending a fatal fountain of blood spurting into the air from the femoral artery, black against the brilliance of the roaring flames. Then he turned back to Kursk and kicked him so that for a moment his body unfurled, exposing his chest. Carver shot him in the left lung.

Kursk was still alive, though the screams were just whispers now. Carver fired twice more.

'Stop!' Alix shouted. 'For God's sake, stop!'

The sound of her voice made Carver stand up straight and look around, a puzzled expression on his face. The storm that had raged in him blew itself out as suddenly as it had appeared. The hand that held the gun dropped to his side. He looked back down at the men at his feet as if he didn't know who they were or how they had got there.

Alix walked across the tarmac and took the gun from Carver's hand.

'Come on,' she said, gently. 'It's over.'

He nodded mutely and let her lead him up the path to the front gate. Alix pressed a button on a keypad attached to a post by the side of the drive, and the big metal gates swung open. They stepped out on to the road outside, and just as they did so a car engine started up and two headlights flared, shining right at them.

Carver was looking straight into the lights when they suddenly went on. He stopped dead in his tracks, then bent over with his head in his hands, moaning softly.

The car door opened and a tall figure emerged. Alix held out the gun in her right hand, shading her eyes with her left.

'Don't move!' she shouted.

'Whoa, take it easy.'

Alix relaxed as she recognized Thor Larsson's voice.

The gangly Norwegian strolled over to where Alix was standing, trying to reassure Carver, who seemed to have reverted to the isolated, unknowing state he'd been in when she first set him free from the torturers' chair.

'I was beginning to get worried about you guys,' Larsson said.

He looked down at Carver.

'What the hell's happened to him?'

Saturday, 6 September

85

The late-summer sunshine dappled the waters of Lake Geneva, sending dancing waves of light across the ceiling of the sanatorium's day-room. It was a large, light, open space, but on this pleasant Saturday lunchtime it was occupied by a solitary patient.

He was sitting in a wheelchair, a few feet away from a television set. The patient seemed lost in a world of his own. He was muttering to himself while his body carried on its own unconscious yet compulsive ritual of ticks and twitches. He was not paying any attention to the pictures on the TV screen.

Eight young soldiers in bright scarlet tunics were carrying a coffin draped in a glorious heraldic banner and covered in wreaths of white flowers down the aisle of a vast and ancient church. The coffin processed towards the altar and the congregation began to sing the slow, dirge-like opening of the British national anthem. As the tune rose to its climax in the middle of the verse, with a triumphant cry of 'Send her victorious!', the patient suddenly became quiet, sat up straight and fixed his eyes on the screen.

He frowned. He gazed at the picture, which was now focusing on an elderly couple, a middle-aged man and two teenage boys wearing formal black suits and ties. Then he screwed his eyes shut and started to scratch his head with both hands. There was something manic about his movements, and also the suddenness with which they stopped as his attention reverted to the screen, then started up again as he retreated back into himself.

He was a relatively young man, showing no signs of physical disease or malnourishment. He was dressed in a pair of cotton pyjama-trousers and a white T-shirt, and it was readily apparent that his body was lean, well muscled and fit. Yet there were red marks around his wrists and ankles – scratches, chafing and bruising that suggested he had been tied up or restrained in some way. He had the swollen, discoloured face of a mugging victim.

That, however, was all just surface damage, from which a man of his age, in his condition, would soon recover. More worrying were his eyes. There was a numb blankness in his stare, as though he found it hard to focus on the world around him, and harder still to make sense of what he saw.

The nurses called him Samuel.

Alix Petrova had to stop for a moment outside the sanatorium entrance. She had visited Carver morning and night since she and Thor Larsson had brought him to this very private, exceptionally discreet and even more expensive facility two days earlier. But still she had to steel herself for what awaited her within.

The receptionist directed her to the day-room. A nurse met her as she stepped through the glass-panelled door into the airy room. A badge on the nurse's crisp white uniform read CORINNE JUNEAU.

'How is Samuel today?' asked Alix.

'A little better today,' Nurse Juneau replied. 'We've got him out of bed, but he's still terribly confused, the poor man. Look at him, watching the funeral. I don't think he knows what's happening at all, bless him.' She watched her patient for a moment, then added, 'He's so full of fear . . .' A cloud passed over her kind, caring face. 'How could anyone do this to another human being?'

The nurse led the way across the room to the wheelchair. 'Wait here,' she said, when they were still a few feet away. She walked on alone. The TV set was mounted on the wall and controlled by a handset that sat on a console just below. Nurse Juneau picked up the remote control and used it to turn down the volume. When talking to Samuel it was important to keep one's voice as low and calm as possible. Even the slightest loud noise seemed to scare him.

Once the sound of the church music had faded away, Nurse Juneau turned to face Samuel. She was still holding the remote control.

'Hello,' she said, with her sweetest smile. 'Your friend has—'

She got no further. Samuel was looking at her, eyes wide, mouth gaping. He was pointing at her and pleading, 'No! No!' She took a pace towards him and he flinched, curling up in his wheelchair. 'Don't hurt me! I'll talk!'

Nurse Juneau's professional composure fractured in the face of such overwhelming terror. She was fixed to the spot, looking around her, trying to find the source of his distress. Alix hurried to her side and took the remote control from her hand. She replaced it on the console, then put a reassuring hand on Nurse Juneau's shoulder, as if she were the professional and the nurse the visitor.

'It's all right,' she said. 'It wasn't you. Don't worry. I'll take care of him now.'

Nurse Juneau hurried away to the far side of the room, casting a couple of nervous looks over her shoulder as she went.

Samuel was watching the women through his fingers. His eyes were still wide and staring, but he seemed fractionally less afraid now.

Alix crouched down by the wheelchair, not wanting to stand over him. 'It's OK,' she murmured. 'You're safe here. No one can hurt you. I will look after you.'

As she spoke, she gently stroked one of Samuel's arms. He gave no sign of understanding what she had said. But her soothing tone and the soft touch of her fingers against his skin seemed to relax him. Gradually, he uncurled. Alix kept talking to him, keeping her voice low, using simple phrases.

'Everything's going to be fine. I'm here . . .'

Samuel seemed more content now. His attention shifted back to the TV screen. He watched in silence for a while, still frowning and scratching and twitching, lost in his own bleak universe.

Then he pointed up at the picture. 'What's that?' he mumbled through his battered mouth. His voice sounded blank and uncomprehending. 'What's happening?' And then, quite clearly, in a voice that could have been mistaken for that of a normal, healthy man, 'Who died?' Samuel's brow furrowed as he tried to make sense of what he was seeing. 'Did someone die?' he asked, though now the anxiety had returned to his voice.

Alix bit her lip and pressed her eyelids together. Then she whispered, 'Yes. She was a princess. She had an accident.'

Samuel thought about what she had said, then turned his attention back to the TV. Alix pulled up a chair next to the wheelchair, and they sat there together in silence.

Later, Samuel Carver watched as a line of black cars drove down an empty road. People were standing on bridges across the road. Whenever the cars went under a bridge, all the people threw flowers down on to them. Some of the flowers landed on the car, but many more fluttered down on to the road, leaving lovely bright colours against the dirty grey surface.

He reached out for Alix's hand. She squeezed it gently, letting him know that she loved him. Then Samuel Carver looked at her, a flicker of recognition danced in his eyes, and he smiled.

Acknowledgements

My sincere and heartfelt thanks go out to the many people without whom this book could never have been written or published.

Charlie Brocket, whose fascination with the events of 31 August 1997 and wonderful skill as a raconteur first sparked my interest and set me on the path to writing this novel.

The team at my literary agency, Lucas Alexander Whitley, in London, notably Julian Alexander, without whose faith, perseverance and creativity over more than two years nothing would ever have happened; Mark Lucas, whose response to my first feeble attempts epitomized the phrase 'creative destruction' (brutal, but dramatically effective!); and Peta Nightingale, whose line-by-line analysis of the early drafts made such a massive difference.

At Transworld Publishers in London, Sally Gaminara and Simon Thorogood had the faith to plunge into this project with incredible speed and absolute commitment, as did Clare Ferraro and Joshua Kendall at Viking in New York. They gave me the kind of encouragement that authors can only dream of.

Nigel Parker provided his usual wise counsel, and Mitchell

Symons was not only a patient and, long-suffering sounding-board, but also supplied one all-important suggestion at a crucial moment.

The management and pilots of Elite Helicopters, Goodwood, West Sussex gave invaluable information on the construction of helicopters; Dr Michael Perring of Optimal Health devised M. Leclerc's medication; Gisela Gruber at Gold Air International drew up the flightplan and likely bill for a journey by private jet from Northolt to Sion and then on by chopper to Gstaad; Trevor Clifton worked out how to sail a Rustler 36 across the Channel and avoid a container ship along the way; and John Smythe took me out on the water in his own 36-footer.

Finally, but most importantly, I owe everything, as always, to my family: to Fred, without whom I might be tempted to take things easy; to Holly and Lucy, whose criticism of their father was (this time!) both asked for and much appreciated; and, of course, to Clare. You are, as always, the beginning and the end of everything I do.